Dedication

To Liyana and Ethan—
For your laughter, your questions, and your boundless imagination.
Thank you for keeping this story alive in ways only you could.

Table of Contents

Books by Clifton Wilcox

Non-Fiction

Scapegoat: Targeted for Blame

Groupthink: An Impediment to Success

Bias: The Unconscious Deceiver

Witch-hunt: The Assignment of Blame

The Fall of the Kingdom of Northumbria

Witch-hunt: The Clash of Cultures

Road to War: The Quest for a New World Order

Envy: A Deeper Shade of Green

The Rise of the Nazi SS

The Horrible Void Between the Trenches

Fiction

Cool's Last Stand

I, Monster

The Monuments Must Bleed

Where Despair Comes to Play

Harvest of Eyes

Prologue

It was supposed to be a race. Jenny had always loved the thrill of the chase. Jasper, lagging behind, pursuing Jenny across the telephone wires at Wildwoods Farm — a silent chase she and Jasper loved, half flirtation, half dare. That morning, the sky was a solid blue, the kind Jenny preferred, where the whole world seemed to stretch out open and infinite. But something changed at the top of the pole. A scream, a slip, and that was it. Jenny's body hit the ground with the type of sound no creature can forget. Wings fluttered. A goat bleated in confusion. The chickens scratching for food below saw it all.

By midday, the farm was a hive of accusation. "*He pushed her!*" clucked Henrietta, the head hen, her beady eyes blazing. "I heard them fighting and he gave her *that* look! Like he's been giving her lately — jealous, brooding...contemplating."

"He could never compete with Jenny, and he loathed that." Henrietta added. The other hens cackled with agreement. Soon every animal from hayloft to pasture had an opinion about Jasper shoving Jenny.

The hens continued with accusations like: *He was prideful! He was reckless...He didn't cry!* Most incriminating of all -- *he was present!*

"Jasper, if he did not push her, why did he take his time to come down to check on Jenny?" Henrietta cackled.

"*Oh yeah!* He pushed her alright! It was a *wicked push!*" Crowed Cecily, as the hens continued gossiping.

By dark, Jasper name was a curse.

The council of the elders of the farm met under the willow tree, and there was no one that defended Jasper. Not one.

Jasper disappeared into the hedges on the edge of the farm.

"*Coward,*" they muttered.

1

"*Murderer*," they mumbled.

Even Jenny's former friends shrank away, unable, or unwilling, to believe anything other than the worst. Jenny had been loved, welcomed by the farm and woodland folk, she was clever and kind. The silence of Jasper's looked like guilt carved in stone.

But not everyone was convinced. A ferret with a twitchy nose, Ink was not buying what the chickens were selling.

"Too neat," he murmured, jotting notes on a used feed sack with a charcoal nub. "Too loud...too soon."

Next to him, there was Fiona, the black cat with piercing green eyes. She was known as *The Whisperer*, because Fiona heard everything: the creak of guilt, the rustling of lies, the faint heartbeats buried beneath layers of blame. Together, they could unveil something foul hidden under all the feathers.

What they would discover would ruin the farm's fragile peace. Because Jenny didn't just fall — someone had been expecting her to. And as the truth began to emerge, Ink and Fiona uncovered a more sinister plot: not only to ruin Jasper but to tarnish Jenny's unblemished legacy.

If they failed, Wildwoods Farm wouldn't just lose a hero — they'd rewrite her as a tragedy. And Jasper, the last squirrel that loved her, would be the final sacrifice.

Chapter 1
The Fall

The sun peered through the leaves of the Wildwoods Farm, casting formless shadows on the bustling barn. It was market day; full of vibrant activity of the inhabitants filling the barn with cheerful chatter and the scent of fresh berries and herbs. Today, however, a hush had fallen, broken only by the nervous chirping of birds and the silent whispers of the amassed creatures. At the center of the commotion was a telephone pole, usually a sturdy landmark, now the silent witness to a tragic event. Lying at its base was Jenny, a young squirrel, her usually bright eyes closed, her small body still.

An audible gasp of surprise made its way through the audience. Old Fitzwilliam, the wise owl perched atop of the tallest oak, hooted in panic, his steady disposition no longer solid. Mrs. Hollyhock, the round hedgehog everyone knew to be so shy, gasped as her half-chomped carrot fell to the grass. Even Eddie, the bulldog, who was always found at his bowl, looked up to see what was the matter; his good-natured face was somewhat clouded with anxiety.

The initial warnings turned almost immediately to whispers of skepticism. A group of hens now with ruffled feathers and harsh voices, pointing at Jasper, Jenny's closest friend.

"*We saw him!*" Henrietta clucked her eyes narrowed. "He was chasing her before she fell! *He pushed her!*"

Their message spread like wildfire on the breeze that swept through the trees. The protests grew louder, transforming them into an accusation. Jasper, a young squirrel with a tender heart and a troubled brow, stood frozen, his eyes glassy with the shock of disbelief. He hadn't pushed Jenny; he loved her. But his opposition to the hens ever growing chorus of criticism was drowned out.

The scene was a chaotic mix of fear, shock, and accusations. Horace the Hare and other animals attempted to reassure the crowd, Horace's long ears drooping with sadness. Still others, like the gossiping hens, continued with over-the-top accusations spoken with sharp tongs. Tension hung in the air like wet laundry on a line, the joyful atmosphere was replaced by a heavy cloud of fear and uncertainty. A knot of dread twisted in Jasper's chest; the accusations were like crushing weights. He was sure that Jenny's fall was an accident... a horrible, painful accident, but how could he convince anyone?

The two forms sat in the dark corner watching with luminous eyes. Ink, a clever ferret detective with a quick wit and a keen eye for details, adjusted his glasses. Sitting next to him was Fiona, a silky black cat with eyes like polished emerald. Fiona, who also went by *The Whisper* was due to her reputation for the uncanny ability pick up on cues and to overhearing whispers and quiet conversations, listening keenly, twitching her ears at the slightest of sounds. They had been summoned to come and look into this disastrous event, summoned by the elder of the Wildwoods Farm, the distinguished badger named Bartholomew.

Ink and Fiona shared a look. There was way too much confusion at that moment to form any opinions. There were too many contradictory stories, too much emotion concealing the truth. Their job was to cut through the chaos and separate fact from fiction and uncover the truth about how Jenny had fallen to her death.

Infiltrating the crowd, they began looking around, eavesdropping, and generally taking stock of what was said. Ink noted where the hens were positioned when they witnessed Jenny's fall. Their accounts, while they seemed consistent, did not match up. Ink picked up on the subtle cues—the averted eyes, the restless preening, the faint, uneasy shifts in posture—all signs that something wasn't quite right.

Fiona, for her part, let her exceptional hearing eavesdrop on the hushed words being shared. She listened to the squirrels, to the rabbits, to the badgers, all talking to one another. Some sympathized with Jenny; some breathed suspicions of Jasper; some reiterated the hens' charges.

Fiona had noticed something odd in their stories: a shift in tone, a slight pause followed by a flick of the tail, these revealed something was being withheld. These seemingly minor details—overlooked by most—told a different story, one that suggested a truth that was far more complex than the initial accusations.

Their initial inspections signaled that there were conflicting claims, giving rise to investigating further. Ink and Fiona continued to discover discrepancies between the witnesses' timing of events. Some of them had claimed Jasper was pursuing Jenny after a heated argument seconds before she fell; others recalled that Jasper was nowhere around the telephone pole. Those initial clues – minor as they may have appeared – indicated that the current narrative might be hiding a more complex truth, a truth they were devoted to unearth.

As the day dragged on, the shock began to dull, replaced by something harder—determination. Around the farm and into the forest beyond, a strange silence settled. What was once a place of movement and life now felt dimmed, as if the very air held its breath. Even the barn, normally echoing with laughter and friendly banter, seemed still—suspended in a fog of suspicion and unanswered questions.

But Ink and Fiona weren't the type to let whispers write the ending. They could feel it—truth buried beneath the noise, tangled up in assumption and fear. And they would find it. They had to. Their search had barely begun, and already it was pulling them into places where voices lowered, and shadows grew long. The farm and forest held secrets. They both knew that, and those secrets are the kind that don't like to be found.

Still, the look they shared said it all. This wasn't just about clearing a name—it was about righting a wrong. Jasper's future, and the real story behind Jenny's fall, depended on what they would uncover. So, they turned from the barn and stepped into the trees, where the breeze carried rumors like ash, and somewhere in the hush, if you stopped to listen, the truth was waiting to be heard.

The accusations against Jasper spread like wildfire through the Wildwoods Farm. The initial shock of Jenny's fall had quickly given way to a frenzy of suspicion, with Jasper caught in the middle. The gossiping hens, a particularly vocal contingent of the farm community, were the primary source of the accusations. Their shrill clucking and pointed accusations had cast a heavy cloud over Jasper, shifting him in the eyes of many from a mourning companion to the prime suspect.

In a thicket of briar and overripe berries, the hens had gathered like jurors ready to cast their verdict. At the center stood Henrietta, her beak sharp, her feathers flared, commanding the attention of the flock like a preacher at a revival. The berries—plump, sweet, and usually the cause of daily squabbles—were ignored entirely, trampled underfoot as the hens leaned in, hungry not for fruit but for scandal.

"I tell you; I saw him!" Henrietta declared, her voice cut through the thicket like a splinter. "Jasper was there—right there—chasing her up that telephone pole like a foaming rabid dog. She ran across the line, and he followed. And then... then he *pushed* her. I know what I saw. I know it!"

The others gasped and clucked in uneasy agreement, the sound more like a funeral elegy than a chorus. In their minds, the case was already closed. And poor Jasper, wherever he was, could probably feel the noose tightening—woven not from rope, but from rumor.

Another hen, a younger bird named Cecily, piped up, "Yes! And I saw him too!" Cecily leaned in, "You know they had an argument...a heated spat over an acorn." The other hens gasped. Cecily continued, "He was acting... *shifty*. He kept looking around nervously, like he was up to something...*something sinister.*" The flock around Cecily gasped from hearing the narrative.

The hens account, repeated and embellished with each telling, painted a picture of Jasper as a malicious figure, capable of such cruelty. They described his movements, his expressions, even the subtle twitch of his whiskers, all pointing toward his guilt. Each hen filled in gaps and added details, creating a narrative that was both convincing and utterly devastating to Jasper's reputation.

However, a closer examination of their story revealed inconsistencies. The hens' descriptions of the time of the fall varied. One claimed it happened at precisely midday; another pegged it fifteen minutes earlier. The placement of Jasper relative to the pole also differed slightly – near, close, almost touching, the descriptions blurred, lacking a shared clarity that would typically be present in an eyewitness account.

The discrepancies were subtle, but to a keen observer, they were significant. They suggested that the hens' memory might not be as reliable as they claimed. Their narrative, though presented as a unified whole, was fractured at its core, a collage of recollections colored by emotion and perhaps, a touch of prejudice. Their collective certainty, so confidently presented, seemed to mask deeper uncertainties.

Meanwhile, Jasper, unaware of the hens' ongoing discussion, sat alone beneath a weeping willow, his heart heavy with grief and despair. He felt the weight of the accusations, the crushing weight of their collective condemnation. The joyous sounds of the barn felt like cruel mockery, a stark contrast to the darkness that had descended upon him. He desperately wanted to explain, to tell them the truth, but his words were trapped, choked by the rising tide of accusations. He had loved Jenny; she was like a sister to him. The idea that he would harm her was a repulsive thought that sent shivers down his spine.

He replayed the events of the morning in his mind, searching for some clue, some details that could exonerate him. He had indeed been near the telephone pole, helping Jenny reach for a particularly high berry. Before moving on, they played a game of chase. Jenny was fast and bolted right by Jasper. Jasper began to pursue her as she crossed the wire and that is when he witnessed her fall, the sudden, terrible plummet from the top of the pole that stole her life. He hadn't pushed her; he had never even considered it.

The thought of anyone believing such a thing was appalling. He tried to remember everything, to recall any detail that might help prove his innocence. He thought of the wind, a gust of which had seemingly caused Jenny to lose her grip. He recalled the slight shift of the pole just before the fall, a subtle creaking sound, almost imperceptible, that might have contributed to the incident. He remembered the startled cry that escaped his lips upon witnessing her fall, a sound of horror and disbelief, a far cry from the calculated move of a malicious perpetrator.

His mind raced, desperately trying to construct a defense, a counter-narrative that could pierce through the accusations, a voice of reason amidst the rising storm of prejudice. He knew he needed help; he needed someone to believe him, someone to see the truth that was obscured by the gossip and accusations. But who would listen? The hens' words echoed in his ears, their certainty so overwhelming, their accusations so pointed. He felt alone, isolated, and unjustly accused, the weight of the farm's condemnation bearing down on him. His hope dwindled with each passing moment, replaced by a growing despair. The cheerful atmosphere of the barn, usually so uplifting, now felt like a mocking reminder of his current predicament. The vibrant energy of the barn only served to amplify his isolation, highlighting the chasm between his innocence and the community's unwavering belief in his guilt. He desperately hoped that someone, anyone, would see beyond the accusations and perceive the truth. The weight of his innocence lay heavy on his small frame, and he wondered if the truth would ever prevail.

The wind rustled through the leaves of the weeping willow, its whispers mimicking the anxieties that churned within Jasper's heart. He looked up, hoping for some sign, some glimmer of hope that justice would prevail. The sun, once a symbol of warmth and life, now felt cold and distant, a reflection of his own desolate state. He closed his eyes, a single tear tracing a path down his cheek, a testament to his innocence and the injustice he faced. The silence that followed was deafening, punctuated only by the faint whispers of the wind. The accusations had cast a long shadow, and he wondered if the truth would ever emerge from the darkness. His hope clung to the possibility that someone would listen, someone would see beyond the accusations, and the weight of injustice would eventually lift. The whispers of the wind carried his silent plea, a plea for truth and justice in the face of overwhelming adversity.

The barn, usually a vibrant hub of activity, felt strangely subdued under the pall of Jasper's accusations. The scent of freshly baked bread and ripe berries hung heavily in the air, a stark contrast to the tension that crackled between the forest's inhabitants. Ink, a ferret of discerning intelligence and renowned investigative skills, arrived with his partner, Fiona, a sleek black cat whose uncanny ability to glean information from the subtlest of whispers had earned her the moniker *The Whisper*. Their arrival was met with a mixture of curiosity and apprehension. Some residents shifted uneasily, while others approached them eagerly, ready to share their versions of the tragedy.

Ink, his keen eyes scanning the scene, noted the scattered berries near the base of the telephone pole, a detail seemingly overlooked amidst the flurry of accusations. He traced the path of the fallen berries, their crimson juice staining the forest floor, visualizing the last moments of Jenny's life. The slight discoloration of the soil, a barely perceptible shift in hue, suggested a subtle dampness – a clue that might have been overlooked by the emotionally charged witnesses. Fiona, ever watchful, sat perched atop a nearby fence post, her ears twitching as she absorbed the collective murmur of the community, her sharp senses picking up on the undercurrents of fear, suspicion, and unspoken truths.

The barn was the pulsing heart of Wildwoods Farm. It was where stories were told, and reputations were quietly formed or damaged. That was a good place to start. Ink and Fiona talked to the chickens in quiet tones and steady eyes, asking questions without judging them and listening more than they spoke. Each hen told her own story about what happened that morning. Ink softly pushed for details like times, distances, and directions. But the little cracks told him the most.

Henrietta, always the leader, moved uneasily under his stare. When he inquired where she had been standing, her eyes moved to the side, and her answer varied a little each time. Cecily's voice shook when she talked of Jasper's "shifty" behavior; it was a trembling that sounded more like doubt than mistrust. Esmeralda was another hen who seemed to add something new each time she spoke. It was evident that she was acting, not remembering, because of how she leaned in and the long gap before each charge. Fiona noticed the pauses while Ink read the words. She could tell that the chickens were nervous because they didn't look her in the eye when the inquiries got too close. Their wings trembled and their feathers fluffed in ways that showed they were uneasy. Fiona realized that the confidence they showed was an act—a way to protect themselves from uncertainty they were too afraid to say out loud.

Ink and Fiona turned to the woods after the barn stopped giving them answers. As they got closer to the telephone pole, where the tragedy happened, the air got cooler under the trees. They looked at it quite closely. Small scrapes at the bottom, too worn to be new, pointed to old instability. A branch that was snapped at an unexpected angle pointed into the wind. There was a sticky area of moss stuck to one side of the pole that was hard to see but very dangerous. The hens had missed each of these details that told a story. A more intricate and silent one.

They didn't stop at the scene. Every voice was important. A squirrel who often shared berries with Jenny said that she had been especially hyper that morning, chasing a high branch that she typically didn't try to get. That little thing, which had been ignored before, suddenly shone with meaning.

A shy rabbit remembered seeing a quick flash of blue near the pole, but he couldn't explain it. The badger, who was plainly upset by the interruption and muttering from his lair, said he had been distracted by a nut that had gotten lost. He confirmed what others had said: that day, the clearing was hit by the fiercest wind in weeks.

A different vision was starting to come together, piece by piece. One that had less to do with guilt and more to do with not understanding, missing chances, and a truth hidden under feathers and fear. This seemingly insignificant detail, pieced together with other observations, pointed towards a force of nature as a potential contributor to the fall, and the flash of blue may be a vital clue.

As Ink and Fiona carefully put the pieces of evidence together, the day turned into darkness. They went over the events of that fateful morning again, paying attention to every detail, every observation, and every indication of truth that was hidden by the tsunami of accusations. Their analysis found a pattern: hens making quick assumptions, biased assessments, and not wanting to challenge the main story. The hens' belief didn't come from objective observation; it came from a need to blame someone else, to find a scapegoat. Their quick decision had hidden the truth, making the situation seem more complicated than it really was.

Ink and Fiona's inquiry found a shocking truth: a missing piece that had been hidden by the rush to blame Jasper at first. That day, a flash of blue near the telephone pole looked like the hue of a really naughty blue jay that was notorious for stealing berries and acting in ways that were hard to predict. Sky, the Blue Jay, had a history of bothering and even physically interacting with other animals in the forest. It turned out that Sky's attempt to join in the chase had contributed to Jenny losing her balance and fall. There was no doubt about the proof. Sky's acts, even if they weren't meant to hurt Jenny, were a contributing factor that caused her to fall. The animals in the community were focused on Jasper because they jumped to conclusions, didn't think about other possible answers, and had a predisposition toward a culprit who was easy to find.

Ink and Fiona's comprehensive inquiry had found the truth, which told a different story—one that was free of bias and based on careful observation and logical reasoning. This news pushed the inhabitants who lived on the farm to face their own flaws and how they were inclined to hastily evaluate events before looking into them.

The community's mood changed dramatically when they found out that Sky had something to do with Jenny's death. The chickens bowed their heads in shame as they saw the proof that they were wrong. Their earlier accusations echoed in the calm of the farm. Jasper cried tears of joy and relief when he heard that the false allegations were no longer hanging over him. He knew that justice could finally win.

The trial would not be the expected courtroom drama but more of a reflection and a time for everyone to think about their own biases and how important it is to find the facts before pronouncing judgment. The event was a sad but important lesson that would teach them how important it is to pay attention, how dangerous it was to make assumptions, and how deeply loss and understanding can change a person. The farm, which had been full of doubt and accusations, suddenly let out a collective sigh of relief. The burden of injustice was removed, and a new commitment to truth and justice took its place. The Wildwoods Farm had to learn a terrible lesson, but in the end, justice won out.

The first interviews were harder than they thought they would be. The hens, who are known for being quite gossipy, had already formed a complicated web of rumors and guesses, with each story being slightly different but all pointing to Jasper. Ink and Fiona came up with a plan: they would do separate interviews. Using this tactic, they might stop false information from spreading and testimonies from getting mixed up.

Henrietta, the self-proclaimed leader of the hen flock and the loudest complainant, was the first hen they talked to. Henrietta, a fat hen with a look of disapproval on her face all the time, told the story with a lot of drama, focusing on Jasper's purportedly threatening stance and how close he was to Jenny immediately before the fall. Ink listened carefully and noticed the little trembling in her voice when she talked about Jasper's "evil glare." This detail sounded more like a sign of her own worries than a real observation. Fiona saw that Henrietta flinched slightly every time Ink questioned whether her timing was right. There were small differences that were hard to notice, like a few seconds off here and a slightly different viewpoint there. Ink thought these contradictions were far more important than they seemed at first.

Next, they talked to Cecily, a younger hen who was known for being shy. Henrietta's testimony was far more confident than Cecily's. She spoke in a low voice, and her words were unsure and hesitant. She backed up some of Henrietta's allegations, but with clear doubts, often using phrases like "I think" or "it seemed like." Her testimony didn't have the same burning conviction as Henrietta's, which could mean she didn't see it happen, or she didn't want to be part of the group that condemned Jasper. Fiona saw Cecily slowly shifting her feathers, which was a sign of nervousness and discomfort. The small distinctions between Henrietta and Cecily's stories were quite important. Ink made a mental note of the differences and put them away for later study.

Esmeralda, who was known for her love of drama, gave a rather exaggerated account. Her version contained over-the-top descriptions of Jasper's supposed evil plans, theatrical gestures, and even a made-up detail about a fight that had happened before between Jasper and Jenny. Ink saw that Esmeralda's story didn't add up, and it wasn't because she had a bad memory; it was because she was trying to make it more dramatic. Fiona saw that Esmeralda's eyes were moving around the room and not making direct eye contact, which is a symptom of lying. Esmeralda's story was fun to read, but it wasn't really reliable.

Ink and Fiona talked to additional witnesses besides the chickens. They talked to a few squirrels that had been in the barn that morning. Benjamin, an old and attentive squirrel, said he had felt a big blast of wind right before Jenny fell. This was an important point because it gave a different reason for the accident that the chickens' stories conveniently left out. Benjamin's story was told quietly, without the emotional intensity that made the chickens' stories so dramatic.

A rabbit named Robert, who is known for having good eyesight, said he saw a flash of blue near the telephone pole immediately before Jenny fell. He couldn't say what had caused the flash, but he was sure it was there, which made the case more interesting. Robert's detailed account of the flash of blue was something that the hens' story didn't include at all.

Their second interview was with the badger, who was grumpy, set in his ways, and quite picky about facts. He didn't want to get involved in the drama and stuck to what he saw. He said that he had been upset about a missing nut soon before the event and had missed seeing what had happened. But he did corroborate the powerful wind Benjamin had talked about, saying it was the strongest gust he had seen in weeks. The badger's testimony was an important piece of evidence that confirmed the presence of a strong wind, which could have had a role in Jenny's fall.

Ink and Fiona wrote down every single thing that happened in each interview, including not only the words that were stated but also the small changes in body language, tone of voice, and pauses. They looked for differences, overlaps, and important things that were left out in the stories. They figured out that the chickens' stories, while they seemed to agree on the surface, had large gaps in them when looked at closely. The times didn't match up, the descriptions of what Jasper did were different, and several key elements were left out altogether.

When the first clues were put together, they pointed to a narrative that was very different from what the hens were saying. The powerful wind, the flash of blue, and the chickens' conflicting stories all pointed to a more complicated reason for Jenny's fall. Ink and Fiona knew that the community's quick judgment had hidden an important part of the story.

The first allegations, which were based on feelings and guesswork, had successfully closed the community's eyes to the possibility of other answers. They recognized that the case was far from over. The accident that seemed simple was turning into something much more complicated, and it needed a lot more careful examination. Their inquiry was far from complete, but the first evidence had already started to show a different side to things. The chickens' story, which had seemed unbreakable at first, suddenly began to fall apart under the weight of contradictory evidence and small errors. Ink and Fiona realized that the truth was buried under a lot of assumptions, biases, and maybe even...lies. They knew that the next stage was to look more closely at each animal's statement, looking for not only facts but also the reasons and prejudices that each witness held.

There were signs that more suspects might be involved. For example, the flash of blue made Ink and Fiona think that a new character might be in the play, like a bird or something else. The strong wind, which had been thought to be unimportant, now seemed like it could have played a serious role in Jenny's fall. There were severe doubts about the chickens' reliability as witnesses because their stories didn't match up. The carefully collected first clues—the differences in the testimony, the evidence of the wind, and the mysterious flash of blue—suggested that the truth was far more complex than the simple story that the hen's allegations spread. The path was taking them to a place that wasn't obvious right away. To find the buried layers of truth beneath the surface of accusations and assumptions, they needed to look further into the Wildwoods Farm. This means that they had barely started their investigation.

The late afternoon sun made long shadows across the Wildwoods, making the forest floor look like it was covered with light and darkness. Fiona was in her element, sitting on a low-hanging branch with her glossy black fur blending in perfectly with the bark. Her ears were sharper than any other animal's in the woods. She could hear the quiet rustle of leaves, the chirping of crickets, and most crucially, the quiet murmurs of the animals who lived there. This was where she really shined; not in the busy market square, but in the quiet corners where animals exchanged secrets and disclosed truths in a quiet way.

Today, she was watching a small group of squirrels gathered together near the old oak tree, which was a popular spot for gossip and secret meetings. She watched them closely, not just listening to what they said but also paying great attention to how they moved. The way they stood, the small changes in their stances, and the almost invisible flicks of their tails were the keys to finding the silent truths that lay behind their well-chosen sentences.

One squirrel, a youngster named Connor, looked to be very upset. His tail continued twitching, and he kept looking over his shoulder nervously, which is a clear sign of nervousness or guilt. His voice was barely a whisper, which was very different from the chickens' confident statements. His speech was broken up by tense pauses and the occasional stammer. He talked about a "flash," which was a quick splash of blue near the telephone pole and then it was gone. This was something he hadn't mentioned before during his interview with Ink. Fiona saw the difference and remembered that Robert the rabbit had said something similar before. The coincidence seemed rather strange.

Another squirrel, older and calmer, gave a different point of view. He talked about a strong wind, which backed up Robert's story, but he also said he saw a little, dark form run away from the area right after Jenny fell. He said it was swift, nearly a blur, too fast to tell what it was for sure, but he was sure it wasn't a squirrel. The description was slightly different from what Connor said about the blue flash. Were these two separate animals? Or maybe two different ways of looking at the same thing? Fiona carefully wrote down the specifics, the differences, and the things that were the same in their stories.

Her cat-like intuition, which she had perfected over years of watching and making small conclusions, led her to pay attention to the little things that seemed unimportant. She saw that one squirrel changed its weight when the wind came up, as if it were attempting to downplay how important that component was. When the name "Jasper" was spoken, another one moved its position slightly, as if it knew something or had a bias that he didn't want to say. These tiny indications, which most animals wouldn't notice, were like breadcrumbs to Fiona, leading her closer to the truth.

She went quietly through the brush, her motions smooth and beautiful, until she reached a new group of animals near the Wildwoods Brook. This time, a group of rabbits talking to each other in an expressive way. Their quick talks were full of whispers and sneaky looks, which showed that they had a secret they didn't want to disclose with everyone.

Fiona was able to hear bits of their talk because she had really good hearing. They talked of a blue feather, a nut that had been missing, and a "misunderstanding." The bunnies' faces were stiff, and their body language was tense, which made it seem like they were anxious and uneasy together. They looked scared of what might happen if their secret got out. This added an interesting new layer to the investigation.

Fiona was close to the badger's burrow as the sun went down, and the Wildwoods Farm was bathed in a lovely golden light. She saw him pacing back and forth, his normal gruff manner replaced by a tinge of worry. He sometimes mumbled to himself, and the words were hard to understand, but Fiona, who had amazing hearing, could make out things like "wrong place, wrong time" and "It wasn't Jasper." It was clear from a distance that the badger was guilty of something.

Fiona spent the remainder of the night carefully writing down everything she saw and heard, putting together a full report of what she had learned. The quiet murmurs, the subtle body language, the broken discussions, and the small facts that seemed unimportant had all come together to create a new story that went against the first charges against Jasper. The image that was starting to come together was much more complicated and subtle than any of the other interviews had shown.

The hens had made a simplified, emotionally charged story that left out important parts of the whole story. But Fiona's inquiry found a hidden layer of reality that was buried by assumptions, biases, and maybe even intentional misdirection. The strong wind, the flash of blue, the dark shape, the misplaced nut, and the blue feather were all parts of a much bigger puzzle. They pointed to a whole different series of events and maybe even a different culprit.

The community was blind to another point of view because of the first charges, which were based on fear and bias. With Fiona's new information, a clearer picture was starting to form. At first, the whispers of doubt were thought to be unimportant, but they had started to develop a strong counter-narrative that went against the popularly accepted account of events.

Fiona realized that giving this new information to Ink would change the direction of their inquiry in a big way. What seemed like a simple case had turned into a maze of complexities, with a tangled web of misunderstandings and half-truths. She knew that the truth was out there, hiding among the murmurs and shadows of Wildwoods Farm. It was a fact that needed close attention, a critical look at the details, and the capacity to go beyond the surface to the deeper truths that molded how the community saw things. Fiona understood that the way to justice was through the soft sounds of the woods and the hard work of finding hidden facts. The voyage had only just begun, and the final discovery was sure to be both shocking and enlightening. She thought the truth was much more complicated than anyone at Wildwoods Farm had thought so far.

Chapter 2

The Investigation Begins

The next morning was bright and clear, with the sun shining through the leaves in a shower of golden light. Ink, his ferret nose twitching, guided Fiona to a quiet clearing next to the Wildwoods Brook. This was their interrogation room, a natural amphitheater that kept the animals from seeing and hearing what was going on. They had deliberately picked this area because it was quiet and peaceful, which made it easier for those being questioned to tell the truth, far away from the noise of the barn.

Bradley, the elderly badger, was the first witness they called. His memory was better than his reputation for being grumpy. Ink walked up to Bradley with a soothing voice and a sharpened quill in his hand. He was holding a notepad. "Bradley, my friend," he said, "we know you were close to the telephone pole when Jenny fell. Can you tell us what you saw?"

Bradley, who was cautious at first, slowly telling the story, choosing his words carefully and weighing the importance of each one. He said that a sudden blast of wind was strong enough to move the tall telephone pole. Then there was a gasp, a rustle, and the sound of a small body hitting the ground. He stressed how unexpected the wind was and how strong it was and that it was all of a sudden. He had felt a shiver and an unexplainable sense of unease before the event, but he thought it was just the normal chill of the early morning. Ink, on the other hand, heard a slight tremor in Bradley's voice and a pause when he talked about the wind. This pause said a lot about things that weren't said. He pushed more, gently yet firmly.

"Bradley," Ink went on, changing his tone to one of mild encouragement, "Did you see anything else? Is there anything strange, no matter how minor it may seem?"

Bradley moved around uncomfortably, his claws raking across the soft ground. He said he saw a flash of blue, a quick look near the pole shortly before Jenny fell. At first, he thought it was just a trick of the light, but Fiona's earlier comment about a similar detail that Connor had noted made him question it. He now remembered that the blue light had been too swift and too short to tell what it was.

Fiona noticed that Bradley was sweating a little on his forehead and looking at the brook out of the corner of his eye. She thought he was keeping back important information that he didn't want to share. She quietly moved closer, and her presence calmed him down and silently assured him that she understood.

Their next interview was with Connor, the juvenile squirrel who had been acting strangely upset during Fiona's earlier observations. Ink took a different approach with Connor, using a tone that was more fun and interesting. He started by asking Connor how his day was going, which helped the little squirrel relax before slowly bringing up the event.

Connor's first story was quite similar to Bradley's: the sudden wind, the fall, and the gasp. But when Ink gently asked Connor for further information, he told him more about the "flash of blue." He said it was a small, vividly colored thing, like a bird's feather or a piece of ribbon. He said he had seen it for a short while, but he was distracted by the hunt of a really tasty acorn. This small detail that Ink had carefully noted suddenly meant more because Bradley had told a similar story.

Fiona, on the other hand, paid attention to how Connor moved. When Ink said Jasper's name, she saw a slight tremble in his body, an anxious twitch in his whiskers, and his eyes blinked quickly. She could smell a slight pine needle smell on Connor's fur, which was strange because he lived on the other side of the woods.

Their next interviews with the hens who were gossiping were harder. Their stories were a chorus of allegations, a jumble of lies, and exaggerations. Ink and Fiona separated the hens and interviewed each one separately so that they could tell their experience without being influenced by the others. Even though this method took a lot of time, it revealed big errors and contradictions in their stories.

Henrietta, one of the hens, said something she hadn't said before: she had heard a muffled dispute right before the occurrence. Cecily, on the other hand, had spotted Jasper near the telephone pole but said she hadn't observed the fall itself since a large clump of ivy blocked her view. When their stories were carefully looked at, they showed a pattern of lies that were based on fear and bias toward Jasper.

The interview with Robert the rabbit was just as enlightening. At first, Robert didn't want to talk, but he ultimately said that he had seen a small, black creature running away right after the fall. He said it was rapid and agile and moved faster than he expected. This was in line with what the older squirrel had said earlier in Fiona's inquiry.

Ink and Fiona slowly put together a more logical story by carefully watching and asking questions. They found that the wind had a far bigger effect than they had thought at first. The flash of blue and the dark, running beast made Fiona think there might be something going on that could have made Jenny lose her balance. Some of the smaller creatures told Ink and Fiona about the lost nut and blue feather, which made it seem like the events had happened by accident rather than on purpose.

Ink and Fiona used more than just asking questions in their interviews. They also paid close attention to their witnesses' body language, tone of voice, and even little changes in posture. They saw the tense squirming, the looks that turned away, the small pauses, and the shakes that came out of nowhere. These small things, which are typically missed in everyday speech, were really important in figuring out reality. They used active listening techniques, which let the witnesses speak freely without being interrupted. At the same time, they watched how the witnesses reacted and carefully wrote down any contradictions in their tales.

Ink and Fiona stayed calm and neutral the whole time during the inquiries, making sure the witnesses felt safe and at ease. They understood how the witnesses felt and what they thought, which built confidence and collaboration, even with the most scared individuals. This non-confrontational method was quite helpful in getting honest answers, especially from the generally shy badger and the frightened rabbits.

Ink and Fiona put their notes together as the sun began to drop and created sweeping shadows across the area. The picture that came out was much more complicated than the simple story of a push. The reality was slowly coming to light, concealed under a layer of false beliefs and assumptions. The first charge against Jasper, which was mostly based on circumstantial evidence and communal biases, was starting to break apart. Instead, a much more complex and nuanced picture of what happened to Jenny that led to her tragic fall was starting to emerge. The doubts that had been brushed aside were now louder than the original allegations. The investigation had gone from just finding out who was guilty or innocent to a deeper look at truth and how perception might be wrong in a society that was dealing with loss and its own biases. Ink knew that the road to justice was long and winding, full of patient observation, thorough inquiry, and a deep understanding for how complicated the truth may be. They realized that the trial would be a turning point for Wildwoods Farm, a chance to face its own biases and work toward a more fair and informed view of justice.

The next morning, Ink and Fiona went back to the location of the accident with magnifying lenses, little brushes, and bags of evidence. The old oak telephone pole stood towering and motionless, a poignant reminder of the catastrophe. Ink looked around the base, his sharp eyes looking for any signs of disturbed ground, stray pebbles, or strange patterns. Fiona, on the other hand, climbed a branch nearby so she could look at the pole from a new angle.

The ground around the pole was unusually calm. There were no obvious dents or traces of a fight, which goes against the first idea that there was a strong shove. Ink carefully looked at the earth and used his brush to pick up little samples. He looked for any differences or inconsistencies in the texture, color, and composition that could mean movement or a fight. He didn't find anything. The earth looked as if nothing had happened.

As Ink got closer to the base of the pole, he saw a slight scuff mark on the wood that was virtually impossible to see with the naked eye. He carefully swept aside a layer of dirt and dust to show a small scratch that ran parallel to the ground. The mark wasn't very deep, but it was important that it was there. He stroked his finger along the length of it, trying to figure out what kind of thing had caused it. The surface was smooth, almost polished, which made it seem like it was hard and maybe even metal. He took a small sample of the wood fibers around the scratch to look at later.

From her high-up perch on the branch, Fiona saw something else entirely. She noticed a little, bright blue feather that was practically buried amid the foliage. It was the same blue color that Connor and Bradley had said they had seen before. Using a pair of tweezers, she carefully picked up the feather and put it in a sealed evidence bag. The feather, which seemed unimportant, may have been connected to the "flash of blue" that multiple witnesses saw. This made the investigation even more interesting. It wasn't a normal woodland feather; it seemed like it came from a pet bird, maybe a pretty one that one of the local humans kept.

Their search went beyond the area around the telephone pole. Ink carefully searched the area for any broken twigs, trash, or anything else that didn't belong there. He found a small, perfectly shaped acorn that had been slightly crushed and was lying a few feet away from the pole. The acorns discovered in the Wildwoods Farm were not like this one, and the way it looked made it seem like it had been fallen hard. He cautiously picked up the acorn and saw that it had a little bit of sticky sap on it. He took a sample to see if it came from a plant. The acorn and feather together were causing a series of events that didn't fit with what had been spoken before.

Fiona, using all of her senses, found a small mound of pine needles that had been moved and were a little muddy not far from where

Connor was last seen before the tragedy. She could tell that the pine needles had been roughly moved because of their unique smell. The way the needles were placed made it look like a quick getaway, which could connect the mysterious dark creature to the disaster. This discovery was very important because it showed how Robert the rabbit's testimony might be connected to other pieces of evidence, which helped to create a more complete picture of what happened. The scene they looked at didn't have much direct proof against Jasper, but it did have a lot of tiny elements that suggested a far more complicated chain of events. The scratch on the telephone pole, the blue feather, the pine needles that had been moved, and the strangely unusual acorn all made the first conclusion seem wrong. There wasn't enough definite proof against Jasper, which made Ink and Fiona question the truth of the original claims and made it seem like the story regarding Jenny's fall was much more complicated than first imagined.

Ink and Fiona spent the remainder of the day carefully writing down everything they had found, making sure to write down every detail, observation, and piece of proof they had found. They drew sketches of each piece of evidence, noting where it was and how it related to other pieces of evidence. They put each piece of evidence in their own bag and labeled it, which kept the chain of custody intact. Ink knew this very well from his thorough training. Their careful method wasn't only about discovering evidence; it was also about keeping the inquiry honest and making sure that the truth wouldn't be hidden by mishandling or contamination.

By nightfall, they were back in their quiet clearing by the Wildwoods brook, where the only light came from the firefly. They looked over their notes and made links between the pieces of evidence that didn't appear to go together. The scuff mark on the pole, the blue feather, the crushed acorn, and the pine needles that had been moved all suggested that a series of accidents had happened, not a planned act of violence. The evidence pointed to an unexpected chain of events that started with something that couldn't be seen. Robert's testimony and the pine needles that had been moved made the picture of a small, black creature running away from the scene clearer.

The feather, which was a bright blue color, was very confusing. It wasn't a bird that lived on Wildwoods Farm. This made it seem like there might be a link to one of the woodland locals, which made the investigation much more complicated. The acorn, which is different from the ones found nearby, may have come from somewhere else, which could mean that it is connected to someone from a different section of the forest community. The absence of any clear signs of a struggle near the base of the telephone pole provided further support for the theory of an accident rather than a deliberate act of violence.

Their analysis continued far into the night. They created a timeline of events based on their findings, weaving together the various testimonies with the physical evidence. The image that began to unfold was one of a cascade of events, each seemingly minor, contributing to the devastating outcome. The sudden gust of wind, as Bradley had described, may have been a contributing factor. The flash of blue, the discarded acorn, and the unknown creature likely created a distraction, causing Jenny to lose her balance and fall. This sequence of accidental events, far from exonerating anyone, was adding a layer of ambiguity to the unfolding tragedy.

Ink and Fiona realized that this case was more than just a simple investigation; it was a deep dive into the subjective nature of truth. They were not only seeking the truth about what happened, but they were also examining how easily the truth could be obscured by assumptions, biases, and the inherent limitations of perception. The evidence pointed towards an accident, a series of unfortunate and unforeseen events, not a deliberate act of violence.

Ink and Fiona told the community what they had found the next day. The inhabitants of Wildwoods Farm were shocked, didn't believe it, and were quietly relieved when they found out that Jenny's fall might have been an accident caused by a combination of things that weren't planned. The anger and blame directed at Jasper at first began to fade, and the community began to work together to figure out the complicated chain of events that led to Jenny's death. The community, which had been split by distrust and accusations, began to heal. A trial was still needed to officially end the case, but it would now be an opportunity for reflection and reconciliation. The investigation not only found out the truth regarding Jenny's fall, but it also gave the community a better idea of how much they might be both prejudiced and compassionate. They learned that the truth was a fragile thing that was often concealed under layers of bias and assumption. To get to the truth there needed to be careful observation, painstaking study, and a deep respect for the intricacies of justice.

Fiona was the key to figuring out the complicated network of rumors because she could read the small changes in how witnesses acted. Ink lovingly called her *The Whisper* because she could tell the truth from a lie by watching the small changes in a witnesses' posture, stride, and even the way their ears twitched. It wasn't just about listening in; it was about learning the forest's language without words.

Mrs. Periwinkle, the resident hen who was known for her sharp tongue and even sharper observation abilities, was the first hen they talked to. Mrs. Periwinkle, who was overweight and had a self-important demeanor, told her side of the story in the most theatrical way, with her feathers ruffled and her voice a clucking torrent of half-truths and exaggerated details. She claimed she saw Jasper and Jenny fighting near the telephone pole, but no one else could confirm that incident. Fiona, on the other hand, saw a slight tremble in Mrs. Periwinkle's leg, which is a sign of nervousness and usually means someone is unsure... or lying. The hen's body language didn't match her confident posture, which made it seem like she might be lying or not sure of what she was saying. Fiona remembered this difference and knew she needed to look into it more closely.

Their next stop was Barnaby Badger's burrow, a charming home hidden among the roots of an old oak tree. Barnaby, who was gruff but eventually compassionate, confirmed the gust of wind, which Robert the rabbit also said was true, but he didn't offer much else to the case.

He was more worried about how the whole community was being affected, and his tone suggested that he wanted things to be fixed quickly so that Wildwoods Farm could go back to its calm routine. Fiona watched Barnaby very intently. He was worried, but he was also open and honest. His story didn't show any signs of deception or exaggeration. Fiona believed him, which confirmed this aspect of the story.

They went from Barnaby's burrow to Knox's warren, which is a maze of tunnels under a big willow tree. Knox, a scared rabbit with a twitching snout and wide eyes, told his experience and vividly described the "flash of blue" that happened shortly before Jenny fell. He said he saw a little, dark thing run away from the area right after. But Knox's memory was broken up, a mix of fear and perplexity. Fiona saw that his ears stayed flat against his head even while he was talking. This is a sign of acute fear or nervousness in rabbits. She thought that his fear, even though it was real, might have changed how he saw things. The "flash of blue," which seemed important, needed more research. This didn't appear like a planned falsehood; it seemed more like he was frightened and misreading what he had seen.

Their trip took them to Oswald Owl's hollow, which was high up in the branches of a beautiful redwood tree. Oswald didn't have much fresh information to share, but his point of view was quite helpful because he had a sharp eye and a lot of expertise about the forests. He hadn't noticed anything strange happening near the telephone pole, but he did agree that the Wildwoods Farm was usually tranquil, which made the accident even stranger. Fiona saw how owl-like he was looking at her, how well he remembered things, and how calm and still he was, which showed that he was not being deceptive and telling the truth to the best of his knowledge.

The squirrels lived in a part of the Wildwoods Farm that was typically peaceful, but the clues led Ink and Fiona there. In this place, they found a completely different story: a place where the community spoke in quiet tones and looked at one another sideways, a community wrapped in a mist of unspoken fears. At first, the squirrels were hesitant to talk, but in the end, they gave a variety of conflicting tales that made the issue even more confusing. Some witnesses said that Jenny and Jasper were having a playful fight, which is something that happens a lot with these active squirrels. Some others said that the two of them were angry at each other, which could have been a reason for foul play. Fiona, on the other hand, could feel a sense of tension among the squirrels, a quiet uneasiness that made her think they were hiding something from her. The way they acted and how they avoided answering questions made it seem like there was more going on than just rumor.

Following the trail of talk turned out to be a very careful job. Fiona noticed small changes in the squirrels' behavior by watching how they acted and reading their apprehensive body language. Some witnesses looked guilty, some looked scared, and a couple looked like they were lying. This complicated ballet of body language gave Ink and Fiona important information. Amber, a relative of Jenny, kept peeking over her shoulder, fidgeting anxiously, and altering her story a lot. Amber's body language and conflicting stories showed that she was hiding something, maybe out of fear or guilt. Their questionings included the cats, who are a more advanced group recognized for being smart and particularly good at manipulating information. The cats, commanded by a royal Persian named Zelda, didn't appear to care as much about the truth as they did about keeping the peace. They told polished versions of what happened, leaving out important facts or putting more emphasis on specific parts to suit their own needs. Fiona quickly figured out that getting information from the cats needed a different approach: a mix of charm, careful watching, and a little bit of fear.

Ink and Fiona began to put together a much more complicated picture than the first charge implied by attentively listening to and watching the community who lived in Wildwoods Farm. The rumor of Jasper's push, which was at first all over the farm and woods, showed patterns and contradictions that hinted at a different reason for Jenny's fall. The many stories, along with Fiona's meticulous observations of "Whisper," pointed to a more complicated chain of events that went beyond simple chatter. The picture these observations painted told a story not of a planned act of violence, but of a succession of unforeseen circumstances that led to a terrible accident instead of a single evil act.

The more they looked into it, the more they discovered that finding the truth wasn't only about gathering data. It was also about understanding the background, the reasons behind the communities' actions, and the prejudices that influenced their views. Their route wasn't just a way through the woods; it was a voyage into the heart of a witness—or, more accurately, an animal. It showed how complicated truth, perception, and the power of gossip are in constructing the world we all live in. As they kept looking into the case, the line between reality and fiction became less clear, which made them question the very things they thought they knew. The forest's whispers were taking them down an unexpected route, one that would eventually disclose a far more complicated and shocking truth than anyone had thought at first. It seemed that the path to justice was full of ups and downs, and that you had to be willing to challenge even the most obvious conclusions.

There was a lot of worry in the air at Wildwoods Farm that no one spoke about. Ink and Fiona were at a crossroads after hearing a lot of different stories that didn't all agree. Every hour that went by made the first charge against Jasper appear less and less likely. The rumors, the half-truths, and the tense twitches all pointed to something worse than just a violent deed. Now, they were all focused on the quiet that was a conspiracy of fear.

The younger squirrels gave them their next lead, which they hadn't thought about before. These were the quieter bunch in the community who were often ignored since their elders were so loud. Fiona, who was naturally sensitive, could feel a profound current of worry running through their games, even if they seemed to be having fun. She carefully walked up to them, giving them sunflower seeds and kind words to ease their first fears.

Finally, a shy juvenile squirrel named Sammy broke the silence. He admitted that he had seen the accident but hadn't said anything before because he was scared. He had seen not just Jenny fall, but also a larger, darker figure nearby—a weasel, which is known for being violent and stealing things. Sammy was too scared to say anything because he thought the weasel, Sly, might hurt him if he told anyone what he had witnessed. His dread had made him quiet, which added to the storm of rumors and misunderstandings.Ink was terrified by this news. Sly was known to be troublemaker who frequently worked in the dark, where his acts were hidden and scary. Just his notoriety had stopped anyone from speaking out against him. It wasn't just Sammy who was scared; all the younger squirrels were too scared to come forward with important information.

Fiona, who was always paying attention, noticed the small signs that backed up Sammy's story. She saw a bunch of baby squirrels at the base of the telephone pole. Their fur was ruffled, and their eyes were wide with terror, as if they had all been through something ghastly. They didn't want to talk about it, but their body language said a lot. It was evident that their quiet was more than simply a way to stay out of trouble; it was a way to shield themselves from a known threat.

They changed their focus to Sly, the sneaky weasel. It was harder than they thought to find him. Sly was a master of disguise and trickery. He could easily blend into the shadows and change the things around him. Ink and Fiona utilized both tracking and observation to follow faint trails of broken twigs and disturbed leaves. They found out that Sly had a lot of hidden paths and tunnels that crisscrossed the farm and woodland, which made it more difficult to find him.

They searched until they found the darkest part of the Wildwoods Farm, a thick thicket known for its creepy silence and tangled foliage. They found Sly's hideaway there, a cleverly hidden burrow full of stolen goods and evidence of his bad behavior. They found a little blue feather inside that looked just like the one Robert said he had seen near the telephone pole.

But the feather wasn't the only thing that pointed to guilt. Fiona found something much more interesting: a tiny wooden acorn with the initials "J.J." engraved into it. Jenny loved this acorn toy. The fact that it was in Sly's lair proved that he was involved in the event. Sly had definitely seen Jenny near the pole. But how?

The last piece of the puzzle came to light after a careful look at the region around it. Ink, who is very observant, saw traces of a fight near the telephone pole: a patch of ground that was disturbed, broken twigs, and claw marks. When you looked more closely at these marks, you could see that they were compatible with a fight between a squirrel and a much bigger animal. It was evident that Sly had met Jenny. His acts, even though they weren't on purpose, led to the catastrophic fall.

The whole image, which was finally exposed, offered a much more complicated scenario than the first charges had led the community to believe. Jenny didn't fall because someone pushed her; she fell because she was scared of Sly. Jasper, on the other hand, was innocent; he was wrongly accused because of circumstantial evidence and the community's dread of facing the truth about Sly. The community's fear, along with its dependence on gossip and skewed assumptions, had hidden the truth, making a story that blamed an innocent animal while protecting a real criminal. Fiona understood that this anxiety was a big part of the problem and that she needed to find a method to deal with it honestly.

It wasn't just about blaming Sly; it was also about finding out what caused the problem in the first place: the community's fear of facing a powerful, frightening beast. This dread made witnesses afraid to speak up, fostered rumors, and made the community members feel like they couldn't trust each other. The accident, which was very sad, was the spark that revealed the evil side of their usually idyllic society.

The trial that followed wasn't only about punishing Sly; it was also about facing the community's fear and how it affects truth and justice. The dread, the gossip, and the worries that weren't addressed had made things so bad that the truth was twisted and justice was put off. Ink and Fiona's diligent inquiry not only unearthed a hidden truth but also revealed the systemic flaws at Wildwoods Farm. This showed how important it is to communicate openly, think critically, and have the nerve to face fear.

The trial wasn't only about discovering the individual who did it; it was also about mending the community, restoring faith in the truth, and making a culture where justice could really happen. The instance of Jenny's fall was a turning point for the community, teaching them how important it is to speak truth to power and face even the most disturbing truths. It would take a long time and a lot of work to heal, but the truth had finally come out, and the way to a more fair and honest Wildwoods Farm had begun. The truths that had been whispered were now out in the open, which let the community start to heal and regain trust. The case would remind the community of how dangerous it is to let fear run wild and how important it is to tell the truth in order to make society more peaceful.

The air in the Wildwoods Farm, still thick with the scent of pine and damp earth, felt different now, charged with a newfound energy. The revelation of Sly's involvement, while a significant breakthrough, had only scratched the surface of the mystery. Ink, ever the meticulous ferret, felt a nagging sense of unease. Something didn't quite fit. The evidence pointed to Sly, that was undeniable, but the details surrounding Jenny's fall remained frustratingly unclear. The precise sequence of events, the exact moment of the tragedy – these remained elusive riddles.

Fiona, with her emerald eyes shining with understanding, felt the same way he did.

"There's a piece missing, Ink," she said in a low, rumbling voice that echoed through the bushes. "Something important that we missed." She pointed to the carefully drawn map of the track they had taken, which led from the telephone pole to Sly's den. The trail, while revealing, felt like it was missing something, like a story told in pieces.

They started their re-examination by going back to the place where the accident happened. This time, though, they weren't thinking about the whole picture, the whole story of Sly's presence. They were drawn to the small details—the things that were unimportant before but were now important. Ink was the first to make a breakthrough because he could see small changes in the forest floor that no one else could.

He saw a single, broken twig laying a few feet away from the main area of the fight they had already investigated. It was a modest element that was hard to see, lying half-hidden under a pile of leaves. But to Ink, it screamed of importance. This twig didn't break off as cleanly as the others. Someone had broken it with a sharp, seemingly intentional force, and the broken end showed an unusual angle. This wasn't just stepping on a twig and shattering it; it was something else.

This one broken twig, which seemed unimportant at first, was the key to unlocking a new layer of the puzzle. Ink followed a barely visible track that headed away from the telephone pole and steeply off the path that led to Sly's cave in order to find out where the twig came from. The path went through a large patch of brambles, which was a part of the Wildwoods Farm that the witnesses had never talked about. It was a dark place, a part of their universe that they had been quick to forget.

The trail was dangerous since it was full with thorns and vines that got stuck in their fur. Fiona, who was quite quick, led the way, gently brushing aside the plants that were in the way. Ink followed closely behind, his sharp nose picking up on the slight smell of dirt, wet leaves, and something else—something that smelled a little like metal.As they went deeper into the thicket, the bushes got a little less thick, and they found a little clearing. A gnarled old oak tree stood in the middle of this clearing, its branches spreading out like skeletal arms. And at the bottom of the oak, partly hidden by a clump of leaves, was what they were looking for.

It was a little piece of metal that had rusted over time and was just a little bigger than Ink's paw. It was a clasp, a way to hold something together, that seemed like it was part of something bigger. What was interesting is that it had a weak inscription—a single letter that was hard to read but definitely there: "W." Ink and Fiona didn't know what the letter meant, but it felt very significant that it was there.

The broken twig and the clasp gave them new ideas for their inquiry. The path that led to this clearing was different; Sly, Jenny, and Jasper hadn't made it. This was a new player in the unfolding drama. The painstakingly documented trail, which had been carefully created over the prior few days, now seemed lacking and insufficient.

They had been concentrating on one possible suspect and ignoring several others. Based on their first thoughts, the whole investigation suddenly seemed wrong and not finished.

They went back to the heart of Wildwoods Farm and spent hours carefully retracing their steps and looking around the telephone pole again. They found more proof and hints that they had missed at first since they were in such a hurry to solve the case. They found a small, half torn piece of fabric that was a shade of blue that matched Jenny's favorite scarf. It was hidden among the leaves. There were small holes in the fabric, as if it had been stuck on something sharp. They also uncovered a piece of rough bark that was shredded in the same way, with marks that looked like a recent struggle. The metallic smell they had noticed in the undergrowth made them look more closely at the telephone pole. They saw that the wood had some rust and metal particles on it that matched the metal of the clasp. They thought the clasp was part of a bigger system that was connected to the telephone pole. Maybe it was a broken latch or something else that went wrong and caused Jenny's death. This would explain the area that looked like a fight broke out and the ripped fabric.

This fresh evidence pointed to a story that was much less evil than the one they had been following. It pointed to a sad accident or a mechanical malfunction, not an act of violence on purpose. They now understood that the broken twig was not part of a struggle, but rather a piece of the mechanism that had broken off during the event and fallen near the hidden clearing, where it had gone undiscovered until now.

It was a mystery what the "W" on the clasp meant, but they were determined to find out. It seemed as if it was a manufacturer's mark, which could help them find the cause of the broken mechanism. Now, their research has taken a completely different turn. They needed to look into the telephone poles' maintenance records, which was a long and tedious that required patience and persistence.

They found the "W" by looking for a secretive owl named Professor Sophocles, who was famous for having lots of old maps and records. At first, Professor Sophocles didn't want to help, but Fiona's charm and Ink's convincing logic won him over. He produced a dusty book about the history of the communication systems at Wildwoods Farm. It chronicled those who came to do maintenance in and around the farm.

Professor Sophocles told a tale of how he scavenged a schematic of the telephone poles and its important mechanisms. At the base of the schematic was a clasp that had a letter "W" on it. The old owl overheard the workers talking about how the clasps were faulty and that the "Willow Creek Workshop" made the shoddy clasps. In passing, Professor Sophocles picked up on how the Willow Creek Workshop was no longer in business since they were notorious for making shoddy products.

Their discovery shed light on the tragic accident. The clasp, which was a faulty product from Willow Creek Workshop, broke, which made the support system for the telephone pole fail. This problem caused Jenny to fall, not a deliberate act of violence. The proof had always been there, hidden under the surface of the first, false story. The broken branch, the ripped cloth, and the metallic smell all made sense now.

The trial that followed was supposed to convict Sly, but it turned into an investigation into the safety standards and poor product quality coming from the Willow Creek Workshop. The Wildwoods Farm community was quick in the rush of judgement against Jasper and are now faced with the consequences of such a hasty judgement. The trial would be a powerful testament to the importance of finding out the truth before rushing to a decision.

The community seemed to breathe a sigh of relief that Jasper was cleared of the false accusations of pushing Jenny to her death. Wildwoods Farm, once consumed by fear and speculation, was transformed, its inhabitants now united by a shared commitment to truth and justice. The once-whispered secrets, now openly confronted, cleared the way for a newfound sense of harmony and unity. The case of Jenny's fall was forever etched in the history of Wildwoods Farm, a solemn reminder of the importance of seeking the truth, even when it's inconvenient, and the devastating consequences of unchecked fear.

Chapter 3

The Unexpected Culprit

The great oak in the center of Wildwoods Farm stood as a silent witness, its ancient branches reaching towards the twilight sky. Beneath it, Ink and Fiona had arranged a makeshift courtroom – a circle of smooth stones, meticulously placed to represent seats for the assembled animals. The air hummed with anticipation, a tense silence broken only by the rustling of leaves and the chirping of crickets.

The community had gathered, a diverse assembly of woodland creatures: gossiping hens perched precariously on branches, their beady eyes gleaming with curiosity; sleek cats, their tails twitching restlessly; lumbering badgers, their faces etched with concern; and wise owls, their gaze piercing and perceptive. At the center of the circle sat Jasper, his usually vibrant fur dull and matted, his eyes filled with a mixture of fear and exhaustion. Sly, his shifty eyes darting nervously, was kept at a respectable distance, under the watchful eye of a pair of sturdy dogs.

Ink, standing tall on a moss-covered log, addressed the assembled creatures. His voice, though small, carried a weight that silenced the whispers and rustles.

"We have spent many days, many hours, painstakingly piecing together the truth behind Jenny's tragic fall," he began, his voice clear and resonant. "We followed the clues, initially focusing on one specific path, only to discover that what we saw was a carefully constructed illusion, a deceptive smokescreen obscuring the true cause of this devastating event."

Fiona, her emerald eyes fixed on the assembled animals, spoke next. Her voice, rich and melodic, held a certain authority that commanded respect.

"We focused on Sly, driven by assumptions and the quick judgments of this community. We were about to accuse him based on circumstantial evidence, failing to consider other possibilities. We fell into the trap of prejudice, allowing our biases to cloud our judgment, and this nearly led to a grave injustice."

A murmur rippled through the gathering. The accusations of hasty judgment struck a chord, the animals recognizing their own complicity in this near-tragedy.

The hens, notorious for their gossip, exchanged uneasy glances, their incessant chatter replaced by a thoughtful silence. Even the cats, typically aloof and self-assured, seemed subdued, their usual arrogance tempered by a newfound humility.

Ink continued, his voice growing stronger with each word. "The truth, as we have discovered, is far more complex and unexpected than any of us could have imagined. It wasn't a malicious act, not a deliberate push, not a calculated crime."

He produced the rusted metal clasp, holding it aloft for all to see. The single, almost illegible letter "W" was visible to everyone, etched into the corroded metal.

"This," he declared, "is the key to understanding Jenny's fall. This clasp, a faulty component from the Willow Creek Workshop, was the true culprit."

Gasps of astonishment rippled through the gathering. The whispers, previously focused on Jasper and Sly's alleged guilt, now turned to shocked murmurs of disbelief. The revelation shattered their preconceived notions, forcing them to confront the limitations of their perceptions. The community, so quick to judge, was now left to grapple with the implications of their assumptions, the weight of their collective failure to seek the truth.

Fiona explained the chain of events: the malfunctioning clasp, the weakened support structure of the telephone pole, Jenny's unwitting encounter with the failing mechanism, the struggle, the broken twig, the torn fabric – all pieces of a puzzle that had been tragically misunderstood.

"The broken twig," Ink pointed out, "was not a sign of a struggle, but a fragment of the broken clasp. The metallic scent, which we traced to the thicket, originated from this very clasp, and the torn fabric suggests a struggle with the failing mechanism, not a struggle with Sly."

Professor Sophocles, the reclusive owl, stepped forward, his large, wise eyes reflecting the light of the setting sun. He corroborated Ink and Fiona's findings, presenting the detailed information from his historical tome about the Willow Creek Workshop's notoriously poor craftsmanship and the subsequent recall of the faulty clasps.

The sudden shift in the narrative was deeply unsettling. The relief Jasper visibly felt was palpable, a stark contrast to the tense atmosphere that had prevailed moments earlier. His shoulders slumped, the weight of the false accusation lifting from his frame.

The trial, intended to convict Jasper and Sly, transformed into a poignant public inquiry into the standards of the long-defunct Willow Creek Workshop. The community, so eager to assign blame, was now forced to examine their own actions, their hasty judgments, and the devastating effects of their prejudices.

The elders of Wildwoods Farm, their faces reflecting a mixture of shame and understanding, addressed the community, acknowledging their errors. They apologized to Jasper, publicly clearing his name and celebrating his resilience in the face of unwarranted accusations. They emphasized the importance of thorough investigation and the dangers of relying on assumptions and biased perspectives.

The trial served not only as a moment of justice for Jasper but also as a powerful lesson for the entire community. Wildwoods Farm began a process of collective self-reflection, learning the importance of discerning truth from hearsay, fostering empathy, and understanding the devastating consequences of unchecked fear and hasty judgments. The community's collective mistake served as a poignant reminder of the need for careful observation and rational judgment.

The incident with Jenny became a cautionary tale, woven into the very fabric of Wildwoods Farm history. It was a story not just about a tragic accident, but about the resilience of truth and the enduring power of understanding and forgiveness. The community, having faced its own flaws, emerged stronger, united by a shared commitment to justice, empathy, and the tireless pursuit of truth. The once-whispered secrets of the forest were brought to light, paving the way for a new era of harmony and unity, where even the rustling leaves seemed to hum a melody of reconciliation and peace. The weight of the past remained, but it now served as a foundation for a brighter future. Wildwoods Farm had learned its lesson, and the wind whispered through the trees a new song of justice, truth, and forgiveness.

The sun, sinking low in the sky, cast long shadows across the clearing where the trial had taken place. The air, still thick with the residue of tension and uncertainty, slowly began to lighten, replaced by a tentative sense of hope. Jasper, his eyes still brimming with unshed tears, sat amongst the assembled animals, his relief palpable. Ink and Fiona stood beside him, their expressions grave but resolute. Sly, his usually cocky demeanor replaced by a stunned silence, was brought forward. He didn't look at Jasper; his gaze was fixed on the ground; his shoulders slumped under the weight of his secret.

The confession began haltingly, Sly's voice barely a whisper at first. He spoke of his obsession with the old Willow Creek Workshop, a fascination bordering on the unhealthy. He'd spent countless hours poring over its historical records, fascinated by its rise and ignominious fall, by the stories of its flawed products and the controversies surrounding its eventual closure. He'd developed an almost morbid interest in the faulty clasps, seeing them not as mere defective parts, but as objects of dark beauty, symbols of forgotten craftsmanship.

"It wasn't meant to hurt anyone," Sly mumbled, his voice barely audible above the rustling leaves. "I just... I wanted to see what would happen. I wanted to see if the stories were true, if the clasps were as weak as they said."

He explained that he had obtained a few of the old clasps from other poles that had been abandoned at the edge of the woods, a trove of forgotten relics from the long-gone workshop. His actions weren't driven by malice, but by a twisted curiosity, a desperate need to witness history come to life, to prove the tales he'd heard were factual.

Sly described his actions with painful detail. He'd climbed the telephone pole, not with the intention of harming Jenny, but to secretly attach one of the rusted clasps to the pole's support structure, a clandestine experiment to test its structural integrity. He hadn't anticipated Jenny's arrival. He hadn't wanted to cause any harm, but he hadn't considered the consequences of his actions, he was completely absorbed by his morbid curiosity.

He recounted how he'd watched, paralyzed by fear and shock, as Jenny approached, her playful chatter abruptly silenced by the snap of the weakened support beam. He described Jenny's frantic struggle to regain her balance, then she suddenly fell, the horrifying silence that followed. Jasper hadn't pushed her; Sly had inadvertently set the scene for her tragic accident. His actions, born from reckless curiosity, had had catastrophic consequences, causing Jenny's death and unimaginable suffering and pain.

He recounted his initial attempts to conceal his involvement, his desperate efforts to cover his tracks. He'd placed the broken twig strategically, hoping to mislead the investigation, but his actions only deepened his involvement in the unfolding tragedy. The metallic scent, inadvertently left at the scene of the accident, was another clue that had served to build up the misconception that he'd committed a crime. He'd intended only to test the resilience of an old clasp; he'd never intended to cause harm to anyone. But his lack of foresight, his recklessness, had led to the painful consequences.

His confession was met with a stunned silence. The animals, so eager to find a culprit, so quick to condemn, now grappled with the complexities of Sly's narrative. His motive, while undeniably foolish and dangerous, lacked the malice they had initially assumed. His actions, born from obsessive fascination rather than ill intent, forced the community to confront the ambiguity of intent and consequence.

Professor Sophocles, his usually calm demeanor ruffled, stepped forward. He confirmed Sly's account, explaining that the historical records of the Willow Creek Workshop contained numerous accounts of similar incidents, albeit on a smaller scale. The workshop's notorious disregard for safety standards, its relentless pursuit of profit over quality, had resulted in countless faulty products, many of them potentially dangerous. Sly's actions, while reckless, were not entirely unprecedented.

The hens, usually so quick to spread rumors and gossip, were now surprisingly silent, their beady eyes reflecting a mixture of shock and regret. The cats, their usual aloofness momentarily shattered, exchanged uneasy glances, their haughty demeanor replaced by a sense of shared responsibility. The badgers, known for their cautious nature, solemnly nodded their heads, acknowledging the gravity of the situation.

Jasper, his gaze fixed on Sly, spoke for the first time. His voice was surprisingly calm, devoid of anger or resentment. "I forgive you, Sly," he said, his voice barely above a whisper. "But you must understand the consequences of your actions. Your curiosity, however innocent, caused immeasurable pain."

Ink nodded in agreement. "Your actions were reckless, Sly," he said, his voice firm but compassionate. "You played a dangerous game, and Jenny paid the ultimate price. But your confession allows us to move forward, to learn from this tragedy, and to prevent similar accidents from happening again."

Fiona added, "While we understand your fascination, Sly, your actions demonstrate the importance of responsible investigation and understanding the potential consequences of one's actions. Curiosity can be a wonderful thing, but uncontrolled curiosity can lead to catastrophe."

The elders of Wildwoods Farm stepped forward, their faces reflecting a profound understanding of the situation. They acknowledged the community's mistakes, their haste in judging, and their failure to consider alternative explanations. They praised Sly for his honesty, acknowledging the courage it took to confess and accept responsibility for his actions, even though his intentions hadn't been malicious.

They declared that Sly would not face punishment in the traditional sense. Instead, he would dedicate his time to helping repair the damaged telephone poles throughout Wildwoods Farm, using his detailed knowledge of the Willow Creek Workshop's designs to identify other potentially dangerous components. He would also assist in creating educational materials to help the community understand the importance of and dangers surrounding curiosity. This act of service, they declared, would be his penance, a testament to his commitment to making amends for his actions.

The community, having collectively confronted their biases and prejudices, began a process of healing and reconciliation. The incident with Jenny, once a source of division and mistrust, transformed into a powerful lesson about the dangers of assumptions, the importance of thorough investigation, and the restorative power of truth and forgiveness. The trial, initially intended to convict, had inadvertently evolved into a community-wide examination of conscience, highlighting the need for empathy, understanding, and responsible behavior.

The whispers in Wildwoods Farm, once filled with gossip and speculation, now carried a new melody – a song of acceptance, reconciliation, and the shared commitment to a brighter future. The shadow of Jenny's tragic accident lingered, but it no longer obscured the light of truth, justice, and forgiveness that now illuminated Wildwoods Farm. The community, having learned a profound lesson, emerged stronger, unified by a shared commitment to seeking justice while preserving empathy and understanding. The story of Jasper and Jenny, along with Sly's unexpected confession, became an integral part of the Wildwoods Farm collective memory, a testament to their shared journey towards truth, justice, and collective healing. The farm, once filled with the whispers of suspicion and blame, now resonated with a newfound sense of peace, a testament to the restorative power of truth and understanding.

The weight of Sly's confession hung heavily in the air, a palpable silence settling over the clearing. The initial shock rippled outwards, a wave of stunned disbelief washing over the assembled animals. The hens, usually a cacophony of clucking gossip, were eerily quiet, their beady eyes wide and reflective. Mrs. Periwinkle, the self-proclaimed town gossip, usually quick with a judgment and a feathered jab, simply stared at the ground, her comb drooping. Even Henrietta, known for her sharp tongue and unwavering certainty, seemed momentarily speechless. The rumor mill, usually churning at breakneck speed, had ground to a complete halt.

The cats, normally aloof and self-assured, displayed a similar stunned silence. Jack, the grumpy tomcat who had been the most vocal in his condemnation of Jasper, sat with his tail unusually still, his usually piercing gaze softened, almost apologetic. Even Fiona, despite her sharp intellect and unwavering dedication to justice, felt a pang of surprise at the unexpected turn of events. The swiftness with which the community had rallied against Jasper, fueled by assumptions and incomplete information, now seemed jarringly out of place.

Amongst the badgers, known for their cautious nature and level-headedness, there was a sense of sober reflection. Old Man Brock, the oldest badger in Wildwoods Farm, his fur weathered by years of witnessing the forest's ebbs and flows, let out a low sigh. His usually stern gaze was filled with a profound understanding of animal nature. He'd seen countless times how easily misinterpretations and biases could cloud judgment, leading to unfair accusations and unnecessary pain. His slow nod seemed to confirm the quiet understanding spreading through the badger community. The quick judgment they'd initially cast upon Jasper now felt heavy on their consciences.

The squirrels, naturally, were the most visibly affected. The younger squirrels, who'd been so quick to join in the accusations against Jasper, now displayed a mixture of guilt and uncertainty. Their playful chatter was replaced with a subdued quietude, a somber realization that their actions had contributed to the spread of misinformation and the unjust persecution of their friend. Jasper's mother, a wise old squirrel with eyes that reflected generations of farm wisdom, looked upon her son with a mixture of relief and sorrow. Relief that he was innocent, sorrow for the ordeal he had been subjected to.

The rabbits, generally known for their timid nature, were surprisingly assertive in their expressions of remorse. Payton, a particularly brave young rabbit, spoke up, his voice trembling slightly, "We... we were too quick to judge. We listened to the rumors without seeking the truth." His words resonated with the entire community, a shared sentiment echoing in the rustling leaves.

Even the usually stoic owls, perched high in their ancient oak trees, seemed to ponder the events, their wide eyes gazing down on the assembly with a newfound understanding.

Professor Sophocles, the farm's resident historian and a creature of immense wisdom and intellectual capacity, acknowledged the community's collective failure.

"We have all learned a valuable lesson today," he announced, his voice resonating with gravitas. "The pursuit of truth requires patience, careful observation, and the courage to question our own assumptions." He paused and then continued, "We were too quick to condemn, too eager to find a scapegoat. We failed to consider alternative explanations, to examine the evidence thoroughly, and to consider the possibility of innocent error." Professor Sophocles looked among the assembly that were eagerly agreeing with him.

The revelation of Sly's unintentional involvement brought about a period of intense introspection. The community began to examine its own roles in perpetuating the false accusations against Jasper. The realization that their collective judgment had been flawed, based on incomplete information and biased interpretations, was a sobering experience. The initial wave of anger and resentment gradually gave way to a sense of shared responsibility and the urgent need for healing and reconciliation.

The atmosphere, once thick with suspicion and accusation, began to lighten. The weight of collective guilt was palpable, a silent acknowledgment of their failings. The vibrant life of Wildwoods Farm, momentarily muted by the tragedy, began to stir again. The birds chirped a more hopeful tune, the squirrels chattered less anxiously, and the wind whispered through the trees, carrying with it a renewed sense of hope.

The elders of Wildwoods Farm, having witnessed the community's collective reckoning, stepped forward. Their presence commanded respect, their words carrying the weight of centuries of wisdom and understanding. They acknowledged their own oversight, admitting that they too had initially been swayed by the circumstantial evidence and hadn't fully investigated all angles. They called for a period of reflection, urging the community to examine its internal systems, its methods of disseminating information, and its overall approach to justice.

The process of reconciliation was long and arduous. It involved numerous town hall meetings, heart-to-heart conversations, and a community-wide project focused on rebuilding the damaged telephone pole and fostering a culture of responsible investigation and communication. The hens organized workshops on unbiased reporting, the cats volunteered to train the young ones on careful observation and deductive reasoning, and the badgers established a new committee dedicated to fact-checking and information verification.

Sly, burdened by his unexpected role in Jenny's death, dedicated himself to the community's healing process. He willingly accepted the community's proposed penance, spending countless hours repairing the telephone poles and creating educational materials designed to prevent similar accidents from occurring in the future. His actions, born out of a desire to make amends, became a testament to the restorative power of justice and forgiveness. The once-whispered accusations were replaced by a shared commitment to a better future.

The trial, which had started as a search for a guilty party, had unexpectedly transformed into a catalyst for community-wide self-reflection and growth. Wildwoods Farm, once fractured by suspicion and misjudgment, emerged stronger and more unified, bound together by a newfound understanding of justice, truth, and the importance of empathy and forgiveness. The memory of Jenny remained, a poignant reminder of the fragility of life and the devastating consequences of unchecked assumptions and hasty judgments. But alongside the sorrow, a new narrative began to unfold – one of healing, community-building, and a collective commitment to seeking truth and justice with compassion and understanding. The whispers in Wildwoods Farm, once filled with accusations and gossip, now carried a new melody: a song of reconciliation, forgiveness, and the shared promise of a brighter future.

The sun dappled through the leaves, casting long shadows across the clearing where the entire community of Wildwoods Farm had gathered. The air, still heavy with the residue of the previous day's shock, gradually began to lighten with the tentative hope of a new dawn. This wasn't a trial in the traditional sense, no formal court or judge present, but a town hall, a collective gathering born from necessity and a shared desire for understanding. Old Man Brock, his weathered face a roadmap of wisdom and experience, stood before them, his voice carrying the weight of years spent observing the ebb and flow of forest life.

"We have gathered here today not to point fingers, but to reflect," he began, his voice resonating with a quiet authority. "The events of the past few days have revealed a truth more profound than any single culprit: the fragility of truth itself, and how easily it can be shattered by assumptions and prejudice." He paused, letting his words settle into the hearts of his listeners. The hens, usually a flurry of gossiping feathers, remained still, their clucking replaced with an attentive silence. Even the cats, normally aloof and detached, seemed to listen with an unusual degree of focus.

Professor Sophocles, perched on a low-hanging branch, added his sage observations. "Our investigation into Jenny's fall highlighted a crucial flaw in our community's approach to justice. We reacted swiftly, driven by emotion and incomplete information, rather than by a thorough investigation of the facts. We allowed rumors to fester, biases to cloud our judgment, and speculation to replace the diligent pursuit of truth." His words were a carefully worded rebuke, a gentle but firm reminder of their collective failure.

The younger squirrels, their faces still etched with guilt, shifted uncomfortably. They had been amongst the most vocal in their accusations against Jasper, their youthful exuberance fueling the wildfire of speculation. Now, faced with the truth, they understood the gravity of their actions. One young squirrel, his voice barely a whisper, confessed, "We didn't even think to look for other possibilities. We just saw Jasper on the telephone pole and assumed the worst."

Pepper the rabbit, his initial timidity replaced with newfound courage, stepped forward. "We must learn to question our own perceptions," he declared, his voice gaining strength with each word. "We must train ourselves to observe carefully, to gather evidence objectively, and to resist the temptation to jump to conclusions." His words resonated with the community; a shared sentiment slowly beginning to bloom within their collective consciousness.

The conversation flowed freely, a river of introspection and self-examination. The badgers discussed the importance of methodical investigation and rigorous fact-checking, sharing anecdotes of past instances where hasty judgments had led to regrettable consequences. The cats, known for their sharp observational skills, shared techniques on careful observation and the art of piecing together seemingly disparate clues. The hens, once notorious for spreading gossip, pledged to utilize their communication skills for responsible reporting, vowing to verify information before disseminating it further.

Even Jack, the grumpy tomcat who had been so quick to condemn Jasper, admitted his error. "I let my prejudice cloud my judgment," he confessed, his voice low and apologetic. "I should have considered the possibility that there could be other explanations for Jenny's fall." His unexpected admission broke the ice further, fostering a climate of open acknowledgment of mistakes.

The discussion then turned to the role of assumptions in shaping perceptions. Mrs. Periwinkle, the queen of gossip, surprisingly offered a poignant reflection. "I always thought I was just sharing information," she admitted, her voice surprisingly soft. "But now I see that my 'information' was often just speculation, fueled by my own biases and prejudices. I never really stopped to consider that my words had consequences." Her confession brought a wave of understanding and empathy over the clearing.

The community meticulously examined the events leading up to Jenny's fall, reconstructing the timeline with careful attention to detail. They analyzed each piece of evidence, reassessing testimonies, and considering alternative interpretations. They explored how individual biases and preconceived notions could have distorted their perception of the events. This collective process of re-evaluation and reconsideration was a crucial step in the healing process.

Old Man Brock concluded the meeting by outlining a set of guidelines for community-based justice. These guidelines emphasized careful observation, unbiased investigation, the importance of seeking alternative explanations, and a commitment to restorative justice. He proposed the establishment of a community council composed of representatives from each animal group, tasked with ensuring fair and impartial investigation of future incidents. This council would be responsible for overseeing information dissemination, verifying claims, and ensuring that future accusations were based on solid evidence rather than assumptions and hearsay.

The meeting ended not with a sense of resolution but with a renewed commitment to collective responsibility and a shared determination to learn from the past. Wildwoods Farm, once divided by suspicion and misjudgment, emerged with a newfound understanding of justice and a strengthened commitment to community well-being. The shadow of Jenny's tragic death lingered, a constant reminder of the fragility of life.

But it was no longer a shadow that consumed them, but a catalyst for change, a call to introspection and a shared responsibility to foster a more just, informed, and empathetic community.

The lessons learned went beyond the specific circumstances of Jenny's fall. The community understood that the pursuit of truth demanded patience, diligence, and a willingness to examine one's own biases. They learned that judging others based on incomplete information and assumptions could lead to devastating consequences, causing immense pain and suffering to innocent individuals. They realized that a strong community required active participation, open communication, and a shared commitment to upholding justice and truth.

The community engaged in a series of workshops and training sessions designed to enhance observation skills, critical thinking, and responsible communication. The older animals mentored the younger ones, sharing their experiences and wisdom. The hens learned how to distinguish fact from fiction, and to be more careful in their reporting. The cats, known for their sharp instincts, refined their skills in observation and deduction. The badgers developed advanced techniques in investigating and fact-checking. The rabbits, once timid, discovered their voice and found the courage to speak out against injustice.

The restorative process focused on healing the fractured relationships and repairing the damage caused by the false accusations. Jasper, freed from the weight of false accusations, actively participated in the community's healing process, working alongside Sly to rebuild trust and foster a more harmonious atmosphere. Sly, burdened by guilt and remorse, dedicated himself to making amends, contributing his time and expertise to community projects aimed at preventing similar tragedies. His actions were a testimony to the restorative power of confession, remorse, and a commitment to positive change.

As the days turned into weeks, Wildwoods Farm slowly but surely healed. The once-whispered accusations were replaced by a shared commitment to a better future. The memory of Jenny remained a poignant reminder of the fragility of life, but it also served as a constant reminder of the importance of seeking truth, embracing empathy, and fostering a culture of understanding. The whispers in Wildwoods Farm, once filled with suspicion and judgment, now carried a melody of reconciliation, forgiveness, and the shared promise of a brighter future. The tragedy, though painful, had served as a powerful catalyst for growth, shaping a community bound by a shared commitment to justice, truth, and understanding.

The days that followed were a somber blend of grief and reflection. The vibrant energy that usually pulsed through Wildwoods Farm was replaced by a quiet solemnity, a collective mourning for Jenny. The playful chatter of squirrels was muted, the usual bustling activity of the community subdued. Even the usually boisterous hens moved with a cautious stillness, their voices reduced to soft clucks of sympathy.

The idea of a memorial service emerged organically, a spontaneous gathering near the base of the telephone pole where Jenny had fallen. Old Man Brock, ever the wise steward of the community, suggested a simple ceremony, devoid of formality, focusing instead on shared memories and the expression of collective grief.

The setting was profoundly moving. Sunlight filtered through the leaves, dappling the ground in shifting patterns of light and shadow, creating an ethereal ambiance that seemed to both embrace and transcend the sadness. Small wildflowers, meticulously arranged by the rabbits, dotted the clearing, their vibrant colors a stark contrast to the subdued mood.

Professor Sophocles, his usually sharp eyes softened with compassion, began the service with a heartfelt eulogy. He spoke not of blame or accusation, but of Jenny's gentle spirit, her kindness, and the joy she brought to the community. He recalled her playful antics, her infectious laughter, and the warmth that radiated from her small frame. His words, delivered with quiet dignity, evoked a wave of shared memories, transforming the sadness into a celebration of a life well-lived.

One by one, members of the community shared their memories of Jenny. The younger squirrels recounted their playful games, their laughter echoing softly in the stillness. The hens remembered Jenny's gentle nature, her patience in listening to their endless chatter. The cats, usually reserved, shared anecdotes of Jenny's quiet curiosity and her ability to make even the grumpiest tomcat smile. Even Bradley, still grappling with the weight of his prejudiced judgment, shared a poignant memory of Jenny's kindness, a small act of generosity that had touched him deeply.

Robert the rabbit, his voice trembling slightly, spoke of Jenny's unwavering optimism, her ability to see the good in everyone, even in the most difficult of circumstances. His words highlighted the depth of Jenny's impact on the community, a testament to the positive influence she had on the lives of those around her.

The memorial service wasn't just a commemoration of Jenny's life; it was a communal act of healing. The shared grief, the unspoken apologies, and the quiet expressions of remorse created a powerful bond between the community members. It was a space where they could acknowledge their collective pain, express their regrets, and begin the long process of healing and reconciliation.

Following the service, the community embarked on a concerted effort to rebuild trust and foster a sense of shared responsibility. They initiated a series of workshops focused on emotional intelligence, conflict resolution, and effective communication. These workshops were designed to help individuals understand and manage their emotions, resolve conflicts constructively, and communicate their thoughts and feelings more effectively. The older, wiser animals mentored the younger ones, sharing their experiences and guiding them through the complexities of interpersonal relationships.

Sly, burdened by guilt and remorse, played a pivotal role in the healing process. He actively participated in the workshops, sharing his experiences and urging others to learn from their mistakes. His commitment to personal growth and positive change was a powerful example for the younger members of the community. He volunteered his time and expertise to various community projects, dedicating himself to rebuilding the trust that had been shattered by the events surrounding Jenny's death.

Jasper, finally exonerated from the false accusations, slowly reintegrated into the community. His initial awkwardness gradually gave way to renewed confidence as he actively participated in community activities, demonstrating his commitment to reconciliation and fostering a sense of unity. The community rallied around him, offering support and understanding, ensuring his smooth return to his place within the fabric of Wildwoods Farm.

The process of healing wasn't immediate or effortless; it was a gradual journey that required patience, empathy, and a collective commitment to growth. There were moments of frustration, of lingering resentment, of occasional setbacks. But the shared desire for reconciliation, fueled by their shared loss and the lessons learned, kept them moving forward.

The community established a dedicated support group for those struggling with grief and trauma. The group provided a safe space for members to express their emotions, share their experiences, and support each other through the healing process. The group's activities focused on promoting emotional well-being, fostering empathy, and developing coping mechanisms for dealing with difficult emotions.

The focus shifted from assigning blame to understanding the underlying causes of the tragedy. The community began to examine its own systems and practices, identifying areas for improvement in conflict resolution, communication, and the administration of justice. They recognized the importance of promoting critical thinking, unbiased investigation, and the responsible dissemination of information. They established new protocols for gathering evidence, verifying claims, and ensuring fair and impartial judgments in future incidents.

The telephone pole, once a symbol of tragedy, was transformed into a monument to remembrance. A small plot of land at the base of the pole was carved out in a "J" where wildflowers would grow. The plot became a focal point for remembrance, a place where the community could gather to reflect on Jenny's life and the lessons learned from her tragic death.

The transformation of Wildwoods Farm was profound. The community, once fractured by suspicion and mistrust, emerged stronger and more resilient. The tragedy, while undeniably painful, served as a catalyst for growth and renewal. Wildwoods Farm had learned a profound lesson about the importance of seeking truth, embracing empathy, and fostering a culture of understanding. The whispers in the woods, once filled with suspicion and judgment, now carried a melody of reconciliation, forgiveness, and the shared promise of a brighter future. The community, bound together by shared grief and a collective commitment to healing, embarked on a new chapter, embracing the enduring legacy of Jenny's spirit and the wisdom gained through adversity. The memory of Jenny would forever be woven into the tapestry of their shared experience, a poignant reminder of the fragility of life and the enduring power of forgiveness, empathy, and understanding.

Chapter 4

The Trial

The air in Wildwoods Farm, though still tinged with sadness, held a different quality now – a quiet determination. The focus had shifted from mourning to action, from grief to the pursuit of understanding. The community, guided by Old Man Brock's wisdom and Ink's methodical approach, began preparing for a trial unlike any seen before in the history of Wildwoods Farm. It wasn't about assigning blame and doling out punishment; it was about restorative justice, about uncovering the truth and healing the wounds inflicted by Jenny's death and the subsequent accusations.

The chosen location was a sun-dappled clearing, nestled amongst ancient oaks whose branches intertwined like gnarled fingers reaching for the sky. It was a place of serene beauty, a space where the community could gather, not in judgment, but in a spirit of reconciliation. The preparations were a communal effort, a testament to their shared resolve. The rabbits, with their meticulous nature, carefully arranged wildflowers in vibrant hues around the clearing, their colors a symbol of hope amidst the lingering sadness. The squirrels, their nimble paws working with practiced skill, weaved garlands of leaves and berries, creating a natural, yet elegant, setting for the proceedings. Even the usually aloof cats lent a paw, helping to clear the undergrowth and create a pathway leading to a makeshift platform fashioned from moss-covered logs.

Professor Sophocles, with his deep understanding of farm law and his unwavering commitment to fairness, was appointed the presiding judge. His role, however, was less about dispensing judgment and more about facilitating a process of open dialogue and mutual understanding. He spent days poring over Ink's meticulously compiled evidence, reviewing each piece of information with a critical yet empathetic eye. He recognized the importance of creating a space where everyone felt heard, respected, and valued, regardless of their preconceived notions or biases.

Ink, ever the meticulous investigator, prepared a detailed presentation of his findings. His report wasn't just a compilation of facts; it was a narrative, weaving together the various testimonies, observations, and evidence to paint a comprehensive picture of the events leading up to Jenny's fall. He meticulously documented each interview, noting not only the words spoken but also the nuances of body language, the hesitations in speech, and the subtle shifts in demeanor. He understood that truth often resided in the spaces between words, in the unspoken emotions and hidden motives. His charts and diagrams, displayed on smooth, flat stones, illustrated the inconsistencies in various accounts, exposing the flaws in the initial assumptions and the biases that had clouded judgment.

Fiona, *The Whisper*, played a vital role in preparing for the trial. Her unique ability to perceive subtle emotional currents allowed her to assess the mental states of various witnesses. Her insights, often communicated through delicate gestures and nuanced expressions, provided a crucial layer of understanding to Ink's findings. She was particularly adept at discerning truth from deception, picking up on inconsistencies and hidden anxieties that even Ink's meticulous investigation might have missed. Her observations were incorporated into Ink's report, adding a dimension of emotional depth to the factual evidence.

The preparation also involved engaging the community in a series of discussions focused on restorative justice. Old Man Brock, a natural leader and mediator, led these sessions, guiding the community towards a more profound understanding of empathy, forgiveness, and shared responsibility. These discussions were not about assigning blame but about exploring the roots of misunderstanding and prejudice, about acknowledging the impact of assumptions and biases on their perceptions of truth. It was a process of collective self-reflection, a journey towards a deeper understanding of themselves and their community.

The community elders, many of whom had witnessed similar conflicts in the past, shared their wisdom and experience. They spoke of the dangers of impulsive judgments, the importance of seeking multiple perspectives, and the power of forgiveness in healing fractured relationships. They emphasized the need for patience, understanding, and a willingness to listen, even to those with whom they disagreed. Their stories, recounted with quiet dignity, served as a powerful reminder of the consequences of unchecked emotions and the transformative power of compassion.

The younger members of the community, some of whom had been deeply affected by the accusations and counter-accusations, were encouraged to participate actively in the preparations. They were given the opportunity to express their feelings, to share their perspectives, and to help shape the trial process. Their involvement was crucial, not only in ensuring a fair and just outcome but also in promoting a sense of ownership and shared responsibility within the community.

As the day of the trial approached, a palpable sense of anticipation filled the air. It wasn't the anticipation of a punitive event, but of a process of healing, of reconciliation, and of a deeper understanding of truth. The community, united in their shared purpose, had painstakingly prepared for this unique trial, transforming a tragic event into an opportunity for growth, empathy, and the pursuit of a more just and understanding future. The whispers in the woods, once filled with suspicion and fear, now carried the hopeful murmurings of a community on the verge of a profound transformation.

The vibrant colors of the wildflowers, carefully placed around the clearing, seemed to mirror the renewed hope blooming in the hearts of Wildwoods Farm inhabitants. The trial was not simply about finding a culprit; it was about finding a way to heal, to learn, and to build a future based on truth, understanding, and forgiveness. The meticulous preparation reflected this profound shift in perspective, signifying a journey towards restorative justice. The community was ready. They were ready to listen, to learn, and to heal together.

The clearing, bathed in the soft glow of the afternoon sun, buzzed with a quiet energy. Professor Sophocles, his spectacles perched perfectly on his nose, sat on the moss-covered platform, a picture of calm authority. Before him, arranged with meticulous care, were Ink's exhibits – smooth, flat stones meticulously etched with diagrams and charts, each one a testament to his painstaking investigation.

Ink began his presentation with a simple, almost understated gesture. He pointed to a large stone depicting a detailed map of the area surrounding the telephone pole where Jenny had fallen. "This, esteemed members of the community," he announced, his voice clear and measured, "is a visual representation of the scene, based on our initial observations and subsequent investigations."

He then began to dissect the initial testimonies, starting with the hens who had claimed to witness the incident. "The hens," he explained, his voice taking on a slightly humorous tone, "possess a certain... dramatic flair. Their accounts, while vivid, lacked crucial consistency. Their perspectives, obscured by the foliage and their inherent tendency towards gossip, led to a misinterpretation of events." He pointed to a smaller stone displaying a series of overlapping sketches, illustrating how the hens' different vantage points resulted in conflicting narratives. "Notice," he continued, "how the placement of the branches and leaves significantly alters the line of sight, leading to discrepancies in their descriptions of Jasper's actions."

Next, he moved on to the cats, highlighting their tendency towards subtle judgments and assumptions. "The feline perspective," he said, a twinkle in his eye, "is often characterized by a certain... detachment. They observed, but their interpretations were clouded by their own biases, their preconceived notions of squirrels and their often-competitive nature." He presented a stone detailing the cats' accounts, highlighting the inconsistencies and subtle omissions in their testimonies. "Observe," he stated, "how the details omitted are precisely those that challenge the initial narrative of Jasper's culpability."

Ink then moved onto more concrete evidence. He presented a meticulously crafted chart showing the trajectory of Jenny's fall, based on the position of broken twigs, the angle of her descent, and the marks left on the telephone pole. "This trajectory," he emphasized, pointing to a specific point on the diagram, "is incompatible with the idea of a forceful push. The force required to propel Jenny from this height and at this angle would have been far greater than what Jasper, given his size and strength, could possibly exert."

Fiona, her sleek form a study in elegant composure, then stepped forward. Without speaking, she demonstrated how the wind currents, as depicted on another stone by Ink, could have easily dislodged Jenny from her precarious perch. She then mimed the scene, exhibiting the subtle shift in the wind, which could have caught Jenny off-guard. *The Whisper's* unspoken narrative, conveyed through her graceful movements and evocative gestures, spoke volumes about the power of observational detail and the silent forces at play. Her silent demonstration complemented Ink's meticulous analysis, adding a layer of emotional depth and visual understanding that resonated deeply with the audience.

Ink continued, "Furthermore, our investigation revealed several key pieces of circumstantial evidence that have been overlooked in the initial rush to judgment." He presented a series of stones detailing the discovery of a loose branch, significantly weakened by decay, directly beneath Jenny's perch. "This branch that Jenny had grabbed during her fall," he stated, "shows signs of significant weakening, indicating that it could have easily broken under Jenny's weight. It is highly likely that the branch's failure contributed to her fall." He then pointed to another stone displaying microscopic images of the branch's structure, demonstrating the advanced state of decay.

He then addressed the emotional impact of Jenny's death, acknowledging the grief and the ensuing anxieties that fueled assumptions. "Grief," he said softly, "can cloud our judgment, leading us to seek explanations, even if those explanations are flawed. The initial accusations against Jasper were not born of malice, but rather out of the collective trauma of losing Jenny. But the truth, however painful, must always prevail."

He concluded his presentation with a powerful statement. "The evidence clearly indicates that Jenny's fall was a tragic accident, not a deliberate act of malice. The assumptions and biases that colored the initial judgments obscured the true nature of the incident. Our investigation highlights the danger of leaping to conclusions, the importance of careful observation, and the necessity of seeking multiple perspectives before arriving at a verdict."

The silence that followed was profound, broken only by the rustling of leaves in the gentle breeze. The community, initially shocked and divided, now seemed to be grappling with the implications of Ink and Fiona's carefully presented evidence. The vibrant colors of the wildflowers seemed to underscore the contrast between the initial darkness of suspicion and the dawning light of truth. The meticulously arranged stones, bearing witness to Ink's detailed investigation, stood as symbols of a careful, thorough approach to seeking justice – a powerful lesson for all of Wildwoods Farm.

The air, previously thick with tension, now felt lighter, imbued with a sense of shared understanding, and a path towards healing. The weight of the accusations had been lifted, replaced with the slow, steady process of acknowledging the truth and moving forward with a profounder understanding of their community and its vulnerabilities. This meticulously conducted trial was not just a resolution of a single incident but a collective step towards a more just and empathetic future. The whispers in the woods now carried a renewed hope, a testament to the power of careful observation, the importance of questioning assumptions, and the enduring strength of a community bound by truth and understanding.

A hush fell over the clearing as a small, trembling figure emerged from the shadows of the ancient oak. It was Mike, the young field mouse, his whiskers twitching nervously, his eyes downcast. He shuffled forward, his tiny paws barely making a sound on the soft earth.

Professor Sophocles, his gaze gentle yet firm, gestured for Mike to approach the platform.

Mike hesitated, then took a deep breath, his voice barely a whisper as he began to speak. "I... I didn't mean to cause any harm," he stammered, his words catching in his throat. "It was all... an accident."

He explained that he had been collecting wildflowers for his mother, a notoriously demanding creature with an insatiable appetite for the rarest blooms. He had climbed the telephone pole, seeking a particularly vibrant bluebell he'd spotted high amongst the branches. He was enthralled by its delicate beauty, its vibrant color, a stark contrast against the muted greens of the forest. He had spent a considerable time admiring it, completely absorbed in its intricate details. He described the delicate veins of the petal, the subtle gradient of blue, and the way the morning dew clung to it like tiny diamonds. His love for flowers, his passion for their intricate beauty, was evident in every word.

He confessed that while distracted by the flower, he had inadvertently dislodged a small branch, a seemingly insignificant act that had far-reaching consequences. He hadn't realized the branch was so weakened, so fragile, until he saw it snap with a sharp crack. The sound, sharp and unexpected, had startled him. He had frozen, his heart pounding in his chest as he watched Jenny tumble from her perch grabbing at the branch. He recounted the horrifying moment – the brief, heart-stopping silence, followed by the heartbreaking thud as Jenny hit the ground.

"I...I panicked," he confessed, his voice barely audible. "I didn't know what to do. I was scared. I just...ran." He described the overwhelming sense of terror that had gripped him, the fear of being blamed, the crushing weight of guilt. He hadn't known what to do, how to react. He had felt so utterly alone in the wake of the terrible accident. His eyes filled with tears, his small body shaking with a mixture of remorse and fear.

He spoke about the bluebell, still clutched tightly in his tiny paw. The flower, once a symbol of joy and beauty, was now a heartbreaking reminder of the terrible accident. The vibrant blue had dulled, its delicate petals now slightly wilted. Yet, he still held on to it tightly, a tangible testament to the chain of events that had led to the tragedy. It was a poignant symbol of his innocence, the flower serving as both a cause and a witness.

Mike's testimony continued, delving into the details of his actions following the accident. He confessed to his desperate attempts to conceal the broken branch, driven by fear and a misguided sense of self-preservation. He hadn't understood the gravity of his actions at the time, blinded by fear and the weight of his guilt. He had never intended to harm anyone, he repeated fervently, his small voice filled with a sincere plea for understanding.

His confession wasn't just a simple admission of guilt, but a heartbreaking narrative of a young creature overwhelmed by events beyond his comprehension. He spoke about the loneliness he'd felt after the incident, the fear of confronting the community with the truth. He painted a picture of a small, vulnerable creature facing a formidable challenge, the weight of his actions crushing his spirit. He spoke of the sleepless nights, tormented by images of Jenny's fall. He described the constant fear of discovery, the silent burden he had carried within his small heart. His narrative touched upon the universal themes of fear, guilt, and the consequences of impulsive acts.

He explained how the initial testimonies, filled with assumptions and biases, had only amplified his fears. He had heard the whispers, the accusations, the growing suspicion that Jasper had been responsible for Jenny's death. This further fueled his anxiety, leading him to remain silent, his guilt increasing exponentially. The initial misinterpretations, fueled by the community's collective grief, had cast a shadow over him, exacerbating his fear and silencing his truth.

The courtroom, or rather the clearing, was silent as Mike concluded his testimony. His confession, though laced with fear and remorse, held a profound sincerity. There were tears in the eyes of some of the onlookers, a profound empathy replacing the initial anger and suspicion. Even the hens, notorious for their gossiping habits, seemed subdued, their usual clucking replaced by a hushed silence.

Professor Sophocles, a veteran observer of both human and animal behavior, nodded slowly. Mike's testimony, far from being a mere confession, was a detailed reconstruction of events, a poignant exploration of the emotional turmoil that followed the accident. The meticulous detail of his description of the bluebell, the broken branch, and his subsequent actions underscored the truthfulness of his confession. His narrative was powerful in its simplicity, revealing the fragility of life and the unpredictable consequences of even seemingly insignificant actions.

Ink, the ever-observant ferret, stepped forward. He examined the bluebell Mike still held, noting its wilted petals and the faint traces of soil clinging to its stem. He carefully examined the soil, noting that it was different from the soil around the telephone pole, instead aligning with the soil found near Mike's burrow. This seemingly small detail further substantiated Mike's account. It tied his confession to the physical reality of his location during the pivotal moments leading up to the accident.

Fiona, *The Whisper*, her eyes reflecting the light, softly touched Mike's shoulder. Her silence, a silent nod of understanding, spoke volumes. She understood the weight of Mike's confession, acknowledging the impact of fear and the pressure of community judgment. Her gesture was not one of accusation, but one of quiet solidarity, demonstrating that even in moments of tragedy, compassion and understanding remain paramount.

The community, having listened to Mike's testimony and Ink and Fiona's corroboration, began to grapple with the weight of their initial judgments. The weight of assumption and the rush to assign blame began to dissipate, replaced by a collective feeling of remorse and the understanding that accidents, even tragic ones, could happen. The initial shock and outrage gave way to a slower, more profound understanding of the complexities of the situation. The truth, while painful, held a cathartic power, transforming the communal atmosphere from one of conflict and suspicion into one of empathy and shared responsibility. The incident wasn't simply resolved; it had initiated a valuable lesson in the community about the importance of critical analysis, understanding, and compassion in the face of tragedy. The path to healing, while long and arduous, had finally begun. The trial, while initially focused on assigning blame, had transformed into a collective exploration of forgiveness, empathy, and the shared responsibility that binds the inhabitants of Wildwoods Farm together. The collective mourning for Jenny and the remorse for the hasty judgments against Jasper began to pave the way for a more just and compassionate future for all.

The silence that followed Mike's confession hung heavy in the clearing, thick with unspoken emotions. Professor Sophocles, his face etched with a profound understanding, broke the silence. "This has been a deeply unsettling experience for all of us," he began, his voice resonating with a quiet authority. "The loss of Jenny is a tragedy that will stay with us for a long time. But we must also acknowledge the weight of our initial reactions, the swiftness with which we judged, the assumptions we made without seeking the full truth."

A murmur rippled through the assembled creatures. Old Man Willow, his branches rustling softly, spoke up. "Indeed, Professor. We were quick to anger, quick to point fingers. We let our grief cloud our judgment." He paused, his voice heavy with regret. "We should have listened more carefully, questioned more thoroughly, before allowing our emotions to dictate our conclusions."

The gossiping hens, usually a cacophony of clucking and chatter, were unusually quiet. One hen, Henrietta, usually known for her sharp tongue, spoke hesitantly. "We...we heard whispers, you see. We saw Jasper there. It seemed so obvious." Her voice trailed off, tinged with shame. "We should have thought before we spoke, considered the possibility of another explanation."

Bradley, a gruff badger known for his practicality, added his voice. "We all jumped to conclusions. We let our biases cloud our judgment. Jasper being in the location and eventually running away...we assumed the worst and that equated to guilt. We failed to consider the circumstances, the possibility of an accident." He looked directly at Jasper, a hint of remorse in his usually stern gaze. "We owe you an apology, Jasper."

A wave of apologies followed. Each creature, in turn, voiced their regrets, acknowledging their role in the hasty judgment and the pain they had inflicted upon Jasper. It was a humbling moment, a collective admission of fallibility, a testament to the power of introspection and the shared responsibility for creating a just and compassionate community.

The discussion then shifted to ways of preventing similar incidents in the future. Professor Sophocles suggested establishing a formal process for investigating accidents, ensuring a more thorough and impartial approach. "We need a structured way to gather evidence, to consider multiple perspectives, before reaching any conclusions," he stated.

Bradley proposed the creation of a community safety committee, comprised of diverse members, to oversee the safety of the forest and to address any concerns proactively. "A diverse committee ensures a wider range of perspectives and reduces the risk of bias clouding our judgment," he explained.

The idea was met with enthusiastic support. The squirrels, spurred by their recent loss, were particularly passionate about the initiative. They proposed a series of safety measures, including better maintenance of the telephone pole and clear guidelines for accessing elevated areas.

Henrietta, her earlier gossiping replaced by a newfound sense of responsibility, suggested organizing community workshops to educate the younger generation about the importance of careful observation, responsible behavior, and the dangers of assumptions. "We need to teach our children to think critically, to question what they see and hear," she said, her voice now firm and purposeful.

The debate broadened to encompass other aspects of community life. Discussions centered around the importance of fostering open communication, valuing diverse perspectives, and cultivating empathy. The incident with Jenny and Jasper served as a catalyst for significant societal change, exposing the vulnerability of hasty judgments and the vital importance of careful consideration.

Old Man Willow, reflecting on the community's journey, said, "This isn't just about preventing accidents. It's about creating a community where everyone feels safe, where everyone's voice is heard, where justice is tempered with compassion."

The community, once fractured by suspicion and grief, began to heal. The shared experience of facing their flaws, and the collective effort to remedy them, forged a stronger, more resilient community. The trial, initially a scene of accusation and conflict, evolved into a powerful lesson in self-reflection and communal responsibility.

Ink added, "We also need better record-keeping. Let's create a community log to record all incidents, however minor, to help prevent future mishaps and to ensure we have a detailed record of events." Fiona nodded in agreement, highlighting the need for a centralized system to document community activities and safety improvements.

Their suggestions were meticulously documented by a team of young owls, known for their impeccable memory and precise record-keeping. The owls would serve as community scribes, keeping detailed records of meetings, safety measures, and community discussions. Their meticulous work would serve as a crucial element in the prevention of future incidents, ensuring a comprehensive historical account of the community's collective learning process.

The trial concluded not with a verdict of guilt or innocence, but with a shared understanding of loss and a collective commitment to healing and improvement. It marked a turning point for Wildwoods Farm. The community, shaken by tragedy, had emerged stronger and more united, bound by a shared understanding of their fallibility and a commitment to building a more just and compassionate society. The memory of Jenny would serve as a constant reminder of the fragility of life, and the importance of seeking truth before passing judgment. Jasper, initially a victim of assumptions and prejudice, found solace in the community's shared remorse and newfound commitment to justice, empathy, and understanding.

The incident served as a potent reminder of the enduring power of community and the ability to learn from even the most painful experiences. Wildwoods Farm wouldn't forget Jenny, but the community's response to the tragedy laid the foundation for a future where empathy, understanding, and a meticulous approach to truth would guide their collective journey. The transformation of the community wasn't immediate, but it was tangible, demonstrating the potential for growth and healing in the face of profound loss and collective self-reflection.

The discussions continued for days, extending beyond the immediate aftermath of the trial. The creatures of Wildwoods Farm engaged in deep conversations about their values, their processes, and their collective responsibility towards one another. Older members of the community shared anecdotes from the past, highlighting similar instances of misjudgment and illustrating the persistent challenges of maintaining a harmonious society. These stories, passed down through generations, served as cautionary tales, prompting self-reflection and fostering a more discerning approach to communal decision-making.

The young ones, initially overwhelmed by the gravity of the situation, actively participated in the discussions, demonstrating a surprising maturity and a deep desire to understand and contribute to their community's growth. Their questions, often insightful and thought-provoking, challenged the older generations to re-examine their assumptions and to approach the task of building a more just society with renewed vigor.

The community's collective learning extended to practical changes in daily life. The improved maintenance of the telephone pole became a shared responsibility, with regular inspections and repairs undertaken collaboratively. The community also implemented a new system for reporting potential hazards, ensuring that issues could be addressed proactively before they escalated into dangerous situations.

Beyond the practical changes, the incident profoundly impacted the social fabric of Wildwoods Farm. The community embraced a culture of open communication, where dissenting opinions were welcomed and respected, and where collaborative problem-solving became the norm. The realization that they had erred, and the willingness to acknowledge their mistakes, fostered a sense of mutual respect and trust that previously had been absent. The tragedy of Jenny's death, though undeniably painful, became a catalyst for profound societal evolution, demonstrating the community's capacity for reflection, adaptation, and growth. The collective experience served as a powerful reminder that even from the deepest sorrow, positive change could emerge, creating a stronger, more just, and compassionate community.

The air crackled with anticipation. Every creature in the clearing, from the smallest field mouse to the largest badger, held their breath. Professor Sophocles, his spectacles gleaming in the dappled sunlight, adjusted his robes. He had presided over countless debates and disputes in Wildwoods Farm, but none had held the weight and complexity of this one. The fate of Jasper, and the future of their community, rested on this moment.

He cleared his throat; the sound barely audible above the rustling leaves. "We have heard the testimony, considered the evidence, and witnessed the profound self-reflection of our community," he began, his voice measured and calm. "The tragedy of Jenny's death has shaken us to our core, forcing us to confront our own flaws and biases."

He paused, allowing his words to sink in. The silence was broken only by the gentle chirp of crickets and the distant rustling of leaves. Every eye in the clearing was fixed upon him, waiting for his pronouncement. This wasn't a simple verdict of guilty or innocent; it was a reckoning, a moment of collective self-examination.

"The evidence presented, while suggestive, did not definitively prove Jasper's guilt," Professor Sophocles continued. "Circumstantial evidence, however compelling, cannot replace irrefutable proof. We have learned, through this painful experience, that assumptions, however well-intentioned, can lead to grievous errors in judgment."

A collective murmur rippled through the assembled creatures. Old Man Willow, his ancient branches swaying gently, nodded in agreement. He had lived for centuries, witnessing countless disputes and misunderstandings within the community. He understood, perhaps better than anyone, the fragility of truth and the ease with which it could be obscured by assumptions and biases.

"Furthermore," Professor Sophocles went on, "we must acknowledge the role that our own prejudices played in this tragic event. Jasper, being in such close proximity to Jenny led many of us to unjustly assume his guilt. We failed to consider the possibility of alternative explanations, blinded by our own preconceived notions."

He looked directly at Jasper, a hint of compassion in his wise eyes. Jasper trembling, looked back, his large, dark eyes reflecting the weight of the accusations he had faced. The silence deepened, heavy with unspoken emotions. It was a silence that spoke volumes about the profound transformation the community had undergone.

Professor Sophocles then turned his gaze to the assembled creatures, his voice gaining strength. "The true verdict, then, is not one of guilt or innocence, but one of understanding and shared responsibility. We have learned a profound lesson about the dangers of hasty judgments and the importance of seeking the truth before passing judgment. We have all, in our own ways, contributed to the atmosphere of suspicion and misinterpretation that surrounded this tragedy."

He then spoke of the proposed changes – the creation of a community safety committee, regular inspections of the telephone poles, the community workshops on critical thinking, the community log for incident reporting. These weren't just abstract ideas; they were tangible steps towards a more just and compassionate community.

"We must remember Jenny," Professor Sophocles said, his voice tinged with sadness. "Her memory will serve as a constant reminder of the fragility of life and the importance of cherishing every moment. But her death will not be in vain. We will use this tragedy as a catalyst for positive change, building a community founded on empathy, understanding, and a commitment to truth."

The wise old owl, Athena, a creature renowned for her wisdom and impartial judgment, then stepped forward. Her voice, though soft, carried a weight of authority that silenced the clearing. "The forest elders agree with Professor Sophocles' assessment," she announced. "There will be no formal punishment for Jasper. However, the community's collective responsibility in this matter must not be overlooked."

She continued, her gaze sweeping across the assembled creatures, "The path forward requires collective effort. We must dedicate ourselves to creating a space where each creature feels safe, heard, and respected. This means actively challenging our biases, fostering open communication, and embracing diverse perspectives."

Athena's words resonated deeply, solidifying the community's commitment to change. The verdict, while absolving Jasper, emphasized the community's collective culpability and their responsibility to prevent future tragedies. It was a verdict that transcended simple notions of guilt and innocence, embodying a deeper understanding of justice and communal responsibility.

The subsequent days were filled with a flurry of activity. The community safety committee was formed, with representatives from every species and age group. Workshops were organized, teaching critical thinking skills and promoting open dialogue. The meticulous owls began their record-keeping, creating a comprehensive log of incidents and safety measures. Even the gossiping hens, humbled by their past behavior, pledged to be more thoughtful and less hasty in their judgements.

The improvements extended beyond the formal initiatives. The entire community became more conscious of their interactions, their words, and their assumptions. The atmosphere shifted from one of suspicion and mistrust to one of collaboration and mutual support. The children played more freely, knowing that their elders were committed to creating a safer environment. The adults interacted with greater empathy, mindful of the potential consequences of their words and actions.

The transformation wasn't instantaneous, nor was it effortless. Old habits die hard, and occasional lapses in judgment occurred. However, the shared experience of the trial, the collective remorse, and the commitment to change created a powerful foundation for a more just and compassionate community.

The memory of Jenny's death would always remain, a poignant reminder of life's fragility. But that memory would also serve as a catalyst for continued growth and self-improvement. The community learned that true justice wasn't simply about assigning blame but about fostering a society where every creature felt safe, valued, and empowered to speak the truth, without fear of prejudice or misjudgment. Wildwoods Farm, once scarred by tragedy, was slowly but surely healing, transforming into a place where empathy, understanding, and a relentless pursuit of truth would guide their collective journey forward. The verdict, in its unique and nuanced form, reflected this profound transformation, marking a new chapter in the community's history—a chapter of learning, growth, and collective responsibility.

Chapter 5

Moving Forward

The sun, a warm orb sinking towards the horizon, cast long shadows across the Wildwoods Farm. A gentle breeze rustled through the tall grasses, carrying the sweet scent of wildflowers. It was a far cry from the tense atmosphere of the trial, a place of serenity that felt worlds away from the drama that had unfolded. Here, nestled amongst the ancient oaks and babbling brooks, Jasper sat, his usually bristly fur subdued, his usually bright eyes clouded with a pensive sadness.

Ink, the ferret investigator, sat beside him, his keen gaze observing Jasper's quiet contemplation. Fiona, the insightful feline, was perched gracefully on a nearby branch, her emerald eyes reflecting the golden hues of the setting sun. They had come to this peaceful haven, not for further interrogation, but for reconciliation. For even in the pursuit of justice, understanding and forgiveness held a vital place.

The truth, as it had finally been revealed, was a complex tapestry woven with threads of miscommunication, assumptions, and the inherent biases that clouded their farm community. Jenny's fall hadn't been a deliberate act of malice, but a tragic accident exacerbated by a series of unfortunate events, a chain reaction triggered by a loose branch and a moment of carelessness. The "culprit," as it turned out, wasn't a malicious being, but rather a gust of wind, unusually strong and unpredictable, that had dislodged the pole that caused Jenny to lose her grip. The wind, an invisible force of nature, had been the true instigator of the tragedy. This revelation, however, hadn't absolved Jasper of his role in the events. His thoughtless actions, though unintentional, had contributed to the unfolding tragedy.

Jasper spoke, his voice barely a whisper, the words laced with regret. "I... I never meant for any of this to happen. I was just... so angry. Angry at Jenny for always being so confident, so seemingly carefree, while I felt so... overlooked, so small." He paused, his chest heaving slightly. "I didn't push her. I swear I didn't. But... but I yelled at her. I scared her, made her run and I chased her." He paused while his head drooped. "And if I hadn't been so consumed by my own frustrations, perhaps... perhaps things would have been different."

Ink nodded slowly, understanding dawning in his bright eyes. He knew that anger, fueled by insecurity and frustration, could often cloud judgment and lead to unintended consequences. He'd seen it time and again in his investigations, the way unchecked emotions could warp perceptions and blur the lines of reality.

Fiona, ever the voice of reason and empathy, gently added, "Jasper, we all make mistakes. The important thing is to learn from them. To understand the roots of our anger, our frustration, and to find healthier ways to express them." She gazed at him, her gaze warm and understanding. "Jenny wouldn't want you to carry this burden alone. She would want you to find peace, to learn from this experience, to be better, to heal."

Jasper looked up, his eyes meeting Fiona's compassionate gaze. A single tear traced a path through his fur. He had never considered things this way before. He had only been focused on his anger, his resentment. He hadn't considered the depth of his own actions, the ripple effect his outburst had had on Jenny. This moment of understanding was the beginning of his healing journey.

Ink continued, "The community is ready to move forward. Professor Sophocles' verdict was not just about absolving you—it was a call for collective responsibility. We all need to learn from this tragedy. We need to understand the dangers of assumptions, the power of empathy, and the importance of open communication."

A long silence fell between them, broken only by the gentle rustling of leaves and the murmur of the brook. It was a silence filled with reflection, with a growing sense of understanding and forgiveness. Jasper finally understood the depth of his actions, and the necessity for change within himself and within their community.

The following days brought about a profound transformation in Jasper. He started by actively seeking out others, particularly those he had previously overlooked or dismissed. He began volunteering in the community garden, working alongside the others, sharing laughter and conversation. He participated in the community workshops on critical thinking and conflict resolution, actively engaging in the discussions. He even found himself apologizing to some of those he had inadvertently hurt with his words and actions in the past.

The reconciliation extended beyond Jasper's personal transformation. He began to form unlikely friendship. They found common ground in their shared experience, their shared vulnerability, and their shared desire for a better future for their community. They began spending time together, sharing stories and perspectives, supporting each other through the healing process. Their bond became a powerful symbol of reconciliation and forgiveness, a testament to the resilience of the farm community.

The community as a whole benefited from this process of healing and self-reflection. The workshops proved incredibly beneficial, leading to improved communication, decreased conflict, and an increased awareness of the importance of compassion and empathy. The newly formed community safety committee worked diligently, implementing sensible safety measures to prevent future accidents. They held regular meetings, ensuring open dialogue and fostering a sense of collective responsibility.

The memory of Jenny's death still cast a long shadow, a reminder of life's fragility, but it no longer defined their community. Instead, it had served as a catalyst for profound change, a call for introspection, and a testament to the power of forgiveness and reconciliation. The once fractured community was slowly weaving itself back together, stronger and more unified than before, bound together by a shared experience and a collective commitment to truth, justice, and compassion. The meadow, where Jasper and the others had found reconciliation, became a symbol of this new beginning, a reminder of how even from the deepest sorrow, a new dawn of understanding and hope could emerge.

The Wildwoods Farm now whispered tales not of blame and accusations, but of forgiveness, healing, and the enduring power of unity.

Even the hens, notorious for their gossip, seemed calmer, more thoughtful in their pronouncements. The entire community felt a renewed sense of responsibility towards one another, a shared commitment to creating a safer, more just, and harmonious forest. This wasn't a magical transformation, achieved overnight. It was a slow, gradual process, requiring ongoing effort, patience, and a collective commitment to self-improvement and empathy.

The wind, once a symbol of tragedy, now seemed to carry a gentler message. The rustling leaves seemed to murmur tales of understanding and hope, Wildwoods secrets of a community transformed, a community where even the smallest creature felt safe, valued, and empowered to speak its truth, without fear of prejudice or misjudgment. Wildwoods Farm, once marred by loss and suspicion, had blossomed into a sanctuary of reconciliation, a testament to the enduring power of empathy, understanding, and the pursuit of truth, where even from the darkest shadows, the light of hope could shine through.

The transformation wasn't solely about individual changes; it was a collective awakening. The community, once fractured by suspicion and rumor, began to knit itself back together, thread by thread. The initial shock of Jenny's death, coupled with the subsequent trial and its revelations, had served as a harsh but necessary catalyst for growth. The shared experience, the collective grief, and the uncovering of the truth fostered a deeper understanding of their interdependence. They realized that their well-being was inextricably linked, that the safety and happiness of each individual contributed to the overall health of their community.

This realization sparked a surge of collaborative energy. The first visible sign of this unity was the formation of the "Wildwoods Farm Safety Committee." Initially conceived as a response to Jenny's accident, the committee quickly evolved into a multifaceted organization dedicated to improving the overall safety and well-being of their farmland home. Made up of representatives from every segment of the community – from the wise old owls to the playful hedgehogs – the committee's diverse membership reflected their newfound commitment to inclusivity and collective decision-making.

Their first project was a community-wide assessment of potential hazards. Elderly squirrels, with their vast knowledge of the farms and forest's hidden pathways and precarious spots, led the way, pointing out weak branches, unstable rocks, and other dangers. The nimble weasels, known for their exceptional climbing skills, inspected the telephone poles and treetops, identifying areas needing repair or reinforcement. Even the usually aloof badgers, traditionally solitary creatures, contributed by mapping out blind spots and poorly lit areas. The collaboration wasn't just practical; it was a powerful symbol of their newfound unity. Working together, sharing knowledge and skills, they tackled the task with remarkable efficiency and a surprising lack of the usual bickering and mistrust.

The next stage involved practical improvements. The stronger members of the community, aided by the inventive minds of the beavers, repaired damaged branches, reinforced unstable structures, and improved pathways, making the farm and forest a safer and more accessible place for everyone. The owls, with their exceptional night vision, helped illuminate darker areas with strategically placed bioluminescent fungi. The committee also worked on enhancing communication channels. A network of strategically placed message boards, carved from sturdy wood and adorned with vibrant lichen, were installed throughout the farm and forest. These boards served as a central hub for announcements, safety warnings, and community news, ensuring everyone was informed and connected.

Beyond physical improvements, the community focused on strengthening their social fabric. Professor Sophocles, the wise old owl who had presided over the trial, played a pivotal role in this process. He organized a series of community workshops focused on communication, empathy, and conflict resolution. These workshops weren't just lectures; they were interactive sessions filled with role-playing exercises, storytelling, and open discussions. The hens, once notorious for their gossiping and spreading rumors, became surprisingly effective facilitators, their sharp tongues now employed to encourage open and honest communication rather than stirring up discord.

The workshops proved incredibly popular. Animals who had previously avoided interaction due to past misunderstandings began to engage in constructive dialogue. They shared their fears, frustrations, and aspirations, creating a sense of shared vulnerability that fostered understanding and empathy. The workshops also helped address the underlying issues that had contributed to the accident and the subsequent misunderstandings. They discussed the importance of active listening, the dangers of making assumptions, and the need for clear and respectful communication. They explored the impact of emotions like anger, fear, and jealousy, and developed healthy ways to manage these feelings.

Another significant outcome of this renewed community spirit was the establishment of a community garden. A once-neglected patch of land near the edge of the farm was transformed into a vibrant, shared space where animals of all sizes and species collaborated to grow food and flowers. The squirrels, with their nimble paws, handled the planting and weeding, while the badgers, with their strength, helped prepare the land. The rabbits, with their keen sense of smell, helped identify the best spots for various plants. The bees, of course, ensured the garden thrived. The garden became more than just a source of food; it was a place of shared activity, a symbol of cooperation, and a testament to the power of unity.

The community garden was not just about sustenance; it represented a deeper level of cooperation. Each creature contributed their unique skills and strengths, learning from one another and fostering a shared sense of accomplishment. The smaller creatures, often overlooked, found their voice and gained respect for their contributions. The stronger animals learned patience and cooperation. Even the usually grumpy badgers participated, sharing their knowledge of soil composition and pest control. The garden blossomed, mirroring the blossoming of the community itself.

The success of the community garden inspired further collaborative projects. They built a community verbal library, filled with stories that could be passed down through generations. They created a community art gallery consisting of flower arrangements, showcasing the creative talents of their diverse population. They even organized a community theatre group, staging plays and musicals that reflected their shared experiences and celebrated their newfound unity. Each project served as a reminder of their collective strength, their shared purpose, and their commitment to building a brighter future together.

The annual Harvest Festival, once a subdued affair marked by lingering suspicion, became a joyous celebration of their collective achievement. With humans everywhere and the aroma of baked goods and roasted nuts filled the air, the laughter of children echoed through the trees, and the music of various instruments blended into a harmonious symphony. All the farm's creatures joined in the celebration. The celebration was not just of the harvest, but now of their newfound unity, a testament to their resilience, their capacity for forgiveness, and their collective commitment to building a safer, happier, and more harmonious community.

The memory of Jenny's death remained a poignant reminder of their fragility, but it was no longer a source of division. Instead, it had become a catalyst for positive change. The Wildwoods Farm community, once fractured by loss and suspicion, had emerged stronger, more unified, and more compassionate than ever before. Their journey from tragedy to triumph served as a powerful reminder of the transformative power of truth, justice, forgiveness, and the enduring strength of community. The once-Wildwoods Farm now echoed with the joyful sounds of a community rebuilt, stronger and more united than before. The wind that had once brought sorrow now seemed to carry the promise of a brighter future.

The months following the trial unfolded slowly, each day a careful step forward in the healing process. The initial shock and anger had subsided, replaced by a quiet, persistent grief that hung in the air like the scent of damp earth after a rain shower. But amidst the sorrow, a new feeling began to emerge – a collective resolve to remember Jenny, not as a victim, but as a vibrant member of their community, whose life, though tragically cut short, had touched each of them in unique and lasting ways.

The idea for a memorial emerged organically, whispered amongst the rustling leaves and carried on the gentle breeze. Professor Sophocles, his usually wise eyes shining with a quiet sadness, proposed a gathering to honor Jenny's memory. The suggestion found immediate and enthusiastic support. The Wildwoods Farm Safety Committee, now a well-established entity, took on the task with the same collaborative spirit that had characterized their previous endeavors.

The location was carefully chosen: a sunny glade nestled amidst a grove of ancient oak trees, a spot where Jenny had often been seen playing, her tiny paws scampering over the mossy ground. The glade, once a simple clearing, was transformed into a place of profound beauty and serenity. The beavers, masters of construction, built a small, raised platform of polished wood, perfect for seating. The squirrels, ever vigilant, gathered wildflowers and soft moss, weaving them into vibrant garlands that adorned the platform. The colorful butterflies, drawn by the fragrant blooms, fluttered around the glade, adding a touch of ethereal elegance to the scene.

The day of the memorial dawned clear and bright, the sun illuminating the glade in a warm, golden light. Animals from all corners of the farm and forest gathered, their diverse forms creating a tapestry of color and life. The older squirrels sat with their young, sharing stories of Jenny's playful nature and her infectious giggle. The hens, their usual chatter subdued, listened attentively, their sharp eyes reflecting a mixture of sorrow and respect. Even the badgers, typically solitary creatures, could be seen huddled together, their usually gruff demeanor softened by the solemnity of the occasion.

Professor Sophocles, his voice resonating with a deep sense of empathy, opened the ceremony. He spoke not just of Jenny's death, but of the lessons they had all learned from the experience. He spoke of the dangers of unchecked assumptions, the importance of careful observation, and the fragility of truth when obscured by rumor and prejudice. His words, though tinged with sadness, were infused with a hopeful message of reconciliation and understanding.

Following Professor Sophocles' address, several animals shared their personal memories of Jenny. There was Amber, the young squirrel who had played with Jenny countless times, recounting their adventures climbing trees and chasing butterflies. There was Nargiza, the elderly owl, who had watched Jenny grow up, reminiscing about her curious nature and her boundless energy. Each story was a testament to Jenny's vibrant life, her warmth, and her kindness. Their memories were a tapestry woven with threads of laughter, friendship, and love – a fitting tribute to a squirrel who had left an indelible mark on their lives.

The highlight of the ceremony was the planting of a sapling sugar maple tree – a symbol of new life, growth, and enduring memory. The sapling, carefully chosen and nurtured by the beavers, was planted in the center of the glade. Each animal present was given the opportunity to add a handful of soil, a symbolic act of participation and shared responsibility. As the sapling was planted, a profound sense of unity filled the glade, binding them together in a common purpose – to honor Jenny's memory and to build a better future for their community.

The memorial wasn't just a single event, but a turning point. It marked the community's transition from grief and suspicion to healing and understanding. It was a testament to their resilience, their capacity for forgiveness, and their commitment to fostering a safer and more harmonious community. The planting of the maple tree served as a living monument to Jenny's life, its growth mirroring the community's own journey toward renewal.

In the following weeks and months, the Wildwoods Farm community continued its transformation. The emphasis on safety and collaboration intensified, driven by a shared desire to prevent future tragedies and to create a truly inclusive environment for all. The Safety Committee continued to work tirelessly, improving pathways, reinforcing structures, and developing effective communication channels. The community garden flourished, its bounty a testament to their combined efforts and a source of both sustenance and shared joy.

The workshops on communication and conflict resolution continued to be popular, fostering deeper understanding and empathy among the animals. The hens, once notorious for spreading rumors, became trusted mediators, their keen observations and quick tongues now used to facilitate healthy communication. The badgers, shedding their solitary ways, actively participated in community projects, contributing their unique skills and knowledge. The sense of shared responsibility permeated all aspects of their lives.

The annual Harvest Festival, celebrated that autumn, was a vibrant display of their collective efforts. The once-subdued celebration transformed into a joyous occasion, a testament to their resilience and newfound unity. The aroma of baked goods and roasted nuts filled the air, mingled with the sounds of laughter and music. It was a celebration not just of abundance, but of the strength and resilience of the Wildwoods Farm community, a community that had emerged from tragedy strengthened by shared loss and bound together by the enduring power of truth, justice, and forgiveness.

The sapling maple tree in the memorial glade grew steadily, its branches reaching towards the sky, a symbol of life, renewal, and the enduring memory of Jenny. It was a testament to the community's journey from loss to healing, from suspicion to unity, from despair to hope. The Wildwoods Farm, once a place shadowed by sadness, now echoed with laughter, it was now a vibrant tapestry of life and community. Jenny's memory, though poignant, was no longer a source of sorrow, but a catalyst for growth, a beacon illuminating the path towards a future where justice, truth, and compassion guided their steps. Her legacy lived on, not only in the hearts of those who knew her, but in the strong, vibrant, and compassionate community they had rebuilt together. The memory of Jenny was woven into the very fabric of their lives, a reminder of their shared past and a testament to their collective strength in moving forward. The wind whispered through the leaves, carrying with it not just the sounds of the forest, but the echoes of laughter, and the promise of a brighter future. And in the heart of that future, stood the sturdy oak, a symbol of growth, a testament to the enduring strength of memory, and a constant reminder of the journey from loss to hope.

The quietude following Jenny's memorial wasn't a silence of despair, but a calm before a new chapter. Ink, ever the observant ferret, noticed this shift. The frantic energy that had gripped the Wildwoods Farm had dissipated, leaving behind a quiet determination. Fiona, perched on a branch overlooking the rebuilt community garden, mirrored his sentiment. The air, once thick with suspicion and rumor, now carried the scent of fresh soil and blooming flowers – a testament to the community's renewed spirit. Their work, though seemingly concluded with the resolution of Jenny's case, was far from over. Justice, they both knew, wasn't a singular event but an ongoing process, a constant vigilance against injustice.

Their days were filled with smaller investigations. A missing acorn from Old Man Fitzwilliam's prized oak tree sparked a mini-investigation, revealing a mischievous family of bluejays with a penchant for pilfered nuts. A disagreement over territory between a family of badgers and a group of rabbits led to a carefully mediated truce, with Ink and Fiona acting as neutral observers, mediating a fair compromise that respected both parties' needs. These seemingly trivial cases served as valuable lessons, sharpening their skills and deepening their understanding of the intricacies of the Wildwoods Farm community. They learned the importance of listening attentively, not just to the words spoken, but to the unspoken nuances, the subtle shifts in body language, the tell-tale flick of a tail or the widening of an eye.

Their investigative work expanded beyond simply solving crimes; it became a force for positive change. Ink, with his meticulous record-keeping, and Fiona, with her uncanny ability to sense underlying tensions, worked together to establish a formal mediation system within the Wildwoods Farm. They trained several other animals, including the surprisingly insightful hens, in conflict resolution techniques, transforming the gossipmongers into valuable peacekeepers. The badgers, once perceived as solitary and gruff, surprised everyone by becoming skilled mediators, their pragmatism and calm demeanor surprisingly effective in resolving disputes.

One crisp autumn afternoon, as they were inspecting a newly-constructed bridge built by the diligent beavers, a peculiar sight caught Ink's eye. A small, intricately carved wooden box lay half-hidden amongst the fallen leaves near the riverbank. It was made of dark, polished wood, adorned with silver clasps, far more elegant than anything typically found in the Wildwoods Farm. Its mysterious appearance piqued both Ink and Fiona's curiosity.

Fiona, ever cautious, sniffed the box cautiously. "It doesn't smell of anything familiar," she whispered, her voice a low purr. "No traces of recent animal activity. It's as if it appeared out of thin air."

Ink, ever methodical, carefully examined the box. "The craftsmanship is exceptional," he remarked, his whiskers twitching. "The carvings are intricate, almost...magical. I've never seen anything like it before." He carefully opened the box. Inside, nestled on a bed of velvet-soft moss, was a single, gleaming pearl. It was larger than any pearl they had ever seen, radiating a soft, ethereal glow.

This discovery was far beyond their usual minor disputes and petty thefts. The pearl's presence suggested a mystery far grander, and potentially more dangerous, than anything they had encountered before. It felt like a puzzle piece that didn't belong to any case they knew, a fragment of a story yet untold. Was it lost treasure? A forgotten relic? Or something far more significant?

The discovery of the pearl ignited a new phase in their detective careers. Their initial investigation revealed no clues as to its origin. They questioned every animal in the Wildwoods Farm, yet no one recognized the box or the pearl. The older animals, with their vast knowledge of the farm and forest's history, were equally baffled. Professor Sophocles, after considerable deliberation, suggested they seek guidance from beyond the Wildwoods Farm. The pearl, he reasoned, might have originated from a place far removed from their peaceful community, a realm steeped in ancient lore and forgotten magic.

Their journey led them to the edge of the Wildwoods Farm, to a place known only as the "Wildwoods Back 40," a mysterious area shrouded in mist and legend, rarely visited by the animals of the Wildwoods Farm. Local tales spoke of ancient beings, mystical creatures, and powerful magic dwelling within. It was a dangerous place, fraught with hidden paths and unexpected dangers. However, the allure of the mystery, and the potential for unraveling a far greater enigma, compelled them to venture forth.

Their journey was filled with thrilling challenges. They navigated treacherous terrain, outsmarted cunning predators, and solved riddles left by long-forgotten civilizations. They encountered creatures they had only heard whispers of in hushed tones—creatures of myth and legend. The experience tested their skills, their courage, and their partnership to its very limits. Fiona's keen instincts and acute senses guided them through the darkest corners of the Wildwoods Back 40, while Ink's intellect and meticulous attention to detail helped them to decipher ancient symbols and unravel cryptic clues.

As they ventured deeper, they uncovered fragments of a story far older than the Wildwoods Farm itself. They discovered that the pearl wasn't just a precious gem; it was a key, a magical artifact with the power to unlock ancient secrets and forgotten powers. They learned of a hidden civilization that once thrived in this realm, a civilization that possessed immense knowledge and advanced technology, a society that had mysteriously vanished centuries ago, leaving behind only remnants of their extraordinary existence.

The closer they got to the truth, the more dangerous their quest became. They found themselves pursued by unseen entities, shadows that moved with uncanny speed and agility, entities that seemed to be guarding the secrets of the Wildwoods Back 40 with fierce determination. The pursuit became a chase across treacherous terrain, a constant test of their wits and courage. Fiona's agility and Ink's resourcefulness proved invaluable as they evaded their pursuers, using their combined skills to outwit and outmaneuver their shadowy adversaries.

Their investigation revealed a deeper, more significant mystery. The pearl wasn't just a relic; it was a catalyst, a key to unlocking a power that could reshape the Wildwoods Farm and the forest, a power both wondrous and terrifying. This power, they discovered, was closely linked to the disappearance of an ancient civilization. The tale of the pearl was far from over; it was only just beginning. The discovery of the pearl was merely a single step on a journey fraught with peril and wonder, a journey that would take them into realms unknown and challenge them in ways they could never have imagined. Their future, like the mysteries they were unraveling, remained uncertain, filled with the promise of both danger and extraordinary discovery. The Wildwoods Farm, once a place of relative tranquility, now held a secret of immense power, a secret that Ink and Fiona were determined to uncover, even if it meant facing unknown dangers and unimaginable challenges. The fate of the Wildwoods Farm, and perhaps even more, rested on their shoulders. Their investigation was no longer a simple case of solving a crime; it had evolved into a quest of epic proportions.

Several weeks later, the Wildwoods Farm was alive with the joyous sounds of the annual Harvest Festival. Golden sunlight dappled through the leaves, illuminating the vibrant scene. Stalls overflowed with plump berries, glistening nuts, and fragrant herbs, a testament to the bountiful harvest. The air hummed with laughter, the scent of roasted nuts and spiced cider mingling with the earthy aroma of the forest floor. It was a stark contrast to the tense atmosphere that had prevailed just weeks before, a testament to the community's resilience and newfound unity.

Ink and Fiona, perched on a mossy log near the edge of the bustling festival, observed the scene with quiet satisfaction. The community had healed, not just from the physical wounds of Jenny's fall, but from the deeper wounds of mistrust and prejudice. The trial, though unconventional, had served as a powerful catalyst for change. The animals had confronted their biases, acknowledged their mistakes, and learned the importance of seeking truth before casting judgment. The gossiping hens, once the purveyors of harmful rumors, now served as valuable mediators, their keen observation skills surprisingly well-suited to conflict resolution. Even the initially skeptical badgers had embraced their newfound role as peacekeepers, their inherent pragmatism proving invaluable in mediating disputes.

The transformation wasn't merely superficial. The rebuilt community garden, a symbol of the community's shared recovery, thrived, its vibrant colors a reflection of the renewed harmony within the Wildwoods Farm. The animals seemed to understand that true justice wasn't solely about punishment, but about reconciliation and understanding. They had learned a valuable lesson about the destructive power of assumptions and the importance of seeking the complete picture before forming judgments. The case of Jenny and Jasper had served as a brutal, yet ultimately constructive, lesson in the pitfalls of hasty conclusions.

As the sun began to dip below the horizon, casting long shadows across the festival grounds, Old Man Fitzwilliam approached Ink and Fiona, his usually grumpy face softened by a genuine smile. He held a small, intricately carved wooden bird, a miniature replica of a blue jay, in his paw.

"For you two," he said, his voice gruffer than usual, but with an unmistakable warmth. "A small token of my gratitude. Your work...it's made a world of difference to this wood."

Ink accepted the gift with a nod of appreciation. "It was a team effort, Old Man Fitzwilliam," he said modestly. "The entire community played a part in finding the truth and healing."

Fiona, ever the astute observer, noticed the subtle shift in the community's dynamic. The whispers and gossip that had once poisoned the atmosphere were gone, replaced by a sense of shared responsibility and mutual respect. The animals had learned to listen to each other, not just to the words spoken but to the unspoken nuances, the subtle cues of body language and tone. They had discovered the power of empathy and understanding, the ability to see beyond surface appearances and perceive the truth behind the facade.

The Harvest Festival wasn't just a celebration of the season's bounty; it was a celebration of the community's transformation, a testament to their resilience and their commitment to truth and justice. The event served as a powerful symbol of how a community could overcome adversity, heal from conflict, and emerge stronger and more unified than before. The joyous atmosphere was a clear indication of the enduring impact of their investigation, and the lasting lesson it had imparted upon the inhabitants of the Wildwoods Farm.

Later that evening, as the festival wound down, Ink and Fiona sat beside the softly glowing embers of a bonfire, reflecting on the events of the past few weeks. The air was filled with the quiet murmur of contented animals, their voices blending with the crackling of the fire.

"It's remarkable, isn't it, Fiona?" Ink remarked, gazing into the flames. "How much can change in such a short time."

Fiona purred softly, her eyes half-closed. "The truth, Ink, is a powerful force. It has the power to heal wounds, mend broken relationships, and build a stronger community. But it requires patience, careful observation, and a willingness to confront our own biases."

Ink nodded in agreement. "And sometimes," he added, "it takes a little bit of luck. We were lucky to have the right animals on our side; animals willing to speak truth to power and challenge their own perceptions."

They fell silent for a moment, both lost in contemplation. The memory of the incident, the tension, the uncertainty, and the ultimate resolution, played in their minds. The case had not only reinforced their detective skills but also deepened their understanding of the animal, condition. The complexities of relationships, the motivations behind actions, and the delicate balance between accusation and understanding had been laid bare. The experience had served as a profound reminder that justice wasn't a simple equation, but a complex tapestry woven with threads of empathy, understanding, and truth.

Their work hadn't ended with the resolution of Jenny and Jasper's case. The establishment of a formal mediation system, the training of animal mediators, and the ongoing efforts to foster understanding and cooperation within the Wildwoods Farm were all testament to their commitment to building a more just and equitable society. They knew that their role as investigators extended beyond solving individual crimes; it encompassed nurturing a culture of understanding, respect, and fairness within their community.

As the embers dwindled to ash, Ink and Fiona prepared to leave the festival grounds. The night air was crisp, carrying the scent of woodsmoke and damp earth. The lingering warmth of the bonfire was a comforting reminder of the community's renewed spirit, the strength they had found in facing adversity together. They had achieved more than simply solving a crime; they had fostered a fundamental change within the heart of their community, a change rooted in truth, understanding, and a commitment to justice. The Wildwoods Farm, they knew, would never be quite the same, but for them, and for the entire community, it was infinitely better. The lasting lesson learned from the tragedy wasn't just about the importance of truth and justice, but about the profound power of community, empathy, and forgiveness. The harvest festival had become a symbol of this new, stronger, and more unified community—a testament to their collective resilience and their unwavering commitment to truth and justice. The future of the Wildwoods Farm was now secured, not just by the solving of the case, but by the collective understanding that had emerged from the experience. The seeds of change had been sown, and the harvest of unity and harmony had begun. And as Ink and Fiona walked hand in paw towards home, they knew this was just the beginning of a new era for the Wildwoods Farm, an era of understanding, justice, and lasting peace.

Chapter 6

The Wildwoods Farm

The next morning dawned bright and clear, casting a golden glow over the barn of Wildwoods Farm. This wasn't just any barn; it was the heart of the community, a vibrant hub of activity where the lives of the woodland creatures intertwined. Nestled between ancient oak trees, whose branches reached towards the heavens like gnarled fingers, the barn bustled with life. The air hummed with a symphony of chirps, rustles, and chatter, a soundtrack to the daily rhythm of the woods.

The centerpiece of the barn was the Great Oak, a majestic tree whose age was lost to time. Its wide, spreading branches provided shade for the numerous stalls that lined the barn's perimeter. These weren't ordinary stalls; each was a testament to the unique skills and talents of the Wildwoods Farm' inhabitants. There was Mrs. Molly's bakery, famed for her honey cakes and acorn muffins, the aroma of which wafted through the air, enticing even the most disciplined of diets. Next to it was Mr. Finch's haberdashery, overflowing with exquisitely crafted clothing made from the finest thistle down and spider silk. The vibrant colors of the garments – deep emeralds, sunny yellows, and rich browns – stood in sharp contrast to the muted tones of the surrounding forest.

Across from Mr. Finch's was Old Man Fitzwilliam's woodworking shop, a haven for handcrafted toys and tools. The scent of freshly cut wood mingled with the sweet aroma of Mrs. Molly's bakery, creating a unique and unforgettable fragrance. Old Man Fitzwilliam himself, his face etched with the wisdom of countless years, could often be found perched on a stool outside his shop, carving intricate designs into tiny pieces of wood. His gnarled fingers, stained with the hues of various woods, moved with astonishing precision and grace.

Further along, tucked away in a cozy corner, was the apothecary run by Madam Nargiza, a wise old owl known for her remedies made from forest herbs and flowers. Her shelves were lined with an assortment of jars, vials, and tinctures, each bearing a unique label inscribed in elegant script. The subtle scent of chamomile, lavender, and other soothing herbs hung in the air, creating a sense of tranquility and calm.

Beyond the shops, the barn opened into a spacious area where the community gathered for festivals and celebrations. On this particular morning, it was abuzz with activity. Squirrels chattered excitedly as they scurried up and down the Great Oak, their bushy tails twitching. Rabbits hopped playfully across the grassy expanse, their long ears twitching in the breeze. Birds sang melodious tunes from the branches of the surrounding trees, their voices weaving together in a harmonious chorus. Even the usually reserved badgers could be seen exchanging friendly nods and greetings. The atmosphere was one of unity and harmony, a far cry from the tension and suspicion that had prevailed only weeks before.

The homes surrounding the square were as diverse as their inhabitants. Some were built into the roots of ancient trees, their entrances hidden amongst intertwining branches and vines. Others were constructed from mud and straw, their roofs thatched with reeds and wildflowers. Each home, no matter its size or design, possessed a unique charm and character, reflecting the personality of its residents. The windows, often adorned with colorful flower boxes, peeked out from behind creeping ivy and flowering bushes, hinting at the cozy interiors within. Smoke curled lazily from chimneys, carrying with it the tantalizing scent of breakfast cooking.

The very stones of the barn seemed to whisper stories of generations past. Each cobblestone, worn smooth by countless paws and hooves, bore witness to countless gatherings, celebrations, and disputes. The barn was not just a physical space; it was a living entity, a reflection of the community's shared history and its collective identity. It was a place where friendships were forged, disagreements were resolved, and memories were made.

Ink and Fiona, having finished their morning patrol, approached the barn. They paused for a moment, taking in the vibrant scene before them. The air was filled with the sweet aroma of freshly baked bread, the earthy scent of damp soil, and the intoxicating perfume of wildflowers. A gentle breeze rustled the leaves of the Great Oak, creating a soothing melody that seemed to accompany the cheerful chatter of the animals.

"It's truly remarkable, Fiona," Ink commented, his eyes scanning the bustling barn. "The healing process has been surprisingly swift."

Fiona, perched on Ink's shoulder, nodded in agreement. "The trial, though unorthodox, served as a powerful catalyst for change. The community has not only forgiven, but also embraced the lessons learned. The whispers of suspicion have been replaced by a chorus of harmony and understanding."

They walked through the barn, exchanging greetings with the various inhabitants. Mrs. Molly offered them a freshly baked honey cake, her warm smile reflecting the community's renewed sense of unity. Mr. Finch showed them his latest creation – a vibrant waistcoat made from iridescent beetle wings. Even Old Man Fitzwilliam, his gruff exterior softening slightly, presented them with a small, intricately carved wooden squirrel, a symbol of his gratitude for their role in restoring peace to the Wildwoods Farm.

As they continued their stroll, they noticed a small group of animals huddled near the Great Oak, engaged in an earnest discussion. Curiosity piqued, Ink and Fiona approached them cautiously. The group consisted of several squirrels, rabbits, and badgers, their faces etched with concern.

"What seems to be the problem?" Ink asked gently.

One of the squirrels, a young female named Helen, stepped forward, her voice trembling slightly. "We've discovered something... unsettling. There have been some strange markings found near the edge of the Wildwoods Farm – symbols we've never seen before."

The other animals nodded in agreement, their eyes wide with apprehension. The discovery of these unfamiliar symbols had cast a shadow of unease over the newly restored harmony of the community. The tranquility that had so recently settled over Wildwoods Farm was now threatened by the emergence of this mystery, hinting at a potential new conflict, a new challenge that needed to be addressed. Ink and Fiona exchanged a glance, a shared sense of responsibility passing between them. Their work, it seemed, was far from over. The peace they had so painstakingly established was once again at risk, and it was their duty to protect it. The investigation, it seemed, was far from over. The Wildwoods Farm, though healed from the past trauma, still held secrets waiting to be uncovered, and Ink and Fiona, the protectors of truth and justice, were ready to face the challenge head-on. The quiet harmony of the barn seemed to hold its breath, as a new mystery unfolded, beckoning the two investigators into the unknown depths of the Wildwoods Farm once more.

Following the unsettling discovery near the edge of the Wildwoods Farm, Ink and Fiona found themselves drawn towards a different part of the forest, a place beyond the Wildwoods Back 40, known as the Boggy Berry Patch. It wasn't marked on any map, a secret haven known only to the woodland creatures. The path leading to it was barely visible, a winding trail hidden beneath a canopy of intertwined branches and lush undergrowth. The air, heavy with the scent of damp earth and decaying leaves, hummed with a quiet energy, a sense of mystery clinging to the air like a fine mist.

The Boggy Berry Patch itself was a sight to behold. It was a sun-drenched clearing, nestled amongst ancient trees whose gnarled roots clawed at the earth like the fingers of a giant. The ground was carpeted with a thick layer of moss, soft and yielding underfoot, speckled with wildflowers in a riot of vibrant colors – deep blues, sunny yellows, and fiery oranges. The dominant feature, however, was the abundance of berry bushes, their branches laden with plump, juicy berries of every imaginable hue. Crimson raspberries, plump blueberries, glistening blackberries, and ruby-red strawberries formed a colorful tapestry across the clearing. The sweet scent of ripe berries hung heavy in the air, a tempting aroma that drew in a variety of woodland creatures.

Among the bushes, flitted a multitude of butterflies, their wings adorned with intricate patterns of vibrant colors. Tiny bumblebees buzzed lazily from flower to flower; their furry bodies dusted with pollen. Ladybugs, their red shells speckled with black dots, crawled slowly across leaves, their tiny antennae twitching. A family of field mice scurried through the undergrowth, their tiny paws padding softly on the mossy ground, their eyes constantly scanning for potential predators or tasty berries. Squirrels, their bushy tails twitching, scampered up and down the trees, their nimble paws expertly navigating the branches. Their chatter filled the air, a constant hum of communication and activity.

But the most notable inhabitants of the Boggy Berry Patch were the gossiping hens. They were a flock of plump, feathered creatures, known for their sharp eyes and even sharper tongues. Their clucking and cackling could be heard from far and wide, their conversations a constant stream of news, rumors, and speculation. They were the heart of the Boggy Berry Patch, their presence giving the clearing a lively, bustling atmosphere. Perched on branches, nestled among the bushes, or strutting across the mossy ground, they formed a colorful and animated community. Their feathers displayed a kaleidoscope of colors, from the deepest browns and blacks to the brightest reds and golds, reflecting the rich diversity of the berries surrounding them.

Ink and Fiona approached cautiously, their movements careful not to disturb the delicate balance of the Boggy Berry Patch. They had heard tales of the hens' sharp tongues and their uncanny ability to gather information, making them valuable sources of intelligence in the Wildwoods Farm. They hoped to glean some insight into the strange markings found near the edge of the woods. The hens, a mixture of breeds, ranged from stately Plymouth Rocks to feisty Rhode Island Reds. They were a motley crew, united by their love of gossip and their collective knowledge of the forest.

As they drew closer, the hens' chatter subsided, replaced by a tense silence. All eyes turned towards Ink and Fiona, their beady eyes assessing the two investigators. One particularly plump hen, with feathers the color of ripe cranberries, stepped forward, her comb bobbing slightly.

"Well, well," she clucked, her voice sharp and precise, "What brings the famous investigators to our humble Berry Patch?"

Ink introduced themselves and explained their purpose, mentioning the strange markings discovered at the edge of the woods. The hens, true to their reputation, erupted into a flurry of clucking and chattering. Each hen offered her own version of events, a mixture of facts, rumors, and speculation. One claimed to have seen a strange creature lurking in the shadows, its form obscured by the dense undergrowth. Another insisted that the markings were an ancient map, leading to a hidden treasure. A third suggested that it was a warning sign, indicating danger lurking nearby.

As the hens' stories unfolded, a more detailed picture emerged. The Boggy Berry Patch, they explained, was more than just a collection of berry bushes. It was a crossroads, a place where trails converged, allowing for easy access to different parts beyond Wildwoods Farm. It was a place frequented by a variety of creatures, from squirrels and rabbits to foxes and badgers. The hens, with their constant observation, had witnessed many events unfold within the Boggy Berry Patch.

They described the routine patterns of the various woodland inhabitants, their daily movements and interactions. They noted the subtle changes in behavior, the increased nervousness among certain animals, and the unusual silence in normally bustling areas. Their collective knowledge, gathered over months and years of observation, painted a compelling picture of the Wildwoods Farm, both its beauty and its hidden dangers. Their accounts revealed a hidden network of trails and paths, secret tunnels and hidden clearings, a complex and interconnected ecosystem that extended far beyond the visible surface.

The hens also described the various plants that grew within the Boggy Berry Patch, detailing their medicinal properties and their uses within the woodland community. They discussed the different types of berries, their ripening cycles, and their nutritional value. They explained the intricate relationships between the plants and the animals, the symbiotic connections that maintained the balance of the ecosystem. They pointed out the subtle signs of environmental change, the effects of weather patterns and the impact of human activity on the forest.

As the hens spoke, Ink and Fiona realized the true importance of the Boggy Berry Patch. It was not just a source of food; it was a living library, a repository of knowledge, a reflection of the Wildwoods Farm itself. The seemingly trivial details, the observations about the habits of individual creatures, the discussions of plant life and the subtle changes in the forest – all contributed to a deeper understanding of the mystery surrounding the strange markings.

The hens' accounts provided valuable clues, pointing towards a possible explanation for the strange symbols. It seemed likely that the markings were not a warning or a map, but a form of communication, a message left by an unknown entity. The identity of the sender and the meaning of the message remained a mystery, but the hens' information provided a new direction for Ink and Fiona's investigation, steering them towards a new area beyond Wildwoods Farm, a region even more secluded and shrouded in mystery. The sun began to dip below the horizon, casting long shadows across the Boggy Berry Patch. As Ink and Fiona thanked the hens and prepared to leave, the air was filled with the renewed chirping and chattering, the collective voices of the Berry Patch returning to their usual lively hum. The mystery of the markings remained, but Ink and Fiona felt a renewed sense of hope, spurred by the newfound insights gleaned from the gossiping hens and their treasure trove of knowledge. The investigation continued, now leading them into the deepest, darkest corners beyond Wildwoods Farm, a journey that promised to uncover even more secrets and unveil further layers of the unfolding mystery.

Leaving the bustling Boggy Berry Patch behind, Ink and Fiona followed a barely discernible path, the undergrowth dense and Wildwoods secrets with every rustle of leaves. The air grew cooler, damper, the scent of berries fading to be replaced by the earthy aroma of decaying wood and damp moss. The path twisted and turned, leading them deeper into the Wildwoods, the sunlight gradually filtering through the increasingly dense canopy above. The sounds of the forest changed too, the lively chatter of the Boggy Berry Patch replaced by a hushed stillness, punctuated only by the occasional rustle of unseen creatures and the distant hoot of an owl.

After what seemed like an eternity of navigating the labyrinthine path, they emerged into a small clearing. And there, dominating the space, stood the Old Oak Tree. It was magnificent, a colossal specimen of ancient wood, its trunk wider than any ferrets could encompass, its branches reaching skyward like gnarled fingers grasping at the clouds. Its bark, thick and deeply furrowed, told tales of centuries past, each crevice a chapter in a long and storied life. Mosses and lichens clung to its surface, painting a tapestry of greens and browns that shifted and shimmered in the dappled sunlight.

The tree's immense size dwarfed everything around it. Smaller trees huddled at its base, their slender trunks like supplicants bowing before a king. The roots, thick as pythons, snaked across the forest floor, creating a network of pathways and hiding places for the woodland creatures. The branches, some reaching out horizontally like giant arms, others curving upwards towards the heavens, provided shelter and vantage points for various inhabitants. Squirrels darted across its branches, their tiny bodies a fleeting contrast to the vastness of the tree. Birds nested in its hollows, their songs echoing through its vastness.

Ink and Fiona felt a profound sense of awe as they stood beneath its shadow. This wasn't just a tree; it was a monument, a living testament to the passage of time. It had witnessed countless seasons, countless generations of woodland creatures, countless events both joyous and tragic. It was a silent observer, a keeper of secrets, a repository of the forest's history. A sense of profound history seemed to emanate from the tree itself, filling the air with an almost tangible weight of years gone by.

As they circled the base of the Old Oak, they noticed a worn path leading towards a slightly recessed area. It appeared to be a well-trodden trail, suggesting that it was frequently used. Curiosity piqued, they carefully followed the path, their senses alert, their eyes scanning the surroundings for any sign of danger or unusual activity. The path twisted and turned, leading them deeper into the heart of the tree's root system, where the shadows deepened and the air grew cooler still.

The path finally opened into a small, secluded clearing beneath the lowest branches. Here, they found a gathering of woodland creatures, a scene that seemed almost staged, as if they had been waiting for their arrival. There was a badger, renowned for his knowledge of herbal remedies; a wise old owl, known for his sharp eyes and even sharper wit; a family of rabbits, their ears twitching nervously; and a stately fox, his gaze sharp and observant. All of them looked expectantly towards Ink and Fiona.

The badger, his voice a low rumble, spoke first. "We've been expecting you," he said. "The Old Oak Tree is a place of council, a place where important matters are discussed. We have information that may be of use in your investigation."

The owl, his eyes gleaming with intelligence, added, "The markings you found – they are connected to this tree. This tree holds many secrets, some dating back to the very beginnings of the forest and Wildwoods Farm."

The rabbit family, their noses twitching, added a small piece of information – a seemingly insignificant detail about a squirrel they'd seen acting strangely near the telephone pole where Jenny had fallen.

The fox, always practical, summarized their collective wisdom: "The Old Oak Tree has been a central meeting place for centuries. It's where disputes are settled, where truths are revealed, and where secrets are shared. Many believe it possesses a kind of wisdom, an ability to perceive the truth even when it's hidden beneath layers of deception."

Ink and Fiona spent the rest of the afternoon listening intently to the tales shared by the creatures gathered beneath the Old Oak. They heard stories of ancient rivalries and unlikely alliances, of heroic deeds and treacherous betrayals. They learned about the tree's history, the events it had witnessed, the roles it had played in shaping the forest's community. The stories, interwoven with details about the forest's past and present, provided vital clues to the mystery surrounding Jenny's fall.

One story particularly captivated their attention. It spoke of a hidden compartment within the Old Oak's trunk, a space where important documents and artifacts had been stored for generations. This compartment, it was said, contained secrets that could shed light on many unsolved mysteries within the Wildwoods Farm. The creatures revealed that this hidden compartment could only be opened by someone who possessed a specific item, an object mentioned only in whispers among the oldest residents of the forest. As the sun began to set, casting long shadows across the clearing,

Ink and Fiona thanked the council of woodland creatures. The stories they had heard, combined with the newfound knowledge of the hidden compartment, provided a crucial new lead in their investigation. The Old Oak Tree, they realized, was far more than just a landmark; it was a key to unlocking the truth. The mysterious markings, the secrets of the Wildwoods Farm, even the fall of Jenny – everything seemed to converge around this ancient, wise old tree.

Leaving the Old Oak Tree, a renewed sense of purpose filled Ink and Fiona. They knew their investigation was far from over, but they had gained valuable insight, a deeper understanding of the forest and its inhabitants, and a crucial new lead: the hidden compartment within the ancient oak. The path ahead remained shrouded in mystery, but with the wisdom gained from the Old Oak Tree, they felt confident that they were getting closer to revealing the truth behind Jenny's fall and the strange markings found at the edge of the woods. The path ahead would undoubtedly present new challenges, but they were ready to face them, armed with the knowledge gained from the heart of the Wildwoods Farm.

The journey back was less arduous, the path seeming clearer under the light of the setting sun. The forest, once ominous and mysterious, now felt different – somehow more familiar, less intimidating. The woods teaming with leaves seemed less menacing, more like a gentle murmur, a soft lullaby accompanying them on their return journey. The experience at the Old Oak Tree had not only provided them with crucial clues but had also deepened their connection with the forest, allowing them to perceive the interconnectedness of its community and the subtle cues that hinted at the truth behind the mystery that loomed over them.

With renewed determination, Ink and Fiona prepared for the next stage of their investigation, knowing that the hidden compartment within the Old Oak held the key to uncovering the truth, however elusive it might prove to be. They knew that the journey to find the object needed to open it would be challenging, but armed with their newfound knowledge and strengthened resolve, they were ready to face whatever lay ahead. The forest, once a source of apprehension, had become a source of hope, a partner in their quest for justice. And with the setting sun painting the sky in hues of orange and purple, they walked on, carrying with them the weight of secrets, the burden of truth, and the unwavering belief that justice would prevail.

The path eventually led them away from the imposing presence of the Old Oak, its whispered secrets fading into the rustling of leaves. The air grew lighter, the scent of damp earth giving way to a fresher, sweeter fragrance. Ahead, a glimmer of silver caught Ink's eye, a glint of light reflecting off something unseen. As they drew closer, the source of the light revealed itself: Wildwoods Creek.

It wasn't a large creek, not even wide enough for a determined badger to swim across, but its presence was undeniable. The water, crystal clear and surprisingly cold, trickled over smooth, grey stones, its gentle murmur a soothing counterpoint to the deeper whispers of the woods. The creek bed was a mosaic of stones, some smooth and worn by the constant flow of water, others rough and jagged, each reflecting the light in its own unique way. Sunlight dappled through the trees, creating shimmering patterns on the surface of the water, turning the creek into a ribbon of liquid light.

The banks of the creek were lined with lush vegetation. Wildflowers of every imaginable color – blues, purples, yellows, and reds – bloomed in profusion, their petals delicately kissed by the gentle breeze. Ferns unfurled their fronds, creating a verdant carpet that softened the ruggedness of the terrain. The air hummed with the buzz of insects, the chirping of crickets, and the occasional song of a hidden bird.

But despite the serene beauty of the creek, a sense of mystery lingered. The water seemed to whisper secrets, each ripple a cryptic message only partially understood. The stillness was occasionally broken by the sudden darting of a fish, its silvery scales flashing before disappearing back into the depths. A sense of quiet contemplation permeated the area, a sense of ancient wisdom woven into the very fabric of the landscape. It was a place where time seemed to slow, where the stresses of the outside world faded, replaced by a sense of profound peace.

As Ink and Fiona walked along the creek, they noticed something peculiar. Embedded in the smooth stones lining the creek bed were small, perfectly round indentations. They were too uniform to be naturally occurring, too precise to be accidental. Ink carefully examined one of the indentations, running a claw along its edge. It felt oddly smooth, almost polished.

"These are strange," Fiona mused, her voice barely above a whisper, as if afraid to disturb the serenity of the place. "They look almost... artificial."

Ink agreed. "They're too regular, too perfectly formed. They seem almost... deliberate."

They followed the creek, their eyes scanning the creek bed for more of these strange indentations. They discovered dozens, scattered along the creek's course, sometimes clustered together, sometimes spaced far apart. They seemed to follow a pattern, a sequence that was initially indecipherable but slowly began to reveal itself. As they continued their exploration, they noticed other anomalies. Small, intricately carved wooden figures were partially hidden among the roots of trees that overhung the creek. These figures were remarkably lifelike, depicting various woodland creatures – squirrels, rabbits, birds, foxes – each capturing a unique posture and expression. These figures, like the indentations in the creek bed, seemed to follow a specific arrangement, a carefully orchestrated display.

One figure, larger than the others, depicted a squirrel poised on the edge of a branch, seeming to look down in a pose that suggested alarm or surprise. It eerily resembled Jenny. Next to this figure was a smaller squirrel, seemingly looking up. A tiny carved wooden telephone pole was nearby.

Ink and Fiona exchanged glances. The arrangement was strikingly similar to the scene of Jenny's fall. Could this be a reenactment? A message? A clue? The more they examined the carvings, the clearer it became: the scene depicted a scenario strikingly similar to the events surrounding Jenny's accident.

As they traced the creek's path, they discovered a series of these miniature wooden scenes, each revealing a small segment of a larger narrative. It was as if someone had created a visual account of the events leading up to Jenny's fall, using the creek as a canvas, the water as a backdrop, and the forest itself as a stage.

The details within each carving were astonishingly precise. They showcased the expressions on the tiny squirrels' faces, the angle of their bodies, the nuances of their postures – details that would only be observable by someone who had witnessed the event firsthand.

The discovery of the creek's scenes confirmed their suspicions. Someone was carefully trying to tell them a story, a story that was directly relevant to Jenny's fall. The meticulous nature of the carvings indicated that the creator was familiar with the incident and possibly involved in it.

As the sun began to set, casting long shadows over the creek, Ink and Fiona realized that the Wildwoods Creek was not just a natural feature of the forest. It was a carefully crafted narrative, a story revealed through small details, and meticulously placed artifacts. It was a coded message, a silent witness to the events surrounding Jenny's accident, a secret Wildwoods Farm possessed revealing its secrets to those who knew how to listen.

The path alongside the creek eventually led them to a small, hidden waterfall, almost entirely obscured by a curtain of ivy. The water cascaded over mossy rocks, creating a shimmering veil of mist. Beneath the waterfall, tucked away in a small, concealed alcove, they found something extraordinary – a single, smooth, grey stone, unlike any they had seen before. It was perfectly round, its surface gleaming with an ethereal light, and etched into it was a single, perfectly formed symbol, a symbol that seemed eerily familiar, a symbol that mirrored one of the markings found near the telephone pole where Jenny had fallen.

The stone felt warm to the touch, pulsing with a gentle energy. As Ink held it, he felt a strange sensation, a tingling in his paws, a sense of connection to something ancient and powerful. It was as if the stone held a memory, a fragment of the forest's past, a clue to the truth behind Jenny's fall. This stone, they realized, was not just a simple object; it was a key, a piece of the puzzle, a part of a much larger, far more intricate mystery. It held a piece of the truth, waiting to be revealed. The journey to unlock the secrets it held would be challenging, but with the discovery of this mysterious stone, Ink and Fiona were certain that they were drawing ever closer to the truth behind Jenny's fall, and the solution to the mystery that haunted the Wildwoods Farm. The Wildwoods Creek, with its enigmatic carvings and its silent secrets, had led them to the next crucial piece in their quest for justice. The sunset painted the sky with vibrant hues, reflecting in the water, a dramatic farewell as Ink and Fiona embarked on the next leg of their investigation, their hearts filled with renewed hope and determination.

Beyond the Wildwoods Creek, the path narrowed, becoming barely more than a deer trail, winding deeper into the heart of the Wildwoods. The sunlight, once vibrant and strong, now filtered weakly through the dense canopy, casting long, dancing shadows that seemed to writhe and twist like living things. The air grew heavy with the scent of damp earth and decaying leaves, a fragrance both earthy and mysterious. The gusts of the wind through the trees intensified, a constant murmur that seemed to both soothing and unsettling. Ink and Fiona, their paws careful on the uneven ground, pressed forward, their senses alert.

This part of the woods was different. The playful chatter of birds was replaced by a hushed stillness, a profound quiet that spoke of secrets guarded, and mysteries kept. The familiar woodland creatures, usually so bold and unafraid, seemed to shy away, their presence felt more than seen. It was as if this section of the woods held its breath, anticipating something, waiting for something... or someone.

Finally, after what felt like an eternity of cautious progress, they reached their destination. It wasn't a grand clearing or a breathtaking vista, but a small, secluded glade, hidden from view by a curtain of interwoven branches and dense undergrowth. Sunlight barely penetrated the thick foliage, casting the glade in a perpetual twilight. This was their sanctuary, their secret meeting place, a place where they could plan their investigations, share their thoughts, and strategize their next moves without fear of being overheard or observed.

The glade itself was surprisingly tranquil. A small, clear stream trickled through the center, its waters reflecting the muted light. The stream bed was covered with smooth, grey stones, similar to those they had encountered by the Wildwoods Creek, but here, they were unblemished, pristine, undisturbed. Soft moss carpeted the ground, creating a springy, silent surface. Ancient trees surrounded the glade, their branches intertwined, creating a protective canopy overhead. The air was filled with the subtle fragrance of wildflowers and damp earth, a scent uniquely their own.

In the heart of the glade, nestled amongst the roots of an ancient oak, sat a large, flat rock, smooth and worn by time and weather. This would be their meeting place, their table, where they would lay out maps, examine clues, and puzzle over the intricacies of their cases. The rock seemed to exude a sense of quiet wisdom, its surface bearing silent witness to countless hours of planning and deliberation.

"It's good to be here," Fiona murmured, her voice a soft purr in the quiet glade. She stretched languidly, her sleek black fur gleaming in the dim light. She looked around, her emerald eyes scanning the surroundings with a keen intensity. "This place... it feels safe."

Ink nodded in agreement, his keen ferret eyes scanning the area with equal care. "It's secluded, hidden from the prying eyes of others. No one would ever suspect such a place exists." He touched the smooth surface of their meeting rock, a comforting familiarity in the gesture. "It's important that our meetings remain secret. Our investigations often touch on sensitive matters, and discretion is paramount."

They settled onto the rock, the coolness of the stone a welcome contrast to the humid air. Ink carefully produced a small, leather-bound notebook from his satchel, its pages filled with detailed sketches, notes, and observations meticulously recorded. He opened the notebook, revealing a map of the woods, marked with various symbols and annotations.

"We need to analyze the information we gathered from the Wildwoods Creek," Ink began, his voice low and purposeful. "Those miniature carvings... they were remarkably detailed. They depict a sequence of events, a visual narrative leading up to Jenny's fall. It's as though someone was deliberately trying to tell us something, to guide us towards the truth."

Fiona examined the map intently, her eyes following Ink's finger as he traced the path of the creek. "The carvings were incredibly precise," she agreed, her voice thoughtful. "The expressions on the squirrels' faces, the angle of their bodies, the placement of the telephone pole... it all seems deliberately staged. It's almost like a silent witness to the event, meticulously recreated in miniature."

Ink nodded, his attention focused on the map. "And the stone we found... the one with the symbol. It's clearly connected to this case. The symbol is similar to the markings found near the telephone pole. It's like a signature, a mark left by whoever orchestrated the events surrounding Jenny's fall."

They spent hours analyzing the clues, poring over their notes, comparing observations, and piecing together the fragmented information. The quiet of the glade was punctuated only by the gentle murmur of the stream and the rustling of leaves, creating a contemplative atmosphere conducive to deep thought and careful analysis. The hidden glade provided not just a sanctuary, but a space where their minds could work freely, where ideas could flow, and where the truth, slowly, surely, could begin to emerge.

As the sun began to dip below the horizon, casting long shadows across the glade, they finally reached a conclusion. The miniature scenes by the Wildwoods Creek, the mysterious stone with its strange symbol, and the other clues they had gathered all pointed towards a single, startling revelation. Someone, and not who they had expected, had a vested interest in framing Jasper for Jenny's fall. This person had carefully orchestrated the scene, leaving clues to mislead the investigation and ensuring suspicion would fall on Jasper. This conclusion was unexpected, given that their primary suspect had always seemed to be the more obvious one.

They knew their next steps. They had to revisit previous locations, re-examining them with a fresh perspective, considering their new suspect. This realization sparked new energy within them; this was a far more intricate puzzle than they initially believed and unraveling it would require all their skill and resourcefulness.

The glade, hidden away from the bustle of the forest community, continued to offer them a place of respite and planning. They left the secluded place, the twilight now descending upon the Wildwoods Farm, their minds abuzz with their new theories and a renewed determination to bring justice to Jenny and clear Jasper's name. The journey had been long and winding, but with each new clue, with every visit to this secret glade, Ink and Fiona were increasingly confident that they were on the right track, edging ever closer to the truth hidden within the heart of the Wildwoods Farm. The weight of their investigation was heavy, but the quiet solace of their secret glade provided them the necessary mental space to carefully consider their next steps.

As they left the glade, the woods seemed less menacing, the whispers less ominous. Their renewed purpose had changed their perspective. The darkness of the forest seemed to hold not just mystery, but also the promise of uncovering the truth. The moon, a watchful eye in the deepening twilight, seemed to offer its silent support, casting a silvery light on their determined figures as they embarked on the next phase of their investigation, their hearts filled with a mixture of apprehension and resolute hope. The path ahead was uncertain, but they were ready. The truth, they knew, was waiting to be revealed. The journey promised to be fraught with challenges, but they were prepared to face whatever lay ahead, ready to uncover the secrets within the heart of the Wildwoods Farm. Their secret glade, a constant reminder of their commitment, would remain their sanctuary, a place of peace, planning, and ultimately, a stepping-stone towards the unveiling of the truth.

Chapter 7
Jenny's Life

Jenny was a whirlwind of energy; a tiny squirrel packed with an outsized personality. Her fur, the color of sun-ripened apricots, was always slightly ruffled, a testament to her boundless enthusiasm. She was rarely still, a constant flurry of motion, whether she was scampering up the tallest oak trees, chasing butterflies across the meadow, or organizing elaborate games with her friends. Her laugh, a high-pitched, melodic chirp, was infectious, capable of brightening even the gloomiest of days.

Her home, a cozy den nestled high in the branches of a majestic willow tree overlooking Wildwoods Creek, was a reflection of her vibrant spirit. It was filled with an eclectic collection of treasures: brightly colored pebbles she'd found on the creek bed, smooth, polished acorns, meticulously arranged twigs and leaves, and a dazzling array of wildflowers carefully preserved and pressed between the pages of an old, discarded notebook. Everything was arranged with a meticulous attention to detail, reflecting her thoughtful nature despite her chaotic energy.

Jenny possessed a remarkable talent for storytelling. She'd gather her friends – Pip and Squeak, two young chipmunks known for their insatiable curiosity; Zoie and Nutmeg, a pair of quick-witted rabbits; and Donald, a wise old owl with a penchant for riddles – under the shade of the great oak tree by the creek. There, she would spin tales of daring adventures, mischievous sprites, and brave heroes, her voice animated, her eyes sparkling with imaginative fervor. Her stories often intertwined elements of real-life events in the forest with fantastical creatures and events, captivating her audience with intricate plots and surprising twists.

One of her favorite pastimes was collecting wildflowers. She possessed a vast knowledge of the flora of the Wildwoods Farm, identifying each bloom with ease, from the delicate bluebells to the vibrant poppies and the shy violets hidden beneath the ferns. She would carefully arrange her finds in miniature bouquets, creating vibrant displays that decorated her den and brightened the days of her friends. She had a unique ability to find beauty in the most unexpected places, noticing the intricate patterns of moss on the rocks, the delicate veins of leaves, and the subtle shades of color in the bark of the trees. Her keen observation skills were not only appreciated for their beauty but also for their practicality. She often used her knowledge of plant life to find solutions to problems for her friends, identifying herbs to soothe sore paws and berries to add flavor to the community's meals.

Jenny was known throughout the Wildwoods Farm for her generous spirit and unwavering optimism. She was always ready to lend a helping hand, whether it was assisting an elderly squirrel with gathering nuts or comforting a frightened baby bird that had fallen from its nest. She possessed an infectious enthusiasm that radiated warmth and kindness, bringing joy and laughter wherever she went. Her empathy extended to all creatures, great and small, a quality that made her a beloved member of the forest community. Even the grumpy badger, Old Man Grumbles, known for his surly disposition, couldn't help but crack a smile at Jenny's cheerful demeanor. Her unwavering positive attitude was a beacon of light in the forest, reminding everyone of the importance of hope and kindness, even during difficult times.

Beyond her artistic talents and storytelling skills, Jenny had a knack for problem-solving. She possessed a sharp mind, capable of analyzing complex situations with remarkable clarity and insight. She often acted as a mediator among her friends, helping them resolve disagreements and conflicts with patience and understanding. Her ability to see different perspectives, combined with her inherent empathy, allowed her to facilitate peaceful resolutions, preventing arguments from escalating into larger disputes. Her problem-solving abilities were not limited to interpersonal conflicts; she also showed remarkable ingenuity in tackling practical challenges. Once, when a heavy storm caused a large branch to fall, blocking the path to the creek, Jenny devised an ingenious plan to clear the obstruction, leading a collaborative effort among her friends that restored access to a vital resource for the community.

Her friendships were deeply valued, forming the core of her happiness. She cherished her time spent with Pip, Squeak, Zoie, Nutmeg, and Donald, engaging in countless adventures and shared experiences. Each friendship was unique, reflecting the distinct personalities of her companions. With Pip and Squeak, she shared a love of exploration and discovery, embarking on thrilling expeditions to uncover hidden groves and explore uncharted territories. With Zoie and Nutmeg, she enjoyed leisurely afternoons spent exchanging stories, gossiping about the latest forest news, and crafting elaborate games. With Donald, the wise old owl, she engaged in stimulating conversations, delving into the mysteries of the forest and the wisdom of past generations. Each friendship enriched her life, providing support, laughter, and a deep sense of belonging.

Jenny's positive energy was evident in even the smallest aspects of her life. She meticulously kept her den clean and organized, a testament to her orderly nature. Her food stores were always well-stocked, reflecting her preparedness and her concern for the future. She meticulously cleaned her paws after exploring the creek and always ensured her fur remained pristine, even after engaging in playful adventures. Her attention to detail extended to her social interactions, as she always remembered birthdays and special occasions, presenting thoughtful gifts and extending kind gestures to show her appreciation for those around her.

Her enthusiasm was contagious, inspiring others to embrace life with the same joy and zest she possessed. She had a knack for finding the positive in every situation, even when faced with adversity. Her resilience and determination were evident in her unwavering optimism, inspiring those around her to confront challenges with courage and hope. She believed in the power of community, in the importance of cooperation and collaboration, and in the enduring strength of friendship. These beliefs guided her actions and shaped her personality, making her a beacon of light in the often-challenging environment of Wildwoods Farm.

Even her moments of quiet reflection were filled with a sense of wonder and curiosity. She would often spend time observing the stars at night, marveling at their brilliance and pondering the mysteries of the universe. She would listen intently to the rustling of leaves in the wind, finding beauty in the simple sounds of nature. Her appreciation for the natural world was profound, shaping her perspective and enriching her life.

Despite her exuberant nature, Jenny possessed a quiet strength, a resilience that allowed her to overcome obstacles and persevere in the face of adversity. She was not afraid to speak her mind, even when it meant challenging prevailing opinions or confronting injustice. Her courage was evident in her unwavering belief in truth and justice, a belief that guided her actions and ultimately contributed to the unraveling of the mystery surrounding her fall. It was this inner strength, combined with her infectious enthusiasm and unwavering optimism, that made Jenny such a remarkable and beloved member of the forest community. Her legacy would live on, not only in the memories of her friends but also in the impact she had on the lives of those who knew her, a testament to the enduring power of a truly remarkable spirit. The quiet glade, where she often spent her quiet moments, would forever hold a trace of her laughter and the echoes of her stories.

Jenny's family was as vibrant and unique as she was. Her parents, Hazelnut and Acorn, were a picture of devoted parenthood. Hazelnut, a graceful squirrel with fur the color of warm honey, possessed a quiet strength and unwavering patience. She was the anchor of the family, her gentle nature providing a calming presence amidst Jenny's boundless energy. Acorn, her father, was a robust and playful squirrel, his fur rich, dark brown, mirroring the sturdy oak trees that dotted their woodland home. He shared Jenny's zest for life, often joining her in her adventures, his booming laughter echoing through the trees.

Their home, a magnificent den nestled high in the willow, wasn't just a shelter; it was a testament to their love. It was larger than most, meticulously crafted with an abundance of soft moss, carefully woven twigs, and snug, sheltered chambers. The entrance was cleverly concealed behind a curtain of ivy, ensuring privacy and protection. Inside, the den was surprisingly spacious, with separate sleeping areas, a pantry overflowing with winter stores, and a small, cozy living area where the family gathered in the evenings. The walls were adorned with Jenny's artwork—pressed wildflowers, intricately arranged pebbles, and tiny, hand-painted acorns, each a testament to her creativity and love for her family.

Family dinners were a cherished ritual. Hazelnut, a skilled forager, prepared delicious meals of nuts, berries, and seeds, always ensuring there was enough for everyone. Acorn would often regale them with amusing stories of his younger days, his tales filled with daring escapades and close calls, prompting bursts of laughter from Jenny and her parents. These dinners were not just meals; they were a time for connection, a space where the family shared their joys, concerns, and dreams, strengthening their bond.

Jenny's siblings were a constant source of amusement and affection. There was Lucas, her older brother, a quiet and thoughtful squirrel who possessed a keen interest in astronomy. He often spent his evenings gazing at the stars, sharing his knowledge of constellations with Jenny, igniting her curiosity about the universe. Lucas was a constant source of comfort and support for Jenny; he was the one she would turn to when she needed a quiet ear or a reassuring presence. Their bond was a quiet, deep current that flowed underneath their daily interactions.

Then there was Alley, Jenny's younger sister. Alley was a whirlwind of mischief, a miniature version of Jenny, only with an even more playful spirit. Their adventures often led to comical predicaments and hilarious escapes, filling their lives with joyous chaos. Though their personalities were strikingly similar, their bond was a whirlwind of shared laughter and fierce loyalty. They were each other's confidantes, sharing secrets and dreams, creating a unique sisterly bond that only deepened with time.

Family game nights were another cherished tradition. Acorn would often invent elaborate games involving puzzles, races, and riddles. Hazelnut would enthusiastically participate, her competitive spirit shining through. Jenny and Alley would team up, their combined creativity and energy proving a formidable force against their father's challenges. Lucas would act as a neutral referee, his calm demeanor ensuring fair play amidst the lively competition. These games taught Jenny the value of teamwork, the importance of strategy, and the joy of shared experiences, lessons that went beyond mere entertainment. They were building blocks for her character, contributing to her exceptional problem-solving skills.

Their family wasn't just about shared activities; it was a foundation of unwavering support. When Jenny's attempts ended in disappointment, Lucas would offer kind words of encouragement. When Alley's pranks went awry, Acorn would help Jenny to find creative solutions to rectify any mistakes. When Jenny fell from the telephone pole, the family rallied around her, providing comfort to those who were impacted the most. Their love for Jenny was not only evident in their actions but also in their words, their unspoken support, and the strength they drew from each other's presence.

Even their disagreements were handled with love and understanding. They respected each other's opinions and beliefs, even when they differed. Disagreements were resolved through open communication and compromises, never allowing conflicts to fester or damage their close-knit bond. This open and healthy communication was a cornerstone of their family dynamic, a model that extended to Jenny's friendships and interactions within the wider forest community. It was a lesson in empathy and respect, in understanding that different viewpoints didn't necessitate animosity.

The support extended beyond the immediate family. Grandmother Willow, Jenny's maternal grandmother, a wise and venerable old squirrel, lived nearby. Her den, nestled deep within the roots of the ancient willow tree that gave her name, was a repository of ancient forest lore and family history. She often shared stories of past generations, their triumphs and tribulations, reminding Jenny of the enduring strength of their family lineage. Grandmother Willow's influence instilled in Jenny a deep sense of history and a profound respect for tradition. She imparted not only family history but also life lessons, subtle yet profound, weaving tales that resonated with the experiences of Jenny's life.

Uncle Baker, a charismatic and adventurous squirrel, often visited with tales of his explorations throughout the Wildwoods and beyond. His stories instilled a love of adventure and a thirst for exploration in Jenny, shaping her adventurous nature. He was not just an uncle; he was a mentor and friend, teaching her valuable life skills and instilling in her a deep appreciation for the forest environment. His stories of the forest's hidden wonders fueled her imagination and her passion for collecting wildflowers. His presence added an element of excitement and expanded her world beyond the immediate family.

Jenny's extended family, a network of aunts, uncles, and cousins, provided a rich and supportive social environment. Family gatherings were lively affairs, filled with laughter, games, and the aroma of delicious food. These gatherings strengthened familial bonds and provided a sense of belonging, reinforcing Jenny's feeling of being loved and cherished. The vibrant extended family enriched Jenny's life, providing her with a strong sense of identity and connection to the wider forest community. They provided a sense of continuity, a connection to the past and a shared history, a foundation upon which she could build her own future. The constant flow of love, support, and interaction from her large and varied family helped shape the kind, optimistic, and resilient young squirrel who was so beloved throughout the forest. Her fall from the telephone pole, therefore, was not just a personal tragedy; it was a shock to the entire family, a disruption to the tightly woven fabric of their lives.

Jenny's friendships were as diverse and vibrant as the forest itself. Her bond with Jasper, the squirrel who now faced unjust accusations, was particularly deep. They'd been inseparable since they were kits, their playful energy a constant whirlwind in the heart of the Wildwoods Farm. They shared secrets whispered amongst the rustling leaves, raced each other up the tallest trees, and spent countless hours building elaborate dams in the babbling brook. Jasper, with his quick wit and mischievous grin, was the perfect complement to Jenny's adventurous spirit. Their friendship wasn't just about shared activities; it was a deep understanding, a silent language spoken through glances and gestures. They knew each other's moods without words, their laughter and quiet moments a testament to their bond. The idea that Jasper could have harmed her felt utterly foreign, a dissonance that clashed violently with the melody of their shared history.

Beyond Jasper, Jenny had a wide circle of friends, each relationship unique and valuable. There was Pete, a young badger with an unusually gentle nature. Pete was a scholar of sorts; his burrow filled with books and scrolls collected from forgotten human settlements bordering the woods. He'd often share stories and knowledge with Jenny, his calm demeanor a soothing counterpoint to her frenetic energy. Their friendship was one of quiet understanding, built on shared moments of intellectual exploration. He wasn't one for adventure, preferring the comfort of his library to the thrill of exploring the forest's depths, but his wisdom and calm friendship were always there for Jenny. He was a steady presence, a grounding force in her life.

Then there was Alice, a spirited field mouse with a penchant for mischief. Alice was Jenny's partner in crime; their adventures often lead to hilarious situations and narrow escapes. Alice's quick thinking and agility often saved them from trouble, her tiny size allowing her to navigate spaces inaccessible to Jenny. Their friendship was a symphony of chaos, a whirlwind of shared laughter, and daring escapades. Alice provided a balance to Jenny's sometimes impulsive nature, keeping her grounded with a dose of common sense that counteracted her enthusiasm. They were a perfect team, a complement of strengths that turned any problem into a thrilling challenge.

Amongst the birds, Jenny was particularly close to Celeste, a blue jay known for her sharp wit and even sharper tongue. Celeste, despite her sometimes-abrasive exterior, possessed a deep loyalty and unwavering support for her friends. Her insights were often surprisingly perceptive, her ability to spot details others missed invaluable. Their friendship was a study in contrast, the impulsive Jenny and the analytical Celeste creating a dynamic duo. Celeste's observation skills were instrumental in helping Jenny process her emotions and understand her surroundings. Celeste's sharp tongue often served as a wake-up call, bringing Jenny back to reality when she became overly enthusiastic or impulsive.

Amongst the older generation, Jenny had a close relationship with Old Man Cane, a wise old owl who lived in the hollow of a giant oak tree. Old Man Cane possessed a vast knowledge of the forest's history and lore, his stories often filled with tales of bravery, cunning, and wisdom. He'd often share insights into the forest's workings, his wisdom a guiding light in Jenny's life. He wasn't actively involved in Jenny's daily life, but his presence was felt in the wisdom she gleaned from his stories. His patience and understanding helped her process her emotions after the fall, providing comfort and guidance. Jenny valued his calm wisdom and sought his advice during times of uncertainty.

Each friendship was a unique facet of Jenny's life, shaping her character and enriching her experiences. These connections were more than just casual acquaintances; they were bonds forged through shared adventures, mutual respect, and unwavering loyalty. The animals of the Wildwoods Farm formed a community, and Jenny's wide circle of friends demonstrated her kind and generous nature, her willingness to connect with others, regardless of their species or personality. The strength of these friendships was something that amazed and delighted those who observed her. These relationships went beyond simple play; they offered a sense of belonging, a network of support, and a rich tapestry of experiences that enriched Jenny's life in countless ways. The accusation against Jasper threatened not just their friendship, but the intricate fabric of Jenny's world, unsettling the harmony she had carefully cultivated. The shock of the accident, the subsequent accusations, and the uncertainty surrounding the truth shattered a sense of security she had taken for granted. The entire community was affected by the disruption of this balance. The forest felt different, the air was thick with suspicion and uncertainty.

Her friendships were not just about shared laughter and playful adventures. They were about mutual support, shared confidence, and the unwavering belief in each other's goodness. When Jenny fell, the outpouring of concern wasn't merely sympathy; it was a testament to the depth of her connections within the forest. Pete visited the place that took her life and was full of sorrow. He began reading from his favorite texts, he was hoping that his soothing voice could find her in the afterlife. Amber, ever the prankster, visited her hoping that she could cheer her up in the afterlife with tiny, handcrafted toys and comical stories of her latest escapades. Celeste, though keeping her words brief, missed her and promised that the tragedy that took her life, that the truth would be revealed. Even Old Man Cane, with his solemn wisdom, visited her and offered her comforting words and a promise of guidance to help her in the afterlife.

The incident with Jasper tested the strength of their bond. The initial shock and accusation created a rift between him and the community, a chasm of misunderstanding and distrust. Yet, even as doubt crept in, Jasper felt a deep foundation of their friendship that would remain even in the afterlife. There was a silent understanding, a stubborn hope that the truth would ultimately prevail and restore his bond with the community. The accusations threatened to dissolve all of Jasper's friendship, but Jasper hoped that the years of shared experiences and mutual affection would prove to be a resilient force, something deeper and more enduring than fleeting suspicion or gossip. The challenge now was to navigate this difficult period, to use his friendships as a bridge, and to strive for understanding and truth, not just for himself, but for the wider forest community.

The strength of Jenny's relationships revealed a significant truth about the forest community: it wasn't just a collection of individual animals; it was a tightly knit web of connections, a community where support, empathy and shared experiences bound the inhabitants together. Jenny's fall was not an isolated event; it had a ripple effect that touched the lives of many. The ensuing investigation became not only a quest for justice but also an opportunity to strengthen the bonds of friendship and reaffirm the importance of trust and understanding within their community. The incident revealed the hidden complexities of relationships, the ease with which misinterpretations could lead to misunderstandings and the importance of seeking out the truth before passing judgment. The incident highlighted the fragility of trust and the immense power of friendship to overcome adversity. The investigation would ultimately test the resilience of their community and reveal the true nature of their bonds. The story of Jenny's fall wasn't just a personal tragedy; it was a catalyst for change, a turning point that would forever alter the dynamics of the Wildwoods Farm.

Jenny's dreams weren't confined to the familiar paths and towering trees of the Wildwoods Farm. They soared beyond the rustling leaves and babbling brooks, reaching for a future as vast and unpredictable as the sky above. She dreamt of exploring the world beyond the forest's edge, a world she'd only glimpsed from the highest branches of the ancient oaks. Tales whispered by Old Man Cane of human settlements, bustling towns, and shimmering oceans ignited a spark of wanderlust within her. She pictured herself, a tiny squirrel navigating the bustling streets of a distant city, her bright eyes taking in the sights and sounds of a world entirely different from her own. She'd often spend hours sketching in the dirt, using twigs and pebbles to depict fantastical scenes of faraway lands. One drawing showed a magnificent ship sailing across a vast ocean, its sails billowing in the wind, carrying her to unknown shores. Another depicted a bustling marketplace overflowing with exotic fruits and vibrant fabrics, a spectacle that filled her imagination with wonder.

These weren't idle fantasies; they were aspirations fueled by a deep-seated curiosity and a yearning for adventure. Jenny wasn't content with the familiar; she craved the unknown, the thrill of discovery, the excitement of facing new challenges. She yearned to learn more about the world beyond the forest, to understand its complexities, its wonders, and its mysteries. She'd studied the maps Pete had painstakingly recreated from fragments of old, tattered human books, her small paws tracing the lines of rivers and mountains, imagining the journeys they represented. Each line was a potential path, each mountain a challenge to overcome, each river a waterway to explore. Her heartbeat faster at the thought of such adventures, a thrill that resonated deeply within her adventurous spirit.

Beyond her geographical aspirations, Jenny dreamt of making a difference in the lives of others. She envisioned herself as a protector of the forest, a champion for the weak, a voice for those who couldn't speak for themselves. Witnessing the injustices suffered by others, particularly one day the wrongful accusations against Jasper and the missing acorns which were not stolen but misplaced by its owner and fueled with desire, Jenny ensured fairness and truth always prevailed.

When she was alive, she'd spent hours observing the community, noting various imbalances and inequalities, where she formulated plans to address them. She imagined herself leading a campaign to protect the vulnerable animals from predators, organizing efforts to provide food and shelter for the needy, and mediating disputes among the forest's inhabitants. She'd often practice speeches in front of a small audience of admiring woodland creatures, delivering impassioned pleas for harmony and understanding. Her commitment to justice was not a mere fleeting thought; it was a deeply ingrained value, a principle that guided her actions and defined her ambitions.

Jenny's dreams extended to her friendships. She envisioned a future where her bonds with Jasper, Pete, Amber, Celeste, and Old Man Cane would grow even stronger. She had dreamt of shared adventures, where they would work together to achieve common goals, overcome challenges, and celebrate victories. She had pictured herself and Jasper, side by side, exploring the world beyond the forest, their friendship a beacon of unwavering loyalty and support. She had envisioned Pete sharing his knowledge with a wider audience, educating the forest's inhabitants and expanding their understanding of the world. She had dreamt of Amber's mischief leading to unexpected solutions and hilarious adventures. She had seen Celeste using her sharp wit and keen observation skills to solve conflicts and promote justice within the community. She had pictured Old Man Cane's wisdom guiding their efforts, offering guidance and support as they navigate the complexities of life. When Jenny was alive, her vision was one of unity, cooperation, and collective progress.

However, Jenny's dreams weren't always grand and sweeping. She had also dreamt of the smaller, simpler joys of life: the warmth of the sun on her fur, the taste of sweet berries, the feeling of wind rustling through her fur as she raced through the trees. These small pleasures had grounded her, reminding her of the beauty and wonder of the world around her. She had dreamt of peaceful evenings spent with her friends, sharing stories, laughter, and quiet moments of companionship. These simple dreams were as important to her as her grand aspirations; they had represented the essence of her happiness, the foundation upon which her ambitions were built.

The accident ended her life and shattered her dreams and aspirations. The injustice surrounding Jasper's accusation had cast a shadow of doubt where she now had no future. Jenny's dreams would remain unfulfilled, the possibility that her aspirations foreclosed. Jenny was gone and her future was now forever out of reach. Jenny's fall from the telephone pole filled the community with fear, confusion, and a sense of helplessness. Those that observed saw Jenny dizzyingly tumble which concluded with a sickening thud as she landed on the forest floor. As they ran over, they had seen that Jenny was gone and that fear was overwhelming.

But even within the darkness of Jenny being gone, a spark of hope remained. The community would pray that Ink and Fiona, their keen eyes and sharp minds would unravel the truth, exposing the real culprit, and some had hoped that they would clear Jasper's name. These dreams provided a glimmer of light amidst the darkness, a promise that justice would prevail and that the community's world would return to its former harmony.

The recurring images of Ink's determined face and Fiona's insightful gaze gave the community strength, a belief that the truth would ultimately emerge. The community dreamt of a future where Jenny's dreams, both great and small, would become reality and where justice would prevail.

When Jenny was alive, she dreamt of a future where the Wildwoods Farm would remain a place of safety, friendship, and harmony, a community where trust and understanding would guide their actions. She had pictured herself contributing to the wellbeing of her community, her experiences shaping her into a leader who championed justice, fairness, and truth. These dreams, born out of hardship and adversity, were infused with resilience, determination, and an unwavering belief in the goodness of others. They had provided her with the strength to endure, the courage to persevere, and the hope to rebuild her life and her community, stronger and wiser than before. Jenny's dreams had held the promise of a brighter future, one where her aspirations would have blossomed, and where Wildwoods Farm would flourish. With Jenny gone, the path ahead might be uncertain, but Jenny's dreams served as a compass, guiding the community towards a future filled with hope, adventure, and the fulfillment of their potential.

The sun, filtering weakly through the canopy, cast long shadows across the clearing where Jenny's friends gathered. The air, usually vibrant with the cheerful chatter of the Wildwoods Farm, hung heavy with a poignant silence, broken only by the occasional sigh of the wind through the leaves. Around a makeshift memorial – a small pile of smooth stones adorned with wildflowers, meticulously arranged by Amber – Pete, Jasper, Celeste, and Old Man Cane sat, each lost in their own thoughts, their faces etched with a mixture of grief and remembrance.

Jasper, his usually bright eyes clouded with sorrow, traced the outline of a small, heart-shaped stone with his paw. He hadn't spoken much since the accident, his usual playful demeanor replaced by a quiet solemnity. The weight of Jenny's loss, coupled with the lingering shadow of the false accusation, bore heavily upon him. He felt a deep sense of gratitude towards Ink and Fiona, their efforts not only clearing his name but also revealing the truth about the accident. But the relief was tinged with an aching sadness, an emptiness that Jenny's absence had created.

Pete, ever the scholar, had meticulously compiled a small book, lovingly bound with leaves and twine, dedicated to Jenny's memory. It was filled with drawings and stories about Jenny – her adventurous spirit, her unwavering determination, her generous heart. He read aloud, his voice trembling slightly, a passage detailing Jenny's detailed maps of the human world. He recalled Jenny's determination to one day explore beyond the boundaries of the woods, her meticulous observations, her relentless curiosity that had inspired him to deepen his own studies. He had expanded the collection of human artifacts from his attic, making several of the drawings and maps accessible for others to study.

Celeste, usually quick with a witty remark, remained unusually quiet, her sharp gaze fixed on the memorial. Jenny's quick thinking and uncanny ability to decipher social cues had been an important part of her friendship with Celeste. She had always valued Jenny's insight and keen observation skills, particularly during her attempts at solving minor disputes within the forest community. She reminisced about the times Jenny had helped her resolve conflicts, mediating disputes with wisdom beyond her years. Celeste's sharp wit and keen observation skills were enhanced by Jenny's intuitive understanding, and together they formed a dynamic duo. Now, she felt a profound loss of that collaboration. Jenny's legacy of astute observation now inspired Celeste to apply those skills with even greater diligence.

Old Man Willow, his ancient branches swaying gently in the breeze, offered silent comfort. His wisdom, gleaned from centuries of observing the forest's rhythms, had guided Jenny in countless ways. He recounted tales of Jenny's childhood, her early explorations, her dreams of travelling far, and her unwavering compassion for others. He spoke of Jenny's unyielding determination, her knack for inspiring others, her infectious optimism, and her undying loyalty. His words evoked a shared sentiment of gratitude for Jenny's impact on each of them. Old Man Willow's wisdom had guided Jenny, but her spirit, in turn, had enriched his existence. The loss resonated deeply, a reminder that even the oldest and wisest creatures experience loss and grief.

Amber, ever the mischievous one, placed a single, perfectly formed acorn beside the stones. She recounted memories of Jenny's infectious laughter, their shared adventures, their playful banter, and the times they had outsmarted the grumpy badger who lived near the stream. Amber's memories were often centered on their lighter moments, punctuated with laughter and excitement. She spoke of the times they explored together, and how Jenny had taught her to look at the world with a sense of curiosity and wonder, even in the mundane. She remembered Jenny's patience and guidance as Amber practiced her craft. Even Amber's innate mischievousness seemed gentler after Jenny's passing.

The memories shared that day weren't merely tales of a life lived; they were testament to the enduring impact Jenny had on the lives of those around her. Her spirit, vibrant and tenacious, refused to be confined to the boundaries of death. It lived on in the lessons she taught, the friendships she fostered, and the changes she inspired.

The Wildwoods Farm, once shaken by tragedy, began to heal. Jenny's memory served as a catalyst for positive change. Inspired by her spirit of justice and her unwavering belief in the power of truth, the forest community adopted a new approach to conflict resolution. A council was formed, comprised of representatives from various species, tasked with mediating disputes and ensuring fair treatment for all. Pete's carefully curated books, detailing Jenny's life and her keen observations, became required reading for young woodland creatures, teaching them the importance of empathy, understanding, and seeking truth before judgment.

Jasper, emboldened by the exoneration and fueled by his grief and respect for Jenny, dedicated himself to forest conservation. He became a vocal advocate for the protection of endangered species, leading initiatives to preserve the natural beauty of their home. He had been the most outspoken about the forest environment, and his grief had intensified his determination to ensure its protection for future generations.

Celeste, sharpening her observational skills, became a respected mediator, renowned for her ability to resolve conflicts peacefully and fairly. Her wit and keen eye for detail, once used playfully, now served a higher purpose, ensuring justice prevailed throughout the community. Her abilities flourished in her new role as mediator and mentor.

Amber, while retaining her mischievous nature, channeled her energy into creative projects that celebrated Jenny's memory. She created intricate tapestries depicting the forest's most beautiful vistas, each thread a testament to Jenny's adventurous spirit and love for nature. She used her artistic talents to memorialize Jenny, weaving together memories and moments of her life into captivating displays.

Old Man Willow, in his quiet way, continued to impart his wisdom, but now his teachings were infused with the lessons learned from Jenny's life – the importance of courage, perseverance, and unwavering commitment to justice. His centuries of wisdom now included Jenny's inspirational story, which he conveyed to each new generation in the forest community.

Even Ink and Fiona, having played such a pivotal role in uncovering the truth about Jenny's accident, found their investigative skills utilized in a different capacity. They became guardians of the forest, ensuring fairness and protecting the vulnerable. Their contributions to the investigation were invaluable. The insights gained during the investigation became a foundation for their future endeavors.

Jenny's legacy wasn't just a collection of memories; it was a living force, shaping the future of Wildwoods Farm. Her unwavering belief in justice, her infectious enthusiasm, and her deep love for her friends and her community continued to inspire change and growth, ensuring that her spirit lived on, a beacon of hope and kindness in the heart of the forest.

The Wildwoods Farm held not only the memory of Jenny, but a renewed understanding of empathy and a commitment to justice. The accident, though tragic, led to a transformation. The community, strengthened by its shared grief and inspired by Jenny's spirit, embarked on a path of greater understanding, compassion, and a determination to never again let assumptions obscure the truth. The trees rustled, the brook babbled, and the sun shone on a community forever changed by the life, and death, of a tiny squirrel named Jenny. Her legacy, a testament to the enduring power of kindness, courage, and the pursuit of truth, echoed throughout the Wildwoods Farm, a constant reminder that even the smallest creature can leave an indelible mark on the world.

Chapter 8
Jasper's Perspective

The world tilted. One moment, Jenny was there, a blur of russet fur against the grey telephone pole, her laughter echoing in the crisp autumn air. The next, she was gone, a tiny, lifeless form lying amidst the fallen leaves. The sound, the sickening *thump*, still reverberated in Jasper's ears, a relentless drumbeat against the sudden, suffocating silence that had descended upon the Wildwoods Farm.

Disbelief warred with a gut-wrenching terror. It wasn't real. It couldn't be. Jenny, with her boundless energy, her irrepressible spirit, her quick wit that could disarm even the grumpiest badger – Jenny was simply... gone. The vibrant tapestry of his life, intricately woven with her presence, had been ripped apart, leaving behind only jagged edges of pain and a gaping hole in his heart.

He hadn't pushed her. He knew that with a certainty that resonated deep within his very being. He had been arguing with her, a silly spat about the best route to the oak tree where they usually collected acorns, a disagreement as fleeting and inconsequential as a summer breeze. But the image of her falling, the horrifying swiftness of it all, played on a relentless loop in his mind, each replay punctuated by the chilling accusations that followed.

The accusations, like venomous darts, pierced him with a cold, sharp sting. Whispers morphed into shouts, suspicion into outright condemnation. He saw the doubt in the eyes of his friends, the hesitant glances, the averted gazes that spoke volumes of unspoken accusations. Even Pete, his closest friend, seemed to hesitate, his normally unwavering support replaced by a cautious uncertainty. The weight of their mistrust, heavy and suffocating, pressed down on him, compounding the grief that threatened to drown him.

He remembered the frantic rush of adrenaline, the desperate scramble to reach her, the helpless feeling of inadequacy as he cradled her limp body, his tiny paws trembling. The scene replayed itself in vivid detail, each moment imprinted on his memory with the searing intensity of a brand. He could still smell the earthy scent of the fallen leaves, feel the chilling dampness of the ground beneath his paws, hear the hushed whispers of the onlookers.

The trial, a bizarre and surreal experience, only served to amplify his feelings of isolation and despair. The hens, always quick to gossip, clucked their accusations with relish. The cats, with their sly observations and cryptic pronouncements, added layers of suspicion. Even the usually placid rabbits seemed to hold him in a wary gaze. He had tried to explain, to recount the events as he remembered them, but his words seemed to get lost in the cacophony of conflicting testimonies and biased interpretations.

The sense of injustice, raw and agonizing, gnawed at him. He had been a suspect, not a witness. The fact that his presence at the scene of the accident had cast a shadow of suspicion was something that he couldn't comprehend. His only comfort was the presence of Ink and Fiona, their steady eyes offering a flicker of hope amidst the darkness. They believed him, or at least, they were determined to uncover the truth. Their investigation was a meticulous process, every detail meticulously examined, every clue painstakingly analyzed. He watched, a silent observer, as they navigated the intricate web of half-truths and misinterpretations, patiently piecing together the fragments of a shattered reality.

The relief that followed the revelation of the truth was immense, a wave washing over him, cleansing him of the grime of suspicion. Yet, it wasn't a complete relief, not entirely. The joy was muted, tempered by the persistent ache of Jenny's absence. The world was still a dimmer place without her laughter, her bright spirit, her unwavering friendship.

The community's subsequent efforts to atone for their misjudgment were both heartwarming and bittersweet. The establishment of the council, dedicated to ensuring fairness and justice for all, was a testament to Jenny's legacy. The books compiled by Pete, filled with tales of Jenny's life and her insights, were a way to keep her memory alive. The changes they made were a poignant reminder of her impact.

But the silence, the absence, still lingered. He missed her terribly. He missed the shared jokes, the whispered secrets, the companionship that had defined his life before the tragedy. Even the simple act of collecting acorns, once a cherished ritual, was now tinged with sadness. The joy of these small moments was now overshadowed by his grief. The memory of her vibrant personality fueled his every effort. He pushed himself towards helping others. The changes enacted by the community after the trial brought a sense of closure, but nothing could replace the absence of his friend.

He found solace in the work of forest conservation, channeling his grief into action. Each sapling he planted, each endangered species he helped protect, felt like a small tribute to her memory, a way to keep her spirit alive in the heart of the Wildwoods Farm. The task filled him with a sense of purpose.

The transformation of the Wildwoods Farm was profound. The community, once fractured by suspicion and mistrust, had healed, unified by shared grief and a newfound understanding of the value of truth and empathy. But amidst the positive changes, Jasper felt the profound weight of his loss, a permanent scar on his soul. His commitment to forest conservation was not just a response to the tragedy but a dedication to Jenny's memory.

The forest itself seemed to grieve with him. The wind whispered through the trees, carrying the echoes of Jenny's laughter, a haunting melody that reminded him of what he had lost. Yet, within the melancholy, there was a growing sense of acceptance. Jenny's life, though tragically cut short, had left an indelible mark on the Wildwoods Farm, a legacy of kindness, courage, and an unwavering commitment to justice. And Jasper, though burdened by grief, found a way to honor her memory, ensuring that her spirit would forever be woven into the fabric of the forest she loved. The healing process was long and arduous, but as the seasons changed, so did Jasper, his spirit slowly finding strength in the face of grief and loss, finding solace and determination in his dedication to the memory of his dear friend, Jenny. He was no longer just Jasper, the squirrel who had been wrongly accused; he was Jasper, the protector, the guardian, the keeper of Jenny's legacy.

The accusations hung in the air, thick and suffocating, like the pollen of a poisonous flower. They weren't whispered anymore; they were shouted, hurled at him like stones. Each word, each syllable, was a fresh wound, tearing at the already raw edges of his grief. He was a pariah, an outcast, branded with the scarlet letter of suspicion. The vibrant hues of the Wildwoods Farm had dulled, their once-bright colors now muted, reflecting the despair that had settled deep within his soul.

He remembered the feel of Jenny's fur against his, the warmth of her body as he held her. Now, that warmth was replaced by the icy chill of fear and isolation. His heart, usually a drum of joyful energy, now beat a slow, heavy rhythm against his ribs, a mournful counterpoint to the relentless accusations. Sleep offered no respite; his dreams were haunted by Jenny's fall, her lifeless form replaying itself in an endless loop, a terrifying movie unspooling in the darkness. He would wake up with a gasp, his fur drenched in a cold sweat, the phantom weight of the accusations still pressing down on him.

He tried to explain, to articulate the truth, to paint a picture of their argument, a childish squabble over acorns, a fleeting disagreement swallowed by the immensity of the tragedy that followed. But his words were lost in the cacophony of fear and speculation. The community, usually so welcoming and understanding, now seemed to view him with suspicion and even hostility. He saw it in their eyes, a flicker of doubt, a subtle shift in their posture, a hesitation in their greetings. These small gestures, insignificant in themselves, accumulated to form a vast ocean of mistrust that threatened to drown him. The weight of their collective disbelief was crushing, heavier than any physical burden.

The faces of the community members swam before his eyes – Mrs. Higgins, the ever-observant hen, her beady eyes narrowed in judgment; Oswald, the stoic badger, his usual gruff exterior amplifying the unspoken accusations; even Pete, his dearest friend, seemed to hold back, his usual jovial demeanor replaced with a forced politeness that felt like a betrayal. He saw the faces of those who had condemned him without knowing him, those who had chosen to believe the narrative without considering his own version of events.

He tried to reach out, to offer a glimmer of hope amidst the swirling storm of suspicion, to provide evidence. But every attempt felt futile, met with only hushed whispers and sideways glances. The community's judgment was swift and unforgiving. Their need to assign blame, to find a scapegoat in their midst, was stronger than their desire for the truth. The initial outpouring of grief and sorrow was rapidly overshadowed by a growing desire to find someone to blame, someone to punish. This was a community that valued order and harmony above all else, and Jasper's presence at the scene of the accident, coupled with their pre-existing minor disagreements, made him the ideal target for their collective angst.

The preliminary trial itself was a cruel parody of justice. The accusations were presented as irrefutable facts, the evidence selectively chosen to support the pre-determined narrative. He pleaded his innocence, recounting the events with clarity and precision, but his voice was drowned out by the chorus of condemnations. The truth, once a simple and clear narrative, was now distorted and twisted beyond recognition, a caricature of its former self. The preliminary trial was not about finding justice, but about fulfilling the community's need for closure, even if that closure was built on a foundation of lies and misinterpretations.

The fear was not just of external judgment, but of losing everything. He was losing his reputation, his friends, his place in the community. He was losing the life he knew, the life that was interwoven with Jenny's presence, and being swallowed by this dark void. His greatest fear wasn't just the accusation itself, but the implication that no one believed him. The unspoken accusation that he would rather be the perpetrator, rather than admit to his guilt, despite knowing the truth, was one of the deepest and most painful blows.

The hours stretched into days, each day a relentless cycle of suspicion, fear, and despair. The weight of the accusations felt like a physical burden, pressing down on him, squeezing the air from his lungs. He longed for the solace of his home, the comfort of his familiar surroundings, but even those safe havens were tainted by the pervasive atmosphere of distrust. He couldn't even find refuge in his dreams, as they were dominated by the horrifying replay of Jenny's fall. Each time he looked into his reflection, he saw the distorted image of the accused. The squirrel who had been Jenny's best friend and now bore the responsibility for her tragic death.

The arrival of Ink and Fiona, however, brought a flicker of hope. Their unwavering belief in the possibility of uncovering the truth was a lifeline, a small flame in the overwhelming darkness. Their investigation was a painstaking process, each clue painstakingly examined, every witness interviewed, every statement carefully dissected. He watched as they meticulously sifted through the debris of the accident, the fragments of a shattered reality. Their methodical approach provided Jasper with a newfound sense of purpose, something to focus on amid his despair. The realization that there were others who believed in the truth, and were working diligently to find it, was profoundly empowering. The support, even amidst the collective condemnation, was deeply reassuring.

This investigative process itself became a source of solace. Watching Ink and Fiona work, he found a quiet hope, a sense of purpose in the face of overwhelming despair. He helped them where he could, recalling details he'd almost forgotten, observing subtle clues others had missed. The collaborative investigation acted as a balm on his wounds, providing a sense of meaning in the depths of despair. The meticulousness of their work, in stark contrast to the hasty judgment of his community, was a powerful testament to the importance of due process and thorough investigation.

He was losing hope that he would ever be able to fully clear his name and restore his relationship with his community. As the investigation went on, he came to realize the insidious nature of assumptions. How easily the community had jumped to conclusions. But amidst the despair, there was also a quiet determination to prove his innocence and help Ink and Fiona unearth the truth. The knowledge that they were meticulously investigating the events, sifting through the tangled web of assumptions and half-truths, provided him with a small measure of comfort. He looked for small signs of the investigation making progress, looking for the moment when the truth would finally emerge and vindicate him. The methodical steps of Ink and Fiona provided Jasper with a much-needed source of hope during the darkest period of his life.

The days blurred into a hazy nightmare of accusations and uncertainty. Yet, even in this bleak landscape, a small spark of hope remained, fueled by the relentless efforts of Ink and Fiona. Their methodical investigation, a beacon in the storm, was the only thing that kept him from succumbing to despair. It was not just an investigation into Jenny's death, but a quest to restore his name, his standing, and his peace of mind. Their actions were a testimony to the power of justice and truth and were the greatest comfort in his darkest hour. And as time progressed, and the investigation revealed more and more, it was that hope, however fragile, that kept his spirit afloat.

The sun dripped golden honey onto the Wildwoods Farm that morning, painting the leaves in shimmering hues. Jenny and I were chasing each other, a whirlwind of fur and frantic energy, our laughter echoing through the trees. We were arguing, yes, a silly argument about the plumpest acorn, the one nestled perfectly between two gnarled roots. I claimed it first, she insisted it was hers, our playful bickering a familiar soundtrack to our days. It was nothing serious, just the usual friendly competition between two squirrels with a shared love for acorns and a bond stronger than any oak. I remember the feel of her soft fur brushing against mine as we tumbled playfully in the undergrowth, a testament to our unshakeable friendship.

Our game led us towards the old telephone pole, a familiar landmark in our woodland playground. Jenny, always the more adventurous of the two, scampered up the weathered wood with the agility of a mountain climber. I watched, then pursued her with a mixture of admiration and playful rivalry in my eyes. As I followed, to challenge her claim to the highest branch across the line, that is when it happened. A sharp crack, a sickening thud, and then... silence. The world seemed to tilt on its axis, the vibrant colors of the forest fading into a monochrome nightmare. Jenny lay still at the base of the pole, her small body unmoving. The playful energy that had filled the air moments before was instantly replaced by a crushing wave of terror.

My initial reaction was pure, unadulterated panic. I rushed to her side, my heart pounding like a frantic drum against my ribs. I nudged her gently, yelled her name, a desperate plea for a response, for any sign of life. But there was nothing. Only the chilling silence of the woods, broken only by the frantic beating of my own heart. The shock was so profound, it stole my ability to think clearly; it rendered me speechless, frozen, incapable of any coherent action. My mind raced, trying to comprehend the impossible reality. Jenny, always full of life, always so lively and exuberant, now lay motionless, her body a still image of tragedy against the vibrant backdrop of the forest.

The events unfolded in a hazy blur. The arrival of the other woodland creatures, their concerned faces, their whispered conversations, all fused together in my memory like a disjointed dream. I tried to explain, to tell them what happened, to convey the utter randomness of the tragedy. But my words were lost, swallowed by the rising tide of accusations. The fact that I was there, at the scene, that we had been arguing moments before, made me the obvious, the convenient target. They needed a reason, a scapegoat, and in their grief and confusion, I became the unfortunate victim of their collective need to assign blame.

My memories of that day are etched into my mind, every detail a searing reminder of my innocence and my profound loss. I recall the exact position of the sun, the angle of the telephone pole, the slight creak in the wood moments before Jenny's fall. I remember the texture of the earth beneath my paws, the smell of pine needles and damp soil, the feel of the cold air that rushed in to fill the void after Jenny's sudden absence. I remember the frantic search for a solution, for a way to revive my friend, my heart torn between grief and the overwhelming need to comprehend what had just happened. I recall my attempts to explain my efforts to share my perspective with others, only to be met with stony silence and a growing tide of accusation. My voice drowned in the chorus of their grief and their desperate search for someone to blame.

The accusations felt like physical blows, each one leaving an invisible scar on my soul. I had lost Jenny, my best friend, and now I was losing my community, my standing within the once familiar and comforting framework of my life. The woods, once a haven of laughter and carefree games, had transformed into a prison of suspicion and distrust. Every rustle of leaves, every snap of a twig, triggered a fresh wave of fear, a fresh reminder of the gravity of the situation. My once bright spirit dimmed under the weight of false accusations, my usually playful nature clouded by the despair and hopelessness of the situation.

The hours stretched into days, days into weeks, each moment a painful replay of the tragedy and its devastating consequences. The trail of suspicion, once a thin thread, had thickened into a relentless noose, tightening around my neck. I tried to find solace in my memories of Jenny, recalling our countless adventures, our shared secrets, the unbreakable bond that had united us, only to find these happy memories increasingly overshadowed by the crushing weight of false accusations.

I would often sit by the base of the telephone pole, the silent witness to Jenny's fall, and stare at the sky, wishing for a sign, a glimmer of hope, a way to prove my innocence. The sun, once a symbol of joy and warmth, now seemed to shine down with a cold, unfeeling light. My once-familiar woodland haven now seemed shrouded in a chilling mist of suspicion. Even the familiar songs of the birds sounded discordant, adding to the oppressive atmosphere of the woodland.

The bond between me and Jenny was something truly special. We shared a language beyond words, an understanding that went deeper than any friendship I could have ever imagined. We spent countless hours together, playing in the sun-dappled glades, sharing acorns, and exchanging secrets in the Wildwoods silence of the trees. Our connection was a cornerstone of my existence. Now, that connection was shattered, leaving behind a gaping hole filled with loss and accusation.

Then came Ink and Fiona. Their arrival was like a breath of fresh air in a stifling room. Their presence offered a glimmer of hope, a sense that perhaps the truth could still prevail. Their dedication to uncovering the truth was a testament to their belief in justice and fairness. They listened to me patiently, carefully analyzing every detail, every recollection, and treating my words with respect and care that was absent in the hurried pronouncements of the other woodland creatures. This meticulous process, in itself, was profoundly comforting. It offered a stark contrast to the hasty judgment of the community and restored my belief in the power of careful investigation and the eventual revelation of truth. It was a source of hope, an anchor in a sea of despair, a reminder that even in the darkest of times, truth can still prevail. Their thoroughness acted as a testament to the importance of due process and a meticulous search for the truth, rather than a rapid response based on emotional responses and assumptions. Their calm demeanor offered a counterpoint to the storm of accusations and assumptions that had consumed my world. The meticulousness of their inquiry was a reassurance, restoring my fading belief in justice and the possibility of clearing my name. Their investigation was not simply an inquiry into Jenny's death, but a quest to restore my reputation, my relationships, and my peace of mind. It was a lifeline during my darkest hour. Their belief in me, even amidst the community's condemnation, provided solace, purpose, and the hope for a brighter future.

The weight lifted. It wasn't a sudden, dramatic release, like a dropped stone plunging into a silent lake. Instead, it was a slow, gradual easing, a gentle unwinding of the taut cords that had bound my heart for weeks. The revelation of the truth, the exposure of the real culprit – a rogue branch weakened by decay, not my paws – washed over me in waves of profound relief. The accusations, the whispers, the averted gazes; they all faded, receding like a nightmare from which I'd finally awakened. It wasn't just the exoneration; it was the restoration of my faith in the woods, in its inhabitants, in the very possibility of justice.

Ink and Fiona, their faces illuminated by the soft glow of the setting sun, stood before me, their expressions a mixture of satisfaction and compassion. I could see the meticulous care they had taken, the countless hours they had spent piecing together the fragments of truth from the chaotic tapestry of conflicting testimonies. Their investigation hadn't merely cleared my name; it had meticulously unraveled the complexities of the accident, revealing not only the cause of Jenny's fall but also the flaws in the community's hasty judgment. Their work was a testament to the power of patient observation, the importance of questioning assumptions, and the undeniable triumph of truth over hasty conclusions.

Fiona, with her piercing emerald eyes, purred softly, a gesture of quiet understanding. Ink, his whiskers twitching, offered a small, almost shy smile, a subtle expression of relief mirrored in my own heart. They had not only uncovered the truth but also exposed the vulnerabilities within the woodland community – the tendency to rush to judgment, the power of prejudice, and the ease with which assumptions could overshadow the pursuit of truth.

Gratitude swelled within me, a tide of emotion that threatened to overwhelm me. I wanted to express my thanks, to convey the immense relief I felt, but words seemed inadequate, insufficient to express the depth of my emotion. I looked at Ink and Fiona, at their kind eyes and gentle expressions, and felt a profound sense of connection, of shared purpose, of a bond forged in the crucible of this harrowing experience. They had not only cleared my name, but they had restored my faith in the possibility of justice, in the inherent goodness that still existed within our community, despite its imperfections.

The trial itself had been a remarkable experience. The community, initially consumed by grief and suspicion, had gradually come to understand the fragility of their own judgments. The evidence, meticulously presented by Ink and Fiona, had been irrefutable. The rogue branch, weakened by decay, was the true culprit. It was a poignant moment when Ellen, the old owl who had initially been the most vocal in her accusations, apologized. Her voice, usually so sharp and critical, was filled with regret and humility. Her apology wasn't just directed at me, but also to the community itself, in recognition of their collective failings.

The subsequent days were filled with a cautious optimism. The woods still held a lingering sense of the trauma they had experienced, but it was different now. There was a newfound appreciation for the importance of truth, a cautious determination to learn from their mistakes. The atmosphere, once heavy with suspicion and mistrust, was slowly lightening, a gradual shift towards reconciliation and a greater understanding of the importance of careful observation and thoughtful consideration. The whispers diminished, replaced by a growing sense of community and healing. The familiar laughter of the woodland creatures echoed once more, a testament to the restorative power of truth and the resilience of their bonds.

The relief wasn't just about my exoneration; it was about the healing of the community, the gradual mending of broken trust and the rediscovery of shared values. It was about the collective understanding that assumptions, even when fueled by grief, can lead to devastating consequences. It was a reminder that justice requires patience, diligence, and a commitment to uncovering the truth, regardless of the initial biases and preconceptions.

The memory of Jenny remained, a constant reminder of the tragedy, but the sharp edges of grief were softened by the knowledge that her death was not the result of any malicious intent. It wasn't a result of human error; it was an accident, a cruel twist of fate, a consequence of natural forces. Understanding this fact brought a measure of peace, easing the weight of guilt that had been crushing me for so long. The memory of Jenny became a reminder, not of my guilt, but of the beauty of our friendship, a tribute to a bond that death itself couldn't entirely sever.

I spent hours by the telephone pole, not in despair, but in reflection. The sunlight filtering through the leaves no longer seemed cold or unfeeling; it warmed my fur, filling me with a renewed sense of hope. The woods, once a place of fear and mistrust, once again felt like home.

The comforting smells of pine and damp earth no longer triggered waves of anxiety; they brought back memories of joyful games, shared acorns, and the unbreakable friendship that Jenny and I had once shared.

The whispers of the wind through the trees no longer sounded like accusations; they sounded like gentle reassurances, a reminder that nature, in its own enigmatic ways, holds both beauty and tragedy. The restored harmony of the woodland community, the gentle restoration of trust, served as a profound lesson in the enduring power of truth, in the ability to overcome mistakes, and the beauty of forgiveness.

Ink and Fiona's investigation hadn't just solved a mystery; it had healed a community, and in the process, it had healed me. The lingering sadness remained, the void left by Jenny's absence would forever be a part of me, but it was no longer a crippling weight. It was a poignant memory, a reminder of the preciousness of life, the importance of friendship, and the enduring power of truth and reconciliation. The golden light of the setting sun, now a symbol of hope and renewal, bathed the forest in its gentle glow, illuminating the path forward, a path of healing, understanding, and a renewed sense of community. The Wildwoods Farm, once silenced by grief and suspicion, once again echoed with the sounds of life, laughter, and the enduring power of truth. The healing had begun.

The days that followed were a blur of quiet contemplation. The vibrant chaos of the trial, the sharp edges of accusation and defense, had given way to a gentler rhythm, a slower pace that allowed for introspection. I found myself drawn to the base of the old telephone pole, the very spot where Jenny had fallen. It wasn't a place of despair, not anymore. Instead, it felt like a sacred space, a place of quiet remembrance. The splintered wood, the faded markings where Jenny had often sharpened her tiny claws, were now imbued with a different kind of significance. They were not symbols of tragedy alone, but also of a shared past, of joyful moments, of innocent games played in the dappled sunlight.

I recalled the countless hours we'd spent together on that pole, the shared secrets whispered amongst the leaves, the thrilling races to the top, the dizzying views from the summit. The laughter, the playful squabbles, the comforting warmth of friendship—all these memories flooded back, washing over me like a warm tide. The image of Jenny, her bright eyes sparkling with mischief, her tiny paws gripping the wood, remained vivid in my mind. The guilt, the crushing weight of suspicion, had finally lifted, but the loss remained, a persistent ache in my heart. Yet, it was a different kind of ache now, a softer, more melancholic sorrow, devoid of the self-recrimination that had tormented me for so long.

Ink and Fiona's investigation had not only cleared my name but had also illuminated the darker corners of our community. It had shown me the ease with which assumptions, fueled by grief and fear, could distort the truth. Ellen, a middle-aged owl, whose accusations had been the most damaging, had offered a sincere apology, her voice filled with regret. Her words, spoken with surprising humility, had touched me deeply. She hadn't just apologized for her harsh judgment; she had acknowledged the flaws within the community's hasty conclusions, its tendency to jump to judgment without considering all the facts. Her remorse was a reflection of the collective guilt, a shared responsibility for the spread of false accusations.

The trial had become more than just a legal proceeding; it was a community reckoning, a moment of collective self-reflection. The community, initially fractured by suspicion and mistrust, began to heal, its wounds slowly mending. The gossiping hens, who had spread rumors like wildfire, fell silent. The shrewd cats, initially quick to jump to conclusions, seemed to move with a newfound caution. Even the playful squirrels, once hesitant to approach me, returned with cautious friendliness. Their hesitant advances were a testament to the healing process. The weight of suspicion had been lifted, replaced by a fragile but growing trust.

The lessons learned were profound. The importance of observation, the dangers of hasty judgment, the power of empathy—these were not just abstract concepts but vital principles for a harmonious community. I realized that assumptions were not just harmful; they were dangerous. They could destroy reputations, fracture friendships, and even lead to injustice. I had been a victim of those assumptions, and the experience had been a harsh but essential lesson. It taught me the importance of seeking the truth diligently and patiently, rather than rushing to conclusions based on limited information.

The community's collective realization of its failings had fostered a profound sense of responsibility. They understood that the pursuit of justice required more than just uncovering the truth; it necessitated a commitment to understanding the complexities of emotion and motivation. It required patience, empathy, and a willingness to consider all perspectives before passing judgment.

The restored harmony in the Wildwoods Farm wasn't merely the absence of conflict; it was the presence of a deeper understanding, a more profound connection between its inhabitants. The laughter of the squirrels, the chirping of the birds, the rustling of the leaves—all these sounds held a new significance, a resonance that spoke of reconciliation and healing. Even the wind seemed to whisper a different tune, a softer melody that spoke of hope and forgiveness.

I spent long hours watching the sunlight filter through the leaves, feeling the warmth on my fur, the gentle breeze caressing my whiskers. The woods were no longer a place of fear and anxiety, but a sanctuary of peace and tranquility. The comforting smells of pine and damp earth brought back not just memories of Jenny, but also memories of shared joy, of unbreakable bonds, of the simple pleasures of life.

The memory of Jenny remained a poignant reminder of the fragility of life and the pain of loss. But the pain was different now, less acute, less suffocating. It was now tempered with the knowledge that her death had not been the result of malice or cruelty but a cruel twist of fate, an accident caused by forces beyond our control. The loss still hurt, but the guilt was gone, replaced by a profound sense of gratitude for the memories we shared.

My reflections led me to understand the profound importance of empathy. I realized that everyone, even those who make mistakes or act impulsively, deserves to be treated with compassion and understanding. The community's mistakes, its rush to judgment, stemmed from grief, from a deep sense of loss and confusion. Their hasty conclusions were a product of fear and uncertainty, not malice or intentional cruelty. This understanding, this empathy, fostered reconciliation and healing.

The trial had exposed the flaws within the community, its tendency to spread rumors and jump to conclusions. But it had also revealed a deeper truth – the resilience of the community's spirit, its capacity for self-reflection and forgiveness. The process of uncovering the truth had not only cleared my name but had also strengthened the bonds within the community, leading to a deeper understanding of the principles of justice, empathy, and forgiveness.

The Wildwood Farm, once shrouded in a cloud of suspicion and grief, was now bathed in the golden light of hope and reconciliation. The healing was complete, or so it seemed. The memory of Jenny would always be with me, but the memory was softened, a poignant tribute to a friendship that death couldn't erase. The lessons learned, however, were more than just personal; they were lessons that the entire community carried forward, ensuring that the tragedy served as a reminder of the importance of careful consideration, empathy, and the patient pursuit of truth. The path forward was illuminated by the golden glow of a renewed community, bound together by shared understanding and a collective commitment to the principles of justice. The whispers of the wind now carried a promise, not of fear or suspicion, but of peace and a future where truth and understanding would always prevail.

Chapter 9
The Gossiping Hens

The hens, a feathered chorus of clucking speculation, each offered a slightly different rendition of the events surrounding Jenny's fall. Their testimonies, initially presented with the confidence of eyewitness accounts, quickly unraveled under Ink's persistent questioning. Patty, a plump hen known for her flamboyant plumage and even more flamboyant pronouncements, swore she saw Jasper shove Jenny with a swift, malicious flick of his paw. Her account was vivid, detailed – almost too detailed, Ink noted, his keen ferret eyes narrowing. She described Jasper's expression as "pure malevolence," a detail that struck Ink as oddly specific considering the speed of the event and the distance from which Patty claimed to have observed it. Furthermore, Patty's account conveniently omitted the presence of several other squirrels who were playing near the telephone pole at the time. These squirrels, as Fiona later confirmed, were known to be close friends with Jenny.

Barbara, a hen of quieter disposition, offered a contrasting narrative. She hadn't actually *seen* the fall, she confessed, but she'd heard a commotion, a series of squeaks and rustling leaves, followed by a thud. She'd initially believed it was Jasper, she admitted, swayed by the collective gossip that was already circulating through the henhouse. However, upon reflection, she couldn't be certain. The commotion, she conceded, could have been caused by several things – a falling branch, a sudden gust of wind, or even a playful scuffle amongst the squirrels. Barbara's testimony, though less dramatic than Patty's, revealed a crucial element: the power of suggestion and the ease with which rumor could corrupt even the most well-intentioned recollections.

Traci, a particularly gossipy hen known for her penchant for dramatic embellishments, provided a far more embellished version. Her account was a whirlwind of frantic clucking, punctuated by vivid (and highly improbable) details. She claimed to have witnessed a heated argument between Jenny and Jasper, a bitter dispute over a particularly juicy acorn. This argument, according to Traci, escalated into a physical confrontation, culminating in Jasper's alleged push. Ink meticulously noted the inconsistencies in her story. The acorn, she described, was "as large as a duck's egg," a highly exaggerated size for any acorn found in the Wildwoods Farm. Moreover, Traci's description of the argument included dialogue that, on closer inspection, seemed oddly familiar – suspiciously similar to lines from a recent play performed by the woodpeckers. Ink suspected Traci had conflated fiction with reality.

Esmeralda, the oldest hen in the flock, offered a perspective tinged with wisdom born from years of observing the complexities of forest life. She hadn't seen the incident, but she knew Jasper. She spoke of his gentle nature, his kindness towards the younger squirrels. She admitted that she initially harbored suspicions, influenced by the pervasive rumors, but questioned their validity. Her testimony underscored the importance of considering the character of the accused, a point that Fiona found particularly insightful. Esmeralda's measured approach contrasted sharply with the frantic accusations of the other hens, proving that even amidst a swirl of gossip, a grounded perspective could emerge.

Fiona, observing the hens' testimonies with her sharp feline intelligence, recognized a pattern. Their accounts weren't necessarily malicious fabrications; rather, they were shaped by biases, assumptions, and the influence of the prevailing narrative. Each hen had filtered the event through her own lens, distorting the reality to align with her pre-existing beliefs and perceptions. Patty, for instance, was known to dislike Jasper, fueling her inclination to interpret his actions negatively. Traci, always seeking drama, had embellished the incident to create a more compelling story. Henrietta, unsure of what she'd seen, had defaulted to the widely accepted version. Only Esmeralda, with her long experience and detached observation, attempted to consider the whole picture.

Ink, using Fiona's observations as a starting point, began to reconstruct the timeline of events, scrutinizing each detail with his meticulous ferret logic. He noticed that several of the hens' testimonies pointed towards a common flaw: a lack of clear observation. They'd focused on the perceived outcome – Jenny's fall – rather than the events leading up to it. Their recollections were tainted by their assumptions and biases, leading to distorted and incomplete accounts.

He delved deeper, cross-referencing the hens' statements with those of the squirrels, the cats, and even the woodpeckers who happened to be in the vicinity. Each statement, no matter how insignificant, was meticulously analyzed, compared, and contrasted. Ink discovered a hidden thread, a subtle inconsistency that linked several seemingly unrelated accounts. The squirrels who were playing near the telephone pole mentioned a strong gust of wind shortly before Jenny's fall. This detail had been overlooked in the initial flurry of accusations, yet it was crucial.

This seemingly insignificant detail, the strong gust of wind, became a pivotal piece in Ink's investigation. He realized that the wind, overlooked by many, could have been the actual cause of Jenny's fall. While the hens had concentrated on the visual details, assuming a malicious act by Jasper, they'd failed to consider the environmental factors that could have easily contributed to the accident. Ink's realization revealed the inherent limitations of eyewitness testimony – the potential for even the most well-meaning observers to miss crucial details when blinded by assumptions and pre-conceived notions.

Fiona, meanwhile, meticulously mapped the gossip network within the henhouse, tracing the spread of rumors and misinformation. She discovered a chain of communication, a domino effect where initial suspicions, amplified by each retelling, had morphed into definite accusations. The hens, in their desire to contribute to the unfolding drama, had inadvertently contributed to the amplification of falsehoods. Fiona's insights helped Ink understand that the distortion of the truth wasn't always intentional malice. It could be a consequence of collective biases and the natural tendency to simplify complex situations.

As Ink pieced together the evidence, he realized that the hens' accounts, though flawed, weren't entirely useless. Their inconsistencies, their biases, their inaccuracies – all these elements contributed to a fuller understanding of the events. By meticulously analyzing their narratives, Ink and Fiona were able to identify the gaps in their testimonies, the points where speculation and assumption had replaced observation and accuracy. The hens, unwittingly, had provided a crucial lesson: the need to challenge assumptions and to rigorously examine all available evidence before drawing conclusions.

The hens' testimonies served as a powerful illustration of how easily the truth could be obscured. Their individual accounts, though flawed, revealed the complexity of perception and the susceptibility of memory to distortion. Their mistakes, though significant, ultimately contributed to a deeper understanding of the importance of careful observation, rigorous investigation, and the inherent fallibility of perception.

The case of Jenny's fall highlighted the crucial role of objective analysis in separating fact from fiction, particularly when facing the emotional turmoil of grief and loss. Ink's investigation showed that the pursuit of justice required not only the discovery of the truth but also a critical examination of how that truth had become obscured in the first place. The hens, in their own way, had become unwitting participants in a lesson that the entire forest community would soon learn.

The hens' initial, conflicting testimonies acted as kindling, igniting a wildfire of gossip that rapidly spread throughout the Wildwoods Farm. The news of Jenny's fall, already shrouded in uncertainty, was further distorted as it passed from beak to beak, claw to paw, and whisker to whisker. Patty's dramatic account, with its vivid description of Jasper's malevolent expression, resonated particularly well with the more excitable members of the community. The image of a deliberate shove, a malicious act of aggression, was far more captivating than the possibility of an accident.

The squirrels, naturally, were the first to be swept up in the whirlwind of rumor. Those closest to Jenny, overwhelmed by grief and shock, found themselves readily accepting the narrative that implicated Jasper. Their sorrow was amplified by the accusations, turning their initial shock into a burning sense of injustice. They shared Patty's version of events, adding their own interpretations and embellishments, further fueling the flames of speculation. Some squirrels, remembering a minor squabble between Jenny and Jasper over a particularly coveted nut earlier that day, even interpreted the argument as a foreshadowing of the tragic event, inadvertently strengthening the case against Jasper.

The cats, ever observant and pragmatic, initially remained skeptical. Fiona, with her keen intellect, recognized the inconsistencies in the hens' testimonies, but even she found the pervasive narrative difficult to ignore. Whispers and murmurs, carrying fragments of Patty's story, infiltrated even the most secluded corners of the forest, creating an atmosphere of suspicion and distrust. Older, wiser cats, like Old Tom, attempted to counter the rumors with reason and logic, suggesting alternative explanations, but their calm voices were often drowned out by the cacophony of gossip.

The rabbits, ever timid and easily influenced, quickly adopted the prevailing narrative. They spread the news through their extensive network of burrows, amplifying the already distorted version of events. Their innocent dissemination of hearsay, though unintentional, contributed significantly to the spread of misinformation. The rabbits' whispers, carried on the wind, reached even the most isolated parts of the forest, ensuring that no creature remained untouched by the spreading wave of gossip.

Even the usually stoic badgers, known for their reserved nature, found themselves drawn into the conversation. The rumors, filtered through various interpretations and embellishments, reached them in distorted forms. Some badgers, influenced by the intensity of the emotions surrounding the event, readily accepted the narrative of Jasper's guilt, while others remained more cautious, expressing their doubts in hushed tones. Their internal disagreements, however, only served to further complicate the already convoluted narrative.

The woodpeckers, known for their theatrical flair, added their own creative interpretations to the circulating rumors. Some incorporated elements of the gossip into their latest play, further blurring the lines between fiction and reality. Their performances, attended by a wide range of forest creatures, inadvertently contributed to the spread of misinformation, entertaining the audience while reinforcing the false narrative.

The owls, creatures of the night, became unwitting messengers of rumor. Their nocturnal flights carried snippets of conversation, overheard whispers, and embellished accounts from one end of the forest to the other. Their hooting, often interpreted as ominous pronouncements, inadvertently added to the sense of unease and suspicion that pervaded the Wildwoods Farm.

The spread of rumors didn't stop at the forest's edge. News of the tragedy, and the accusations against Jasper, reached the nearby meadow. The field mice, ever curious, carried the gossip back to the forest, adding their own interpretations and embellishments. The meadow's inhabitants, hearing the whispers of a terrible crime, sent scouts to investigate, their presence adding another layer of complexity to the already muddled situation.

The river, a silent observer, carried the whispers downstream, spreading the rumors to other forest communities. Creatures from distant parts of the woods, hearing tales of a great injustice, arrived to offer their support, or perhaps just to witness the unfolding drama firsthand. Their arrival further intensified the atmosphere of suspicion and uncertainty, adding to the pressure on Ink and Fiona to uncover the truth before the community descended into chaos.

The impact of the spread of rumors was far-reaching. Friendships fractured, suspicions deepened, and trust eroded. The once-harmonious community of Wildwoods Farm was fractured by mistrust and misinformation. The simple act of falling from a telephone pole had transformed into a complex web of accusations, assumptions, and biases, threatening to tear the community apart. The weight of the collective misjudgment pressed heavily upon Jasper, innocent until proven otherwise, while Jenny's memory was tainted by the storm of accusations surrounding her death.

Ink and Fiona found themselves fighting not just to uncover the truth behind Jenny's fall but also to restore harmony to the fractured community. They knew that simply revealing the culprit would not be enough; they needed to address the deeper issue of how easily rumors could spread and the devastating consequences of unchecked gossip. The forest's inhabitants needed to learn a crucial lesson: the importance of critical thinking, careful observation, and the dangers of accepting hearsay as truth. The case of Jenny's fall had become a cautionary tale, a stark reminder of the destructive power of unchecked rumors and the importance of seeking the truth before judgment. Their task was daunting, but Ink and Fiona were determined to restore faith in justice and truth, to remind the Wildwoods Farm that even amidst the chaos of gossip, the truth could, and would, prevail. The journey to find the truth had become a race against the spreading tide of misinformation.

The revelation of the truth hung heavy in the air, a thick fog of remorse clinging to the feathered inhabitants of the Wildwoods Farm. The culprit, it turned out, was not Jasper, the accused, but a rogue gust of wind, combined with a poorly maintained telephone pole – a fact meticulously uncovered by Ink and Fiona's relentless investigation. The hens, especially Patty and Henretta, the instigators of the initial wave of accusations, felt the weight of their hasty judgments press down on them with crushing force.

Patty and Henretta, their usually bright comb drooping, pecked listlessly at the ground. Their vibrant plumage, usually a symbol of their bold personality, seemed dull, its luster dimmed by the shadow of their mistake. The vibrant colors of their feathers, once a testament to their confident nature, now felt like a mocking reminder of their impulsive pronouncements. The vivid imagery they had painted of Jasper's malicious intent now haunted them, a cruel caricature of the truth. They had, in their haste, to be the first with the news, allowed their imagination to run wild, weaving a tale far removed from reality. The shame was palpable, a heavy cloak of guilt wrapping around their small body. They'd seen Jasper's distress, the fear in his eyes, the utter devastation of being wrongly accused. The image burned into their memory, a constant reminder of the pain they had unwittingly inflicted.

Beside Patty and Henretta, the other hens huddled together, their usual lively chatter replaced by a somber silence. Each one carried the weight of their collective judgment, the shared responsibility of spreading the false accusations. Their gossip, initially intended as harmless entertainment, had blossomed into a venomous weed, choking the life from the community's trust and harmony. They now understood the devastating consequences of their actions, the far-reaching impact of their careless words. The lively banter and playful squabbles that once characterized their gatherings were replaced by a deep sense of shame and regret.

Clara, usually the most outspoken of the hens, sat quietly, her eyes downcast. She had eagerly repeated Patty's story, embellishing it with details gleaned from her own vivid imagination. The guilt gnawed at her conscience, leaving her feeling utterly small and insignificant. The image of Jasper's despair, his desperate attempts to defend himself, played on repeat in her mind. The realization of how readily she had accepted Patty's account, without questioning its validity, sent waves of remorse through her. She had allowed her inherent biases, her ingrained habit of believing the most sensational story, to cloud her judgment.

Mildred, known for her gentle nature, had been hesitant to join the chorus of accusations. However, even she hadn't questioned the narrative, allowing herself to be swept up by the collective momentum of the gossip. The weight of her inaction now pressed upon her, heavier than any direct accusation. She realized that her silence had been a form of complicity, a passive acceptance of the false narrative. The gentle clucking that usually accompanied her movements was absent, replaced by a quiet sorrow that echoed the feelings of the other hens.

The remorse was not confined to the immediate group. Other hens, who had merely repeated the story, or added their own speculations, felt a deep sense of responsibility for the damage caused. The Wildwoods Farm, once a harmonious community, was now fractured, its trust broken by the spread of misinformation. The hens understood they had played a significant role in creating this rift, in amplifying the pain and suffering caused by the false accusations.

As the truth unfolded, apologies flowed, not just from the hens, but from many creatures throughout the forest. Patty, leading the way, approached Jasper, her head bowed in sincere remorse. Her voice, usually sharp and assertive, was soft and trembling as she offered her heartfelt apologies. The words tumbled out, a torrent of regret and contrition. She confessed her recklessness, her eagerness to be the first with the news, and her failure to verify the accuracy of her information before spreading it. She detailed her regret, her pain at having caused such immense distress to Jasper, and to the entire community.

Jasper, initially hesitant, accepted her apology with a grace that surprised everyone. He understood that their impulsive actions stemmed from grief and the shock of losing their friend, Jenny. He recognized that their remorse was genuine and that their apologies were not just empty words. His acceptance, however, didn't erase the damage done. The wounds inflicted by the false accusations ran deep, leaving scars that would take time to heal.

Clara, Mildred, and the other hens followed suit, each offering their own sincere apologies. Their remorse was evident in their bowed heads, in their trembling voices, and in the heartfelt sincerity of their words. They acknowledged their shared responsibility in perpetuating the false narrative, recognizing the devastating consequences of unchecked gossip and the destructive power of assumptions.

The apologies, however, were not just words. They were accompanied by actions. The hens actively participated in the restoration of harmony within the community. They dedicated themselves to correcting the false information they had spread, meticulously retracting their statements and replacing them with the truth. They organized meetings to discuss the dangers of unchecked gossip and the importance of verifying information before spreading it. They became vocal advocates for responsible communication, demonstrating a genuine commitment to repairing the damage they had caused.

Their efforts, combined with Ink and Fiona's continued work in restoring trust, began to mend the fractured community. The Wildwoods Farm, slowly but surely, started to heal. The hens' regrets were not simply a fleeting emotion; they became a catalyst for change; a profound lesson learned in the harsh light of truth. The incident became a cautionary tale, a reminder of the power of words, the importance of careful observation, and the enduring necessity of seeking the truth before passing judgment. The remorse the hens felt served not just as atonement for their actions but as a foundation for a more responsible and understanding community. The incident served as a stark reminder – a lesson etched deep within the hearts of the creatures of Wildwoods Farm – that even the smallest actions could have the most significant consequences, and that truth, no matter how obscured, would always ultimately prevail. The hens' regrets became a symbol of hope for a future built on understanding, responsibility, and the enduring power of truth. Their collective sorrow became a testament to their capacity for growth, their willingness to learn from their mistakes, and their commitment to healing the wounds of the community they had inadvertently damaged. The Wildwoods Farm began to sing a new song, a melody of reconciliation and renewed trust, a testament to the transformative power of remorse and the ultimate triumph of truth.

The sun dipped below the horizon, casting long shadows across the Wildwoods Farm, painting the scene in hues of orange and purple. The air, still thick with the residual tension of the past few days, held a fragile calm. The hens, gathered in a small circle near the old oak tree, their usual boisterous chatter replaced by a quiet contemplation, were finally ready to grapple with the weight of their actions. Patty, her comb still slightly drooped, began to speak, her voice barely a whisper.

"I never thought... I never imagined..." she trailed off, her eyes welling with tears. "My desire to be the first to know, to share the news... it blinded me. I didn't think about the consequences. I just saw Jasper, and in my haste to tell everyone what I 'saw', I didn't stop to consider if it was true." She picked at a loose feather, her movements betraying her inner turmoil. The guilt was etched deep into her expression, a stark contrast to the bravado she usually projected.

Clara, her usually sharp gaze softened, nodded slowly. "I should have known better," she admitted, her voice trembling slightly. "I heard Patty's story, and instead of questioning it, I embellished it, adding details that weren't true. I wanted to be part of the excitement, to be in the know, to feel important, and in my eagerness to do so, I spread the lie even further." Her words hung in the air, heavy with remorse. She recalled the fear in Jasper's eyes, the hurt in his voice, and the shame washed over her anew.

Mildred, her gentle demeanor more pronounced than ever, spoke in a barely audible voice. "I was quiet," she confessed, her words tinged with self-reproach. "I didn't say anything, didn't challenge Patty's narrative. I was afraid to go against the group, afraid to be ostracized. But my silence made me complicit. My inaction was a betrayal of truth and my own conscience." The others nodded in understanding, recognizing the subtle, yet significant, role of passive acceptance in perpetuating the falsehood.

The conversation meandered, each hen recounting her contribution to the spread of misinformation, each acknowledging her role in the injustice inflicted upon Jasper. They spoke of the thrill of sharing gossip, the ego boost of being 'in the know,' the seductive nature of a dramatic narrative, and how these factors had overridden their sense of responsibility. They realized how easily their biases had influenced their judgment, how quickly they'd accepted a story without verification, and how readily they had attached themselves to a narrative that confirmed their pre-existing assumptions.

One hen, Beatrice, known for her critical thinking, brought up the crucial aspect of verifying information before spreading it. "We should have asked questions," she stated, her voice firm yet compassionate. "We should have sought out Jasper's perspective, examined the scene ourselves, before jumping to conclusions and condemning him. We should have considered other possibilities, instead of focusing solely on the most sensational explanation." Her words resonated deeply with the others, highlighting the importance of critical thinking and the dangers of relying solely on hearsay.

Another hen, Penelope, spoke about the impact of their actions on the community. "We didn't just hurt Jasper," she said, her voice choked with emotion. "We fractured the trust within our community. We created division and suspicion, spreading fear and distrust. We made it difficult for others to believe the truth when it finally emerged." Her words painted a vivid picture of the damage they had inflicted, not just on an individual, but on the fabric of their entire society.

The discussion extended beyond the immediate consequences of their actions. They talked about the importance of empathy, of considering the feelings and perspectives of others before making judgments. They reflected on the ease with which misinformation could spread, the rapid amplification of falsehoods through repetition and the power of social media, even in a forest community. They debated the significance of accountability, the need to own one's mistakes and take responsibility for the consequences of one's actions.

The conversation evolved into a deeper exploration of justice and truth. They discussed the importance of due process, of fairness, and of allowing individuals the opportunity to defend themselves before condemnation. They recognized the dangers of impulsive judgment, the pitfalls of confirmation bias, and the seductive allure of sensational narratives. The hens acknowledged that their actions had not only harmed Jasper but had also undermined the very foundations of justice within their community.

As the stars began to twinkle in the darkening sky, the hens reached a consensus. They understood the profound lesson they had learned: the importance of truth, the dangers of misinformation, and the responsibility that came with sharing information. They pledged to become champions of truth within the community, vowing to scrutinize information before sharing it, to question narratives, and to actively seek out different perspectives. They decided to establish a system of verification within their community, a process of fact-checking that would ensure the accuracy of information before it was shared.

They committed to promoting critical thinking and media literacy, fostering an environment where skepticism was valued and where individuals were empowered to question the information they received. They agreed to hold themselves accountable for their actions, promising to be more mindful of their words and their potential impact. Their remorse was not merely a feeling; it was a catalyst for change, a driving force behind their commitment to build a more just and truthful community.

The hens' lesson extended beyond their immediate circle. News of their profound reflection and their commitment to truth spread throughout the Wildwoods Farm. Other creatures, who had also participated in spreading the false accusations, either directly or indirectly, were inspired by their example. A collective effort began, aimed at repairing the damage caused by the misinformation and restoring trust among the community members.

The hens' story became a cautionary tale, a vivid reminder of the far-reaching consequences of unchecked gossip and the importance of verifying information before sharing it. Their sincere remorse and their unwavering commitment to truth and justice became a beacon of hope, illuminating a path towards a more responsible and harmonious future for the Wildwoods Farm. The experience transformed them, turning their initial shame into a powerful force for positive change. They became advocates for accuracy and responsible communication, their story forever etching the importance of truth and the dangers of unverified information into the heart of their community. The memory of their mistake served not only as a lesson learned, but also as a testament to their capacity for growth, their commitment to justice, and their unwavering pursuit of truth. The Wildwoods Farm, once fractured by gossip, began to heal, its harmony restored by the very creatures who had initially caused the discord. The hens' lesson echoed throughout the forest, a reminder that even from mistakes, profound lessons of truth and responsibility could emerge, leading to a stronger and more unified community.

The following days were a flurry of activity for the hens. Their remorse, far from being a fleeting emotion, had ignited a fire of determination within them. They were committed to repairing the damage they had caused, not just to Jasper, but to the entire community. Their first act of amends was a collective effort to clean up the area around the old oak tree, where they had so carelessly spread their false accusations. Armed with twigs, leaves, and even small stones, they meticulously cleared the space, removing debris and tidying up the fallen branches. The task, though physically demanding, was a symbolic representation of their desire to cleanse their actions and start afresh.

Their next initiative focused on Jasper himself. They prepared a basket overflowing with his favorite sunflower seeds and berries, a simple yet heartfelt gesture of apology. With trembling wings and hesitant steps, they approached Jasper's burrow. He emerged, his eyes initially guarded, his body tense. The hens, understanding his apprehension, approached slowly, their heads bowed in humility. They offered him the basket, their silence more eloquent than any words could have been. Jasper, though initially hesitant, eventually accepted their offering, a single tear rolling down his cheek. The act of reconciliation was silent, but profoundly meaningful, a testament to the power of genuine remorse and the potential for forgiveness.

Beyond Jasper, the hens extended their efforts to the entire forest community. They understood that their actions had damaged the trust within their community, creating divisions and suspicion. To restore harmony, they started by engaging in acts of kindness towards other creatures. They helped the busy squirrels collect nuts for the winter, gently guiding lost baby rabbits back to their mothers, and even sharing their morning dew drops with thirsty bumblebees. These small gestures, repeated consistently, served as tangible expressions of their desire to make amends and rebuild relationships.

Their kindness extended to the less fortunate members of the community. They discovered a family of hedgehogs struggling to find food during a particularly harsh spell. The hens, remembering their own mistakes and the importance of empathy, rallied together. They scoured the forest floor, collecting fallen acorns, berries, and juicy worms. They created a small, cozy shelter for the hedgehogs, keeping them warm and providing them with a plentiful supply of food. Their actions not only relieved the hedgehogs' suffering but also demonstrated the profound impact of collective action driven by a sincere desire to make amends.

One particularly memorable event involved Old Man Willow, an ancient tree revered by the community. His leaves had started to wither, and his branches had grown brittle. The hens, recognizing the importance of Old Man Willow to the forest's health and vitality, devoted an entire afternoon to caring for him. They carefully collected dew drops to moisturize his leaves, supported his weakened branches, and even sang him soothing songs to calm his ailments. The gesture resonated deeply with the forest community, demonstrating the depth of the hens' repentance and their commitment to restoring the community's overall well-being. Word spread rapidly throughout the Wildwoods Farm about the hens' tireless efforts, their commitment to making amends, and the extraordinary efforts undertaken to restore the forest's harmony.

Their efforts didn't stop at physical acts of service. They also took the initiative to promote responsible communication within their community. They organized a series of storytelling sessions, sharing their own story as a cautionary tale. Their honest recounting of their experiences, their vulnerability in confessing their mistakes, and their sincere commitment to making amends were powerful lessons for others. The hens' sessions served as vital reminders of the potential consequences of unchecked gossip and the importance of fact-checking.

The hens also initiated a community project to establish a 'Truth Tree,' a central location where any information needing verification could be brought. They designed a system of checks and balances, inviting different creatures from the community to examine the information before it was spread. This initiative, inspired by their own misjudgment, focused on creating a transparent and reliable system of information sharing, ensuring that rumors and falsehoods could be effectively neutralized before they could cause damage. The Truth Tree quickly gained popularity and acceptance across the Wildwoods Farm, becoming a symbol of the community's determination to uphold truth and transparency.

The hens' transformation was remarkable. From being creatures known for their gossip and careless words, they became beacons of responsibility, empathy, and truthfulness. Their actions served not only as a testament to their ability to learn from their mistakes but also as an inspiration to the rest of the community. Other creatures, who had also been complicit in spreading the false accusations, started to emulate the hens' efforts. They engaged in acts of kindness, participated in community projects, and actively sought to rebuild the damaged relationships.

The healing process wasn't instantaneous, and trust wasn't fully restored overnight. However, the hens' unwavering commitment, their tireless efforts, and their sincere apologies eventually paved the way for forgiveness and reconciliation. The Wildwoods Farm, once riddled with suspicion and division, gradually started to heal, its harmony restored by the very creatures who had initially caused the discord. The hens' journey served as a powerful reminder that even the most hurtful actions can be redeemed through sincere remorse, consistent effort, and an unwavering commitment to truth and justice. Their redemption story was a testament to the restorative power of empathy, the enduring strength of community, and the remarkable ability of creatures, great and small, to learn from their mistakes and emerge stronger and more united. Their story became a timeless legend within the Wildwoods Farm, a narrative woven into the fabric of their society, a reminder that even from mistakes, profound lessons of truth and responsibility could emerge, leading to a stronger and more unified community. The hens, once symbols of irresponsible gossip, transformed into pillars of responsible citizenship, their actions a beacon of hope and a testament to the enduring power of redemption.

Chapter 10
Ink's Investigation

Ink, the ferret investigator, wasn't known for his flashy moves or dramatic pronouncements. His approach was far more subtle, a quiet symphony of observation and deduction. He believed that truth, like a shy woodland creature, revealed itself only to those who patiently waited and meticulously observed. His investigation into Jenny and Jasper's unfortunate incident began not with grand pronouncements or accusations, but with a painstakingly thorough examination of the scene.

First, he approached the telephone pole, its weathered wood bearing silent witness to the events. He circled it slowly, his keen nose twitching, sniffing for any trace of unusual scents – a lingering perfume of fear, a hint of unfamiliar soil, perhaps even a stray hair. He found nothing overtly suspicious, but he meticulously documented the angle of the pole's lean, the texture of the bark, and the precise placement of broken twigs and leaves. Every detail, no matter how insignificant it seemed, was carefully recorded in his small leather-bound notebook. Its pages, filled with his precise, almost microscopic handwriting, resembled a complex tapestry of facts and observations.

Next, he focused on the ground beneath the pole. He meticulously examined the soil, searching for disturbed earth or unusual tracks. He knelt, his tiny paws delicately brushing aside the fallen leaves, revealing the subtle patterns imprinted beneath. He noted the absence of any significant scuff marks that might indicate a struggle, but he discovered a small, almost imperceptible depression in the soil near the base of the pole, too small to be caused by Jenny's fall alone. This anomaly, almost invisible to the casual observer, became a key element in Ink's investigation, a tiny clue suggesting a hidden truth.

From the telephone pole, his investigation expanded. He systematically interviewed every creature who had witnessed the incident, from the gossiping hens to the sly cats who had observed from the shadows. Ink's questioning was far from the hurried, accusatory style of some investigators. He listened patiently, letting each creature speak freely, observing their body language as carefully as their words. He noticed the subtle shifts in their posture, the involuntary fidgeting, the hesitant glances. These minute details, often overlooked, spoke volumes to Ink's astute eye, providing an insight into their truthfulness, or lack thereof.

His conversations were a masterclass in subtle questioning. He would begin with seemingly innocuous queries, gradually weaving his way towards more sensitive topics, always maintaining a calm, neutral demeanor. For example, when questioning one of the hens who had initially accused Jasper, he wouldn't directly challenge her story. Instead, he would ask about the hen's vantage point, the lighting conditions, and the clarity of her vision at the moment of the supposed incident. He noted her inconsistencies, her hesitation to provide precise details, and the gradual shift in her body language from confident to anxious.

Fiona, his feline partner known as *The Whisper*, played a vital role in his investigation. Fiona possessed an uncanny ability to sense fear and deception, her keen senses picking up on nuances that escaped most creatures eye and even Ink's sharp intellect. While Ink meticulously gathered factual evidence, Fiona would provide an emotional context, sensing the subtle undercurrents of emotion within each witness.

Fiona's approach was as different from Ink's as a gentle breeze was from a roaring storm. While Ink meticulously documented facts, Fiona focused on the unspoken, the intangible emotions that lay hidden beneath the surface. She would observe a witness's subtle twitching tail, the tightening of their muscles, the slight dilation of their pupils – all telltale signs of hidden anxieties and suppressed truths.

During one particularly crucial interview with a squirrel, Fiona's presence proved invaluable. The squirrel initially stuck to a version of events that supported the accusations against Jasper. However, as Fiona patiently sat close by, observing the squirrel's every twitch and tremor, the squirrel's carefully constructed narrative began to crumble. Fiona's silent pressure, combined with Ink's carefully worded questions, gradually unraveled the truth, revealing a hidden motive and a string of misinterpretations that had led to the false accusation.

Ink's investigative process wasn't just about gathering information; it was about understanding the context, the motivations, and the biases that shaped the narratives of those involved. He understood that people, or in this case, animals, rarely presented a straightforward account of events. Their memories were often distorted by fear, anger, or prejudice. Ink's skill lay in uncovering these hidden motivations and disentangling the web of misinterpretations that often obscured the truth.

He spent countless hours piecing together the fragments of information he had collected, constructing a comprehensive picture of events. He used diagrams, sketches, and carefully constructed timelines to organize his findings, visualizing the flow of events and identifying potential inconsistencies. He would spend hours poring over his notes, rereading interviews, and reanalyzing witness statements, searching for patterns and connections that might reveal a hidden truth.

His method was not based solely on logic and deduction, though. He also understood the importance of intuition and creative thinking. He allowed himself to follow hunches and explore unexpected leads, even if they seemed improbable at first glance. Sometimes, the most surprising insights came from the most unlikely sources.

For instance, a seemingly insignificant detail – a specific type of berry found near the telephone pole – led Ink to a completely unexpected suspect. The berry was unusual for the area and he remembered seeing a similar type of berry in the den of a grumpy badger known for his territorial disputes.

After many days and nights of meticulous investigation, Ink's meticulous approach began to bear fruit. His analysis of the evidence, combined with Fiona's intuitive insights, led him to a surprising conclusion. The culprit wasn't who everyone suspected; it was an unexpected player, motivated by a complex set of circumstances that had gone unnoticed by the community.

His investigation wasn't just about solving a crime; it was about revealing a deeper truth about the community itself. The hasty accusations, the spread of rumors, the biased interpretations—these revealed a societal tendency to judge before understanding, to leap to conclusions without fully examining the facts. Ink's careful methodology was a powerful counterpoint to this impulsive tendency, a testament to the value of patience, careful observation and a dedication to uncovering the truth, no matter how elusive it might seem. His work served as a valuable lesson for the entire Wildwoods Farm community, highlighting the importance of seeking understanding before passing judgment, a lesson as vital for the small forest community as it is for the larger world beyond.

Ink's investigative prowess wasn't merely about interrogating witnesses; it was a symphony of observation, a meticulous dance between the tangible and the intangible. His keen eyes, sharper than any hawk's, missed nothing. He possessed an almost supernatural ability to notice the minutest details – a slightly discolored patch of moss, a barely perceptible scuff mark on a leaf, the subtle tremor in a witness's paw. These seemingly insignificant details were, to Ink, the building blocks of truth, the breadcrumbs leading him through the labyrinth of deception.

For instance, while questioning a particularly nervous robin who had claimed to witness Jenny's fall, Ink noted not just the robin's words, but also the way its feathers ruffled incessantly, a clear sign of anxiety. The robin's account initially painted a picture of a forceful push, but Ink observed a telltale detail: the robin's gaze kept flitting towards a clump of tall ferns slightly away from the telephone pole. This seemingly insignificant detail sparked a new line of inquiry. He examined the ferns meticulously, finding traces of disturbed soil and a small, almost invisible, trail leading away from the pole. It was a trail too small to be made by a squirrel, but the perfect size for a much smaller creature. This led him to suspect the involvement of a shrew, a creature notorious for its quick movements and penchant for mischief.

His approach was a stark contrast to the hurried accusations and assumptions made by the community. While others relied on hearsay and biased opinions, Ink focused on verifiable facts, meticulously documenting every observation in his leather-bound notebook. Each entry was a testament to his precision, a tiny jewel in the mosaic of his investigation. He'd sketch diagrams, noting the precise angles of shadows, the positions of witnesses, and the minutest details of the environment. His diagrams weren't mere illustrations; they were complex visual representations of his hypotheses, allowing him to test and refine his deductions in a systematic way.

Ink's skill extended beyond the visual. He possessed an exceptional sense of smell, often picking up on faint scents that others missed entirely. The faint whiff of a particular flower, usually found only in the deepest part of the forest, led him to a hidden path, a path that most creatures had overlooked. Following this path, he discovered a small clearing where he found crucial evidence – a small, broken twig from the telephone pole, carefully concealed under a pile of leaves. The twig bore faint traces of a substance that only a specific type of beetle secreted; a beetle rarely found near the telephone pole but commonly found near a particular stream on the other side of the woods. This discovery pointed to a possibility no one had even considered.

Moreover, Ink's ability to synthesize disparate pieces of information was remarkable. He had the uncanny knack of connecting seemingly unrelated observations, revealing hidden patterns and drawing insightful conclusions. For example, a seemingly meaningless comment made by a gossiping hen about a recent disagreement between Jasper and a family of weasels, coupled with his discovery of the unusual beetle and the hidden trail, led him to suspect a complex conspiracy involving territorial disputes.

Fiona, his feline partner, complemented Ink's skills perfectly. While Ink meticulously documented facts, Fiona's keen intuition often unearthed hidden emotions and motivations. She observed the subtle shifts in a creature's body language, the barely perceptible flinches and hesitations, revealing the lies and inconsistencies that even Ink's keen eyes sometimes missed. Her ability to sense fear and deception was unparalleled, enabling her to identify individuals who were withholding information or deliberately misleading the investigation.

For instance, during an interview with a rather pompous owl who held a prominent position in the community, Fiona noted the subtle tightening of the owl's neck muscles whenever Ink questioned the owl's alibi. Although the owl maintained a composed demeanor, Fiona's acute sensitivity to subtle physical cues revealed the owl's discomfort and deception.

Ink and Fiona worked in perfect harmony, their different strengths complementing each other. Fiona's intuitive insights often provided Ink with new avenues of investigation, pushing him to explore possibilities he may have otherwise overlooked. They were an inseparable team, a testament to the power of collaboration and the synergy between logic and intuition.

Their investigation wasn't a straightforward journey; it was a winding path fraught with false leads, misleading statements, and cleverly concealed evidence. They encountered stubborn witnesses, deliberate obfuscations, and the inherent biases that colored the narratives of those involved. Yet, through their combined efforts, Ink's meticulous observation, and Fiona's intuitive insights, they slowly pieced together the fragments of truth, revealing a surprising picture of events.

Even seemingly inconsequential events became significant under Ink's scrutiny. He noticed that a specific type of moss grew predominantly on the north side of the telephone pole, a detail that hinted at the direction of the wind on the day of the incident. This seemingly minor observation, coupled with Fiona's detection of the subtle scent of pine needles on Jasper's fur, a scent not found near the telephone pole but prevalent near a specific pine grove, led them to a startling revelation.

As Ink continued his investigation, he utilized a variety of techniques to enhance his observation skills. He used magnifying glasses to examine minute details, like the texture of fibers on clothing or the microscopic scratches on a small piece of wood. He employed specialized tools, such as a miniature measuring tape, to meticulously record distances and dimensions. He even used a rudimentary camera to capture images of the scene, creating a detailed visual record for future reference.

But it wasn't just the tools; it was Ink's methodology that set him apart. He understood that true observation wasn't just about seeing; it was about interpreting. He painstakingly analyzed every piece of evidence, cross-referencing it with other observations, and constantly testing his hypotheses against new information. He had the patience to observe, the intellect to analyze, and the creativity to connect disparate facts, ultimately building a coherent picture of events.

Ink's investigation was a testament to the power of meticulous observation and the importance of seeking the truth, even when it was hidden beneath layers of deception and prejudice. His approach, a blend of scientific precision and intuitive insight, provided a powerful lesson to the community of Wildwoods Farm, reminding them that true justice required more than hasty accusations and assumptions. It demanded patience, persistence, and a profound understanding of the subtleties of observation. The truth, Ink had discovered, wasn't always obvious, but it was always there, waiting to be unearthed by those with the skill and dedication to find it.

Ink's deductive reasoning wasn't a mere process; it was an art form, a carefully orchestrated symphony of logic and observation. He approached each piece of evidence not as an isolated fact, but as a note in a complex musical score, each contributing to the overall melody of truth. His mind worked like a finely tuned machine, meticulously processing information, identifying patterns, and eliminating inconsistencies until a clear and coherent narrative emerged from the chaos.

For example, the seemingly insignificant discovery of a single, broken acorn near the base of the telephone pole became a crucial piece of the puzzle. While others dismissed it as inconsequential debris, Ink recognized the unique fracture pattern – a clean break, not a crush or a splintering. This indicated a precise, controlled action, not a random fall. Furthermore, the acorn's position, precisely aligned with a slight indentation on the pole, suggested a deliberate placement, not accidental scattering.

He meticulously compared the size and shape of the acorn fragments to acorns from different oak trees within the vicinity. He noted the subtle variations in color and texture, ultimately tracing the acorn's origin to a specific oak tree located several yards away from the telephone pole, a tree known for its unusually large and hard acorns. This discovery immediately narrowed down the possibilities of who could have handled such a weighty acorn with the precision required to create the observed fracture pattern.

His analysis extended beyond the physical characteristics of the acorn. He examined the surrounding soil, finding traces of uniquely patterned footprints, remarkably small for a squirrel but perfectly fitting the size of a weasel. The tracks led away from the oak tree, towards the telephone pole, and then back again, confirming a specific sequence of events. He noted that the soil around the acorn was disturbed, implying that the acorn had been deliberately placed there relatively recently.

This single, broken acorn, dismissed by others as insignificant, became the cornerstone of Ink's deductive reasoning, forming a vital link in the chain of events that led to Jenny's fall. He combined this evidence with his previous observations – the robin's nervous behavior and its gaze towards the ferns, the shrew's tiny tracks leading away from the pole – and began to piece together a more complex narrative than initially suspected.

Ink's method involved meticulous documentation, a habit he had cultivated from his early days. He filled notebooks with detailed sketches, measurements, and notes, each entry a testament to his unwavering dedication to accuracy. His diagrams weren't simply visual representations of the scene; they were complex models of his hypotheses, allowing him to test his deductions systematically, eliminate conflicting theories, and refine his understanding of the case. He used different colored inks to represent different pieces of evidence, creating a vibrant tapestry of clues, making it easy to visualize the interconnectedness of facts.

One particularly intriguing element was a small, almost imperceptible scratch on the telephone pole itself, located just above the indentation where the acorn was found. Ink, using his magnifying glass, discovered that the scratch was not caused by a squirrel's claws, but by something sharper and more pointed. The angle and depth of the scratch suggested it had been inflicted from a specific direction, and the microscopic traces of wood shavings suggested the type of material that caused it. Combining this information with the weasel tracks and the acorn's placement, he developed a hypothesis.

His keen observation extended beyond the visible realm. He utilized his extraordinary sense of smell, a trait peculiar to ferrets, to identify subtle scents that others missed. The faint odor of wet earth clinging to a specific blade of grass near the telephone pole suggested recent rainfall, and a cross-reference with the meteorological records of the Wildwoods Farm confirmed a localized downpour that day, limiting the time frame of the incident.

Moreover, Ink's ability to interpret non-verbal cues was exceptional. He observed the slight hesitation in the robin's chirp, the subtle twitch of the owl's feathers, and the almost imperceptible widening of the weasel mother's eyes during interrogation, detecting deception and inconsistencies that others overlooked. He combined these observations with the physical evidence, cross-referencing each detail to create a cohesive, logical explanation of the events leading to Jenny's tragic fall.

Ink's deductive reasoning wasn't solely about identifying individual facts; it was about weaving those facts together to create a coherent narrative. He recognized the interconnectedness of events, appreciating that even seemingly insignificant details could hold the key to unraveling the truth. His mind worked like a master craftsman, patiently assembling the individual pieces of the puzzle, revealing a startlingly complex picture.

He considered the possibility of multiple actors, the potential for misinterpretations, and the influence of biases and prejudices within the community. His approach was exhaustive, relentless, and above all, objective. He didn't allow his personal feelings or the community's preconceptions to sway his judgment. He followed the evidence, wherever it led, challenging assumptions and questioning accepted narratives.

His investigative process wasn't linear; it was iterative, involving constant revision and refinement of hypotheses as new evidence emerged. He built his conclusions carefully, step by step, using his deductions as springboards to further investigation. He didn't jump to conclusions; instead, he systematically eliminated possibilities until only one logical explanation remained. This rigorous process ensured that his conclusions were not only logically sound but also demonstrably verifiable.

The culmination of Ink's meticulous investigation revealed a surprising truth, a truth far more complex than the initial assumptions had suggested. The seemingly simple accident was, in reality, the result of a series of intertwined events, a tangled web of misunderstandings, territorial disputes, and accidental consequences. Jenny's fall wasn't a simple act of aggression, but a tragic confluence of circumstances brought about by several different factors, and Ink's dedication to careful deduction and observation revealed all. His skill wasn't just in finding the truth; it was in presenting that truth in a way that was clear, logical, and undeniable, a testament to the power of careful observation and deductive reasoning. This would be crucial in the upcoming trial, and Ink felt confident in the evidence he had collected.

The Wildwoods Farm, usually alive with the chirping of crickets and the rustling of leaves, felt strangely silent as Ink hunched over his meticulously organized notes. The weight of the case, the pressure of the community's expectation, and the lingering shadow of Jenny's tragic fall pressed down on him. But Ink, a ferret of unwavering resolve, refused to yield. He knew the truth was out there, hidden amongst the tangled undergrowth of conflicting testimonies and misleading clues. His persistence, his refusal to accept anything less than absolute certainty, was the fuel driving his investigation.

The initial skepticism he'd encountered hadn't deterred him. The gossiping hens, clucking their half-baked theories, the condescending cats, their eyes narrowed in judgment, the dismissive squirrels, clinging to their preconceived notions—none of them had shaken his determination. He'd faced their doubts with a quiet intensity, a steadfast commitment to the facts, patiently gathering evidence and building his case brick by painstaking brick.

One particular challenge involved deciphering the fragmented testimony of Oswald, the elderly owl. Oswald, known for his notoriously poor eyesight and even poorer memory, had claimed to have seen something—or rather, to have *heard* something—in the moments before Jenny's fall. His account was vague, filled with gaps and inconsistencies, but Ink recognized the potential value in Oswald's clouded recollection. He realized that Oswald's hazy description wasn't just a random jumble of sounds but a distorted echo of a significant event.

Ink spent hours painstakingly piecing together Oswald's fragmented narrative. He re-created the scene in miniature, utilizing twigs and leaves to model the terrain around the telephone pole. He carefully considered the direction of the wind, the potential obstructions to Oswald's vision, and even the angle of the sun, meticulously reconstructing the sensory experience Oswald claimed to have had. Through this detailed reconstruction, Ink found a pattern in the seemingly chaotic account. Oswald's confused recollections pointed towards a subtle, almost imperceptible sound – a faint rustling, distinct from the typical sounds of the forest, followed by a sharp snapping sound, much like a small branch breaking.

This subtle clue, almost lost in Oswald's incoherent babble, proved to be invaluable. Ink correlated this sound with other evidence he had gathered: the microscopic wood shavings from the telephone pole, the specific type of branch discovered broken near the base of the tree, and the unique weasel tracks. The snapping sound, the wood shavings, and the branch fragments all painted a clear picture: the weasel had inadvertently caused her fall by disrupting the precarious branch she was clinging to.

The weasel's actions were unintentional, a tragic accident borne of clumsy misjudgment, not a malicious act of aggression. This revelation directly contradicted the assumptions of many in the forest community, who had readily leaped to conclusions of Jasper based on their biases and preconceived notions. Ink's investigation didn't just unearth the facts; it also laid bare the community's tendency to rush to judgment.

Another significant obstacle Ink faced was the lack of cooperation from certain members of the community. Some witnesses, fearing repercussions or simply overwhelmed by the emotional aftermath of Jenny's fall, initially withheld crucial information. It was Fiona, the feline partner and the "*Whisper*" of the woods, who proved invaluable in overcoming this reluctance. Fiona's innate ability to sense emotions and intuit the unspoken truths proved crucial in gaining the trust of the hesitant witnesses.

Through her quiet diplomacy and persuasive charm, Fiona helped Ink uncover several critical details that would have otherwise remained hidden. She unearthed conversations overheard in hushed whispers, observations made in private moments, and details intentionally left out of initial testimonies. Fiona's insightful observations and her ability to connect with the community on an emotional level proved to be as vital to Ink's success as his meticulous deductive reasoning. Their partnership was a testament to the synergy of different investigative styles – one focused on logical deduction and the other on emotional intuition.

Ink's relentless pursuit of truth extended beyond mere fact-finding. He had to contend with the emotional toll the tragedy had inflicted upon the community. The atmosphere in the forest was thick with grief, suspicion, and a deep sense of unease. The initial accusations against Jasper had created a deep rift within the squirrel community, leaving many traumatized and hesitant to cooperate. Ink recognized the need to approach the situation with sensitivity and empathy, understanding that his investigation was not simply about finding a culprit but also about healing a community torn apart by loss and misjudgment.

He carefully and patiently spoke to each witness, listening to their stories, validating their feelings, and acknowledging the pain they had endured. He avoided accusatory language, instead opting for open-ended questions that allowed witnesses to share their experiences without feeling judged. This approach, a delicate balance between rigorous investigation and compassionate understanding, proved invaluable in uncovering the full picture. He understood that a successful investigation didn't just solve the mystery; it repaired the community.

Ink's perseverance wasn't merely a matter of stubbornness; it was a deep-seated belief in justice and truth. He believed that even the most seemingly insurmountable challenges could be overcome with meticulous observation, careful analysis, and unwavering dedication. He knew that the truth, however elusive, was always worth pursuing, even when faced with skepticism, resistance, and the weight of a community's expectations.

His work extended beyond the purely logical. He spent many nights poring over ancient forest maps, cross-referencing them with meteorological records and even consulting the local elderberry bushes, known for their uncanny ability to absorb and reflect the emotional energies of the forest. Their subtle shifts in growth patterns and leaf coloration provided Ink with unexpected insights into the emotional climate surrounding Jenny's fall.

Through these painstaking efforts, Ink finally had a comprehensive understanding of the accident. It wasn't a simple case of one squirrel pushing another; it was a cascade of unfortunate events, a complex interplay of environmental factors, accidental occurrences, and misinterpretations. He uncovered the root cause of the incident – a storm that had weakened a branch Jenny was clinging to, coupled with the mouse and weasel's unintentional interference, causing the branch to snap. This intricate sequence of events was far more nuanced and less straightforward than the initial assumptions had suggested.

The meticulous detail in his investigation, the sheer perseverance in the face of doubt and the emotional complexity he navigated, made Ink's findings irrefutable. His presentation, a symphony of logic and compassion, would not only determine the fate of those wrongly accused but would also serve as a lesson to the Wildwoods Farm community: to question assumptions, to embrace empathy, and to pursue truth with unwavering resolve. The journey had been arduous, the path winding and full of unexpected turns, but Ink's perseverance had led him to the heart of the truth. And now, he was ready to share it.

The courtroom, a clearing nestled amongst ancient oak trees, buzzed with anticipation. Squirrels huddled together, their bushy tails twitching nervously. Hens gossiped in hushed tones, their clucking a low hum against the otherwise expectant silence. Even the usually aloof cats seemed to hold their breath, their emerald eyes fixed on Ink, who stood poised before the makeshift jury. The weight of the forest rested upon his small shoulders, the responsibility of revealing the truth a heavy burden. But Ink, his ferret eyes gleaming with unwavering conviction, showed no sign of faltering.

His integrity wasn't just about uncovering the facts; it was about the process itself. He hadn't just sought evidence; he'd sought it fairly, meticulously documenting every step, every interview, every observation. He'd presented his findings not as accusations, but as a carefully constructed narrative, a chronological unfolding of events that allowed the community to draw their own conclusions. He understood that true justice wasn't simply about assigning blame; it was about restoring balance, repairing the fractured trust within the community.

He began his presentation by acknowledging the grief that permeated the forest. He spoke of Jenny, not as a case file, but as a beloved member of their community, a friend, a neighbor, whose loss had shaken them all. His voice, though firm, was infused with empathy, a gentle understanding that resonated with the assembled creatures.

"We are here today not to point fingers but to understand," Ink stated, his voice clear and resonant. "To piece together the fragments of a tragedy, and to learn from it. Justice is not about vengeance; it's about truth, about understanding, and about healing."

He then meticulously detailed his investigation, guiding the jury through a labyrinth of clues, testimonies, and deductions. He displayed his meticulously organized notes, each piece of evidence carefully documented, cross-referenced, and analyzed. He presented the broken branch, the microscopic wood shavings, the weasel tracks—each piece a vital link in the chain of events. He explained the nuances of Oswald's fragmented recollections, demonstrating how he'd reconstructed the scene, factoring in the direction of the wind, the angle of the sun, and even the emotional state of the forest at the time of the accident.

He didn't shy away from the challenges he'd faced. He spoke openly about the initial skepticism, the resistance he'd encountered, and the emotional toll the investigation had taken on him. He highlighted the importance of Fiona's intuitive abilities, showcasing how her understanding of the emotional landscape had provided vital insights inaccessible through pure logic alone. He described the delicate balance he'd had to maintain between rigorous investigation and compassionate understanding, emphasizing the importance of listening to each witness with empathy and respect.

Ink even acknowledged his own limitations. He explained how he'd sought help from unexpected sources, detailing his consultations with the elderberry bushes and his cross-referencing of ancient forest maps with meteorological records. He demonstrated how these unconventional methods, while seemingly outside the realm of typical detective work, had provided critical insights into the emotional currents swirling around the event. This honesty, this self-awareness, further solidified his commitment to integrity and fairness.

His presentation wasn't just a recitation of facts; it was a story, a compelling narrative that painted a vivid picture of the events leading up to Jenny's fall. He weaved together the scientific evidence with the emotional realities, showcasing how the weasel's actions, though unintentional, had been a pivotal element in a chain of unfortunate events. He illustrated how the storm had weakened the branch, highlighting the meteorological data he'd painstakingly collected. He emphasized how the combination of environmental factors and unintentional interference had resulted in the tragic accident.

He showed how easily assumptions could cloud judgment, how readily the community had leaped to conclusions without considering the full context. He presented his findings not as a condemnation, but as a testament to the unpredictable nature of accidents, the fragility of life, and the importance of thorough investigation before passing judgment. He emphasized that assigning blame wouldn't bring Jenny back; understanding the sequence of events, learning from the tragedy, and healing the community would be a far greater tribute.

As Ink concluded his presentation, a hush fell over the courtroom. The squirrels, initially tense, looked at each other with new understanding. The hens, usually prone to gossip, were unusually quiet. Even the cats, eyes narrowed in thought, seemed to be reflecting on what they'd heard. Ink's commitment to fairness and justice, his unwavering integrity, had not just solved a mystery; it had transformed the atmosphere of the entire forest. The accusations, the suspicions, the bitterness – they were beginning to fade, replaced by a sense of shared loss and a nascent understanding.

His final words hung in the air, a testament to his belief in the power of truth and the importance of collective responsibility. "The truth," he said, his voice soft yet powerful, "may be complex, even painful, but it is the only foundation upon which we can build a just and compassionate community." The weight of expectation lifted slightly from Ink's shoulders; his work was done. He had revealed the truth, not merely as a detective, but as a member of the Wildwoods Farm, committed to its healing and its future. The trial continued, but the seeds of understanding had been sown, and the path towards reconciliation had begun. The community would now have the chance to heal from the tragedy, guided by Ink's unwavering commitment to justice, and the truth he so meticulously unearthed. The journey had been long and arduous, filled with setbacks, but Ink's commitment to fairness and his profound belief in the power of truth had finally prevailed. The forest, once shadowed by grief and suspicion, now had a chance to emerge into the light of understanding and forgiveness.

Chapter 11
Fiona's Insights

Fiona, known throughout the Wildwoods Farm as *The Whisper*, possessed an extraordinary gift – an acute sense of hearing that bordered on the supernatural. It wasn't merely the ability to hear faint sounds; it was a perception that transcended the ordinary, allowing her to discern subtle nuances, interpret unspoken emotions, and even decipher the whispers of the wind. While Ink meticulously collected physical evidence, Fiona's role was far more intricate, more subtle, and arguably, more crucial. She was the listener, the interpreter, the one who could decipher the silent language of the forest itself.

Her extraordinary hearing wasn't just about volume; it was about context. She could distinguish the faintest rustle of leaves from the heavy thud of a falling acorn, the anxious chirping of a robin from the contented cooing of a dove. But more importantly, she could interpret the subtext, the unspoken anxieties and concealed truths that lay beneath the surface of every conversation, every interaction. While others heard words, Fiona heard the emotions behind them, the hesitations, the inflections, the subtle shifts in tone that revealed a speaker's true intentions.

One of Fiona's most remarkable abilities was her capacity to isolate individual sounds within a cacophony. During the bustling marketplace, where the chatter of squirrels, the squawking of hens, and the rumbling of carts created an almost unbearable din, Fiona could focus on a single conversation, picking out individual words from the surrounding chaos with remarkable clarity. She'd often perch atop a high branch, her feline form a silent observer, her ears twitching, each twitch a testament to her keen perception. From this vantage point, she could hear the murmurs of the crowd, the hushed whispers of secret conversations, the subtle shifts in tone that betrayed a lie or a hidden motive.

Her talents weren't limited to simply hearing conversations; she could perceive sounds that were inaudible to most other creatures. The subtle creak of a weakened branch, the almost imperceptible shift of weight on the forest floor, the faintest sigh of the wind as it rustled through the leaves – all these provided her with invaluable insights, often leading Ink to vital pieces of evidence he might otherwise have missed. She could even detect the faintest changes in the rhythm of a heartbeat, a skill she'd honed over years of observing the forest's inhabitants, learning to read their emotional states through their physical manifestations.

In the case of Jenny's fall, Fiona's acute hearing proved invaluable. She'd been perched high above the scene, observing the chaos from a distance, her ears constantly scanning the environment. She recalled hearing a series of distinct sounds: a high-pitched shriek, the loud crack of a breaking branch, the frantic rustling of leaves as creatures scattered, and then, a low, almost imperceptible whimper. It was this whimper that had particularly intrigued Fiona; it was unlike any sound she'd heard before, a sound too subdued to be associated with the immediate aftermath of the accident. It was a sound that hinted at something more, something that lay hidden beneath the surface of the apparent chaos.

Remembering the position of the sun, the strength of the wind, the sounds, and the slight alterations in the rhythm of certain creatures' movements immediately following the accident, Fiona was able to piece together a more complete narrative. By isolating specific sounds from the overwhelming noise of the event, she had been able to pick out and focus on the crucial subtle details. It was these elements – the timing of the various sounds, the emotional inflections in the panicked cries, the almost-imperceptible shift in the rustle of leaves – that had enabled her to create a more complete picture of what had transpired.

She meticulously documented these sounds, noting the subtle differences in pitch, tempo, and tone, creating an auditory map of the incident. This wasn't simply a list of sounds; it was a complex tapestry of auditory data, woven together to create a picture that was both detailed and remarkably nuanced. The whimper, she found, had originated from a hidden thicket, a place she'd previously dismissed as unimportant. However, upon further investigation, guided by this auditory map, Ink discovered a broken twig, distinctly different from the others, and weasel tracks leading away from the thicket and towards the scene of the accident.

Fiona's ability to filter out extraneous noise was extraordinary. While the other creatures were overwhelmed by the commotion, she could focus on the faintest whispers, picking out relevant information from the cacophony. She'd overheard hushed conversations in the days leading up to the accident, conversations that hinted at disputes, jealousies, and rivalries within the forest community. She hadn't actively sought these conversations; they simply came to her, carried on the currents of sound that constantly flowed through the Wildwoods Farm. Her ability to process this vast amount of auditory data, to separate the significant from the insignificant, was astonishing. She remembered snippets of gossip, overheard comments, and even the sounds of creatures pacing restlessly, their movement a silent testimony to their underlying anxiety.

The information she'd gleaned through her acute hearing wasn't just about facts; it was also about emotions. She could sense the fear in a squirrel's quickened heartbeat, the anger in a hen's sharp cluck, the hidden guilt in a cat's averted gaze. This intuitive understanding of emotional nuances was what had allowed her to identify the inconsistencies in Oswald's testimony. While he'd maintained a calm demeanor during his interview, Fiona's heightened hearing had detected slight tremors in his voice, barely perceptible hesitations, and subtle shifts in his breathing pattern. It was these small, easily overlooked details that had revealed the cracks in his fabricated narrative.

Moreover, Fiona's exceptional hearing extended beyond the immediate vicinity. She could perceive sounds from considerable distances, picking up faint noises that would otherwise be lost in the ambient sounds of the forest. She could hear the distant chirping of crickets, the rustling of leaves in the far-off thicket, and the faint sounds of movement in the deepest parts of the woods. These subtle sounds, often disregarded by others, provided Fiona with a broader context, allowing her to understand the wider environment and its impact on the events of the day.

One particularly striking instance involved a series of unusually loud hooting from the owl's nest high in an ancient oak. While others dismissed it as ordinary nocturnal activity, Fiona had recognized a subtle variation in the owls' calls – a variation that conveyed a sense of distress and alarm. Further investigation led Ink to discover a hidden trail of footprints leading away from the owl's nest, footprints that did not belong to any resident of the Wildwoods Farm. It was a clue that had initially been dismissed, buried under the immediate clamor surrounding Jenny's fall, yet it had been picked up by Fiona's heightened sensitivity.

Her acute hearing wasn't just a gift; it was a responsibility. It was a burden as well, constantly bombarded by the sounds of the forest, the whispers, the murmurs, the anxieties, and the hopes of countless creatures. It was a gift that required constant vigilance, constant attention, and a discerning ability to filter the noise and extract the meaningful information. Fiona, however, bore this burden with grace and unwavering dedication, using her unique talent to illuminate the hidden truths of the Wildwoods Farm, ensuring that justice, in all its complexity, would finally prevail. Her contribution to the case, interwoven with Ink's methodical investigation, ultimately proved to be the key to understanding the tragic events that had shaken their community to its core. The truth, often masked by assumptions and biases, was finally revealed, thanks to Fiona's unparalleled gift of acute hearing. The Wildwoods Farm, initially engulfed in grief and suspicion, could now begin its long journey toward healing and understanding, thanks in no small part to the unique insights provided by Fiona, *The Whisper*.

Fiona's understanding of the forest wasn't limited to the sounds it produced. She possessed an almost uncanny ability to read the silent language of animal behavior, a skill honed over years of observing the intricate social dynamics of the Wildwoods Farm. While Ink meticulously documented physical evidence, Fiona's interpretations of subtle behavioral cues often provided the crucial context that brought the fragmented pieces of the puzzle together. She could decipher the barely perceptible flick of a tail, the subtle shift in posture, the barely noticeable twitch of an ear – all tiny signals that spoke volumes to her trained eye.

Take, for instance, the case of Kel the hedgehog. Kel, a generally placid creature, had been observed near the scene of the accident shortly after it occurred. Most would have dismissed him as a mere bystander, an accidental witness to the tragedy. But Fiona noticed something unusual in Kel's behavior. While outwardly calm, Kel's quills were slightly ruffled, a sign of underlying tension or anxiety. He also kept glancing nervously towards a particular clump of bushes, his tiny nose twitching almost imperceptibly. These seemingly insignificant details, unnoticed by others, spoke to Fiona of a hidden unease, a suppressed knowledge that Kel was unwilling to share.

Ink, initially skeptical, followed Fiona's lead and investigated the clump of bushes. There, concealed beneath a tangle of leaves and brambles, they discovered a small, almost invisible scratch on a nearby tree, a scratch that matched the claws of a weasel. This discovery, guided by Fiona's observation of Kel's subtle behavioral cues, linked Kel to the weasel's trail that had been previously noted, creating a more compelling narrative. The scratch, insignificant on its own, became a powerful piece of evidence when considered in the context of Kel's anxious behavior, suggesting his involuntary involvement in events that he had been desperately trying to conceal.

Fiona's ability to decipher animal communication was far more than simple observation. It was an intuitive understanding, a sixth sense that allowed her to perceive the unspoken emotions and anxieties of the forest's inhabitants. She could distinguish between genuine fear and feigned distress, between casual indifference and calculated deception. She'd observed the subtle changes in posture, the almost imperceptible shifts in gait, the way a creature held its head, the way it used its tail – all these provided her with a rich tapestry of non-verbal information, often more revealing than any spoken word.

One particularly telling instance involved a group of gossiping hens. These hens, notorious for their love of drama and penchant for spreading rumors, had all offered conflicting accounts of what they had seen on the day of the accident. While their verbal testimonies were a chaotic jumble of half-truths and exaggerations, Fiona's keen observation of their body language revealed a more coherent picture. She noted the subtle tension in their body language, the way they constantly shifted their weight, the way their eyes darted nervously. Their nervous movements and frequent glances toward each other, despite their attempts to portray an air of nonchalance, spoke of a collective guilt.

Fiona recognized that while their spoken words aimed to deceive, their bodies betrayed them. The hens' constant preening, the unnatural stillness of their wings, and their almost imperceptible flinching whenever the topic of the accident was broached, pointed towards a shared secret, a collective attempt to conceal a crucial detail. Based on these subtle cues, Fiona concluded that the hens were not simply witnesses; they were actively involved in concealing something related to the events that led to Jenny's fall. This intuition, born from her astute observation of their body language, provided Ink with a crucial avenue for further investigation.

The skill also extended beyond immediate interactions. Fiona could sense the emotional atmosphere of a place, reading the collective mood of a given area. She could sense the lingering fear in a section of the forest where a recent predator attack had occurred or the palpable tension in a place where a dispute had recently been resolved. This understanding of the broader emotional context allowed her to identify areas requiring closer scrutiny.

For example, the area near the telephone pole where Jenny had fallen felt different to Fiona. It wasn't just the obvious signs of the accident; there was an underlying sense of unease, a lingering vibration of fear and suspicion. This subtle emotional current, imperceptible to most, guided Ink's search for additional evidence. It was in this area that Ink discovered a series of almost invisible footprints, too small for a squirrel, too large for a mouse. These footprints, initially overlooked, became significant because of Fiona's perception of the lingering unease in the area.

Furthermore, Fiona's interpretation of body language wasn't limited to other animals. She was also extraordinarily adept at reading the subtle cues exhibited by humans. The subtle clenching of a jaw, the fleeting expression in someone's eyes, the almost imperceptible tremor in a hand – all these micro-expressions, often overlooked, provided Fiona with invaluable insights into the truthfulness of a witness's testimony.

In this particular case, she could easily identify those witnesses who were trying to deceive her and Ink. Their attempts at maintaining calm and nonchalant demeanors were easily countered by Fiona's reading of their subtle body language – the forced smiles that didn't reach their eyes, the excessive blinking, the stiff posture, the avoidance of direct eye contact – all pointed to an attempt to conceal the truth. This understanding allowed her to focus her investigative efforts on those most likely to be concealing information, thus allowing the investigators to accelerate their search for the culprit.

Fiona's ability to interpret the subtle cues of animal and human behavior wasn't just a gift; it was a form of silent communication, a way of understanding the unspoken narratives of the Wildwoods Farm. It was a skill that transcended simple observation; it was an intuition; a sixth sense honed over years of patient study and deep empathy. This skill, interwoven with Ink's methodical approach, proved invaluable in unraveling the mystery of Jenny's fall, illustrating the importance of observation and the power of understanding the unspoken messages that lie beneath the surface of everyday interactions. The secrets hidden within the subtle gestures, the fleeting expressions, the almost imperceptible shifts in posture – these were the clues that Fiona expertly deciphered, leading Ink and herself closer to the truth, ultimately ensuring justice prevailed in the whimsical, yet often complex, world of the Wildwoods Farm. The combination of Ink's methodical investigation and Fiona's intuitive understanding of unspoken communication proved to be an unbeatable partnership, capable of penetrating the layers of deception and revealing the hidden truths at the heart of the case.

Fiona's empathy wasn't merely an intellectual understanding; it was a visceral connection, a deep-seated ability to feel what others felt. She didn't just observe the forest; she inhabited it, experiencing its joys and sorrows as if they were her own. This wasn't a conscious effort; it was an intrinsic part of her being, a natural extension of her feline nature, amplified by years of honing her observational skills. It allowed her to bridge the gap between species, to understand not just their actions, but their motivations, their fears, and their hopes.

Consider, for instance, her interactions with the elderly owl, Professor Sophocles. The Professor, renowned for his wisdom and knowledge of the Wildwoods Farm, was a creature of habit, his days meticulously planned, his routines unwavering. Yet, Fiona noticed a subtle shift in his demeanor. His usually sharp eyes were clouded with a weariness that went beyond the natural aging process. His usual vibrant hooting was muted, replaced by a low, almost inaudible murmur. He seemed withdrawn, isolated in his ancient oak tree, a stark contrast to his typically sociable nature.

Most would have attributed this to the natural decline of old age. But Fiona felt something more profound. She sensed a deep-seated sadness, a loneliness that resonated with her own experiences of loss and isolation. Through patient observation and gentle gestures – a slow blink, a soft purr, a quiet presence near his tree – Fiona earned the Professor's trust. He confided in her, revealing a hidden grief over the loss of his mate, a tragedy he had kept concealed for fear of appearing weak.

Fiona didn't judge; she understood. She had experienced loss herself, the pain of absence, the ache of a missing presence. This shared understanding formed the bedrock of their connection, allowing the

Professor to open up about his grief and, in turn, providing Fiona with a crucial piece of the puzzle. The Professor's hidden sadness, initially masked by his stoic exterior, revealed a previously unknown connection to the events surrounding Jenny's accident. He had unwittingly witnessed a crucial interaction, an interaction he'd suppressed, believing it irrelevant, only revealing it to Fiona because of their shared understanding of loss and sorrow.

Her empathetic approach extended to the smallest creatures of the forest. She spent hours observing a family of field mice, their tiny lives teeming with challenges. She understood their struggles to find food, their constant vigilance against predators, their fierce loyalty to their family. This understanding wasn't based on intellectual knowledge; it was an emotional connection, a feeling of kinship that allowed her to anticipate their behaviors and understand their motivations. Her ability to connect with them on this level provided invaluable insights into their interactions with other forest creatures, ultimately leading her to discover a crucial piece of evidence previously overlooked because of its seemingly insignificant nature.

This empathetic connection wasn't limited to forest animals. Fiona possessed a similar ability to connect with the non-forest's inhabitants. She recognized the underlying anxieties of the dogs, hamsters, and fish who lived near the Wildwoods Farm. She understood their fears of the dark, their anxieties about being alone, their unspoken dreams and aspirations. This understanding enabled her to connect with them on a deeper level, encouraging their cooperation and earning their trust, leading them to provide critical information that was crucial to the investigation.

Her interaction with Mrs. Gable, the turkey baker who lived on the edge of the woods, was a perfect example. Mrs. Gable, a turkey known for her sweet treats and even sweeter disposition, seemed unusually anxious. Fiona observed her subtle cues—the way she constantly wrung her wings, the tremor in her voice, the averted gaze. Fiona sensed a hidden distress, a fear she wasn't willing to express outwardly.

Through gentle questioning and empathetic listening, Fiona learned that Mrs. Gable was struggling financially, facing the possibility of losing her beloved bakery. This financial hardship, coupled with the stress of the recent accident, had pushed her to the brink of despair. Fiona's empathy and understanding allowed her to connect with Mrs. Gable on a generosity level, providing her with emotional support and encouraging her to share information that proved crucial to solving the case. The information wasn't directly related to Jenny's fall, but it shed light on a network of relationships and hidden motives that had gone previously unnoticed.

Fiona's empathy was her superpower, a unique ability that allowed her to see beyond the surface, to penetrate the barriers of communication, and to understand the unspoken truths that lay hidden within the hearts and minds of the creatures of the Wildwoods Farm. It wasn't magic; it was a deep and intuitive understanding; a gift of perception coupled with the capacity for genuine compassion. This empathy, combined with her remarkable observational skills, transformed her into an unparalleled investigator, a creature capable of uncovering even the most carefully concealed secrets.

It allowed her to navigate the complex web of relationships, to distinguish between genuine remorse and feigned innocence, to uncover the subtle nuances of deception and manipulation. She didn't merely gather information; she understood the context, the motivations, the unspoken desires and fears that drove the creatures of the Wildwoods Farm. Her insights weren't based on simple observation; they were born from an intimate understanding, a profound empathy that allowed her to see the world through the eyes of others, to inhabit their experiences, to feel their emotions, and to unlock the hidden truths that lay concealed beneath the surface.

This innate ability allowed Fiona to perceive the subtle shifts in the collective consciousness of the Wildwoods Farm. She could sense the collective anxiety following the accident, the ripples of fear and suspicion spreading through the community. This wasn't just an intellectual understanding; it was a felt experience, a visceral connection to the emotional landscape of the forest. She felt the collective sorrow, the shared grief over Jenny's fall, but also the simmering currents of suspicion and resentment that threatened to tear the community apart.

Understanding this collective emotional state allowed Fiona to focus her investigation; to identify those individuals and groups whose behavior deviated from the norm, whose actions betrayed their outward demeanor. She could sense the disharmony, the dissonance between what was being said and what was being felt. This ability to read the emotional undercurrents of the forest was crucial in her investigation, providing her with an invaluable guide to navigate the complex web of lies and half-truths surrounding Jenny's fall.

Fiona's empathy also allowed her to connect with the accused, Jasper. While Ink focused on the physical evidence, Fiona sought to understand Jasper's emotional state. She observed his subdued demeanor, the tremor in his voice when he spoke of Jenny, the guilt that shadowed his eyes despite his denials. She didn't judge him; she sought to understand his perspective, his fears, and his motivations. This empathetic approach allowed her to gain his trust, ultimately leading him to reveal a critical detail that had previously escaped his conscious memory, a detail that would turn the tide of the investigation.

In essence, Fiona's empathy wasn't just a tool; it was the very foundation of her investigative prowess. It allowed her to connect with every creature in the Wildwoods Farm, to understand their perspective, to tap into their emotions, and ultimately to uncover the truth behind Jenny's fall. Her capacity for empathy, her ability to feel what others felt, was the key to unlocking the mystery and bringing justice to the Wildwoods Farm. It was a testament to the power of understanding, the importance of compassion, and the extraordinary potential of empathy in uncovering even the most elusive truths.

Fiona's intuition wasn't simply a hunch; it was a sixth sense, a finely-tuned radar for the unspoken truths that shimmered beneath the surface of the Wildwoods Farm. While Ink meticulously collected physical evidence – a stray acorn, a displaced twig, a feather out of place – Fiona delved into the emotional landscape of the community, sensing the subtle tremors of guilt, the whispers of deception, the unspoken anxieties that rippled through the forest's inhabitants.

This intuitive ability manifested in myriad ways. One evening, while observing the gathering of gossiping hens near the accident site, Fiona noticed a peculiar detail. The hens, known for their incessant chatter and sharp observations, were unusually subdued. Their usual cacophony was replaced by hushed tones, furtive glances, and nervous clucking. While their words danced around the edges of the truth, their body language spoke volumes. Their postures were tense, their wings slightly drooped, a clear indication of suppressed anxieties rather than simple curiosity. This subtle shift in their demeanor, easily overlooked by a less perceptive observer, triggered an instinct in Fiona. She sensed a collective knowledge; a shared secret being concealed beneath their feathery exterior.

Intrigued, Fiona subtly shifted her focus. She observed a young hen, Heather, who usually dominated the flock with her boisterous pronouncements. Heather, however, was unusually quiet, avoiding eye contact and pecking nervously at the ground. Fiona sensed a shift in her demeanor, a nervousness that suggested more than mere fear of involvement. Heather's guilt was a subtle thing, a barely perceptible tremor in her movements, the slight way she shifted her weight from one leg to another, the way her eyes darted nervously around the gathering.

Following her intuition, Fiona approached Heather with caution, using soft purrs and gentle blinks to approach her cautiously. It took time, but eventually, Heather, overwhelmed by Fiona's calming presence, confessed a fragment of truth. She'd seen something, she murmured, something she'd tried to forget, a detail that would turn the investigation on its head. While Heather's recollection was fragmented and fear-laden, the image she painted - a brief glimpse of a flash of blue near the telephone pole at the precise moment of Jenny's fall - was a crucial piece of the puzzle, a detail that contradicted the initial assumptions and pointed towards a previously unconsidered suspect.

Fiona's intuitive insights also extended to inanimate objects. During her investigation, she discovered a partially hidden trail camera, cleverly disguised amongst the undergrowth. While Ink meticulously examined the camera's footage, Fiona felt a strange resonance emanating from the device, a feeling of hidden information that pulsed out from its mechanical heart. This sensation, a physical response to an unseen energy field, guided her to a specific point in the camera's footage, highlighting a crucial detail that Ink had missed.

The footage itself showed a blurry sequence at a critical moment. While Ink focused on the blurry faces, Fiona, through her intuitive sense, perceived a faint, almost imperceptible shimmer in the background. It seemed insignificant - a flicker of movement within a patch of reeds. But Fiona understood; to a keen observer like her, the slight movement wasn't just accidental; it represented a deliberate attempt at camouflage, a subtle deception. Further investigation into the area where the movement was detected revealed a small, hidden burrow, perfectly concealed and camouflaged among the reeds, indicating the precise spot where the culprit may have been hiding during the accident.

The discovery of the burrow led to the apprehension of the unexpected culprit: Barkley, a seemingly harmless badger known for his sweet disposition and generous nature. Barkley had been secretly competing with Jenny and Jasper for the coveted supply of acorns stored in the hollow of the old oak tree. The acorn supply was a significant source of sustenance during the approaching winter, creating a silent, competitive battle among the forest's inhabitants. Driven by his fear of losing the acorns, Barkley had devised a plan to get rid of his competitors, a scheme that accidentally resulted in Jenny's tragic fall.

Fiona's intuition wasn't just limited to solving the mystery of Jenny's fall. It allowed her to sense the underlying currents of tension and deception that rippled throughout the Wildwoods Farm. She could feel the collective sigh of relief that swept through the community once Barkley confessed, the gradual easing of the tension that had gripped the forest. She sensed the deep-seated regret of those who had prematurely judged Jasper, the shame in the gossiping hens' eyes as they realized the extent of their own assumptions and unwarranted accusations.

Through this experience, Fiona learned to trust her intuition even more. It wasn't a matter of mystical powers or clairvoyance; it was an intuitive skill honed by her years of close observation and deep understanding of the emotions and motivations of the forest's inhabitants. It was a testament to the power of empathy, the ability to not only observe but to truly feel the emotions of others, thereby uncovering the hidden truths that lie beneath the surface.

This ability allowed her to navigate the complex social dynamics of the Wildwoods Farm, to distinguish between genuine remorse and feigned innocence, to understand the unspoken anxieties and hidden motives that shaped the behavior of the forest's creatures. She had learned to listen not only to their words but to the silent language of their bodies, the subtle shifts in their demeanor, the barely perceptible tremors in their voices. It was a skill that transformed her into an exceptional investigator, capable of uncovering the truth even in the most intricate and carefully constructed webs of deceit.

Moreover, Fiona's intuition helped her understand the psychological impact of the accident on the community. She sensed the pervasive fear that gripped the forest, the underlying anxiety that threatened to tear the community apart. She perceived the collective grief, the shared sorrow over Jenny's death, but also the simmering currents of suspicion and resentment that shadowed the collective mourning. She understood how easily rumor and speculation could escalate into prejudice and injustice, how quickly assumptions could obscure the truth.

Fiona's sensitivity to these undercurrents helped her to manage the aftermath of the trial. While Ink focused on the legal aspects, Fiona focused on the emotional healing of the community. She helped the community members address their prejudices, their fear-based assumptions, and the guilt that stemmed from their participation in the swift judgment of Jasper. She guided the community towards forgiveness and reconciliation, fostering empathy and understanding through quiet conversations and gentle encouragement.

Her insights extended beyond the immediate aftermath of the trial. She realized that Barkley's actions weren't simply a result of his competitive spirit. There was a deeper issue at play: the scarcity of resources and the resulting competition that threatened to destabilize the forest's delicate ecosystem. This realization led her to advocate for a more sustainable approach to managing the forest's resources. She initiated a community-based project aimed at improving resource management, ensuring equitable distribution of the forest's bounty, preventing future conflicts and mitigating the risk of further tragic events.

Finally, Fiona's intuitive approach extended to a broader understanding of justice itself. She understood that justice wasn't simply about punishment; it was about understanding the root causes of conflict, about repairing the damages caused by misjudgment and prejudice, about fostering a sense of shared responsibility and community healing. Her investigation transcended the simple resolution of the mystery; it facilitated a profound transformation of the community's understanding of justice, leading to a more equitable, compassionate, and harmonious forest society. The case of Jenny's fall became a catalyst for change, a transformative experience that highlighted the vital importance of empathy, understanding, and the pursuit of truth in achieving true justice. The Wildwoods Farm, once shaken by suspicion and grief, began to heal, its inhabitants united by a newfound appreciation for the intricate web of life and the importance of understanding one another.

Fiona and Ink, despite their contrasting approaches, formed a partnership as seamless as the intertwining branches of the Wildwoods Farm. Ink, with his methodical nature and keen eye for detail, meticulously documented every clue, every footprint, every misplaced twig. He was the architect of the investigation, building a solid foundation of concrete evidence upon which Fiona's intuitive insights could flourish. He'd meticulously chart the locations of each witness, cross-referencing their statements with the physical evidence, creating a complex web of interconnected facts and probabilities. His notes, filled with precise measurements, detailed sketches, and meticulously cataloged observations, were a testament to his dedication and unwavering commitment to accuracy.

Fiona, on the other hand, operated on a different plane. While Ink focused on the tangible, Fiona perceived the intangible – the unspoken anxieties, the hidden resentments, the subtle shifts in demeanor that hinted at concealed truths. She was the artist, painting a vibrant picture of the community's emotional landscape, adding depth and nuance to Ink's factual framework. She was not simply observing; she was actively feeling the pulse of the Wildwoods Farm, sensing the collective anxieties that clung to the air like morning mist.

Their collaboration was a beautiful dance of logic and intuition, a harmonious blend of science and art. Ink's meticulous documentation provided Fiona with a framework, a solid foundation upon which she could build her intuitive interpretations. His findings guided her investigations, allowing her to focus her empathetic skills on the individuals most likely to hold the key to the mystery. For instance, after Ink had mapped the movements of the hens near the accident site, Fiona was able to focus her attention on Heather, the subdued hen who displayed such obvious signs of hidden guilt.

Conversely, Fiona's insights often pointed Ink in new directions. Her intuition, for example, led them to the hidden trail camera. While Ink meticulously analyzed the footage, identifying blurry forms and analyzing the time stamps, Fiona's perception of a subtle shimmer in the background led them to the badger's hidden burrow, a detail that had completely escaped Ink's keen eye. Her intuition didn't replace his meticulous analysis; it enhanced it, adding another layer of understanding to his already comprehensive investigations.

Their communication wasn't always verbal. A shared glance, a subtle nod, a knowing purr – these non-verbal cues formed a sophisticated language between them. They understood each other's strengths and limitations, compensating for each other's shortcomings with effortless grace. Ink, for instance, was occasionally overwhelmed by the sheer volume of information, his analytical mind struggling to sort through the myriad details. At such times, Fiona would offer a calming presence, subtly guiding him toward the most pertinent information with quiet confidence. Her gentle reassurances helped keep Ink focused amidst the chaotic complexities of the investigation, providing crucial emotional support.

On other occasions, Fiona would stumble upon a detail that sparked her intuition, only for Ink to offer a critical counterpoint, grounding her observations in logical possibility. He would examine her hunches with his characteristic methodical thoroughness, testing her insights against the hard evidence. He acted as a vital anchor to Fiona's intuitive leaps, ensuring that her insights were not merely subjective impressions but were grounded in the reality of the situation.

Their combined skills extended beyond the investigation itself. Their partnership was a masterclass in collaborative problem-solving, demonstrating how different perspectives, approaches, and skills could be interwoven to achieve a shared goal. They taught each other; Ink learned to trust his intuition a little more, to see beyond the hard facts, while Fiona learned to appreciate the value of detailed evidence and the necessity of a solid logical framework.

One evening, huddled together by the crackling warmth of a firefly lantern, Ink recounted his findings from the interviews with the other squirrels. He described the conflicting accounts, the inconsistencies in their testimonies, and the evident tension between them. Fiona listened intently; her emerald eyes gleaming with thoughtful concentration. As Ink spoke, she began to notice patterns in his accounts, subtle shifts in emphasis, and fleeting expressions that hinted at unspoken truths. She detected a faint undercurrent of resentment and rivalry within the squirrel community, a competitive spirit that ran far deeper than simple jealousy over acorns. It was a subtle detail, easily missed, but Fiona recognized it as a key to unlocking a deeper layer of understanding within the case.

This realization, inspired by Ink's meticulous documentation, allowed Fiona to revisit her earlier observations. She recalled a specific interaction she had witnessed between two squirrels, Amber and Pete, during a previous investigation. While seemingly insignificant at the time, this interaction now took on a new significance in light of Ink's recent discoveries. Amber, usually gregarious, had been unusually withdrawn, her demeanor suggesting a deep-seated anxiety and fear. This new understanding enabled Fiona to re-interview Amber with a far more focused and insightful approach.

Their partnership transcended the merely professional. A deep respect and affection had grown between them, built upon their shared experiences and mutual admiration for each other's unique skills. They were friends, colleagues, and partners in the pursuit of justice. They celebrated each other's successes, offering comfort and support during moments of frustration and uncertainty. They were the yin and yang of investigation – the meticulous detective and the intuitive empath, perfectly balanced, an unstoppable force in the pursuit of truth within the Wildwoods Farm.

Their collaborative efforts had far-reaching consequences. Not only did they solve the mystery surrounding Jenny's death, but they also brought about a profound change in the Wildwoods Farm community. The trial presided over by the wise owl, Judge Hoot, highlighted the dangers of prejudice and assumptions, promoting a culture of empathy and understanding. The community's ability to move beyond its own biases and embrace the truth, in large part, was a testament to the investigative duo's unwavering pursuit of justice and their dedication to ensuring that the truth was not only discovered but also understood.

Fiona and Ink's partnership became a legend in the Wildwoods Farm, a testament to the power of collaboration, the value of diverse perspectives, and the profound impact of a shared commitment to justice. Their story served as a reminder that the pursuit of truth often requires a multifaceted approach, a blend of meticulous investigation and intuitive understanding, a harmonious collaboration of intellect and empathy. The Wildwoods Farm was a safer, more just, and more compassionate place, thanks to the unwavering dedication of Ink and Fiona, the unlikely pair who proved that even the smallest of creatures could make a monumental difference in the pursuit of justice.

Chapter 12

The Broken Twig

The damp earth clung to Ink's paws as he knelt beside the base of the ancient oak, the afternoon sun filtering weakly through the dense canopy above. He'd spent the better part of the morning meticulously examining the area around the telephone pole where Jenny had fallen, his keen eyes missing nothing. He'd measured the distances between footprints, analyzed the soil composition for any unusual disturbances, and even cataloged the types of moss growing on the surrounding rocks. Yet, the crucial piece of the puzzle remained elusive.

Fiona, perched gracefully on a low-hanging branch, watched him with a patient, knowing gaze. Her feline senses, far more attuned to the subtleties of the forest than Ink's, had already picked up on a faint scent, a trace of something unusual near the base of the oak. It was a subtle aroma, almost imperceptible to a less sensitive nose, a faint whiff of disturbed earth mixed with something else... something faintly metallic.

Ink, engrossed in his detailed analysis of a particularly unusual pattern of squirrel droppings, failed to notice Fiona's subtle shift in position. He was meticulously sketching the arrangement, noting the precise orientation of each pellet, when a tiny, almost invisible object caught his eye. It was a small, broken twig, no larger than his little finger, lying half-buried in the soft earth. It was unusually dark, almost black, as though charred or stained.

He carefully picked up the twig with his delicate paws, examining it under the dappled sunlight. The break was clean, almost precise, as if snapped rather than broken by natural forces. There was a slight discoloration near the break, a faint smudge of a brownish substance. Ink's keen eyes registered the detail instantly. He recognized it from his previous investigations – it was the residue of a particular type of berry, one known to be highly toxic to squirrels. A dangerous berry commonly found only on the far side of the woods outside Wildwoods Farm, a territory rarely visited by Jenny.

He carefully placed the twig in a small, airtight container, his mind already racing. This small, seemingly insignificant piece of debris could be the key to unlocking the entire mystery. The break was too clean, too precise for a simple accident. It was a deliberate act. But who would deliberately snap a twig at the scene of an accident? And why?

Fiona, sensing the significance of Ink's discovery, leaped down from her branch and joined him. She sniffed at the twig, her head tilted slightly to one side. She confirmed the metallic scent he'd detected, a faint trace of blood mixed with the soil and berry residue. The blood was so diluted, it would have been undetectable without her acute sense of smell.

"The berry residue," Ink murmured, his voice barely a whisper. "It's from the Nightshade berries. Highly toxic. But why would anyone place a Nightshade berry near the scene of an accident?"

Fiona purred softly, a low rumble in her chest. "Perhaps it wasn't an accident at all, Ink. Perhaps it was a deliberate attempt to frame someone."

The possibility hung between them, heavy with unspoken implications. If Jenny had been poisoned, the broken twig could be a crucial piece of evidence, linking the culprit to the scene of the crime. The deliberate placement of the twig, combined with the Nightshade berry residue and the trace amounts of blood, suggested a calculated plan to incriminate someone else. But who?

Ink meticulously examined the surrounding area again; his attention now focused on finding other potential clues related to the Nightshade berries. He carefully brushed away the loose soil near the oak's roots, revealing a tiny, almost invisible trail leading away from the broken twig. It was a barely visible path, so faint that only Fiona's keen senses and Ink's unwavering attention to detail would have noticed it.

The trail led to a dense thicket of bushes, a place rarely visited, secluded and hidden from the main pathways of the Wildwoods Farm.

As they cautiously pushed aside the tangled branches, they discovered a small clearing. In the center lay a single Nightshade bush, its dark, ominous berries glistening in the weak sunlight. And beneath the bush, nestled amongst the fallen leaves, lay another clue – a small, intricately carved wooden acorn.

The acorn was too finely crafted to be a simple toy. It was clearly a piece of artisan work, far more sophisticated than anything a typical squirrel would produce. It was adorned with tiny carvings, intricate designs that resembled a stylized representation of a telephone pole and a squirrel, almost as if depicting the scene of the accident itself. The acorn, upon closer inspection, bore a faint scent of the same metallic blood Fiona had detected on the broken twig.

The discovery of the acorn provided a crucial link to a suspect previously overlooked. It belonged to Amber, a squirrel known for her exceptional craftsmanship and her quiet, reserved nature. Amber had been initially dismissed as a mere witness; her subdued demeanor interpreted as indifference. But now, the acorn provided undeniable evidence that she was somehow involved. The subtle artistry, the faint bloodstains, the connection to the Nightshade berries – it all pointed to her. This was not a coincidence; this was a deliberate act.

Ink and Fiona exchanged a look. The broken twig wasn't just a piece of evidence; it was a meticulously placed clue, designed to mislead the investigators. The killer had tried to frame someone else, but the meticulous nature of their crime had ironically betrayed them. The broken twig, so seemingly insignificant, had revealed a truth far more sinister and complex than they initially imagined. It revealed a plan, a calculated attempt to create a false narrative, to shift blame, to obscure the true events of that fateful day.

The next step was to confront Amber and confront her with the evidence. But Ink and Fiona knew they had to proceed cautiously. Amber's quiet demeanor masked a hidden depth, a potential for both cunning and despair. They had to approach her with tact and understanding, allowing her to confess her actions willingly, rather than forcing a confession which could yield false information. The truth, they understood, was far more precious than a simple conviction. They had to uncover the motive, the reasons behind Amber's actions. Only then could they truly understand the tragedy of Jenny's death and bring a sense of closure to the Wildwoods Farm community. The investigation was far from over.

The broken twig had opened a door, but the path beyond it was shrouded in shadows and secrets yet to be revealed. The true story was yet to unfold, and Ink and Fiona, hand-in-paw, were ready to face whatever lay ahead. The justice of the Wildwoods Farm depended on their ability to unravel the complicated web of deceit and lies that lay at the heart of this tragic mystery. The weight of the community rested on their tiny shoulders. They were not just investigators; they were the guardians of truth and justice in the Wildwoods Farm.

Ink carefully held the broken twig, its surface cool and smooth against his sensitive paws. The break was undeniably clean, almost surgical in its precision. He rotated it slowly, examining the fractured ends under the dappled sunlight filtering through the leaves. There was a subtle discoloration, a faint, almost invisible stain near the break – the residue of the Nightshade berry, a detail he'd noted earlier. But this wasn't just any Nightshade berry; it was a specific variety, one with a particularly potent toxin, found only in the deepest, darkest parts beyond the Wildwoods Farm, far beyond Jenny's usual foraging grounds.

Fiona, ever vigilant, circled the base of the oak, her tail twitching rhythmically. Her keen senses were working overtime, picking up on the faintest of scents, the subtle whispers of the forest floor. She detected a trace of something else, a subtle metallic tang that mingled with the aroma of the disturbed earth and the Nightshade residue. It was a faint scent of blood, so diluted it would have been imperceptible to an ordinary nose, yet clear as day to her heightened feline senses.

"Blood," she murmured, her voice a low purr. "And not just any blood, Ink. Squirrel blood, I think."

Ink nodded grimly. The combination of the Nightshade berry residue and the trace amount of blood pointed to a deliberate act, a carefully planned crime. The broken twig wasn't just a random piece of debris; it was a crucial piece of evidence, a meticulously placed clue. But why? Why would anyone plant a Nightshade-stained twig near the scene of an apparent accident? The answer, he suspected, lay in the deliberate nature of its placement, the precision of its break, the carefully chosen location. It was a calculated attempt to mislead, to point the finger of suspicion towards someone else.

He spent the next hour painstakingly analyzing the surrounding area. He examined the soil, searching for any signs of disturbance, any footprints that might have been overlooked. He meticulously measured the distances between the twig and other objects, searching for patterns, for clues that might reveal the culprit's movements. He even examined the insects, carefully observing their behavior, looking for any indication of recent activity near the twig.

The insects, he noticed, were oddly clustered around a particular area near the twig. Upon closer inspection, he realized why. There was a small patch of unusual discoloration in the soil, a slightly darker shade than the surrounding earth. He carefully dug at the spot, revealing a tiny, almost imperceptible depression, barely noticeable unless one knew what to look for.

Inside, nestled amongst the loose soil, he found a minute fragment of something hard and smooth. He carefully extracted it, revealing a tiny piece of a polished acorn, barely larger than a grain of rice. The fragment was intricately carved, adorned with tiny, almost microscopic details – a stylized representation of a squirrel, clinging precariously to a telephone pole.

He recognized the style immediately. It was the unmistakable work of Amber, a talented squirrel known for her exquisite craftsmanship and her exceptionally quiet demeanor. Amber had been considered a mere witness, her reserved nature mistaken for indifference. But this tiny fragment of a carved acorn, found near the poisoned twig, changed everything. It placed her directly at the scene of the crime.

Fiona, who had been patiently observing Ink's meticulous examination, let out a soft meow. She had detected a faint scent on the tiny fragment of acorn – the same metallic scent of blood she had detected on the twig. This was no longer a circumstantial link; this was conclusive evidence.

The broken twig, meticulously placed, served as a cunning distraction, diverting attention away from the true culprit. The placement of the Nightshade berries, the subtle trace of blood, the tiny fragment of the acorn – each element was part of a carefully orchestrated plan to frame someone else, to create a false narrative. The killer had been remarkably thorough, but their meticulousness was their undoing. Their eagerness to ensure a perfect crime had ironically revealed their guilt.

The question now was, who was being framed and why? Ink and Fiona began to delve deeper into Amber's life. They learned she had a history of quiet rivalry with Jenny, a competition born not of malice but of a shared ambition – to be the finest acorn carver in the Wildwoods Farm. Jenny's recent success, winning a prestigious acorn-carving competition, might have sparked a simmering resentment, a quiet jealousy that festered beneath Amber's quiet exterior. The pressure, coupled with her own deep-seated insecurities, might have driven her to an act of desperation.

But even with this suspicion solidifying, Ink and Fiona knew they couldn't jump to conclusions. They needed more evidence, more confirmation before confronting Amber. They spent the next few days quietly observing her, watching her interactions with the other forest creatures, paying close attention to her demeanor, searching for any signs of guilt or remorse.

They discovered that Amber hadn't been merely rivaling Jenny, she was also deeply insecure about her craft, always comparing her own work to Jenny's flawless artistry. This insecurity had grown into a sense of inadequacy, making her believe she was a failure compared to Jenny. Jenny's victory had broken Amber. The accident, they found, was a desperate attempt to sabotage Jenny's reputation. This wasn't murder, but a desperate cry for help, a twisted attempt to steal Jenny's success.

Armed with this understanding, they approached Amber, not as investigators seeking a confession, but as friends seeking to understand. The careful way they approached her, considering the emotional fragility of the situation, allowed Amber to admit to her act, the guilt weighing heavily upon her heart. She confessed to her involvement with the Nightshade berries and the broken twig, not as an act of malice, but as a misguided attempt to prove herself, a desperate act born out of insecurity and a deeply wounded pride.

The community, upon hearing the truth, showed both compassion and justice. Amber's punishment was not a harsh judgment, but a path towards healing, a chance to confront her insecurities and find peace. The trial itself was a community effort, a chance for everyone to acknowledge their own biases and assumptions. The Wildwoods Farm learned a valuable lesson about the importance of understanding and empathy, the dangers of quick judgments, and the fragility of truth when clouded by prejudice and assumptions. The broken twig, a seemingly insignificant piece of evidence, had become a symbol of the forest's journey towards understanding, acceptance, and a renewed commitment to truth and justice. The incident highlighted how easily assumptions could cloud judgment and how even a seemingly insignificant detail can hold the key to solving the most complex of mysteries.

The journey to trace the twig's origin began not in the bustling heart of the Wildwoods Farm, but at its quietest edge, near the murmuring stream where Amber, the meticulous acorn carver, often sought solace. Ink, his keen eyes scanning the ground, noticed the faintest impression in the soft earth, a barely perceptible drag mark, almost invisible to the untrained eye. He followed the almost imperceptible trail, his sensitive nose twitching, picking up the faint, earthy scent of the twig, a scent unique to the specific type of oak it originated from. The trail, barely more than a ghost of a path, led him away from the scene of the apparent accident, towards a secluded grove of ancient oaks, their branches draped with thick moss and shimmering with the morning dew.

The grove was Amber's sanctuary, a place where she honed her craft, her tiny hands shaping acorns into exquisite works of art. Ink found the specific type of oak he was searching for, its leaves rustling gently in the breeze. He circled the tree, his gaze sharp, his senses heightened. He discovered a small, almost imperceptible gouge in the trunk of the oak, a fresh wound where a twig had been snapped off. The size and shape of the wound were a perfect match for the broken twig found near Jenny's fall. The evidence was undeniable. The twig had indeed originated from this tree, within Amber's private grove.

But the discovery raised more questions than it answered. Why would Amber, the quiet and unassuming acorn carver, break a twig from her beloved oak? And what was the significance of the Nightshade berry residue found on the twig? Ink and Fiona knew they needed to delve deeper, to uncover the hidden motives behind this seemingly insignificant act.

Fiona, with her unparalleled sense of smell, began to investigate the immediate vicinity of the broken twig's origin. She sniffed at the base of the oak, her whiskers twitching as she detected a faint, unfamiliar scent mingled with the earthy aroma of the forest floor. It was a subtle fragrance, almost imperceptible, a blend of crushed herbs and something else... something metallic.

The metallic scent, Fiona realized, was faint traces of blood. But this wasn't the fresh, vibrant scent of a recent injury; it was old, dried blood, barely clinging to the earth, almost lost to time. It suggested that the twig had not been broken recently, but perhaps days or even weeks prior. This contradicted the timeline of events surrounding Jenny's fall. The broken twig was clearly placed strategically; it wasn't a random piece of debris, but a meticulously chosen element in a much larger scheme.

Ink, his mind racing, realized that the Nightshade berry residue and the trace of blood weren't simply coincidental elements; they were carefully orchestrated clues. They were pieces of a puzzle designed to mislead, to deflect suspicion towards someone else. But who? And why?

Following the faint trail of dried blood, Ink discovered a partially concealed depression in the ground, hidden beneath a cluster of ferns. Inside, nestled amidst the loose earth and decaying leaves, he found a tiny, intricately carved acorn, almost identical to those created by Amber but unfinished, its surface stained with the same metallic blood. The acorn was significantly different, its design more primitive than Amber's usual work. The carving style was strangely inconsistent, a rougher attempt in comparison to Amber's precise and delicate work.

It wasn't Amber's usual precision, indicating either a rushed attempt or an act performed in duress. The blood stains corroborated Fiona's earlier findings. The acorn had been carved near the time of the blood spill. This was crucial evidence. This piece, however crude, indicated a hidden hand at play. Someone had not only placed the broken twig but also carefully concealed the remnants of their work, a piece that tied them to both the crime and the original injury.

Their investigation now broadened, shifting from focusing solely on the broken twig to understanding the context surrounding this hidden acorn. Who would have used Amber's design, even crudely imitating it? The answer, Ink and Fiona realized, lay in the deeper social dynamics of the Wildwoods Farm.

They discovered a secret rivalry amongst the acorn carvers, a hidden competition not of malice but of artistic ambition. Jenny, the squirrel who had fallen, was known for her exceptionally skilled craftsmanship, her delicate and flawlessly executed work consistently winning accolades. Amber, while immensely talented, always lived in Jenny's shadow, her creations, though exquisite, often overshadowed by Jenny's stunning pieces.

Ink and Fiona then uncovered a series of events: a long-standing tension between Amber and Jenny, fueled not by outright hostility, but by a simmering resentment fueled by Amber's perceived lack of recognition despite her immense talent. The acorn carving competition, which Jenny recently won, was the catalyst for Amber's actions. The pressure to keep up with Jenny's successes, the subtle snipes from other squirrels about her seeming lack of progression—all these factors had taken a toll.

The broken twig, the Nightshade berries, the crude acorn—they weren't tools of murder, but desperate attempts to sabotage Jenny's reputation, to prove herself worthy. The blood belonged to Amber herself. The Nightshade berries, planted to misdirect blame, were a result of a panicked attempt to destroy evidence, and the broken twig was a misdirection, a red herring. Amber's actions weren't malicious; they were borne from desperation and a profound sense of inadequacy.

Amber, when confronted, didn't try to deny her actions. Instead, she confessed to the events that transpired, her voice trembling with a mixture of guilt and relief. She had not intended to harm Jenny, but her actions, though misguided, were ultimately acts of self-sabotage and deep-seated insecurity.

The community, guided by Ink and Fiona's thorough investigation, responded not with judgment but with compassion. Amber's punishment wasn't harsh retribution, but a path to healing, to address her insecurity and find peace and acceptance within the community. The trial was a turning point for the Wildwoods Farm, a collective reckoning with their biases and assumptions. They learned a profound lesson about empathy and the danger of hasty judgments. The incident, a tragedy initially, transformed into a journey of communal understanding, acceptance, and healing. The broken twig, once a symbol of suspicion and deceit, became a testament to the power of truth and the restorative potential of empathy and justice.

The significance of the broken twig, initially seemingly insignificant, now resonated deeply within Ink's analytical mind. It wasn't merely a piece of debris; it was a meticulously placed clue, a deliberate piece in a larger, more intricate puzzle. The twig, its delicate structure fractured, held a story within its very grain. Its position, near Jenny's fallen body, had immediately pointed suspicion towards Jasper. Yet, upon closer examination, it revealed a different narrative, a carefully crafted deception. The Nightshade berry residue clinging to its splintered surface served as a crucial marker, a deliberate attempt to mislead the investigation.

Ink recalled the subtle, almost imperceptible drag marks in the soft earth leading away from the scene, a trail that only a keen eye like his could have noticed. He retraced his steps, his mind meticulously piecing together the sequence of events. The twig's origin wasn't random. The almost invisible trail led to Amber's secluded grove, a sanctuary hidden amidst the ancient oaks. There, amidst the rustling leaves and the soft earth, the exact type of oak from which the twig originated stood, its trunk bearing a fresh wound—a perfect match for the broken piece. It was undeniable; the twig had been deliberately broken and placed. But why?

This wasn't a simple act of vandalism; it was an orchestrated act, a complex maneuver designed to implicate Jasper falsely. The presence of Nightshade berries, known for their potent, hallucinogenic properties, served to strengthen this theory. Their inclusion was not accidental; they pointed to a deliberate attempt to obscure the truth, to create a misleading narrative. Someone had carefully selected the twig, added the Nightshade berries, and strategically positioned it near Jenny's fallen body. The precision of the act spoke of careful planning, a deliberate strategy, a calculated attempt to frame Jasper for Jenny's unfortunate fall.

Fiona, ever vigilant, chimed in, her feline senses adding another layer to the mystery. "The blood," she purred, her emerald eyes fixed on Ink, "it was old, dried blood. Not fresh. The scent was faint, almost gone, indicating it had been there for some time, possibly weeks." This contradicted the immediate timeline surrounding Jenny's fall. The placement of the twig wasn't spontaneous; it was a calculated act of deception, meticulously planned and precisely executed.

The old, dried blood was a critical piece of the puzzle. It suggested the twig's breakage and subsequent placement weren't directly linked to the accident. This shifted the focus of the investigation away from a simple act of malice towards a much more elaborate scheme, a plot involving misdirection and calculated deception. The initial impression—a straightforward case of accidental death complicated by a malicious act—was now unraveling to reveal a far more complex scenario.

The combination of the broken twig, the Nightshade berries, and the old, dried blood created a compelling case of circumstantial evidence, each piece pointing toward a deliberate attempt to frame an innocent party. But who was behind this meticulously planned deception? And what was their motive? The answer, Ink realized, lay not only in the physical evidence but also in the intricate web of relationships within the Wildwoods Farm.

Ink and Fiona delved deeper into the social dynamics of the community, uncovering a hidden rivalry between the acorn carvers, a silent competition fueled not by malice but by ambition. Jenny, renowned for her impeccable craftsmanship, had consistently overshadowed Amber, whose talent, while considerable, remained largely unrecognized. The recently concluded acorn carving competition, won decisively by Jenny, seemed to have triggered a profound sense of inadequacy in Amber.

The unearthed unfinished acorn, crudely carved in imitation of Jenny's style, provided a crucial link. It was a piece of unfinished business, a symbol of Amber's suppressed frustration and a desperate attempt to compete, to finally achieve recognition. The blood found near the acorn belonged to Amber herself. She'd been injured while attempting to create a piece worthy of acclaim, her self-inflicted injury a desperate act.

The Nightshade berries, a clumsy attempt to destroy evidence, and the broken twig, a calculated misdirection, were all desperate attempts to shift blame away from herself. Amber's actions were driven by self-doubt and a yearning for acceptance, not by malicious intent. Her desperate act, though misguided, was not an attempt to harm Jenny, but to elevate her own standing. The carefully staged evidence was a cry for recognition, a desperate attempt to find her place within the community.

The broken twig, therefore, was not a tool of murder, but a desperate plea, a misplaced attempt to rectify a deep-seated sense of inadequacy. It was a symbol of Amber's internal struggle, a testament to the destructive power of self-doubt and the lengths to which an individual may go to gain recognition. It was a powerful metaphor for the hidden pressures within the community, showcasing how ambition, if left unchecked, can lead to desperate and self-destructive actions.

The careful examination of the twig, along with the other seemingly insignificant pieces of evidence, led Ink and Fiona to a surprising conclusion: a conclusion that shifted the narrative from accusation and judgment to understanding and compassion. Their investigation, far from being a simple pursuit of justice, became a profound exploration of human nature, highlighting the complexities of motivation and the fragility of truth when distorted by self-doubt and societal pressures.

The case of the broken twig, initially presented as a simple piece of circumstantial evidence, transformed into a powerful allegory, illustrating the importance of careful observation and the dangers of jumping to conclusions. Ink and Fiona's meticulous investigation not only brought justice to the accused but also exposed the underlying emotional turmoil within the Wildwoods Farm community, proving that even in the most seemingly straightforward cases, the truth can often be far more nuanced and complex than it initially appears.

The trial that followed was not a judgment, but a healing process. The community, confronted with the truth, reacted not with anger but with empathy, understanding the pressure and insecurities that drove Amber to such desperate actions. The focus shifted from assigning blame to fostering understanding and healing. The incident, once a source of division, became a catalyst for unity, a testament to the power of empathy and forgiveness.

The broken twig, initially a symbol of deception, became a potent symbol of transformation. It served as a stark reminder of the importance of understanding the underlying causes of behavior, the dangers of quick judgments, and the potential for healing and reconciliation when truth is uncovered with compassion and understanding. It was a lesson learned not only by the community of the Wildwoods Farm but by all who heard their tale. The truth, meticulously uncovered, paved the way not for retribution, but for forgiveness, understanding, and the ultimate triumph of empathy and justice.

The broken twig, a seemingly insignificant piece of debris, had become the linchpin of Ink and Fiona's investigation. Its symbolism extended far beyond its physical form; it represented the fragility of truth, the ease with which it could be manipulated, and the crucial need for careful observation. The initial impression – a simple piece of evidence pointing towards Jasper's guilt – had dissolved under the weight of meticulous scrutiny. The twig's placement, the Nightshade berry residue, the faint traces of old blood – each detail, once seemingly isolated, now formed a cohesive narrative, a story far more complex than initially perceived.

Ink, ever the pragmatist, revisited the scene of the accident. He examined the soil again, his keen eyes scanning for any overlooked clues. He noticed the subtle variations in the earth's texture, the minute differences in the compaction of the soil near the base of the telephone pole. This suggested a struggle, a subtle push and pull, not a forceful shove as initially assumed. The initial reports of a loud thud followed by a scream now seemed less definitive, their accuracy clouded by the panicked responses of the witnesses. He realized that the witnesses' accounts, while well-intentioned, were filtered through the lens of their own biases and pre-conceived notions. Fear, shock, and the natural human tendency to simplify complex events had led to inaccurate recollections.

Fiona, ever perceptive, focused on the sensory details. The faint scent of pine needles masked the lingering odor of the Nightshade berries, suggesting a deliberate attempt to cover the scent trail. She meticulously examined the twig itself, noting the specific type of oak from which it originated and its peculiar fracture pattern, suggesting a specific kind of force, not a sudden break from a fall. She noticed the almost imperceptible scratches on the twig, marks too small to be visible to the naked eye, but readily detectable through her acute feline senses. These marks, she theorized, were made by something small and sharp, perhaps a small carving tool.

The broken twig, therefore, wasn't just a piece of evidence; it was a meticulously crafted tool of deception. It was a symbol of the manipulative power of circumstantial evidence, highlighting the dangers of relying on assumptions and the importance of questioning every detail, every seemingly insignificant observation. It became a potent metaphor for the complexities of truth and the seductive nature of fabricated narratives.

Ink and Fiona's investigation broadened beyond the immediate vicinity of the accident. They explored the social fabric of the Wildwoods Farm, delving into the relationships between its inhabitants. They discovered a simmering tension between the acorn carvers, a hidden rivalry masked by polite cordiality. Amber, a talented but underappreciated carver, had been overshadowed by Jenny's brilliance. The recent acorn-carving competition, where Jenny's artistry had eclipsed Amber's, had cast a long shadow over Amber's self-esteem.

Their investigation unveiled a hidden narrative, a tale of unacknowledged ambition and thwarted aspirations. Amber's deep-seated insecurities, fueled by the competitive spirit of the Wildwoods Farm, had driven her to desperate actions. The broken twig, the Nightshade berries, the subtle manipulation of the scene – these were not acts of malice, but desperate cries for recognition.

They discovered Amber's unfinished acorn, a piece of work abandoned mid-creation, reflecting her struggle to match Jenny's skill. The carving style, a clear imitation of Jenny's distinctive technique, revealed Amber's intense desire to surpass her competitor. The marks on the twig mirrored the tool marks on the unfinished acorn, suggesting a possible connection. Moreover, a small amount of Amber's blood, dried and barely visible, stained the underside of the unfinished sculpture.

The old, dried blood on the twig, initially a confusing anomaly, now fell perfectly into place. The injury was self-inflicted, a result of Amber's frustrated attempts to carve an acorn worthy of recognition. Her desperate act of self-harm was not an attempt to hurt herself permanently but a manifestation of her internal struggle, a symbol of her self-doubt and the intense pressure she felt to achieve success.

The Nightshade berries, previously interpreted as a sinister attempt to mislead the investigation, were now viewed in a different light. They were a clumsy, desperate attempt to destroy evidence, to erase the signs of her struggle and inadvertently implicate another. The placement of the berries near the twig was not a calculated act of malice but rather a panicked attempt to cover her tracks, a desperate act of self-preservation fueled by shame and regret.

The broken twig, once a symbol of deception and potential murder, transformed into a powerful symbol of Amber's internal struggle. It represented the vulnerability of truth under the weight of intense pressure and the desperate measures individuals may take when feeling unseen, unheard, and undervalued. It was a metaphor for the insidious nature of self-doubt and the potential for self-destructive behavior when ambition overshadows rational thinking.

The trial that followed was a stark contrast to the initial atmosphere of suspicion and accusation. It was a process of reconciliation, a journey towards understanding and empathy. The community, armed with the full understanding of Amber's motivations, responded not with anger but with compassion. They recognized the pressure to succeed, the crushing weight of comparison, and the destructive nature of unacknowledged insecurity. The focus shifted from assigning blame to nurturing healing and fostering compassion.

The broken twig, presented as evidence in the trial, became a symbol of transformation and forgiveness. It served as a reminder of the importance of understanding the underlying causes of actions before passing judgment. The community learned a valuable lesson about the dangers of jumping to conclusions and the power of empathy in resolving conflicts. The case of the broken twig transformed from a simple mystery into a profound exploration of the human condition, highlighting the complexities of motivation, the fragility of truth, and the importance of understanding before judging. The Wildwoods Farm, once divided by suspicion, found unity through shared understanding and compassion. Justice was served not through punishment, but through healing, fostering a sense of community stronger than before. The broken twig, a symbol of deception initially, ultimately became a beacon of hope, reminding everyone of the potential for reconciliation and the healing power of empathy. The narrative of the broken twig ended not with a condemnation but with a shared understanding, paving the way for forgiveness and renewed community spirit. The tale of the broken twig served as a powerful reminder that even in the darkest of situations, the light of understanding and compassion can illuminate the path towards healing and reconciliation.

Chapter 13

The Culprit's Motive

Amber's motive, initially shrouded in a fog of circumstantial evidence, gradually revealed itself as a complex tapestry woven from ambition, insecurity, and a desperate yearning for recognition. It wasn't a premeditated act of malice, but a desperate cry for help, a silent scream lost in the bustling clamor of the Wildwoods Farm. The competitive spirit that infused the community, while often inspiring, had also cultivated a climate of intense pressure, where success was measured not by personal growth but by the overshadowing of others.

Jenny, with her innate talent and effortless artistry, had become an unwitting symbol of Amber's own perceived failures. The acorn carving competition, the culmination of months of intense preparation, had become a battleground for Amber's suppressed insecurities. Jenny's triumph had not merely been a victory for one squirrel; it had been a stark and painful reminder of Amber's perceived shortcomings, a public acknowledgment of her inability to match her rival's skill.

This wasn't about jealousy, though a trace of it undoubtedly lingered in Amber's heart. It was deeper, more profound; it was a desperate longing to be seen, to be acknowledged, to finally break free from the shadow of Jenny's brilliance. Amber had poured her heart and soul into her own acorn carving, striving to match Jenny's elegance and precision. But the more she tried, the further away her success seemed. The pressure mounted, transforming into an agonizing weight that threatened to crush her spirit.

Days bled into nights as Amber toiled away, her hands aching, her eyes bloodshot. Each imperfect carve was a blow to her self-esteem, a painful reminder of her perceived inadequacy. Her unfinished acorn, a testament to her struggle, lay abandoned amidst a pile of discarded wood shavings—a silent confession of her failure. The very act of imitation, the deliberate replication of Jenny's unique style, was an expression of her desperation. She wasn't merely trying to create a beautiful piece of art; she was attempting to possess a piece of Jenny's success, to absorb her talent, to finally attain the validation she so desperately craved.

The act of mimicking Jenny's style was not an act of betrayal; it was a desperate attempt to gain recognition, to achieve a sense of self-worth that had eluded her for so long. It was a cry for attention, a desperate plea for approval. It was as if, through imitation, she hoped to magically acquire the talent and recognition that she felt had been unjustly bestowed upon her competitor. It was an attempt to gain some measure of control in a situation she felt completely powerless to change.

The Nightshade berries weren't a calculated attempt to mislead the investigation; they were a desperate, impulsive act born from shame and regret. Their placement, seemingly deliberate, was actually a haphazard attempt to erase the traces of her struggle, to eliminate the evidence of her desperate efforts to attain the recognition she so craved. Amber's clumsy manipulation of the scene wasn't the mark of a seasoned criminal; it was the frantic act of someone overwhelmed by guilt and consumed by the fear of exposure.

The broken twig itself was not a weapon, but a casualty of Amber's internal conflict. The subtle marks, visible only to Fiona's keen eyes, were not the result of malicious intent, but rather the byproduct of Amber's frustrated attempts to perfect her own carving. The tool used to make these marks, almost identical to those on her unfinished acorn, was further evidence of this desperate attempt to bridge the gap between her aspiration and her ability. In her haste and desperation, she had unintentionally created a piece of evidence that would later be misinterpreted as a tool of murder.

The self-inflicted injury, the dried blood barely visible on the unfinished acorn, was not a deliberate act of self-harm, but a manifestation of the intense pressure and self-doubt that had consumed her. The wound was a physical representation of her internal struggle, a manifestation of her deep-seated insecurities. It was a desperate attempt to alleviate the emotional pain of her perceived failure, a self-punishment for her inability to match Jenny's talent.

The seemingly calculated placement of the berries and the broken twig near the base of the telephone pole was not a strategic move to frame Jasper, but a desperate attempt to conceal her own involvement, to deflect attention away from her own failings. She didn't intend to harm anyone; she simply wanted to erase the evidence of her struggle, to obliterate the remnants of her perceived inadequacy. The fear of exposure, the shame of failure, had driven her to these desperate measures, blurring the lines between intention and consequence.

The truth, once revealed, wasn't a simple matter of guilt or innocence; it was a complex narrative of ambition, insecurity, and the desperate yearning for recognition. Amber's actions, while misguided and ultimately harmful, were rooted in a deeper, more profound struggle—a struggle with self-doubt, a struggle with the pressures of a fiercely competitive community, and a struggle to find her own worth independent of external validation. Her motive, far from being malicious, was a desperate attempt to find her place in the sun, a place she felt she had been unfairly denied.

The community of the Wildwoods Farm, initially consumed by suspicion and quick judgment, ultimately embraced empathy and compassion. They understood the pressure Amber had been under, the crushing weight of comparison, and the destructive nature of unchecked ambition. They recognized the fragility of the truth, how easily it could be distorted by fear, prejudice, and the innate human desire to simplify complex situations. They learned the importance of looking beyond surface appearances and understanding the underlying causes of behavior before passing judgment.

The broken twig, once a symbol of potential murder and deception, became a symbol of transformation and forgiveness. It became a testament to the restorative power of understanding, a reminder that even the most seemingly heinous actions can be rooted in a desperate need for love, acceptance, and recognition. The Wildwoods Farm, healed by the revelation of Amber's true motives, emerged stronger and wiser, united by a newfound appreciation for compassion, empathy, and the importance of seeking the genuine truth before rendering judgment. The tale of the broken twig was not simply a mystery solved, but a lesson learned—a lesson about the intricate nature of the heart, the destructive power of unchecked ambition, and the profound capacity for forgiveness and redemption.

Amber's story, however, didn't begin with the acorn carving competition or the tragic fall of Jenny. It began much earlier, in the quiet, shadowed corners of the Wildwoods Farm, where the sunlight rarely reached, and the whispers of insecurity held sway. Amber was not always the ambitious, intensely competitive squirrel she had become. In her youth, she was a timid creature, easily overshadowed by her more boisterous siblings. While they clambered for attention and playfully vied for the best nuts, Amber preferred the solitude of the ancient oak tree at the edge of the woods, her days filled with quiet observation rather than boisterous competition.

She possessed a keen eye for detail, a talent for noticing the subtle nuances of the forest. While her siblings chased butterflies and played games, Amber would spend hours studying the intricate patterns of the bark, the delicate veins in leaves, the subtle shifts in the woodland light. This wasn't a lack of social interaction; it was simply a different way of engaging with the world. Amber found solace in quiet contemplation, finding beauty and satisfaction in the hidden details that most squirrels overlooked. Her natural inclination was towards artistic expression, a talent she discovered in the art of acorn carving.

Unlike her siblings, who pursued more conventional squirrel ambitions—gathering nuts, building nests, and participating in the community's lively social gatherings—Amber found solace in her art. The intricate detail of her carvings became her form of self-expression, her silent conversation with the world. She carved tiny creatures from acorns, each one unique, each one a reflection of her contemplative nature. However, her quiet solitude often left her feeling invisible, her talents unappreciated. While her siblings received praise and attention for their athletic prowess and social skills, Amber's artistic endeavors went largely unnoticed.

This lack of recognition began to gnaw at her self-esteem. She yearned for the same validation that her siblings seemed to effortlessly receive. She began to crave the attention she felt she deserved, a longing that transformed into a deep-seated insecurity. She started to question her worth, wondering if her talents were truly valuable, or simply a quiet hobby, insignificant in the grand scheme of the Wildwoods Farm. The seeds of her ambition were sown in this fertile ground of insecurity and unacknowledged talent.

The arrival of Jenny, a young squirrel with natural talent and an outgoing personality, further exacerbated Amber's feelings of inadequacy. Jenny was immediately embraced by the community, her cheerful disposition and effortless artistic skill winning over the hearts of all who met her. Amber watched, a mixture of admiration and resentment swirling within her. She couldn't deny Jenny's talent; it was undeniable, captivating. But the community's constant praise and accolades for Jenny served as a painful reminder of Amber's own quiet existence.

It wasn't simply jealousy, although that certainly played a part. It was a deeper, more profound feeling of being overlooked, a feeling of being unworthy of recognition. Amber began to compare herself to Jenny, measuring her own progress against her rival's success, leading to an ever-growing sense of self-doubt. The more she tried to compete, the more she felt she was falling short. The pressure to succeed, to match Jenny's effortless brilliance, became an unbearable weight, fueling the insecurity that had simmered within her for so long.

The acorn carving competition wasn't just a contest; it was a crucible, a testing ground for Amber's fragile self-esteem. She poured her heart and soul into her own carving, desperately striving to match Jenny's elegance and precision. She spent countless hours honing her skills, but the more she worked, the more she felt the gap between her aspirations and her ability widen. She struggled to replicate Jenny's unique style, not out of malice, but out of a desperate need to prove her worth, to finally achieve the recognition she so deeply craved.

The night before the competition, Amber worked herself into a state of near-exhaustion. Her hands were aching, her eyes bloodshot, and her spirit weary. The unfinished acorn lay before her, a testament to her struggle, a physical manifestation of her inner turmoil. The thought of failure was unbearable, the prospect of being forever overshadowed by Jenny, a bitter pill to swallow. In her desperation, she resorted to imitation, attempting to replicate Jenny's style, a desperate act born from insecurity and the crushing weight of unmet expectations.

The Nightshade berries, the misplaced twig, the self-inflicted wound – these weren't acts of premeditation or malicious intent; they were desperate attempts to cope with the overwhelming pressure she felt. They were impulsive actions driven by fear, shame, and regret, stemming from a deep-seated insecurity and a desperate yearning for recognition. Amber's actions were not the actions of a seasoned criminal, but the frantic maneuvers of someone overwhelmed by guilt and consumed by the fear of exposure.

Her past experiences, her quiet childhood, her unacknowledged talents, and the overwhelming presence of Jenny, all contributed to the culmination of events that led to the tragic accident. Her motive wasn't to harm Jenny; it was to achieve recognition, to break free from the shadow of her own insecurities and finally claim a place in the sunlight. Her story was not simply a tale of a culprit, but a story of a misunderstood soul, grappling with the crushing weight of ambition, insecurity, and the desperate yearning for recognition in a world that often overlooks the quiet voices. It was a story of how easily ambition, left unchecked, can lead to unintended consequences, blurring the lines between aspiration and destruction. And ultimately, it was a story about the need for understanding, compassion, and forgiveness, even in the face of tragedy. The Wildwoods Farm would learn this lesson, a lesson as vital and intricate as the carvings Amber had once so painstakingly created.

The weight of her actions pressed down on Amber like the heavy branches of the ancient oak tree. The vibrant hues of the forest, once a source of solace, now mocked her with their cheerful indifference. The sunlight, which had once filled her with a sense of quiet contentment, felt harsh and accusatory, highlighting the shadows that now clung to her like a second skin. She had never intended for Jenny to fall; it hadn't been a calculated act of malice, but a desperate, clumsy attempt to seize the attention she craved, a frantic reach for a spotlight that had always seemed just out of her grasp.

The memory of Jenny's fall played on an endless loop in her mind; a horrific film reel she couldn't stop watching. The sharp crack of the branch, the gasp of surprise, the sickening thud – each detail seared itself into her consciousness, a constant, throbbing reminder of the consequences of her actions. The remorse wasn't a fleeting pang of guilt; it was a deep, gnawing ache that settled in her chest, a constant companion that weighed her down, sapped her strength, and left her feeling utterly alone.

Sleep offered no escape. Her dreams were haunted by the image of Jenny's lifeless form, her bright eyes dimmed, her once vibrant fur dull and lifeless. She dreamt of frantic whispers, of accusing eyes, of the community's judgment weighing her down. She would awaken in a cold sweat, her heart pounding, the chilling reality of her actions washing over her once more. Even in wakefulness, the forest seemed different, charged with a palpable sense of judgment. The rustling leaves seemed to whisper accusations, the gentle breeze carried the murmurs of condemnation, and the very shadows seemed to deepen, reflecting the darkness that had taken root within her heart.

Amber tried to find solace in her art, returning to the acorn carving, the activity that had once brought her peace and satisfaction. But the delicate tools, once extensions of her creativity, felt heavy and unwieldy in her trembling hands. The smooth, hard surface of the acorn offered no comfort, only a constant reminder of the clumsy, fatal miscalculation that had altered the course of her life and shattered the peace of the Wildwoods Farm. The once-familiar comfort of the ancient oak tree, where she had found solitude and inspiration, now seemed like a place of exile, a stark reminder of her failure and her isolation.

She attempted to speak to her siblings, to confess her actions, to share the crushing burden of guilt she carried, but the words caught in her throat. The shame was too overwhelming, the fear of rejection too profound. She knew they would be disappointed, perhaps even disgusted. The thought was unbearable, and so she remained silent, alone with her remorse, her guilt a heavy cloak wrapped tightly around her. She observed the other squirrels, their lives continuing, seemingly untouched by the tragedy that had befallen them all, yet the tragedy remained at the heart of Amber's world, a constant and pervasive reality.

The community's reactions were, to her, a constant reminder of her culpability. She had unintentionally caused so much pain, so much chaos. The whispers and hushed conversations followed her like shadows, and though no one directly accused her, she felt their judgment as acutely as if they were shouting her name. Every sideways glance, every hushed word, was a dagger twisting in her already wounded heart. She yearned for forgiveness, but feared that it was beyond her reach, an unattainable dream lost in the depths of her despair.

The image of Ink, the ferret investigator, and Fiona, the insightful feline, persistently haunted her thoughts. She knew they were searching for the truth, piecing together the fragments of a devastating puzzle, and the thought that they might discover the truth—her truth—filled her with a terror that rivaled the regret she already felt. She lived in constant fear of exposure, the dread making it difficult for her to maintain a semblance of normality. Even the most mundane activities, like gathering nuts or grooming her fur, seemed an insurmountable challenge under the weight of her secret. She had traded the quiet solace of her solitude for a suffocating solitude of her own making, a prison built of her own guilt and remorse.

The nights were the worst. The darkness amplified her fear and regret, transforming the familiar sounds of the Wildwoods Farm into a cacophony of accusations. She tried to find comfort in the starlit sky, searching for some sign of hope or forgiveness amidst the celestial bodies. But even the stars seemed to mock her, cold and distant, their brilliance unable to penetrate the darkness that had enveloped her soul. The days were little better; sunlight, once a source of joy, now served only to highlight the emptiness within her, the hollowness that had replaced the quiet contentment she had once known.

Her appetite dwindled. The nuts she once cherished now tasted like ash. Sleep offered little escape, her dreams filled with horrifying visions of Jenny's fall, the accusing eyes of the forest community, and the relentless pursuit of Ink and Fiona. She had lost her zest for life, her vibrant spirit extinguished by the weight of her guilt and the unrelenting dread of exposure. Her actions had not only brought tragedy to Jenny, but had also destroyed a part of herself, leaving behind a hollow shell filled with nothing but regret and despair.

Even the small joys she once found in life – the intricate beauty of the forest, the warmth of the sun on her fur, the camaraderie of her siblings – now seemed to mock her, harsh reminders of what she had lost and the irreparable damage she had caused. She tried to find a way to atone for her actions, but the path to redemption seemed impossibly long and arduous, a daunting journey fraught with self-doubt and uncertainty. She was lost in a labyrinth of her own making, trapped in a cycle of regret, with no clear path towards forgiveness, either from herself or from the community she had betrayed. The thought that her ambition and her longing for recognition had led her down such a devastating path—that her desire for recognition had ultimately resulted in loss, devastation, and a life steeped in regret—was a constant torment. It was a lesson learned at too great a price, a testament to the catastrophic consequences of unchecked ambition and the profound importance of honesty and integrity. The quiet solitude she had once cherished was now a stark reflection of her own internal isolation, a consequence of her actions, a punishment self-imposed in the depths of her despair. And so, Amber waited, bracing herself for the inevitable consequences of her actions, living each day as a penance for the life she had irrevocably altered. The burden she carried was immense, a weight that threatened to crush her, leaving her only with the bitter taste of regret and the stark realization that some mistakes, once made, can never truly be undone.

The days bled into weeks, each sunrise a fresh reminder of the darkness that clung to Amber. The forest, once her sanctuary, felt like a cage, its beauty dulled by the weight of her guilt. She longed to undo her actions, to rewind time and prevent the tragedy, but the past remained immutable, a stark and unforgiving reality. The vibrant colors of the wildflowers seemed to mock her, their cheerful brilliance a stark contrast to the grayness that had settled over her spirit. She found herself drawn to the quietest corners of the woods, seeking solace in the solitude of the deepest shadows, the rustling leaves a constant, mournful accompaniment to her internal turmoil.

One evening, as the sun dipped below the horizon, painting the sky in hues of orange and purple, Amber stumbled upon a clearing she'd never noticed before. Nestled amongst the ancient trees was a small, dilapidated birdhouse, its once vibrant colors faded and chipped. A sudden inspiration sparked within her. She would rebuild it, a small act of restitution, a gesture of atonement. The thought filled her with a fragile hope, a flicker of light in the suffocating darkness of her despair.

Over the next few days, Amber worked tirelessly. She gathered twigs and leaves, carefully selecting the strongest branches and the most vibrant foliage. She spent hours smoothing the rough edges of the wood, her nimble paws working with a newfound purpose. It was slow, painstaking work, but each carefully placed twig, each meticulously woven leaf, represented a step towards redemption, a tangible manifestation of her remorse. As she worked, she allowed herself to remember Jenny, not just the tragedy of her fall, but the joyful times they had shared, the innocent games they had played, the warmth of their friendship.

The rebuilding of the birdhouse became a form of therapy. It was a way to channel her grief and guilt into something constructive, a tangible expression of her regret. The meticulous work demanded focus, keeping her mind occupied and preventing her thoughts from wandering towards the crushing weight of her guilt. With each completed task, a small measure of peace settled over her, a fragile hope that perhaps, just perhaps, she could find a way to make amends.

The birdhouse wasn't just a physical object; it became a symbol of her journey towards redemption. It represented her commitment to rebuilding what she had broken, not just the birdhouse, but also the trust and harmony of the Wildwoods Farm community. She envisioned the birds returning to their home, their cheerful chirping a testament to her effort, a tiny melody of hope in the symphony of the forest. The project helped to channel her pent-up emotions, transforming her despair into productive action.

As the birdhouse neared completion, Amber began to think about how she could make amends to the community. She knew that simply rebuilding a birdhouse wouldn't erase the pain she had caused, but it was a start, a tangible symbol of her remorse. She resolved to perform acts of kindness, to help others whenever she could. She began by assisting her siblings with their chores, sharing the burdens she had previously avoided. She helped gather nuts and berries, offering her assistance to those who needed it. She offered words of comfort to the grieving squirrels, listening to their stories of loss and offering a quiet presence of support. She didn't expect immediate forgiveness, but she hoped that her actions would, over time, demonstrate the sincerity of her remorse.

She also began to cultivate a small garden near the old oak tree, planting wildflowers and herbs. The vibrant colors and delicate fragrances of the flowers provided a comforting contrast to the somber feelings she had carried for so long. It was a slow process, but with each tiny seed she planted, she felt a sense of hope blossoming within her. The garden became a sanctuary, a space where she could reconnect with nature and find solace in the beauty of creation. It was a tangible representation of her efforts to rebuild, to nurture, and to restore harmony to her surroundings. It was a quiet and understated attempt to contribute positively to the community she had hurt, an expression of her desire to heal not just herself but the wounds she had inflicted on others.

One day, while tending her garden, she saw Ink and Fiona observing her from a distance. Her heart pounded in her chest; the fear of exposure threatened to overwhelm her. She braced herself for their questions, their accusations. But to her surprise, their expressions were not those of judgment. There was a quiet understanding in their eyes, a sense of empathy that touched her deeply.

They approached her slowly, their movements gentle and respectful. Fiona purred softly, a comforting sound that soothed Amber's anxious heart. Ink spoke, his voice soft and understanding. He didn't accuse her; he simply listened as she recounted her actions, her motivations, and the profound regret she felt. He listened attentively, his keen eyes studying her, not with suspicion, but with a compassionate understanding.

Their acceptance wasn't a sudden erasure of her guilt, but it was a lifeline, a signal that forgiveness was possible. It was the start of a long and difficult journey towards reconciliation, but it was a journey she was now prepared to embark on. The weight of her guilt remained, but it no longer felt quite so crushing. There was now a flicker of hope, a belief that she could earn the community's forgiveness through actions and consistent effort to demonstrate genuine remorse.

The act of rebuilding the birdhouse and her ongoing efforts to help the community became a testament to her transformation. The seeds of remorse she had planted within herself had begun to blossom into acts of kindness and selflessness. The forest, once a source of overwhelming guilt, gradually became a space of healing and renewal. The vibrant colors of the wildflowers, the fragrant herbs in her garden, the cheerful chirping of birds in the restored birdhouse, all reflected her slow but steady progress on her journey towards redemption. It wasn't an overnight miracle; it was a long and difficult process that required consistent effort, sincere repentance, and a steadfast commitment to making amends. The community, observing her actions, began to understand the depth of her remorse and the sincerity of her efforts.

The journey towards complete forgiveness was far from over, but Amber's transformation and her relentless efforts to make amends had begun to heal the wounds she had inflicted. The Wildwoods Farm, once scarred by tragedy, was slowly beginning to heal, a testament to the restorative power of sincere remorse and the enduring strength of community. Amber's story became a quiet reminder that even the most grievous mistakes can be atoned for, that even the darkest shadows can yield to the light of redemption, and that forgiveness, though a difficult path, is ultimately possible. The forest, in its quiet wisdom, offered her a second chance, a testament to the capacity for hope, healing, and forgiveness even in the face of great loss and profound regret. The scent of wildflowers and the gentle rustle of leaves now carried a quiet message of hope, a testament to the transformative power of remorse and the enduring possibility of healing.

The weight of her secret pressed down on Amber like the heavy winter snows that once blanketed the Wildwoods Farm. She'd lived with the lie for weeks, the silent accusation in the eyes of the other animals a constant torment. Even the playful chatter of the young squirrels, usually a source of joy, now grated on her nerves, a constant reminder of her role in Jenny's accident. Sleep offered no escape; her dreams were filled with the horrifying replay of that fateful afternoon, the sickening thud, and Jenny's lifeless form at the base of the telephone pole.

One morning, she awoke to find a single, perfect acorn nestled beside her. It was a small thing, insignificant, yet it held a power that resonated deep within her. It was a gift, a silent offering from the forest, a gesture of hope in the midst of her despair. That acorn became a symbol; a reminder that even in the darkest of times, life finds a way to persist, to grow, to renew.

She began to spend her days observing the forest with new eyes. Before, she'd only seen the things that served her purpose, the nuts she could gather, the paths she could traverse. Now, she noticed the intricate details, the delicate dance of the sunlight through the leaves, the patient growth of the moss on the ancient trees, the silent communication between the creatures of the woods. She saw the interconnectedness of everything, the delicate balance that sustained the community. Her actions, she realized, had irrevocably disrupted that balance, jeopardizing the very harmony she had taken for granted.

This newfound understanding sparked a profound sense of remorse. It wasn't just about Jenny's death; it was about the damage she had inflicted on the community, the erosion of trust, the spread of suspicion and fear. She'd acted out of selfishness, driven by a childish desire for attention, a desperate need to prove herself. Her actions had been thoughtless, reckless, and ultimately devastating. The realization filled her with a deep and abiding sorrow. She wasn't merely sorry for the consequences; she was truly sorry for who she had been, for the choices she had made.

Amber's transformation began subtly. She started by confessing to her family. The initial shock and disappointment were profound, but eventually, understanding dawned in their eyes. They saw the genuine remorse etched on her face, the depth of her regret. Their forgiveness wasn't immediate, but it was offered, a small act of grace that fueled her desire for redemption. They helped her to channel her sorrow into constructive actions.

She began by quietly helping others. She offered assistance to the older squirrels, carrying heavy nuts and berries, lending a helping paw to those struggling with their tasks. She offered words of comfort to grieving families, listening patiently to their stories of loss and sharing their pain. She started mending things – broken branches, damaged nests, tattered leaves. These small acts of service, performed without fanfare or expectation of reward, became her penance, her way of making amends for her past transgressions.

Her transformation extended beyond simple acts of service. She began to cultivate an empathy she hadn't possessed before. She observed the way the birds built their nests, the patience and care they invested in their homes. She listened to the whispered secrets of the wind rustling through the leaves, the silent language of the forest unfolding around her. She learned to understand the subtle cues of the animals around her, their unspoken anxieties and vulnerabilities. She began to see the forest, not as a source of resources to be exploited, but as a complex and interconnected community deserving of respect and protection.

Her once selfish desires were gradually replaced by a deep-seated compassion. The need for self-aggrandizement faded, replaced by a genuine desire to contribute positively to the life of the community. The constant need for external validation dissipated as she found internal satisfaction in acts of kindness and selflessness. She found joy not in boasting or showing off, but in quietly assisting those in need. Her desire to prove herself transformed into a desire to be a valuable member of the community.

The transformation wasn't easy. Days of deep sorrow and self-recrimination were followed by moments of fragile hope and renewed determination. She still carried the weight of her actions, but the burden felt lighter, eased by the progress she was making. Her actions weren't intended to erase the past, but to demonstrate the depth of her remorse and her sincere commitment to making amends.

Her garden, initially a solitary refuge, became a symbol of her growth. It flourished with vibrant wildflowers and herbs, attracting bees and butterflies, a quiet testament to her commitment to nurturing life. The garden represented not only her own personal healing but also the restoration of balance within the community. The growth of her flowers mirrored the growth within her, a slow and steady process of renewal and regeneration.

One evening, Ink and Fiona found her tending to her garden. They didn't approach with accusations but with a quiet understanding, a recognition of her sincere efforts to atone for her past mistakes. Their acceptance wasn't a sudden absolution; it was a confirmation that her journey towards redemption was genuine, that her transformation was real. It was a profound affirmation of the power of remorse, and the possibility of forgiveness.

Amber's story became a cautionary tale, but also a testament to the power of transformation. Her journey, though arduous, was a testament to the resilience of the animal spirit, the capacity for growth, and the enduring possibility of redemption. Her story served as a reminder that even in the wake of profound loss and devastating mistakes, the path to healing and forgiveness is always open. The forest, in its quiet wisdom, had offered her a second chance, a testament to the enduring power of hope and the restorative nature of community. The Wildwoods Farm leaves carried not only the memory of tragedy but also the quiet promise of a brighter future, a future built on remorse, understanding, and the enduring power of forgiveness. The scent of wildflowers and the gentle rustle of leaves now carried a hopeful melody, a testament to the enduring possibility of healing and the transformative power of a heart changed by remorse.

Chapter 14

Restorative Justice

The concept of restorative justice, as it unfolded in the Wildwoods Farm, wasn't something explicitly codified in laws or scrolls. Instead, it emerged organically from the very fabric of the community, a reflection of their interconnected lives and their shared understanding of interdependence. It wasn't about punishment, not in the traditional sense of retribution or revenge. Instead, it focused on repairing the harm caused by Amber's actions, healing the wounds inflicted on Jenny's family, and restoring the fractured trust within the community.

Ink, the ferret investigator, with his sharp mind and even sharper nose, played a pivotal role in guiding the community toward this restorative approach. He understood that simply identifying Amber as the culprit wasn't sufficient. The real challenge lay in addressing the root causes of her actions, the underlying reasons that led her to behave so recklessly. He subtly steered the community's response away from anger and condemnation, and towards a process of dialogue, understanding, and reconciliation.

Fiona, the insightful feline known as *The Whisper*, contributed her unique skills by facilitating communication. She had an uncanny ability to sense the unspoken emotions swirling beneath the surface of interactions. Her gentle demeanor and quiet observations allowed her to navigate the complex emotional landscape of the situation, creating a space where vulnerable truths could be shared without fear of judgment. She helped Amber, Jenny's family, and the community as a whole to express their feelings, anxieties, and needs, fostering a sense of empathy and mutual understanding.

The restorative justice process started with a series of carefully orchestrated meetings. These weren't formal trials with rigid procedures and accusatory pronouncements. Instead, they were intimate gatherings, facilitated by Fiona and Ink, where all those affected by the accident—Amber, Jenny's family, and other community members—were invited to participate.

The first meeting focused on Amber's confession. She didn't simply reiterate her actions; she delved deep into her motivations, explaining the underlying insecurities and anxieties that had fueled her recklessness. She spoke of her desperate need for attention, her yearning for acceptance, and the crippling self-doubt that had clouded her judgment. Her honesty, raw and vulnerable, stunned the community into silence. There were tears, not of anger, but of empathy and shared understanding.

Jenny's parents, initially consumed by grief and rage, found themselves grappling with Amber's confession. They saw not a malicious intent but a misguided plea for recognition, a cry for help from a troubled young squirrel. The process allowed them to process their own grief, to express their pain and loss without resorting to blame. Fiona helped them to articulate the depth of their sorrow, allowing the community to bear witness to their suffering and offer comfort.

Following Amber's confession, the meetings shifted to focus on the harm caused and the ways it could be repaired. It wasn't just about Amber making amends for Jenny's death; it was about healing the damage she had inflicted on the entire community. The erosion of trust, the spread of rumors, and the pervasive sense of fear – all of these needed to be addressed. Discussions revolved around the community's shared responsibility in fostering a culture of empathy, understanding, and support. They talked about the dangers of making assumptions, the importance of clear communication, and the need to cultivate a culture of responsible behavior.

One of the key elements of the restorative justice process was the creation of a community project dedicated to Jenny's memory. This wasn't a somber memorial, but a collaborative effort designed to embody the spirit of community and resilience. The community decided to plant a beautiful meadow filled with Jenny's favorite wildflowers, creating a vibrant space where the community could gather, celebrate Jenny's life, and reaffirm their collective commitment to supporting one another.

Amber played a central role in this project, dedicating her time and energy to nurturing the meadow, transforming it into a symbol of hope and renewal. This work wasn't merely an act of penance; it was a way for her to contribute positively to the community, a tangible demonstration of her remorse and commitment to making amends. The process of creating the meadow became a shared experience, fostering collaboration and healing among community members who had previously been divided by suspicion and mistrust.

In addition to the communal project, Amber engaged in a series of individual acts of service. She helped the elderly squirrels with their daily tasks, assisted families in need, and shared her skills in nut gathering and food preservation. These acts weren't forced or obligatory; they were expressions of genuine care and a desire to contribute meaningfully to the community's well-being.

The restorative justice process in the Wildwoods Farm wasn't a quick fix; it was a long, arduous journey of healing and reconciliation. There were moments of tension, of lingering resentment, and of emotional setbacks. But the underlying principle—the focus on repair, understanding, and shared responsibility—remained constant. It was a process that required patience, empathy, and a willingness to engage in difficult conversations, to confront uncomfortable truths, and to work collaboratively toward a shared vision of healing and restoration.

Over time, the community transformed. The initial grief and anger gradually gave way to compassion, understanding, and forgiveness. Amber's actions served as a catalyst for profound change, pushing the community to examine its own flaws, to address its weaknesses, and to cultivate a stronger sense of interconnectedness. The meadow, blooming with vibrant wildflowers, became a symbol of this transformation, a testament to the enduring power of restorative justice to heal wounds, repair fractured relationships, and nurture a more just and compassionate community.

The success of this restorative approach wasn't solely measured by the absence of punishment or retribution, but by the tangible changes within the community: the stronger bonds, the enhanced empathy, and the increased sense of collective responsibility. The community learned that justice wasn't simply about punishing wrongdoers but about restoring harmony, promoting healing, and fostering a culture of mutual support and understanding. This experience served as a powerful lesson, not just for Amber, but for the entire community of the Wildwoods Farm, demonstrating the profound transformative potential of restorative justice.

Ink and Fiona, having observed the process unfold, realized that their role was not merely to uncover the truth but to guide the community towards a more compassionate and restorative form of justice. They learned that real justice was not about retribution, but about healing and reconciliation. It wasn't about assigning blame but about understanding the complex interplay of factors that contributed to the tragic accident. The restorative process they facilitated was a testament to the power of empathy, compassion, and shared responsibility in resolving conflicts and building a stronger, more resilient community. The Wildwoods Farm, once fractured by grief and suspicion, began to heal, its collective spirit strengthened by the shared experience of restorative justice. The sound of rustling leaves, once a somber reminder of loss, now carried a melody of hope and renewal. The scent of wildflowers, once a poignant symbol of tragedy, now represented the promise of a brighter future, a future built on understanding, forgiveness, and the enduring power of community. The story of Jenny, Amber, and the Wildwoods Farm became a quiet testament to the transformative potential of restorative justice, a beacon of hope for other communities struggling to find their way to healing and reconciliation. The forest itself, in its quiet wisdom, seemed to breathe a sigh of relief, its ancient trees swaying gently in the breeze, as if celebrating the enduring power of compassion and forgiveness. The whisper of the wind carried not just the memory of Jenny, but the promise of a future where justice and compassion walked hand in hand.

The trial, if it could even be called that, unfolded not within a formal courtroom, but under the dappled sunlight filtering through the leaves of the Wildwoods Farm. There was no judge's gavel, no raised hand swearing oaths. Instead, there was a circle of mossy stones, carefully arranged by Fiona, creating a space for shared reflection and dialogue. This wasn't a contest of guilt or innocence, but a gathering aimed at understanding, healing, and restoring balance within their interconnected community.

At the heart of the process was the principle of shared responsibility. It wasn't just about Amber's actions; it was about the community's role in creating an environment where such an accident could occur. The discussions weren't accusatory; they were introspective, exploring the unspoken pressures, the subtle biases, and the systemic issues that had contributed to the tragedy. Ink, ever the meticulous investigator, had compiled a detailed record of statements, meticulously documenting inconsistencies and highlighting the spread of misinformation. He presented this not as evidence against Amber, but as a collective reflection of their community's flaws. He pointed out the assumptions made, the gossip spread, the lack of empathy that had clouded their judgment. This wasn't about assigning blame; it was about fostering collective understanding and acknowledging shared shortcomings.

Fiona's role was crucial in guiding the emotional currents of the gathering. She wasn't just facilitating; she was actively weaving a tapestry of empathy, her calming presence allowing for vulnerability and honest self-reflection. She encouraged each participant to share their feelings—grief, anger, guilt, remorse—without judgment. She created a space where even the most deeply buried emotions could safely surface. This wasn't about assigning blame; it was about understanding the emotional landscape that had shaped everyone's responses to the accident. Fiona's gentle guidance allowed individuals to see beyond their initial reactions and begin to understand the perspectives of others. She encouraged active listening and empathetic responses, subtly nudging the community toward a more cohesive and understanding approach.

The trial's structure was fluid and organic, adapting to the shifting emotional landscape of the participants. There were moments of intense emotion, tears shed, voices raised in frustration. But Fiona and Ink expertly navigated these tumultuous moments, guiding the conversation back to the central goal: healing and reconciliation. They used creative methods to facilitate understanding. They asked participants to imagine themselves in each other's shoes, to articulate their feelings from different perspectives. This imaginative exercise helped break down ingrained biases and prejudices, creating a path towards mutual empathy. Through carefully structured questions and thoughtful prompts, they ensured everyone felt heard, understood, and validated.

The process wasn't a linear progression; it was a cyclical journey of reflection, revelation, and reconciliation. There were moments of relapse, instances where old wounds resurfaced, and tensions flared. However, Fiona and Ink's unwavering commitment to the process, their steadfast belief in the restorative approach, helped guide the community through these challenges. They emphasized the importance of patience and perseverance, reminding the participants that healing was a journey, not a destination.

One of the remarkable aspects of the trial was its ability to address the broader systemic issues underlying the accident. The community's tendency toward gossip, their quick judgments based on incomplete information, and the lack of support for individuals struggling with emotional challenges – all these issues came to the forefront during the discussions. The trial wasn't just about resolving the immediate conflict; it was about facilitating community-wide growth and change. This broader perspective on restorative justice transformed the focus from the narrow issue of the accident to a holistic examination of their collective well-being.

The trial was interspersed with moments of creative expression. The community's artists created vibrant murals depicting the healing process, reflecting the stages of grief and reconciliation. Their musicians composed haunting melodies that captured the pain of loss and the hope of healing. This artistic collaboration transformed the process from a purely verbal exercise into a multi-sensory experience of healing and reflection. It created a shared narrative; a collective memory that transcended individual experiences and helped foster a shared sense of purpose and resilience.

Amber's participation was crucial. She didn't simply confess; she actively engaged in the process, expressing genuine remorse and taking ownership of her actions. She wasn't simply the "culprit"; she became a vital contributor to the healing process, an active participant in building a stronger, more resilient community. Her active involvement wasn't about punishment; it was about rehabilitation, about allowing her to contribute positively to the community and to earn back the trust she had lost.

The trial culminated not in a verdict, but in a collective commitment to change. The community established a dedicated support system for those struggling with emotional or mental health challenges. They developed clear guidelines for communication and conflict resolution, emphasizing empathy, understanding, and respectful dialogue. The meadow, dedicated to Jenny's memory, became a living symbol of this commitment, a testament to their shared efforts towards healing and transformation.

The Wildwoods Farm trial was unique not for its legal innovations, but for its profound humanity. It was a testament to the power of collective reflection, empathy, and restorative justice. It demonstrated that true justice wasn't about assigning blame and punishment, but about healing wounds, restoring trust, and strengthening the bonds of community. It demonstrated that even in the face of immense loss, a community could find the strength to reconcile, rebuild, and emerge stronger and more compassionate than ever before. The rustling leaves whispered not of judgment, but of forgiveness, healing, and the enduring strength of the community's collective spirit. The story of Jenny, Jasper, and Amber became a legend, a tale recounted to future generations, a reminder of the transformative power of restorative justice. It was a story that whispered of hope, reminding them that even in the darkest of times, the light of compassion and understanding could illuminate the path towards healing and reconciliation. The gentle breeze carried the scent of wildflowers and the promise of a brighter future, a future where justice and compassion danced hand-in-hand, weaving a tapestry of harmony and understanding throughout the Wildwoods Farm.

The air thrummed with a quiet energy, a palpable sense of anticipation hanging heavy in the meadow. The mossy stones, arranged in a perfect circle, seemed to hum with the collective weight of the community's hopes and anxieties. This wasn't a courtroom, with its rigid hierarchies and adversarial procedures. This was a gathering, a communal effort to unravel the tangled threads of misunderstanding and sorrow that had woven themselves into the fabric of their lives since Jenny's fall. The trial, if it could be called that, was a testament to the Wildwoods Farm unique approach to justice—a process built not on blame and punishment, but on understanding, empathy, and collective responsibility.

Unlike a traditional court proceeding where the judge holds absolute authority, this gathering was profoundly democratic. Every member of the Wildwoods Farm community, from the wise old owl perched high in the oak tree to the smallest field mouse scurrying through the undergrowth, had a voice. Their participation wasn't simply passive observation; it was active involvement, a shared responsibility in the pursuit of truth and healing. Fiona, with her gentle guidance and insightful questions, facilitated the process, ensuring that every voice was heard, every perspective considered. She navigated the delicate balance between individual expression and collective understanding, ensuring that the conversation remained focused on the shared goal of reconciliation.

The process began with a moment of silence, a shared acknowledgment of the loss and grief that bound them together. Then, slowly, cautiously, the stories began to emerge. Each individual recounted their experience of the day Jenny fell, their recollection shaped by their unique perspectives and biases. The gossiping hens, initially quick to judge, confessed their role in spreading unsubstantiated rumors, their clucking chorus of speculation echoing the community's tendency to jump to conclusions without sufficient evidence. The shrewd cats, known for their observant eyes, admitted their initial suspicions, while acknowledging their failure to fully investigate the situation before passing judgment. Even the seemingly impartial squirrels recounted their own observations, revealing subtle details that had been initially overlooked.

The community's participation extended beyond mere testimony. They actively engaged in the process of uncovering the truth, challenging assumptions, and confronting their own biases. They shared their interpretations of the events, questioned inconsistencies in accounts, and collaborated to create a more complete and nuanced picture of what transpired on that fateful day. It was a collective detective story, with each individual playing a vital role in solving the mystery. The process was not without its difficulties. Emotions ran high, tensions flared, and old rivalries resurfaced. However, under Fiona's careful guidance, the community collectively navigated these emotional currents, focusing on fostering mutual understanding and building bridges instead of erecting walls of accusation.

The discussion moved beyond the immediate circumstances of Jenny's fall to address the deeper systemic issues that had contributed to the tragedy. They explored the dynamics of their community, examining their patterns of communication, their tendency towards gossip, and their approach to conflict resolution. This introspection was crucial in understanding the roots of the misunderstandings and biases that had clouded their judgment. They acknowledged their flaws as a community, recognizing their collective responsibility in fostering an environment where assumptions and prejudices could flourish unchecked.

This recognition of shared responsibility wasn't simply an abstract concept; it had practical implications. The community decided to implement a comprehensive program for communication and conflict resolution. They established clear protocols for verifying information before spreading rumors, encouraging mindful communication and active listening. They developed strategies for conflict resolution, focusing on restorative measures rather than punitive actions. These changes were not just a response to Jenny's accident; they were a collective commitment to building a healthier and more resilient community, preventing similar tragedies in the future.

Furthermore, the community actively worked to address the emotional needs of its members. They established a support network for individuals struggling with emotional distress, providing a safe and supportive space for sharing feelings and seeking help. They organized workshops on empathy, communication skills, and conflict resolution, empowering every member to contribute to a more harmonious community. This focus on emotional well-being reflected a fundamental shift in their approach to justice, recognizing that true justice requires not only addressing the external circumstances but also nurturing the emotional health of individuals within the community.

The creative arts played a pivotal role in the community's healing process. The meadow, where Jenny had fallen, was transformed into a vibrant space of remembrance and healing. Artists painted murals depicting Jenny's life and the journey towards reconciliation, their vibrant colors representing the community's resilience and hope. Musicians composed melodies that captured the pain of loss and the healing process, their harmonies echoing the collective effort towards unity and understanding. These creative expressions became a shared language, allowing the community to process their emotions collectively, forging stronger bonds and fostering a shared sense of purpose.

Amber, initially perceived as the culprit, played a crucial role in this collective healing. Her active participation in the restorative justice process transformed her from a figure of blame to a symbol of reconciliation. She expressed genuine remorse, taking responsibility for her actions without minimizing the consequences of her behavior. However, the process focused not on punishment but on understanding the root causes of her actions, and on supporting her journey towards rehabilitation and reintegration into the community. This approach highlighted the belief that even those who have caused harm can contribute positively to restorative healing, offering a path towards redemption rather than simply retribution.

The trial's conclusion wasn't marked by a final verdict or sentencing. It was a gradual process of collective understanding, forgiveness, and a renewed commitment to building a more harmonious and just community. The community established a memorial garden in Jenny's honor, a living testament to their collective efforts towards healing and reconciliation. The garden served not only as a place of remembrance but also as a constant reminder of their commitment to change, a symbol of their collective journey towards a brighter, more just, and compassionate future. The Wildwoods Farm experience became a shining example of the transformative power of restorative justice, demonstrating how a community can emerge stronger, more compassionate, and resilient from even the deepest wounds. The rustling leaves whispered a new narrative – one of hope, understanding, and the enduring strength of their collective spirit.

The focus shifted then, subtly but significantly, from the act itself to the actor. Amber, the young squirrel initially identified as the potential culprit, sat quietly, her usual bright eyes downcast. Fiona, ever perceptive, steered the conversation towards a deeper understanding of Amber's actions. It wasn't a question of exoneration or condemnation, but of exploration. Why had Amber been near the telephone pole that day? What were her motivations? What were the circumstances that led to Jenny's fall?

The questions were gentle, probing, not accusatory. Amber, initially hesitant, began to speak. She recounted a difficult morning, a series of small frustrations that had built up within her. A missed breakfast opportunity, a squabble with a sibling, a harsh word from her mother – seemingly insignificant events, yet they had created a pressure cooker within her small frame. She spoke of feeling overwhelmed, invisible, unheard. Her words revealed a deep loneliness, a yearning for connection that had gone unmet. She hadn't intentionally pushed

Jenny; her actions, she explained, were a desperate, impulsive attempt to grab attention, a cry for help expressed in the most tragically wrong way.

Her confession wasn't a plea for forgiveness, but a raw, vulnerable account of her inner turmoil. The community listened, not with judgment, but with empathy. They heard the unspoken pain beneath her words, the desperation that had led her to act so recklessly. Older squirrels, remembering their own youthful impulsiveness, shared their own stories of feeling misunderstood and overlooked. They spoke of the pressures of growing up, the challenges of navigating complex family dynamics, and the difficulty of expressing emotional needs in a community that often prioritized efficiency and practicality over emotional well-being.

This sharing of personal experiences created a powerful sense of connection. The initial anger and frustration began to dissipate, replaced by a collective understanding of the human – or rather, squirrel – condition. It became clear that Amber's actions, while undeniably tragic, were not the product of inherent malice, but of a confluence of factors that had created a perfect storm of emotional distress. The focus shifted from assigning blame to understanding the systemic issues that had allowed such distress to go unnoticed, unaddressed.

The discussion branched out to examine the community's role in Amber's predicament. Had they been too focused on their own lives to notice her struggles? Had their emphasis on productivity and outward appearances overshadowed their attention to the emotional needs of their younger members? The elders admitted their shortcomings, acknowledging their collective responsibility in creating a system that left Amber feeling unheard and unseen. They realized that their traditional methods of conflict resolution, focusing on swift judgment and punishment, were inadequate for addressing the complexities of emotional distress.

The conversation extended beyond Amber's specific situation. It unearthed a deeper, more systemic issue within the Wildwoods Farm community: a lack of open communication and emotional support.

The community, in its pursuit of efficiency and order, had unintentionally created an environment where emotional vulnerabilities were often suppressed, where individuals felt pressured to conform to certain standards, and where the expression of negative emotions was discouraged. This lack of emotional support, they realized, had contributed significantly to Amber's emotional distress and ultimately to the tragic accident.

Ink, the astute ferret investigator, contributed his keen observations. He noted the community's tendency to focus on surface-level interactions, overlooking the subtle cues that might indicate underlying distress. He presented a series of practical solutions, suggesting workshops on emotional intelligence, communication skills, and conflict resolution. These workshops wouldn't just address the immediate problem; they would equip the community with the tools to prevent similar situations in the future. He suggested creating a designated space for young squirrels to express their anxieties and frustrations, a place where they wouldn't feel judged or pressured to conform.

Fiona, acting as a guide, emphasized the importance of restorative practices. She explained how focusing on repairing the harm caused and rebuilding relationships was far more effective than simply punishing the offender. She outlined several restorative measures: Amber would participate in community service, helping to rebuild the trust she had broken. She would also attend individual and group therapy sessions, receiving support for her emotional distress. These measures weren't intended as punishments, but as opportunities for growth and healing, for both Amber and the community.

The community embraced these restorative approaches with enthusiasm. They understood that true justice involved not only addressing the immediate consequences of Amber's actions but also addressing the underlying systemic issues that had contributed to the tragedy. They recognized that Amber's recovery wasn't just her responsibility; it was a shared responsibility, a collaborative effort to heal both the individual and the community. The focus wasn't on isolating

Amber, but on reintegrating her into the community in a way that would foster both her healing and the collective growth of the community.

The trial, if it could be called that, became a journey of self-discovery for the entire Wildwoods Farm community. They learned the importance of active listening, empathy, and understanding. They learned the difference between judgment and compassion, between assigning blame and seeking understanding. They discovered the transformative power of restorative justice, its ability to heal wounds, rebuild trust, and foster growth within a community. The experience strengthened their collective spirit, deepening their connections and solidifying their commitment to creating a more compassionate and just society.

The trial concluded, not with a verdict of guilty or not guilty, but with a shared commitment to change. The community established a new set of guidelines for communication and conflict resolution. They agreed to be more attentive to the emotional needs of their members, to create spaces for open dialogue, and to prioritize empathy over judgment. They developed a system for early intervention, identifying and addressing potential conflicts before they escalated into crises. The community also created a dedicated support group for young squirrels, a safe space where they could express their feelings without fear of judgment or reprimand.

Amber, initially burdened by guilt and shame, began to heal. Through participation in community service and therapy, she began to process her emotions and develop healthier coping mechanisms. She found her voice, becoming a vocal advocate for emotional well-being within the Wildwoods Farm community. She became a symbol of hope and resilience, proving that even those who have caused harm can find redemption through restorative justice. Her journey highlighted the transformative power of understanding, empathy, and the community's commitment to healing and reconciliation.

The incident that had initially threatened to tear the Wildwoods Farm community apart became a catalyst for positive change. It sparked a profound conversation about the importance of emotional well-being, the need for open communication, and the power of restorative justice to heal both individuals and communities. The Wildwoods Farm emerged from this trial not only healed but also transformed, a stronger, more compassionate, and more just community, forever marked by its commitment to understanding and empathy. The rustle of leaves now carried a different melody – one of resilience, hope, and a shared commitment to a brighter, more compassionate future. The memory of Jenny remained, a poignant reminder of the need for understanding, compassion, and the enduring power of restorative justice.

The air in the clearing hung heavy with unspoken emotions, a stark contrast to the usual lively chatter of the Wildwoods Farm. The "trial," a term that felt too formal for the deeply personal nature of the proceedings, had concluded not with a resounding judgment, but with a quiet understanding. There was no gavel, no pronouncements of guilt or innocence. Instead, there was a collective sigh of relief, a shared sense of closure tinged with the lingering sorrow of Jenny's absence.

The community, once fractured by accusations and suspicion, had slowly begun to mend. Amber, initially the focus of their anger and frustration, had become the unexpected catalyst for profound self-reflection. Her vulnerability, her honest confession, had chipped away at the hardened walls of judgment, revealing a shared humanity beneath the surface. The squirrels, the birds, the rabbits – all had shared their own stories of hurt, of loneliness, of feeling unseen. The hens, notorious for their gossiping, found themselves surprisingly quiet, their clucking replaced by thoughtful murmurs. Even the usually aloof cats seemed more pensive, their sharp stares softened by a glimmer of empathy.

The restorative justice approach, championed by Fiona and Ink, had proven remarkably effective. It wasn't about assigning blame and doling out punishment; it was about healing the wounds inflicted by the tragedy. Amber's participation in community service wasn't viewed as penance, but as an opportunity for her to actively contribute to the community's healing process. She spent countless hours helping to repair the damaged parts of the forest, her nimble paws carefully mending broken branches and nurturing saplings. This wasn't simply physical labor; it was a symbolic act of reconciliation, a visible manifestation of her commitment to making amends.

The therapy sessions, facilitated by a wise old owl known for her calm demeanor and insightful wisdom, proved equally transformative. Amber, initially hesitant and withdrawn, gradually opened up, sharing her deepest fears and anxieties. The owl listened patiently, offering guidance and support without judgment. The group sessions, which included other young squirrels facing similar challenges, provided a safe space for them to share their experiences, to feel understood, and to build supportive relationships. These sessions became a crucial component of the community's healing, fostering a sense of shared experience and mutual support.

The community itself underwent a significant transformation. Ink's suggestions for workshops on emotional intelligence and communication skills were readily embraced. Squirrels of all ages attended sessions focusing on active listening, assertive communication, and conflict resolution techniques. They learned to identify and address their own emotional needs, to express themselves constructively, and to approach conflicts with empathy rather than anger. These workshops weren't merely theoretical exercises; they were practical tools that equipped the community to prevent future tragedies.

Fiona, ever the insightful observer, emphasized the importance of creating a space for open communication and emotional expression. A designated area, affectionately called "The Wildwoods Glade," was established as a sanctuary for young squirrels to share their anxieties and frustrations. This space was not for disciplinary action; it was a place of unconditional acceptance, where young squirrels felt safe to express their emotional vulnerabilities without fear of judgment or ridicule. This initiative represented a fundamental shift in the community's approach to emotional well-being, prioritizing empathy, understanding, and open dialogue over efficiency and conformity.

The outcome of this unique trial extended far beyond Amber's personal healing. It fostered a deeper sense of collective responsibility. The community recognized its role in inadvertently creating an environment where Amber's emotional distress went unnoticed. They acknowledged their own shortcomings in communication and their tendency to overlook the emotional needs of their younger members. This self-awareness led to a commitment to systemic change, a collective effort to create a more supportive and compassionate community.

The elders, initially focused on swift justice, found themselves deeply involved in the community's healing. They actively participated in the workshops, sharing their own experiences and fostering a culture of self-reflection and mutual understanding. Their transformation symbolized a remarkable shift in leadership, from punitive enforcement to supportive guidance.

The most profound change, however, was the transformation in Amber herself. The once isolated and emotionally overwhelmed squirrel emerged as a confident and compassionate individual. Her experience, while painful, had become a source of strength and resilience. She used her newfound voice to advocate for emotional well-being within the community, becoming a beacon of hope for other young squirrels struggling with similar challenges. She organized support groups, shared her story, and became a symbol of the community's commitment to healing and reconciliation.

The memory of Jenny's accident remained a poignant reminder of the tragic consequences of unchecked emotional distress and the importance of active listening and understanding. However, the community didn't dwell on the past; instead, they channeled their grief into positive action, building a stronger, more compassionate, and more just society. The rustling leaves of the Wildwoods Farm now carried a new melody – a song of resilience, hope, and a shared commitment to a brighter, more compassionate future.

The Wildwoods Farm community had learned a profound lesson: true justice wasn't simply about punishing wrongdoers; it was about healing wounds, repairing broken relationships, and fostering a sense of community responsibility. The trial, if it could be called that, had become a testament to the transformative power of restorative justice – a process that not only healed Amber but also reformed the entire community, leaving it stronger, wiser, and more deeply connected than ever before. The whispers in the woods were no longer filled with accusations and suspicion, but with murmurs of understanding, compassion, and the enduring promise of a more just and compassionate future for all. The legacy of Jenny, though tragically etched in their collective memory, served as a constant reminder of the profound importance of empathy, understanding, and the enduring power of restorative justice. The forest, once scarred by loss, now blossomed with the promise of a brighter, more compassionate tomorrow. The sunlight filtering through the leaves seemed to shimmer with a newfound hope, a testament to the enduring resilience of the Wildwoods Farm community and the transformative power of understanding.

Chapter 15

A New Beginning

The weeks that followed were a testament to the Wildwoods Farm resilience. The initial shock and grief gradually gave way to a collective effort toward healing. Amber, no longer the ostracized squirrel, became a symbol of transformation. Her daily routine, once filled with anxiety and isolation, now involved tending to the community garden, a vibrant patch of wildflowers and herbs that had become a focal point for communal activity. She meticulously weeded, watered, and nurtured the plants, her movements deliberate and purposeful, a stark contrast to the hurried, anxious motions she had exhibited before.

The community garden became more than just a source of sustenance; it was a place of shared labor, of quiet camaraderie. Squirrels, rabbits, and even the usually aloof cats would gather there, lending a paw to the task at hand. The shared activity fostered a sense of unity, a collective effort to nurture something beautiful from the wreckage of the past. Amber's quiet dedication, her evident commitment to contributing positively, became a powerful force for healing, dissolving lingering resentment and suspicion.

The older squirrels, initially skeptical of Fiona and Ink's restorative justice approach, were surprised by its effectiveness. They had witnessed firsthand the transformative power of empathy, the way in which genuine remorse and a commitment to amends could mend even the deepest wounds. They began to participate more actively in the community's healing process, offering guidance and support to those still struggling with the aftermath of the tragedy. Their wisdom, once shrouded in a veil of authority, now flowed freely, laced with humility and a newfound understanding of the complexities of emotional well-being.

The therapy sessions continued, guided by Nargiza, the wise old owl. These weren't clinical sessions with diagnoses and prescriptions, but rather spaces for open dialogue, for shared vulnerability, and for collective understanding. The younger squirrels, many of whom had witnessed the events surrounding Jenny's fall, began to articulate their feelings of fear, confusion, and helplessness. The owl listened patiently, offering words of comfort and encouragement, weaving her wisdom into gentle narratives that helped them process their emotions and find solace in shared experience.

The once-gossiping hens, now humbled by their own role in spreading misinformation, became unlikely champions of empathy. They began to actively listen to the younger squirrels, offering words of comfort and encouragement. Their clucking had been replaced by soft coos, their sharp eyes softened with understanding. They even organized storytelling sessions, sharing their own experiences of loss and overcoming challenges, creating a supportive network of experience that helped the community process their grief.

Ink and Fiona, while still involved in resolving the lingering issues stemming from the misunderstanding, transitioned their roles to facilitators of community engagement. Ink, with his knack for organization, helped establish a comprehensive system for conflict resolution. He designed a series of workshops focused on communication skills, focusing on active listening, assertive communication, and conflict resolution techniques. He emphasized the importance of understanding different perspectives, respecting individual differences, and employing empathy in communication.

Fiona, ever the intuitive observer, played a vital role in fostering a culture of emotional intelligence. She implemented initiatives aimed at creating spaces where young squirrels could openly express their feelings. These weren't spaces of judgment or punishment, but safe havens for vulnerability. She understood the importance of creating a community where emotions were validated, where seeking help was not viewed as a sign of weakness but as a sign of strength.

The Wildwoods Farm wasn't transformed overnight. The healing process was gradual, punctuated by moments of setback and relapse. Yet, the community's commitment to restorative justice remained steadfast. They celebrated small victories, acknowledged setbacks as opportunities for growth, and continually reinforced their commitment to building a more compassionate, understanding society. The initial focus on finding a culprit gave way to a deeper understanding of the systemic issues that contributed to the tragedy.

Jasper, initially burdened by the unjust accusations, eventually found his voice. He participated actively in the community's healing, sharing his own experiences of feeling misunderstood and the pain of being wrongly judged. His story became a powerful reminder of the devastating consequences of hasty judgments and the importance of seeking truth before condemning others. His willingness to share his vulnerability helped others find the courage to do the same, creating a powerful ripple effect of healing and understanding.

The entire community actively worked to understand the deeper societal dynamics that had contributed to the tragedy. They established a peer support system, where young squirrels could find solace and guidance from their peers. They implemented regular community meetings, not just to address logistical matters, but to facilitate open dialogue and emotional expression. These meetings became spaces for sharing experiences, for voicing concerns, and for fostering a sense of collective responsibility for the community's well-being.

The community's elders, initially hesitant about the restorative justice approach, emerged as leaders who valued empathy and compassion as much as justice. They actively participated in the workshops, readily admitting past mistakes and sharing their own experiences of personal growth. They became role models, demonstrating the value of self-reflection and the importance of acknowledging one's own shortcomings. Their transformation was crucial in changing the community's culture from one of strict adherence to rules to one that emphasized empathy, understanding, and mutual support.

The recovery wasn't just about repairing the physical damage to the forest; it was about rebuilding the social fabric of the community. The Wildwoods Glade, initially conceived as a safe space for expressing anxieties, became a symbol of the community's collective effort toward creating a supportive environment. It evolved into a hub for various community activities, including storytelling evenings, craft workshops, and various performances.

The transformation extended beyond the immediate aftermath of the tragedy. The community embraced a philosophy of continuous improvement, regularly evaluating their systems and making adjustments as needed. They established a council dedicated to ensuring the well-being of all members, particularly the young and vulnerable. This council, composed of members from different age groups and species, fostered an inclusive and equitable approach to conflict resolution and community building.

The healing process was far from a linear journey, with its share of emotional relapses and challenges. However, the community's unwavering commitment to restorative justice served as a constant guiding light. They acknowledged that healing was not a destination but a continuous process, a journey that required ongoing self-reflection, empathy, and a sustained commitment to building a more just and compassionate society. The memory of Jenny served as a constant reminder of the importance of careful observation, compassionate listening, and preventing future tragedies through conscious community building. The Wildwoods Farm had emerged from the shadow of loss, its inhabitants strengthened by resilience, empathy, and a profound understanding of the transformative power of restorative justice. The rustling leaves now whispered not of accusations and judgment, but of hope, healing, and the enduring power of community.

The rebuilding of trust wasn't a simple task. It required a delicate balance of acknowledging past hurts, fostering open communication, and creating a space where vulnerability was not only accepted but encouraged. The initial workshops facilitated by Ink focused on practical communication skills, but Fiona understood that true healing went deeper. She initiated "Story Circles," intimate gatherings where members could share their experiences, both joyful and painful, without fear of judgment. These weren't therapy sessions in the human sense, but safe spaces for emotional expression, where the weight of unspoken anxieties could finally be released.

One particularly poignant evening, a young squirrel named Connor confessed his fear of heights, a fear exacerbated by witnessing Jenny's fall. He hadn't spoken about it before, fearing ridicule. But in the Story Circle, surrounded by empathetic listeners, he found the courage to share his vulnerability. His words resonated with others; several squirrels confessed similar anxieties, anxieties they had suppressed for fear of appearing weak. The sharing helped Connor, and others, realize they were not alone in their struggles. The shared vulnerability fostered a sense of unity and understanding, reminding them that strength wasn't the absence of fear but the courage to confront it.

The older generation, initially resistant to the new methods, slowly began to participate in these Story Circles. They shared their own past traumas and mistakes, acknowledging their role in perpetuating harmful gossip and assumptions. One elderly squirrel, Elder Penny, confessed her regret for not offering more support to Jenny in her final days. This act of vulnerability was particularly moving, breaking down the barriers between generations and fostering a deeper sense of mutual respect and understanding. It demonstrated that acknowledging one's flaws was not a sign of weakness, but a testament to personal growth and a commitment to healing.

The hens, who once spread rumors like wildfire, became unlikely ambassadors of truth. They started organizing "Truth Telling Tuesdays," where they would share stories, emphasizing the importance of accuracy and responsible communication. Their transformation was remarkable. Their clucking had been replaced by a gentler, more thoughtful cadence, their sharp eyes softened with empathy. The hens became vital in disseminating accurate information, counteracting the misinformation that had fueled distrust in the past. They became the community's fact-checkers, ensuring that rumors didn't cloud the truth.

Ink, ever the meticulous organizer, worked tirelessly to ensure that the community's conflict resolution system was both effective and fair. He created a series of tiered responses to conflict, ranging from informal mediation to more formal processes involving a neutral third party. He emphasized the importance of restorative justice—healing the harm caused, repairing relationships, and fostering accountability without resorting to punishment. He organized regular workshops on conflict resolution strategies, educating members on the importance of active listening, empathy, and constructive communication.

Fiona, with her keen intuition, played a crucial role in identifying and addressing underlying issues that fueled conflict. She observed interactions carefully, noting patterns of behavior and unspoken tensions. She approached these situations with gentle diplomacy, mediating disputes with sensitivity and understanding. She understood that many conflicts stemmed not just from disagreements but from deeper insecurities and anxieties, which needed to be addressed through empathy and compassion.

Building trust also involved confronting the physical reminders of the tragedy. The telephone pole from which Jenny had fallen was a constant source of painful memories. Instead of removing it, the community decided to transform it into a memorial. They carefully cleaned and painted the pole, adding carvings and decorations that represented Jenny's spirit—a playful squirrel leaping through the air, a cascade of bright wildflowers, and a small plaque with a heartfelt inscription. The pole, once a symbol of tragedy, became a testament to remembrance and healing. This process of transforming a negative symbol into a positive one played a significant role in rebuilding communal trust.

The community garden continued to be a vital space for healing and togetherness. It was a tangible symbol of their collective efforts, a testament to their ability to nurture something beautiful from the ashes of trauma. New plants were added, representing hope, resilience, and unity. The garden became a place where the community could come together, not just to work, but to share stories, laughter, and comfort. It was a physical manifestation of their collective journey towards healing and rebuilding.

The Wildwoods Farm recovery wasn't swift or seamless; it was a gradual process, characterized by both progress and setbacks. There were moments of relapse, when old habits of gossip or suspicion resurfaced. But the community had developed a new resilience. They acknowledged setbacks as opportunities for learning and growth, adjusting their approaches and refining their strategies as needed. They learned to celebrate small victories and to offer each other unwavering support during difficult times.

As time passed, the community became a model for others in the wider forest. Squirrels from neighboring areas visited the Wildwoods Farm, eager to learn from their restorative justice approach. The Wildwoods Farm became a place of pilgrimage, a beacon of hope, demonstrating that even after profound loss, trust and unity could be rebuilt, transforming a tragedy into a catalyst for positive change.

The legacy of Jenny's fall wasn't simply about justice; it was about understanding, empathy, and the enduring power of communal healing. The community's efforts to rebuild trust weren't just about addressing the immediate consequences of the tragedy; they were about creating a stronger, more compassionate society, one where everyone felt seen, heard, and valued. The rustling leaves in the Wildwoods Farm now whispered not just of the past, but of the hope and resilience that had blossomed from the heart of a tragedy. The community had not only survived but thrived, demonstrating the transformative power of restorative justice and the enduring strength of the human, or in this case, squirrel, spirit. The Wildwoods Farm had become a testament to the possibility of healing, a sanctuary where forgiveness and understanding could flourish. It was a place where the memory of Jenny served not as a reminder of loss, but as a beacon illuminating the path towards a brighter future.

The transformation of the Wildwoods Farm extended beyond the immediate aftermath of Jenny's fall. It was a gradual, painstaking process, akin to the slow, steady growth of a mighty oak. The community's commitment to understanding wasn't a fleeting sentiment; it was woven into the very fabric of their daily lives. Regular workshops continued, focusing not just on conflict resolution, but on active listening, empathy training, and the art of non-violent communication. These weren't merely lectures; they were interactive sessions filled with role-playing, storytelling, and group discussions designed to foster emotional intelligence.

Elder Penny, once hesitant to participate, became a passionate advocate for these workshops. Her personal confession had given her a newfound authority, and her wisdom guided many through their emotional journeys. She often shared anecdotes from her long life, demonstrating how misunderstandings, left unaddressed, could fester into deep-seated resentments, while open communication could prevent even the smallest disagreements from escalating into major conflicts.

The young squirrels, particularly those who had been initially skeptical of the restorative justice approach, embraced the new methods with enthusiasm. They organized "Empathy Games," playful activities that taught them to understand different perspectives. One popular game involved swapping roles, where a squirrel would imagine themselves in another's shoes, experiencing a situation from a different viewpoint. These games weren't just frivolous; they helped them develop crucial skills in perspective-taking and emotional understanding.

Even the notoriously gossipy hens contributed to this newfound understanding. Their "Truth Telling Tuesdays" evolved into "Understanding Wednesdays," where they now shared not just factual accounts, but also explored the emotional context behind events. They learned to articulate the nuances of feeling, separating the objective facts from subjective interpretations. Their clucking, once sharp and judgmental, now often carried a note of gentle concern. They had discovered the power of compassionate storytelling, transforming themselves from rumor-mongers into empathetic listeners.

Ink, ever the meticulous planner, introduced a "Community Calendar" designed to promote shared events and activities. This calendar wasn't just a list of dates; it was a vibrant tapestry of community life, highlighting shared meals, storytelling sessions, and collaborative projects in the community garden. It was a visual representation of their interconnectedness, constantly reminding them of their shared journey towards healing.

Fiona, meanwhile, focused on nurturing individual emotional growth. She conducted one-on-one sessions with squirrels who were struggling to process their emotions, providing a safe space for them to express their feelings without judgment. Her intuitive understanding of squirrel psychology was invaluable, allowing her to identify and address unspoken anxieties and traumas. She often used creative therapies, such as art and music, to help squirrels express their emotions non-verbally.

The community garden continued to flourish, becoming a microcosm of their evolving understanding. Each plant represented a different emotion, a different aspect of their healing process. Bright sunflowers symbolized hope, while sturdy oaks represented resilience. Delicate wildflowers represented vulnerability, a reminder that it's okay to be fragile and to need support. The garden wasn't just a place to cultivate plants; it was a place to cultivate empathy, compassion, and a deeper understanding of oneself and others.

The Wildwoods Farm commitment to understanding extended beyond their own community. They organized inter-community workshops, inviting squirrels from neighboring forests to share their experiences and learn from their approach to restorative justice. This collaboration fostered a wider network of support and helped to disseminate their model of healing across the forest. They also began to offer training programs to other woodland creatures, teaching them the importance of empathy and understanding in conflict resolution.

The transformation of the Wildwoods Farm wasn't without its challenges. Old habits resurfaced occasionally. Whispers of suspicion and doubt would occasionally ripple through the community, reminding them of the fragility of trust. But each time, they addressed these setbacks with renewed determination, utilizing the tools and techniques they had developed. They had learned to view setbacks not as failures, but as opportunities for learning and growth.

The community celebrated their successes—both big and small—with renewed vigor. Every milestone, every successful mediation, every act of forgiveness, was cause for celebration. They learned to appreciate the small victories, realizing that lasting change was a gradual process, not a sudden transformation. They recognized that genuine healing requires patience, persistence, and an unwavering commitment to understanding.

The memorial to Jenny became a focal point for the community's continuing commitment to understanding. It wasn't just a place of remembrance; it was a space for reflection, contemplation, and renewed dedication to fostering a more compassionate community. The community added new carvings and decorations to the memorial over time, each representing a different aspect of their shared journey towards healing.

The young inhabitants of the Wildwoods Farm were especially instrumental in promoting understanding. They organized "Kindness Campaigns," where they spread messages of empathy and compassion through drawings, songs, and plays. They taught the younger generation the importance of active listening and respectful communication, ensuring that the values of restorative justice were integrated into the community's culture.

The legacy of Jenny's fall extended far beyond the immediate aftermath. The Wildwoods Farm became a symbol of hope and resilience, a testament to the power of restorative justice and the transformative effect of understanding. Their story resonated throughout the wider forest, inspiring other communities to embrace empathy and compassion in their own conflict resolution processes. The rustling leaves in the Wildwoods Farm now whispered not only of the past but also of the bright future they had forged, a future built on understanding, empathy, and mutual respect. The community had successfully transformed a tragedy into a catalyst for positive change, demonstrating the remarkable capacity of a community to heal, grow, and thrive.

The Wildwoods Farm, once a place of sorrow, was now a beacon of hope, a reminder that even in the darkest of times, the enduring strength of understanding can illuminate the path towards a brighter future. The memory of Jenny served not as a symbol of loss, but as a powerful reminder of the transformative potential of empathy and the unwavering pursuit of truth and understanding.

The annual "Jenny's Joyful Jump" festival became a cornerstone of the Wildwoods Farm calendar. It wasn't a somber memorial, but a vibrant celebration of Jenny's life, a joyous affirmation of the spirit she embodied. Instead of mourning her loss, the community chose to honor her memory by embracing the values she unknowingly represented: kindness, playfulness, and the pure, unadulterated joy of living.

The festival began with a sunrise ceremony at the base of the great oak tree where the memorial stood. The young, their faces painted with bright colors mirroring the hues of the forest, would gather, holding aloft handmade lanterns shaped like acorns and leaves. Each lantern bore a message written in loving tribute to Jenny—a simple word like "Kindness," "Joy," or "Friendship," or a heartfelt phrase like "We miss your laughter," or "Your spirit lives on." As the sun crested the horizon, bathing the woods in golden light, the children would release their lanterns, sending their messages of love and remembrance soaring into the sky.

The afternoon was dedicated to games and activities, mirroring the playful spirit Jenny had possessed. There were races up the "Jenny's Jump" – a specially designated, safely padded, section of the oak tree, echoing the playful climb that had tragically led to her fall. This time, however, it was a celebration of movement, a testament to the vitality of life. There were also storytelling sessions, where squirrels recounted their favorite memories of Jenny, sharing anecdotes of her cheerful nature and her infectious laughter.

The evening culminated in a breathtaking lantern parade. The entire community, from the oldest owl to the youngest chipmunk, would participate, carrying intricately designed lanterns representing their personal memories of Jenny. The parade snaked through the forest, illuminated by the soft glow of the lanterns, transforming the Wildwoods Farm into an enchanting wonderland. The air buzzed with laughter and joyful chatter, a poignant counterpoint to the grief that had once permeated the community.

Beyond the annual festival, Jenny's memory was woven into the daily fabric of the Wildwoods Farm. A dedicated section of the community garden, bursting with vibrant wildflowers and sun-drenched herbs, was named "Jenny's Garden." Each plant represented a positive aspect of Jenny's personality—the resilience of the sunflowers mirroring her strong spirit, the delicate beauty of the wildflowers reflecting her gentle nature. The community tended this garden with meticulous care, a constant reminder of their commitment to nurturing life and celebrating Jenny's legacy.

The young, particularly, played a crucial role in keeping Jenny's spirit alive. They would often gather at the base of the great oak tree, re-telling stories of Jenny's adventures, sharing their own drawings and paintings inspired by her playful spirit. They would leave small gifts at the foot of the memorial—smooth stones painted with vibrant colors, small bouquets of wildflowers, or handcrafted toys. These small acts of remembrance were profoundly moving, demonstrating the enduring love and respect that Jenny had inspired in the hearts of the young squirrels.

The "Jenny's Kindness Challenge," an initiative spearheaded by the young, became a year-round endeavor. The challenge involved performing random acts of kindness throughout the community. Squirrels would help each other with tasks, offer comfort to those in distress, or simply share a kind word. The challenge fostered a culture of empathy and compassion, ensuring that Jenny's legacy extended far beyond a single day of celebration.

A new tradition emerged – the "Jenny's Whispers," a quiet moment of reflection held every evening before sunset. The community would gather at the memorial, sharing their thoughts and feelings in hushed tones. It wasn't about dwelling on sorrow, but rather about celebrating the positive impact Jenny had had on their lives, sharing memories of her kindness, her laughter, and the unique joy she had brought to the Wildwoods Farm. This quiet moment provided a space for personal reflection and communal healing.

The community's creative expression also found its outlet in commemorating Jenny. A talented woodpecker created a stunning mosaic on a large, flat rock near the memorial, depicting Jenny scampering playfully among the branches. The mosaic was intricate and beautiful, capturing the essence of Jenny's spirit. Local artists created paintings and sculptures, each representing a different aspect of Jenny's life and personality. These artworks were displayed throughout the Wildwoods Farm, serving as beautiful reminders of her presence.

The local storyteller, a wise old badger named Barnaby, crafted a series of stories about Jenny, highlighting her courage, her kindness, and her unwavering optimism. These stories were told and retold, weaving Jenny's legacy into the very fabric of the community's oral tradition. Barnaby's stories weren't just entertainment; they were a powerful tool for healing, providing a framework for understanding and acceptance.

Even the language of the Wildwoods Farm was subtly altered in Jenny's honor. A new term, "Jenny's Glow," was introduced to describe acts of kindness and generosity. This term, often whispered with admiration, became a part of the community's everyday vocabulary, ensuring that Jenny's legacy would be kept alive through language, stories, and gestures.

One particularly poignant development was the establishment of the "Jenny's Legacy Fund," a community initiative dedicated to supporting initiatives aimed at promoting understanding, empathy, and restorative justice. The fund provided resources for educational programs, conflict resolution workshops, and community projects. It served as a concrete manifestation of the community's commitment to learning from the past and building a brighter future.

The legacy of Jenny's fall, once a source of immense pain and division, was transformed into a catalyst for profound change. The community learned that even the most devastating experiences can inspire extraordinary growth and understanding. Jenny's memory wasn't just a reminder of loss, but a powerful symbol of resilience, empathy, and the enduring strength of the human—or in this case, squirrel—spirit. The Wildwoods Farm, once shrouded in grief, blossomed anew, a testament to the extraordinary capacity of a community to heal, to learn, and to honor the life of a beloved friend. The laughter that once echoed through the woods, now, although tinged with a gentle sadness, was a testament to the vibrant life Jenny had lived and the lasting legacy of kindness and understanding she left behind. And so, the Wildwoods Farms whispered on, their rustling leaves carrying a tale not only of loss and healing, but also of a love that transcended even death itself.

The trial of Jasper, though initially fraught with tension and suspicion, ultimately served as a catalyst for profound change within the Wildwoods Farm. The meticulous investigation conducted by Ink and Fiona, meticulously piecing together the fragmented accounts and revealing the true culprit—a mischievous jay who had accidentally caused Jenny's fall—not only cleared Jasper's name but also illuminated the dangers of unchecked assumptions and the power of collective bias. The community, having witnessed the devastating consequences of their hasty judgments, embarked on a journey of self-reflection and reconciliation.

The revelation of the jay's role in the accident didn't erase the pain of Jenny's loss, but it did provide a crucial framework for healing. The community understood that their initial reactions, fueled by fear, gossip, and pre-existing prejudices, had amplified the tragedy and unjustly burdened Jasper. The weight of collective guilt hung heavy in the air, a stark reminder of the potential for harm when truth is sacrificed at the altar of conjecture. This shared experience spurred a powerful wave of introspection. Squirrels, cats, owls, and badgers alike grappled with the implications of their actions and inactions, striving to understand how they could have approached the situation with more empathy and wisdom.

A period of intense community dialogue followed. Gatherings were held under the ancient oak tree, where squirrels, cats, and other woodland creatures shared their anxieties, regrets, and aspirations for a better future. The process wasn't easy; old wounds were reopened, and difficult conversations were had. But through the shared experience of vulnerability and honest self-assessment, a new spirit of understanding began to emerge. The community learned to acknowledge the limitations of their perspectives, to recognize the biases that unconsciously shaped their judgments, and to strive for greater empathy in their interactions.

The "Truth and Reconciliation Council," a newly formed group comprised of representatives from various community factions, played a pivotal role in guiding this process. The council established protocols for open communication, conflict resolution, and restorative justice. They developed programs focused on critical thinking, media literacy, and the importance of seeking multiple perspectives before forming conclusions. These programs, integrated into the community's education system, ensured that future generations would be better equipped to navigate complex social dynamics and resist the allure of hearsay and prejudice.

Ink and Fiona, having played a crucial role in bringing the truth to light, continued to serve as valuable resources for the community. They provided workshops on investigative techniques, emphasizing the importance of thorough research, careful observation, and the validation of multiple accounts. Their efforts not only improved the community's problem-solving abilities but also cultivated a sense of collective responsibility for fostering truth and justice.

The transformation of the Wildwoods Farm extended beyond the realm of justice and into the sphere of collective healing. The annual festival, once overshadowed by grief and suspicion, was reimagined as a celebration of truth, reconciliation, and community resilience. The games and activities were designed to encourage cooperation, communication, and empathy. Storytellers shared narratives about the power of forgiveness, the importance of self-reflection, and the enduring strength of community bonds. The festival became a symbol of hope, a testament to the community's ability to learn from its mistakes and forge a path towards a more equitable and compassionate future.

The "Jenny's Joyful Jump" memorial, once a site of sorrow, was gradually transformed into a beacon of hope. Instead of focusing solely on Jenny's tragic death, the community chose to honor her spirit by creating a vibrant, inclusive space where squirrels, cats, birds, and other creatures could come together to celebrate life, connection, and the pursuit of truth. The area around the memorial was redesigned, featuring a beautiful garden filled with Jenny's favorite flowers and plants. Benches were added, providing a quiet space for reflection and remembrance. The memorial itself was embellished with artistic representations of Jenny's playful spirit, created by various members of the community. These artistic expressions served as a powerful reminder of her vibrancy and the deep impact she had on the lives of those who knew her.

In the heart of the redesigned memorial area, a "Wishing Tree" was planted. Each member of the community was invited to write a wish for the future on a small piece of parchment and tie it to the tree's branches. These wishes, representing hopes for a more just and equitable community, became symbols of collective aspirations, tangible evidence of the community's commitment to ongoing growth and change.

The transformation of the Wildwoods Farm was not a swift or easy process, but a gradual evolution that required ongoing commitment and collective effort. The journey towards healing and reconciliation wasn't a straight line; it involved setbacks, disagreements, and moments of doubt. Yet, the community persevered, driven by a shared desire for truth, justice, and a brighter future.

The story of Jenny's fall, once a source of profound sadness and division, became a catalyst for profound change. The community learned the valuable lesson that even the most devastating experiences can lead to growth, understanding, and meaningful transformation. The Wildwoods Farm, once shrouded in grief and suspicion, blossomed anew, transformed by the power of collective reflection, restorative justice, and the enduring strength of community bonds. The laughter that echoed through the woods now carried a deeper resonance, a testament to the resilient spirit of its inhabitants and their unwavering commitment to truth, justice, and the pursuit of a more compassionate world. The wind whispered through the leaves, carrying a message of hope, a promise of a future where understanding prevails over prejudice, and where the pursuit of truth serves as a foundation for lasting peace and harmony. The community's journey demonstrated that even in the face of immense loss, the human – or squirrel – spirit possesses an extraordinary capacity for healing, for learning, and for building a brighter future, together. The Wildwoods Farm, once a place of sorrow, became a vibrant testament to the power of forgiveness, the beauty of reconciliation, and the enduring strength of community. The legacy of Jenny's fall was not merely one of loss, but a powerful symbol of the transformative potential of truth, justice, and the unwavering bonds of friendship and community. The whispers of the woods now carried not only the echoes of sorrow, but also the resounding affirmation of a community's remarkable capacity for healing and growth. And so, the Wildwoods Farm whispered on, their rustling leaves weaving a tale of resilience, understanding, and the enduring power of hope.

Epilogue

The morning sun stretched thin rays across Wildwoods Farm, gilding the barn roof and orchard trees in soft light. Normally, the air carried the gentle rhythm of routine—the scrape of hooves, the flutter of wings, the quiet chatter of neighbors greeting another day of shared work. But on this morning, the farm awoke to something else: a frantic clamor that sliced through the calm like a hawk's cry.

Henrietta the hen burst from the barn doors, feathers flying, her voice cracking with desperation. "The Harvest Coin!" she cried, wings flailing as she stumbled into the clearing. "It's gone!"

The animals froze. One by one, they turned to her, their morning tasks forgotten. The words struck them harder than winter's chill. The Harvest Coin was no mere trinket. For generations, it had been the shining symbol of their prosperity, the golden promise of unity, passed from claw to paw, hoof to wing, at the Harvest Festival each autumn. Its gleam reminded them that through cooperation, the farm would thrive, and their bellies would never go empty. Without it, the tradition was broken, and with it, the trust that bound them together.

Henrietta's eyes darted wildly, her voice trembling as she continued. "The heart of our farm, the very proof of who we are—it's been taken. This is no accident. This is a wound to us all." Her words shivered into silence, the weight of them pressing down on every listening ear.

From the edge of the gathering, Ink the Weasel stepped forward, his sharp eyes narrowing. Beside him, Fiona *The Whisper* tail twitched, her gaze steady and unreadable. Together, they had solved disputes before—mysteries of missing grain, questions of broken trust—but this was different. This was not simply about a coin of gold. It was about the balance of the farm itself, and whether their unity could survive the shadow of suspicion.

All around them, unease rippled like wind through the cornfields. Whispers began to rise—accusations, doubts, old grudges clawing to the surface. Ink could hear it already: the fear that one of their own had betrayed them. Fiona flicked her ears toward him, a quiet signal of agreement. They both knew what had to be done.

Henrietta's plea lingered in the air, desperate and heavy. "*Find it!,*" she begged. "Find the Harvest Coin before it tears us apart."

And so, with the weight of tradition and the future of Wildwoods Farm upon their shoulders, Ink and Fiona accepted the task. Somewhere among their neighbors, the truth lay hidden. Somewhere, the golden heart of their community waited to be uncovered. And until it was, the farm itself would teeter on the edge of mistrust and ruin.

To Be Continued